BOOK TWO:
THE SPIRAL PATH

GREG WEISMAN

SCHOLASTIC INC.

To my high school history professors,
Mr. [James] Ackerman and Dr. [John] Johnson,
who transformed facts into history, antiquity into
relevancy, cause into effect, and human beings
into the threads of a vast tapestry . . .

©2018 Blizzard Entertainment, Inc. All rights reserved. Traveler is a
trademark, and World of Warcraft and Blizzard Entertainment are
trademarks and/or registered trademarks of Blizzard Entertainment, Inc.,
in the U.S. and/or other countries.

All rights reserved. Published by Scholastic Inc., *Publishers since 1920*.
SCHOLASTIC and associated logos are trademarks and/or registered
trademarks of Scholastic Inc.

ISBN 978-1-338-02937-6

10 9 8 7 6 5 4 3 2 1   18 19 20 21 22

Printed in the U.S.A.   40
First printing 2018

Book design by Rick DeMonico
Cover and interior illustrations by Aquatic Moon

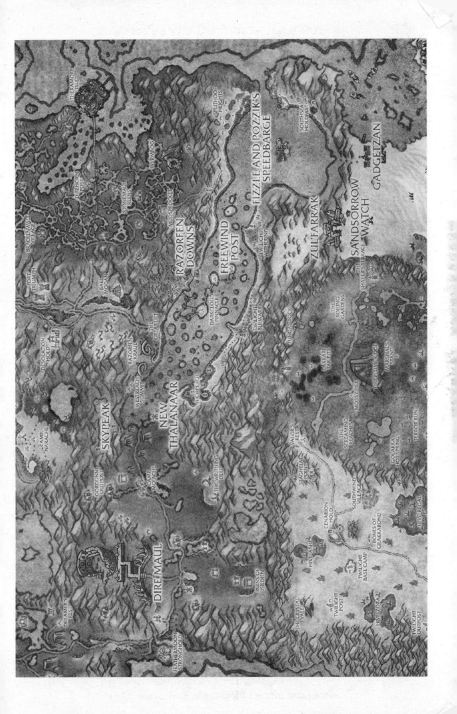

PART ONE:

SKIRTING FERALAS

CHAPTER ONE
LADY AND CHILD

Azeroth's largest moon, the White Lady, was waning now, but its second, smaller moon, the Blue Child, remained full, and these orbs provided—despite the lack of a campfire—more than enough light for Aramar Thorne's current undertaking. Aram had his sketchbook on his lap and his dwindling coal pencil in his hand, and was finally sketching the one person in his life missing from this volume's pages.

Makasa Flintwill posed uncomfortably. He had told her, "You don't have to pose. Just don't move around too much."

She had said, "Fine. Good," but her posture remained upright, stiff, and painfully awkward. The upright, he was used to. But he knew Makasa to be a woman supremely at ease in her own skin, so the stiff and awkward was something he was making an effort to compensate for in his drawing. Makasa Flintwill was seventeen years old, with the demeanor of a woman of thirty—or maybe of a military general of fifty. She was five feet, ten inches tall, lean and muscular, with sable skin, dark-brown eyes, and short black kinky hair. On board the *Wavestrider*, she had kept her trimmed hair very short indeed, to match the shape of her skull. But they had been in Feralas's trackless rain forests for close to a month, and—though no objective observer could think of it as anything but still quite short—Aram knew his sister well enough to believe she must already regard the length of her hair as "completely out of control."

"His sister." It seemed so natural to think of her that way now—and almost impossible to believe that, only a month ago, the words he would have used to describe her were closer to "my nemesis." They had been through so much since then, and both of them had the scars—external *and* internal—to prove it. As he sketched in thin, dark scratches across her left cheek and forehead, he thought of their first meeting seven long months past . . .

Aramar Thorne was the captain's son, officially brought aboard Wavestrider *as a cabin boy, but really there to finally get to know the father who had abandoned his family when Aram was six.*

While Captain Greydon Thorne attempted to teach his son everything from life lessons to swordsmanship to knowledge and trivia about the flora, fauna, and sentient species of Azeroth, Second Mate Makasa Flintwill took on the task of making a sailor out of a twelve-year-old child who had never before seen the ocean, let alone shipped out upon it. Aram was, he had to admit, a poor and resentful student to both of them. He flat out didn't want to be there with either of them and made no attempt to hide that fact.

And worse, he had inadvertently come between Makasa and Greydon, whom she also regarded as a father. To say, in those first six months, that Aram and Makasa had not gotten along was practically the definition of understatement.

Aram sketched in multiple scratches on her bare arms and wondered how or when she had gotten them. He detailed her weapons: the cutlass and hatchet on her belt, the iron chain crisscrossing her chest, and the shield—an iron circle covered with layer upon layer of impact-absorbing rawhide—kept within easy reach.

But everything had changed over the last month. Tragically severed from Greydon and Wavestrider *when the ship was attacked, Aram and Makasa escaped in a lifeboat and were left marooned and alone in a hostile land—where they had finally found each other. How many times had he pulled out his sketchbook only to have her growl, "You better not be putting me in that blasted book"?*

He had always responded by intoning, "I promise I won't sketch you unless you ask me to."

And, of course, she never had. Not until this morning, when she surprised him with a smile and an "I might ask you. I've heard it's good magic."

"Good magic." That's what they had between them now. They had been through hardship and loss, danger and tragedy. But together they had survived and, along the way, not simply made peace with each other but recognized their common bond. Their true kinship. Their . . . siblingness.

Aram paused and looked up. The White Lady was sinking behind Skypeak's rocky spire, where their friend, the night elf Thalyss Greyoak, had died the night before—after extracting one last promise, giving them one last charge.

Makasa moved for the first time, following Aram's eyes to look over her shoulder. Though they were now a long day's walk from Skypeak's heights, both of them could still see the Blue Child's light glistening across the waterfall, at the foot of which Thalyss had been laid to rest that morning. Makasa turned back to Aram and nodded sadly, knowing instinctively where his thoughts had flown. Forgetting to pose, she was herself again, and Aram raced to capture the hard-earned sympathy in his sister's eyes.

It didn't matter now that Makasa hadn't had the time or opportunity to know and love Thalyss as Aram had. It was enough that she knew how Aram felt. Frankly, it was enough that the kaldorei had sacrificed his centuries-long life saving her brother, taking two crossbow bolts in the back that had been meant for Aram. That was more than enough to forever enshrine the elf in her memory as a friend, compatriot, and hero.

Aram felt Thalyss's absence more acutely, more personally; the companionship of the wise, perpetually amused night elf had briefly filled the void created by the death of his father. Now, both Greydon and Greyoak were lost to him. *Not lost*, Makasa would say. *Dead. They're dead. Face it. Don't sugarcoat it.* She was a hard woman, that Flintwill, unfailingly honest and direct. But he had come to appreciate those qualities.

"Mrksa?" a strange little voice called out hopefully. It was Murky, their young, small, green, and gangly murloc companion—with a body that was practically one big head, including large, soulful puppy-dog frog eyes. He and their other current traveling companion, Hackle, had returned to their camp with firewood.

Makasa shook her head impatiently. "No. No fires. I told you we're still too close to Dire Maul. We're not sending up a column of smoke that'll lead our enemies right to us. I thought you were off looking for windblossom berries."

"No berries," Hackle said, dumping the unwanted pile of wood between Aram and Makasa. The furry hyena-man was a gnoll warrior—though little more than a pup himself (if a strong and broad-shouldered pup).

They all paused then to look about their camp, a rocky clearing by a tiny creek, near the border between Thousand Needles and the dense forests of Feralas, its trees leaning, looming in the moon-lit night. The not-to-be-used woodpile now sat where a campfire might have been, where—if there had been time to hunt or fish and not just flee—they might have cooked and enjoyed an evening meal. Almost as one, their four stomachs growled.

Aram remembered then that he was hungry. Very hungry.

Murky said, "Urum n Mrksa mlgggrrr. Murky n Ukle mlgggrrr. Murky mrrugl frunds mmgr mmm mmmm flllurlok, nrk nk mgrrrrl. Nk mgrrrrl!"

Makasa squinted at the murloc, then turned a questioning glance on Aram.

He shrugged. "I don't know. I think I've figured out a few of his words. I know I'm Urum, and you're Murksa—"

"Mrksa," Murky corrected.

"Hackle is Ukle," Hackle said.

"And we're all his frunds. Friends. But beyond that, I really don't know."

Murky just shook his head and repeated, "Nk mgrrrrl, nk mgrrrrl . . ." three or four more times. His stomach grumbled loudly to punctuate his lament.

When did we last eat anything at all? Aram wondered. *Three days ago?* And there had been plenty of exertion during the interval: forced marches, gladiatorial combat, daring escapes. He knew he should be clawing at roots by now. Desperate. But strangely, he felt more at ease than he had in weeks. Months, even. His belly might gnaw at him, but his soul was calm. Yes, they were hungry and hunted. But the enemy was a distance away, and—because Aram and his friends had escaped through the air on the back of an actual wyvern—had only the vaguest idea of their heading and no logical way to pick up their trail. So for now, Aram could relax under soothing moonlight with his companions.

He finished the sketch by signing his name to it with a slightly exaggerated flourish, before dropping his pencil into his shirt pocket. Makasa scowled—an all too familiar expression to Aram. He said, "Would you like to see it?"

Hackle and Murky practically climbed over each other to get to Aram and see his latest endeavor.

"Mmmm mrrrggk," Murky said, cooing, which Aram knew from Thalyss to mean *good magic*.

Hackle nodded firmly and echoed Murky's praise. "Good magic," he said with confidence.

To the murloc and the gnoll, the "good magic" of Aram's sketchbook was not a metaphor. To them, there was something truly mystical about the way Aram and his pencil captured the likenesses of the people and places and things around him. If he had materialized some actual windblossom berries in his hand, Murky and Hackle could hardly have been more impressed.

Aram just knew he liked to draw. He liked to think he was

pretty good at it, too. His stepfather had thought him talented enough to spend a week's wages to purchase this leather-bound sketchbook for Aram's twelfth birthday, and it was Aram's most prized possession. Or at least it used to be, before his father gave him the compass and Thalyss gave him the acorn.

But Aram didn't want to think about compasses and acorns now. He wanted Makasa to *want* to see her picture. But she hadn't made a move to look at it. Nor, it occurred to him, had she responded to his asking her if she'd like to.

Suddenly insecure, he asked again, "*Don't* you want to see it?"

She scowled again. "I don't know. Do I?"

He resisted the temptation to roll his eyes, since he knew that particularly aggravated her. He got up, sidestepped the firewood, and moved toward her. "I hope so," he said.

He held the book under her nose. She studied it in the moonlight for a suspenseful minute. Finally, she said, "Is that what I look like?"

Murky said, "Mrgle, mrgle," which Aram knew meant *yes*.

Hackle said only, "Makasa." To him, it was definitive.

Aram scrunched up his face. He said, "Well, that's what you look like to me, anyway. Don't you like it?"

"She's too soft," Makasa said.

Not "I'm too soft," Aram thought. *"She."* He said, "You don't look like this every second. It's just how you looked in one particular moment. But . . . but this is the *you* I see when I close my eyes."

Makasa

A. Thorne

"If you see me with your eyes closed, why'd I have to pose for you?"

"No, see . . ."

"It's good, I guess," she allowed.

But now he felt like she was simply trying to placate him. "You don't have to like it," he said, trying to hide his disappointment. He closed the book and wrapped it in its oilskin cloth. He stuffed it into the back pocket of his breeches and returned to his seat.

"No, it's good." But she sounded less convincing than ever.

"You're impossible," he muttered.

She smiled then. It angered him. She said, "Brat."

"Me?"

"If we're not all singing your praises, you sulk."

"No one asked you to sing. Do you even know how to sing?"

"I don't sing. Not for you. Not for anyone."

"And that's our loss, I suppose." He shook his head. "What are we even talking about now?"

"My sulky brat of a little brother."

Aram stared at her. She was still smiling.

And soon enough, he was smiling, too.

CHAPTER TWO
SHADOW 'CROSS THE LIGHT

ackle volunteered to take the first watch. Murky was already asleep, snoring softly, air bubbling out—puttering—from between his green fish-lips.

With no fire, this summer night on the Feralas–Thousand Needles border was chilly and getting chillier. Aram pulled on another birthday present: the grey woolen cable sweater his mother had knit to honor his eleventh year. Their travels and adventures had left it quite filthy, but it was still warm. Next, he pulled his father's worn leather coat up to his chin like it was a blanket from his bed back home in faraway Lakeshire. The coat still smelled of the sea, or at least Aram imagined it did. It was the second-to-last gift his father gave him before they parted. Aram reached up to check that Greydon Thorne's final gift—the compass—was still secure on the chain around his neck.

It was.

He lay back on grassy turf, already a bit wet with dew. He glanced over at Makasa, who seemed reluctant to leave the waking world (with its marauding ogres, murderous compass-seekers, and poisonous snakes) in Hackle's yellow, spotted paws. Aram knew she didn't much like trusting in anyone save herself. (Aram not excepted.) He watched the internal conflict gnaw at her. She sucked on her lower lip, then bit it between her white teeth, as Hackle stood at the alert, gripping and re-gripping the stolen ogre war club he now claimed as his own. Something about the gnoll's anxious hold on the weapon seemed to reassure her—that, and the valor he had shown during their escape from Dire Maul. She nodded once at Aram, and then laid her head back against her shield, which was propped up against a large rock. She would sleep in this position. Barely reclining. Ready for action at a moment's notice, with her right hand resting on her cutlass. Her left hand flinched, unconsciously reaching for the iron harpoon she had been forced to abandon some days ago. Aram knew she felt nearly naked without it. Or not naked—but *amputated*—like a piece of herself was missing.

But it wouldn't keep her awake. She would sleep like she did everything, lightly but efficiently. She'd wake herself before Hackle could, and take the next watch.

Aram turned over. His hunger, easily ignored before, was gnawing at his gut now. He felt fairly certain it would keep him awake. But he hadn't reckoned with the fact that it had been forty-plus hours since he had slept at all. In no time, he drifted off . . .

"Aram," the Voice said. "Can you hear me?"

"Yes. Clearer now than before."

"Do you know who I am? What I am?"

"You're the Light. The Voice of the Light. And I'm to . . . 'save you' somehow. That's all I know. Can you tell me more? I want to know—need to know—more."

"Turn to me. Look upon me, Aramar Thorne, and much will be revealed."

Aram turned toward the Light. He had seen it many times before in his dreams—even prior to all his strange new troubles—and every one of those times, it had nearly blinded him. Now, it was brighter still, and yet Aram steeled himself and did not turn away. Did not blink.

"The answers you seek," the Voice said, "are in the Light. Approach."

Aram walked forward. It wasn't easy. The Light seemed to have substance, and moving through it was like swimming through molasses. But a determined Aram persisted. "I have so many questions," Aram said.

"The answers you seek," the Voice repeated, "are in the Light."

"No," a new voice said grimly. "Only death lives in that Light." A looming silhouette interposed itself between Aram and the Light, *blocking Aram's way. "You will receive no answers, learn no secrets here," the silhouette said in a dark, angry baritone. "You will sur-render the compass and give up this quest—or you* will *die."*

"No!" Aram shouted defiantly. "My father gave me that compass!"

Striking like a cobra, the silhouette grabbed Aram by his torn shirtfront and pulled him in close enough so that the boy could make out the features of this obstacle, this opponent. They were nearly as familiar as those of his father. The bushy black eyebrows, the wide forehead and square jaw, the nearly black eyes, glaring at him with a look of pure fury. It was Captain Malus. The man who had killed Greydon Thorne. "Boy," Malus croaked, "if you miss your father that much, I can easily arrange for you to join him." His free hand wrapped around the compass and snapped it off its chain.

Aram woke with a start and a gasp that made Hackle wheel about in place and snapped Makasa out of her light slumber. (Murky, however, bravely bubbled on.)

"What is it?" Makasa asked as Aram threw off his father's coat and frantically reached under his sweater and shirt until he could feel the cold metal of the compass in his grip. And even that wasn't enough. He pulled it out from under his clothes so he could confirm it still remained in his possession.

To all appearances, it was nothing all that special. The compass, which hung from a gold chain around his neck, had a white face in a brass setting. Gold initials—*N, E, S, W*—labeled its four points. The only thing at all unusual about it was the crystal needle, which pointed not north but to the southeast. So mostly, it appeared broken.

But appearances can be deceiving.

How had Thalyss described it?v

"It is a shard of pure starlight from the heavens," the druid had said, "imbued with the celestial spark . . . Simply put, the crystal needle is not of this world. There is an enchantment of some kind upon it."

And *that* had proven itself true, a hundredfold. Aram's father had given him the compass in the most desperate of circumstances, as practically his last act on this world. He had charged Aram to protect it at all costs, and had promised it would *"lead you where you need to go!"*

Aram had thought that meant it would lead him home to Lakeshire. Then, as now, he desperately missed his mother, Ceya, his stepfather, Robb, his half siblings, Robertson and Selya, and his dog, Soot. Aram missed their old, uneventful life in the cottage beside the forge, where Robb Glade had been teaching him to be a simple town blacksmith—not a sailor, and certainly not some kind of unwilling traveler across the blasted wilderness. He missed his mother's cooking and her gentle embrace. He missed roughhousing with Robertson and cuddling with Selya and rambling along the shores of Lake Everstill with Soot.

But the compass was not a ticket home. Its needle had eventually led Aram to another crystal shard, a slightly larger sibling of its own. In fact, the closer the compass had come to the new shard, the more, well . . . *alive* the device had seemed. The needle had begun to glow, and when Aram was very close, the compass literally moved of its own volition, snapping off its chain and flying through the air to meet its kin or kind.

These shards, Aram knew, were part of the Light. The Light he had seen and heard in his dreams and visions. The Light he was somehow meant to save.

"Another dream?" Makasa asked.

Aram nodded, not yet able to speak, not yet able to do much more than turn the compass over and over in his hands.

"Of this Light?" she prompted again.

Aram swallowed and found his voice. "Yeah," he said. "But not just the Light. He was there, too."

"Who? Your father?"

"No. Malus."

Fury flooded over her face at the mere mention of the name. But she said nothing.

"I know why he wants the compass now," Aram said. "He wants to stop me—stop *anyone*—from saving the Light."

And that, as far as it went, was true. But when it came to Malus, it wasn't going nearly far enough.

GORDOK'S ELITE

At that very moment, torches blazed in Dire Maul, the Gordunni ogre stronghold, as Captain Malus marshaled his now considerable forces to hunt Aram down.

Having killed the ogre king Gordok in single combat, the human Malus had declared himself the *new* Gordok, putting every single ogre under his single command, in service of his single-minded cause.

The one ogre that Malus had brought with him, Throgg of the Shattered Hand clan, had been tasked with supervising the complete and total evacuation of Dire Maul: emptying each and every hut and stone dwelling, and scattering each and every ogre— male and female, ancient and child—into the wilderness, across the rain forests of Feralas, the flooded canyon of Thousand Needles, and the simmering desert of Tanaris, to search for Aram and the compass.

*　　*　　*

Throgg performed these tasks, for Throgg was loyal to Malus. Of this, there could be no question. But Throgg also believed in the traditions of Throgg's people, and Throgg knew Throgg's captain had abused those traditions by declaring Malus king. And, yes, Throgg would follow Malus to the ends of Azeroth and into the very jaws of death—whatever jaws there might be. But pledging Throgg's service to Malus had been *Throgg's* choice.

This was different.

For as Throgg watched females, infants bundled on their backs, ushering their young from their homes for the cold night's forced march, Throgg knew deep in Throgg's substantial chest that *this was not right!*

Throgg of the Shattered Hand slowly screwed Throgg's mace attachment onto the metal stump of Throgg's right wrist, as Malus—*Gordok*—approached to supervise Throgg's supervision. As Gordunni ogres marched past, Malus said, "I know we killed most of their elite warriors last night, but pull out the best of what remains and bring them to Gordok's throne room. I'll meet you there."

Throgg nodded, but Throgg's discomfort—even resentment—was plain to see on Throgg's face.

Malus patted Throgg on Throgg's arm and said, "When we have the boy—or, at any rate, the compass—this will all be over. I will hand Gordok's crown to whichever ogre *you* choose, Throgg. And the Gordunni will return to Dire Maul."

Throgg considered this for a little while, slowly screwing the notion into Throgg's brain. Finally, Throgg nodded again, satisfied. *For now.*

Malus turned away before Throgg could see the contempt in his captain's eyes. Malus needed to maintain the loyalty of Throgg the Truly Dim, since he was the *only* member of the Hidden who was truly loyal to Malus. Thus, it was no great sacrifice to be reasonable with the ogre and feign respect for what Throgg held sacred. But it was a genuine annoyance, not to mention a distraction from the man's greater concerns.

The rest of the Hidden had already gathered before the old king's massive stone throne. Here was Zathra, their tracker; Valdread, their swordsman; and Ssarbik, their sorcerer. The first two were mercenaries, loyal only to Malus's purse. The last wasn't loyal at all. Or at least not to Malus. Ssarbik served the same master Malus served and could rarely go five minutes without expressing his contempt for the substance and style of Malus's command.

"What do you hope to accomplish with theezze brainlesss ogrezz?" Ssarbik hissed through his beak.

Malus had covered this ground already. He glared down at the hunchbacked, birdlike arakkoa and growled his explanation again: "We know the boy heads for Gadgetzan."

"You do not *know* thissss. You merely sssurmizze it."

"And you surmise something different, I suppose?" asked

Valdread in a whisper, emerging from the shadows of his hooded head like sand blowing across the desert. The overstrong scent of jasmine water also emerged from under his hood, hiding the stench of his decay. For Baron Reigol Valdread was one of the Forsaken, raised into undeath by dark sorcery—but with his mind and free will restored by further magicks.

His whispered query to Ssarbik had held more than a hint of a wry smile. The baron had little respect for the arakkoa, but Malus hardly appreciated the support. Valdread's greatest enemy was boredom, and Malus knew that his undead swordsman would do anything to break up the monotony of his undead existence. Sowing dissent among the Hidden was one of his favorite pastimes, which—like Throgg's scruples or Ssarbik's insubordination—was just another distraction that Malus didn't need.

So he didn't wait for the flustered, sputtering Ssarbik to respond. As Throgg entered the chamber, followed by half a dozen more ogres, Malus said, "We are confident of the child's destination, but not of his route. By scattering the Gordunni across three regions, we reduce the risk of missing him."

"And if dem ogres catch da boy? Or if *we* grab him up?" asked Zathra, the sinewy, orange-skinned Sandfury troll.

Ssarbik perked up, happy to have been handed a new club with which to bash his captain. "Then our fearlesss leader will find another exxcusse to ssspare him!"

"No," Malus shot back, cold and merciless. "I gave Aramar

Thorne every chance to hand over the compass and walk away with his life. But he's as stubborn as his fool of a father and has made his choice. So I wash my hands of him. We've told the ogres. Now I'm telling all of you. Find the boy. Do what you have to do. But bring me that compass."

The troll seemed pleased with that response. She stroked her breastplate and it shimmied and clicked, causing a couple of the new ogres to take a step back. Malus smiled darkly. He knew Zathra's living armor was actually a three-foot-long scorpid female, which the sand troll called Skitter and treated as a beloved pet.

Zathra said, "Good ta know, mon. I gonna feed my loa wid dat boy's blood. Dat boy an' all a his friends make some meal for da gods. Wid maybe a bit left over for Skitter an' me." She licked her lips, hungrily.

Malus ignored her bloodlust. He was studying the six ogres Throgg had collected. One of them—a striking female warrior, seven feet tall with ashy blue skin—stepped forward, her hand resting easy on her broadsword's hilt. Throgg nodded his head toward her, saying, "This Karrga. Karrga got . . ." He searched for the word.

"Information," she prompted.

"Yeah. That."

Malus liked her already. *First word out of her mouth and it has four syllables. As ogres go, she must be a genius.*

21

Karrga bowed her head slightly and spoke: "New Gordok know old Gordok like his fun." There was no love for her former king in her tone. "Fun mean slaves to fight, so old Gordok send raiders to get more slaves. Send Wordok west. Send Marjuk east. Wordok come back with your boy."

"He's not *my* boy," Malus said, slightly cross.

She shrugged but otherwise ignored the interruption. "Boy's friends killed Wordok last night. But Marjuk still not back. Marjuk big stinking ogre. Won't serve human Gordok."

"Why are you telling me this?" the human Gordok asked.

She smiled. "Marjuk wanna be Gordok. But Karrga no want that. Marjuk killed Karrga's father over a pig. Human Gordok be ready, so human Gordok can kill Marjuk, right?"

"Right," Malus said. They understood each other. "Except tonight *you* will be heading east with Throgg of the Shattered Hand. Your path may cross Marjuk's before his crosses mine. So I give you my permission. You may kill Marjuk."

She frowned slightly and slid her sword—an unusual weapon for an ogre—a few inches out of its scabbard. "Karrga may kill Marjuk. Or Marjuk may kill Karrga. Karrga not afraid. But Karrga not sure." She slid her sword home again.

She's even smart enough to know her limitations.

Throgg stepped forward stiffly and declared, "Throgg of Shattered Hand will kill Marjuk. Throgg sure."

KARRGA

A. Thorne

Karrga glanced at her new king for confirmation. Malus nodded, glancing with amused curiosity at Throgg. *Was Throgg being . . . chivalrous?*

Karrga seemed satisfied. "Throgg kill Marjuk. Karrga sure now."

Throgg smiled stupidly . . . more stupidly than usual. To hide it, he scratched his forehead horn with one of his mace spikes. It belatedly occurred to Malus that this Karrga was capable of wrapping Throgg around her not-so-little finger. Still, Malus liked her. She was smart, which meant she could be useful. Plus, if Throgg killed her blood enemy under the flag of the new Gordok, that could cement her loyalty to both Throgg *and* Malus. Nevertheless, he'd have to keep his eye on her. *It's a fine line between useful and dangerous.*

Malus turned to face the other five newcomers as Throgg made introductions. The new Gordok wasn't particularly interested in learning his subjects' names—but was canny enough to fake it.

Throgg identified two eight-foot-tall male identical twins as Ro'kull and Ro'jak. Both were ruddy-skinned and held massive identical battleaxes.

Next was Short-Beard and Long-Beard, a two-headed ogre with skin the color of a mottled peach. Each head was bald and sported a single thick horn from its brow. They had white beards of eponymous lengths. Long-Beard, on the right, also had a long neck, topping him out at about nine feet tall. On the left, Short-Beard was a couple of inches shorter. He (or they) held an iron mace in either hand.

Slepgar was a pale-red giant of an ogre, easily twelve feet in height, with muscles piled upon muscles. He cradled a tremendous war club in his arms and yawned as if Malus were keeping him up past his bedtime.

Last, there was Guz'luk, an older, potbellied ogre with dark-grey skin and a round, jowly face. He was small relative to the others at only six feet. Guz'luk had a ram's horn tied to his belt and a morningstar that Malus recognized as the former property of the late Gordok. Obviously, the potbellied ogre had salvaged it from the arena after Malus had taken it from Gordok and used it to end his predecessor's life. *Well, what of it?* Malus himself had kept Gordok's long curved dagger. *No sense letting a perfectly good weapon go to waste.*

Malus knew that in their rapid conquest of the Gordunni, the Hidden had been forced to kill most of Gordok's best warriors. Nevertheless, he was impressed with Throgg's selections. They were still ogres and—perhaps with the exception of Karrga—probably as dim as Throgg himself, but as warriors (*or, if necessary, as cannon fodder*), they had real potential.

Malus addressed them now, Gordunni and Hidden alike: "The boy travels with a gnoll, a murloc, and a human woman."

"A human woman of no little skill," Valdread whispered.

Malus nodded. He didn't want them underestimating Thorne's allies. "They may also be in the company of a night elf shape-shifter and perhaps even a wyvern. Together, they may be a match for the rest of the Gordunni hunting parties. *But you are my Elite.* You will find the boy, and no matter who protects him, you will bring me the compass he carries. Head southeast. Make your way to Gadgetzan. One way or another, we'll rendezvous there."

Eight ogre heads nodded solemnly. The troll nodded, too, while absently stroking Skitter. Valdread was enigmatic under his hood. The arakkoa grumbled something unintelligible.

"Zathra, you're in command," Malus said.

"Yes, mon."

"Zzathra? Zzathra?!" Ssarbik squawked. "Why put *her* in command?!"

"Because you and I will be aboard the *Inevitable*, sailing into port. The Thorne boy has a substantial head start and may still be riding that wyvern. If he avoids the hunting parties and reaches his destination, I want to be waiting in Gadgetzan . . . to greet him. Open a portal."

Now, finally, the arakkoa smiled. "A portal to the ship musst needzz take uhss through Outland," he said, barely concealing his glee. "And if we passs through Outland, the Masster will want a report. He will demand one."

"Why do you tell me what I already know?" Malus asked rhetorically. *"Open a portal."*

Ssarbik's head bobbed happily, and he began to chant: "We are the Hidden, the voyagerzz of Shadow. We ssserve and will conquer. What we conquer will Burn. Burn down the barrierzz that divide uhss from the Masster. Burn azz the Masster willzz. Burn for the Hidden. Burn. Burn."

The very air before the arakkoa burst into dark flame. The ogres and troll stepped back. Zathra's breastplate skittered up and over her shoulder to armor her back. Only Valdread, Ssarbik, and Malus didn't retreat. But Malus could feel Ssarbik's borrowed power, and as the hairs on his arms stood at attention, the new king of the ogres willed himself not to move a muscle, not to reveal any weakness or trepidation—not at Ssarbik's display of magic or in anticipation of facing Ssarbik's "Masster."

The airborne flames expanded swiftly into a purple-black oval, a portal just big enough for Malus to walk through if he ducked his head a bit.

Rubbing his feathered hands together, Ssarbik shuffled through the mystic gate, disappearing into the black. Malus watched Long-Beard stretch his neck, expecting to see the arakkoa emerge out the other side. But the bird-man did not emerge. He had vanished into the portal.

Malus strode forward and through, and an instant later the portal collapsed upon itself. The sorcerer and the ogre king were gone.

Come dawn, Aram, Makasa, Murky, and Hackle broke camp, taking inventory of their stores and possessions. Well, of their possessions. They had no stores at all.

Hackle didn't have much to reckon: just the large ironwood war club, studded with three or four iron nails, that he had liberated from the brutal Wordok after Makasa had wounded the broad-backed ogre, giving Hackle the opportunity to finish him off. Considering Hackle's history with that particular ogre, it had been a moment of tremendous satisfaction for the gnoll, and Wordok's club was Hackle's spoils. True, it was a tad too big, a tad too heavy for the adolescent gnoll, but Hackle was already growing broad of shoulder, and he would grow into it yet.

Murky had nothing to reckon at all. He just looked around the camp, again muttering, "Nk mgrrrl, nk mgrrrl . . ." Now, Aram understood. To entangle and delay Valdread the Whisper-Man during their escape from Dire Maul, Murky had sacrificed his fishing nets. Thalyss once said that a murloc has no more valuable possession than his or her nets. Murky's nets had been his *only* possession, and he was more than a little bereft without them.

Makasa had her shield, chain, cutlass, hatchet, two gold coins, Thalyss's canteen, and her abiding *longing* for her harpoon. (She looked around the campsite much as Murky did, as if somehow it would yield up to them the items that had never been there in the first place. In fact, Aram would not have been surprised to hear her murmuring, "Nk harpoon, nk harpoon . . .")

Aram, by far, had the most to keep track of. Of chief importance was the compass on the chain around his neck. The chain's fastening had snapped the other day and had been only crudely repaired, so Aram confirmed it was sure.

Next, he pulled on his boots and, as the day was already growing steamy, tied both his mother's sweater and his father's coat around his waist. His linen shirt was shredded in back and sliced open in front, but the pocket was intact, and his coal pencil was still safe inside it.

The four pockets of his breeches contained two more gold coins, his oilskin-wrapped sketchbook, an oilskin-wrapped case of flints, and three oilskin maps. A used cutlass, taken from the dead hand of a pirate and traitor, hung at his belt.

A purple-dyed leather pouch was also securely tied to his belt. In it was the newly found crystal shard *and* an oilskin-wrapped acorn the size of his fist. This last item was the "Seed of Thalyss," which Aram had seen the night elf use to magically grow everything from tasty vegetables to a massive oak tree. As life was slipping away from the druid, he had extracted a promise from Aram and the others to bring the Seed to Gadgetzan and deliver it safely to a night elf druid tender named Faeyrine Springsong. Along with that final request, Thalyss Greyoak had used his final breath to relay a final admonition: *"Do not . . . let it . . . get . . . wet . . ."* Aram wasn't sure why that mattered—but he was determined to keep the acorn safe and dry, and to honor his friend's dying wish.

Aram unfolded the oilskin map of Kalimdor and knelt to consult it with Makasa. After a little study, she reckoned it would take their small band about two weeks to walk to Gadgetzan along the shore of the Cataclysm-flooded Thousand Needles. Less time, if they somehow managed to find a way to convey themselves via water.

Aram stood, folded the map, and returned it to a pocket. Then he checked the compass, which pointed to the southeast—toward Gadgetzan, though perhaps only incidentally. Aram now knew the crystal needle was actually pointing toward the *next* crystal shard. But perhaps the next shard was *in Gadgetzan* (or perhaps somewhere en route).

In any case, their course was clear enough for now.

Looking over Aram's shoulder, Makasa stated, "It still points southeast toward Gadgetzan."

"Uh huh," he said as he slipped the compass down between his shirt and his slim chest.

"Then southeast we will go, as Captain Thorne would have us go." She spoke as if their captain—their father—were still alive and had given the order half an hour past.

"Southeast," Hackle said.

"Mrgle, mrgle."

They headed out.

As they hiked along the Feralas–Thousand Needles border, the rain forest to one side and the flooded canyon to the other, Aram still wished he were on a true path home to his native Lakeshire. Yet everything he'd been through over the last seven months suggested it would be a long time before he'd see his family cottage again.

He'd lived in that cottage—and hardly gone two miles' distance from it—for the first twelve years of his life. For the first six of those years, his existence had been nothing short of idyllic, snugly ensconced between his mother, Ceya, and his father, Greydon Thorne. Then, early on the morning of Aramar's sixth birthday, his father had abandoned his small family to return to the sea. Years passed with no word from the man. Years passed before Aram could bring himself to believe that his father had really chosen to leave—and had not been spirited away by orcs or murlocs. Years passed before Ceya Northbrooke Thorne gave up on waiting for her husband's return and married the kind blacksmith Robb Glade.

Robb had moved into their cottage—and had even built his new forge alongside it—so that Aram's life would not be further disrupted by having to relocate all the way *around the corner* to Robb's own cottage and forge. (That was the kind of man Robb was. His own convenience meant nothing when reckoned against the needs of his family.) But at the time, Aram hardly appreciated the gesture. The burly, ash-covered smith seemed an interloper, casting a wide, dusky shadow between Aram and Ceya, and—if the boy was being honest—between Aram, Ceya, and the vain hope that Captain Thorne might someday return from the glistening sea.

When Aram's little brother, Robertson, was born nine months later, Aram was sure he'd be out on the street. *After all, isn't that what evil stepfathers do?* Yet through it all, Robb was a paragon of patience, always attentive to Aram, whether the boy was ready for those attentions or not. The broad-shouldered blacksmith with the strong hands and warm heart eventually won Aram over, and by the time his baby sister, Selya, was born, the five of them—or six, if you counted the coal-black dog Soot—were quite the happy little family.

Still, Aram dreamt of someday seeking out and joining his father for great adventures on the high seas! Instead, the lad drew in his sketchbook, apprenticed at the forge, and settled into his comfortable life.

Then one day, about a month after his twelfth birthday, all his dreams came true—and not at all to his liking. Greydon returned, without explanation or apology, to take Aram with him to sea. Suddenly, all of Aram's dreams felt foolish (on the rare occasions when he acknowledged ever having dreamt them at all). He loved Lakeshire, loved his family, and owed no loyalty whatsoever to the man who had abandoned him. Aramar Thorne flat out refused to go with his father.

But Ceya and Robb actually sided with Greydon!

They insisted Aram spend a year as a cabin boy aboard his father's ship. His mother had all sorts of reasons: "You need to get to know your father, understand him, see the world ... Explore that piece of you that is just like Greydon Thorne ... Open your heart to him again . . . Know him to know yourself."

Aram was unconvinced and thus determined to spend his year on *Wavestrider* proving to all three of his parents that they had been dead wrong. During his first six months aboard ship, Aram was—as he now realized—a resentful brat, at war with Captain Greydon Thorne, at war with Second Mate Makasa Flintwill, at war with his own childhood fantasies. Yes, there were members of the crew he was fond of: the brawny, jovial dwarf, First Mate

Durgan One-God, who rarely failed to bring a smile to Aram's face; and the lithe and beautiful ship's lookout, fifteen-year-old Duan Phen, who rarely failed to bring a very *different* kind of smile to Aram's face.

But for the most part, Aram had resisted smiling. He resisted the lessons Robb and Ceya had imparted upon his departure. He resisted the many lessons Greydon tried to teach him. (Or so he believed at the time. He now found that much of his father's teachings had somehow sunk in despite the boy's efforts to keep them at bay.) He had felt acutely that Greydon's attempts at parenting were too little, too late.

Now, he felt nothing more acutely than regret. There was so much he didn't appreciate then that he desperately missed now. He felt nostalgia for the smell of the ocean, for the sound of *Wavestrider*'s iron bell, and for the elegant, angular lines of her unusual figurehead. He missed and mourned nearly every member of the crew. Not just One-God and Duan Phen, but also Third Mate Silent Joe Barker, cook's assistant Keelhaul Watt, helmsman Thom Frakes, and all the rest. He could barely think of any of them without crying.

Well, all save Old Cobb.

For Greydon had a secret. A reason why he had left his family behind in Lakeshire. A reason why he had wanted his son aboard ship now. All the training, all the lessons, was designed to prepare Aram. Prepare him, Aram now knew, for something to do with the compass and the crystal shards and the Light-That-Needed-Saving. But time had run out before Greydon had taken the opportunity to explain.

The ship's cook, Jonas Cobb, had betrayed his captain, his ship, and his crew by selling *Wavestrider*'s route to Valdread, Malus, and their fellow piratical compass-seekers. Malus's ship attacked. Aram witnessed the horrible deaths of Keely, Thom, and many others. He saw the ogre Throgg chop down *Wavestrider*'s mainmast. (The only saving grace being that when the mast came down, it squashed the traitorous Cobb just as he was about to run Aram through. In fact, it was Cobb's villainous cutlass that Aram now wore upon his belt.) He saw his father's ship set aflame; he saw its powder stores explode.

In those last seconds, Greydon had put Aram in the ship's lone dinghy, had given his son his coat and the compass, and had commanded Makasa to go with the boy and protect him, overcoming her objections by invoking the life debt she owed her captain, saying, "There's more at stake than either of you realize." The dinghy was lowered into the water. A storm quickly separated it from the ship and its attackers. The fates of Greydon, One-God, Duan Phen, and the rest were left to the gods. (But Valdread later acknowledged that the gods had not been kind. "Your father . . . ?" he had whispered. "I'm afraid you'll never see him again in this world, my boy.")

Aram and Makasa had come ashore in Feralas. The compass,

which Greydon had said would lead Aram where he needed to go, seemed to point straight to Lakeshire. And also toward Gadgetzan, where Aram was sure he could book passage on a ship home. He had convinced Makasa to take him there, and she had agreed, mostly so she could be free of him. But somewhere along the way, Aram and Makasa had found common ground, had become—both of them—Greydon's children. Aram had been the eldest of three; Makasa, the youngest of four. But now she was truly his older sister in every way but blood.

During their travels, they had stumbled upon Murky and Thalyss. (Stumbled, unless one credited Thalyss's theories on destiny: "There is a harmony to nature," the druid had said. "A way and a flow. Like the path of a river, like the path through the soil that a stem takes to find the sun. Do you think it is any different for beings such as we four travelers?") The murloc and the night elf became traveling companions, much to Makasa's initial frustration.

Then Malus and his minions had resurfaced, abducting Murky and offering to trade the murloc for the compass. Before Aram could comply or resist, he and Thalyss were captured by the Gordunni ogres. They were taken to Dire Maul, where Aram was forced to fight Hackle in Gordok's arena. Instead, the boy and the gnoll had formed an alliance. When Malus showed up with Murky to get the compass, Aram and his friends took advantage of Malus's battle against Gordok to free all of the ogre king's slaves and escape.

But there was a cost.

Malus's troll had fired off two crossbow bolts at Aram's back. Thalyss had intervened, taking the fatal injuries meant for the boy.

Thalyss died that night, but even in his final moments, he attempted to soothe Aram's torment. Thalyss had called Aram's path "a wide road," saying, "It will draw in many souls. I am honored to be among the first."

Now, as Aram walked behind Makasa and between Hackle and Murky, the night elf's words seemed to hold much truth. Aram had known Murky for less than a week; Hackle, for less than two days. Yet he already counted both as fast friends. When the time finally did come to leave them behind and return to Lakeshire, he knew he'd miss them terribly . . .

As morning turned to afternoon, and the sun began to sink low in the sky, its light filtering through the tall trees, Aram remained lost in thought, focused on memories of the recent past and a painful longing for home—most especially, thanks to the growling of his stomach, for his mother's cooking.

Preoccupied as he was, Aram hadn't noticed Hackle's growing anxiety over their current forested location. But Makasa was more astute. She could feel the fear—practically smell it—as it washed over her in waves from behind. She glanced back over her shoulder, expecting to see Aram looking nervous. But her brother's eyes looked inward. Murky glanced up at her and grinned cheerfully.

So Makasa glanced back over her other shoulder at Hackle, and his face instantly revealed the source of what she had felt. The one lower incisor that stuck out even when his mouth was closed was working his upper lip. His head jerked left; it jerked right. His eyes scanned the area relentlessly.

They found themselves crossing a wide-open road between virtual walls of trees, and Makasa dropped back, even with the others. As they continued forward, Hackle shifted the war club from his left shoulder to his right. Then back. Then back again. He sniffed the air with every other step. When a low growl vibrated in his throat, beneath the level of his own awareness, she grabbed the young gnoll by the shoulder and wheeled him around to face her.

"What?" she said.

Aram and Murky stopped. Hackle growled again.

Aram said, "Makasa . . . ?"

"Something troubles this gnoll," she said, her voice nearly as low as Hackle's vocalizations. Her eyes maintained their focus on his.

"What is it, Hackle?" Aram asked. "What's wrong?"

Hackle didn't respond. But Makasa saw his eyes shift back and forth, on the alert. He sniffed the air again.

"You know this territory," she stated. It was more accusation than question.

Aram said, "Sister, leave him alone."

Makasa recognized that Aram had taken to calling her "sister" as a way to influence her. It made her cross, for it seemed an abuse, a cheapening of their genuine fealty to each other. But she also recognized it as a trick she herself had used as a child with her older sibling Akashinga, calling him "brother" when she wanted a ride on his back. She thought Aram a little old to be using such a ploy, even unconsciously, but her memory of one brother tempered her annoyance with this other. So she ignored Aram.

To Hackle, she repeated, "You know this territory."

He nodded curtly but said nothing still.

Murky said, "Ukle flllur mmmrrglllmmm?"

They all ignored the murloc. Now, Aram was studying the gnoll, too.

Makasa asked, "Is this your homeland?"

Aram chimed in: "Is it? Is this Woodpaw clan territory?"

Hackle nodded absently. Then shook his head violently. Then sighed heavily.

Makasa barked, "Do I have to pry open those jaws? Speak, gnoll. Your silence puts us all in danger."

Hackle nodded sadly, grunted to himself, and finally found his voice. "This not Woodpaw lands, but this where Woodpaw clan live now. Gordunni drive us east to here. To the west, ogres chop down our trees. Drive out our game. Take gnolls as slaves. So Woodpaw come here."

Aram said, "But you're free now! You can go back to your people."

The gnoll scowled. "No."

Aram started to speak, but there was something in Hackle's tone that Makasa recognized. She put a hand on her brother's shoulder to silence him. She waited. But like Hackle, she scanned the area, on the alert for trouble.

Finally, the gnoll told his story . . .

CHAPTER FIVE
RUNT

Hackle was pup. *Hackle not pup now!* But Hackle was pup back in Woodpaw lands. Not *so* long ago.

Woodpaw lands sweet then. Much game. Boars. Many boars. Deer. Even bear sometime. Much game. Enough game for hyenas to run with gnolls. Not just follow gnolls and eat leavings, but run with gnolls, hunt with gnolls. Share camp with gnolls.

Then hyenas leave. Hackle wonder where hyenas go. Hackle pup, but Hackle wonder. But Matriarch Greasefang no care. Woodpaw brute Claw no care. "Hyenas in way. Good that hyenas gone," Claw say. "Gnolls no have to share Woodpaw grub with hyenas no more."

But gnolls should have known then.

Hackle walk in woods—in forest. Not *so* long ago. Hackle like woods. Woods cool on hot day. Streams run through. Hackle drink. Squirrels run through. Hackle eat. Woods give shade. Hackle sleep. Easy life for pup.

But Hackle train, too. Hackle's father, Jawstretcher, and mother, Gnaw, were great warriors for Greasefang, for Claw. Gnaw was Claw's littermate. Gnaw and Claw were close. Gnaw train pups to be warriors. Train Hackle. Train Jaggal, son of Greasefang. Jaggal older than Hackle. Jaggal bigger than Hackle. But Jaggal and Hackle good friends. Jaggal and Hackle were close. Not *so* long ago.

But hyenas gone. Then trees gone. Not all trees. But many. Then more and more. Gnolls should have known then.

But gnolls blame yetis. Greasefang blame yetis. So Claw blame yetis. Jawstretcher blame yetis. Gnaw blame yetis. Jaggal blame yetis.

Hackle no see that. Yetis *push* down trees. Sometime, yes, yetis push down trees. But more and more trees *chopped* down. With axes. Not yetis, Hackle say.

"What, then?" Jaggal say.

Hackle no know. But not yetis.

"Greasefang say yetis," Jaggal say.

"Greasefang say yetis," Jawstretcher say.

Gnaw silent.

Hackle say, "Greasefang not right."

Jaggal cuff Hackle then. Hard. Hackle small pup. Mouth bloody. And knocked back hard. Hackle smack back of head on den wall. Much blood from back of head. Hackle silent then.

Yetis move east into Woodpaw lands. Next, yetis attack. Feral Scar is yeti brute. Yetis no call him brute. Yetis no talk. But Feral Scar is like brute for yetis. Like matriarch, too. Not matriarch, though. Feral Scar is male yeti. But Feral Scar lead yetis like Woodpaw matriarch Greasefang. Feral Scar lead in battle like Woodpaw brute Claw. Feral Scar is matriarch and brute for yetis. Feral Scar lead attack. Yetis attack Woodpaw clan. Feral Scar attack Woodpaw clan. Some gnolls die. Three or four gnolls die. One yeti die. Not Feral Scar. Feral Scar no die. Yetis move on. Move east. Feral Scar move on. Move east. Not dead yeti, though. Dead yeti no move. No move on. No move east. Dead yeti feed gnolls. Yeti meat good. Like bear meat. Better maybe.

Greasefang say, "See, yetis chop trees. Then yetis attack. Trees were start of yetis' attack." All gnolls agree with Greasefang.

Hackle silent. But Hackle shake head, and Jaggal cuff Hackle again. Jawstretcher and Claw nod at this. Jawstretcher and Claw think Jaggal right to cuff Hackle.

Gnaw silent. But Gnaw talk to Claw. Gnaw walk with Claw. Hackle follow. Hackle watch Gnaw show Claw tree. Tree pushed over, root and all. "Yeti push tree," Gnaw say.

Claw nod. "Greasefang right," he say.

Gnaw show Claw other tree. Hackle follow and watch. Gnaw show Claw other tree, but there no tree. Just stump. Short stump. Shorter than Hackle, and Hackle is pup then.

"Stump," Gnaw say. "No root. No tree. Just stump. And look. Tree cut with axe. Feral Scar no use axe. Feral Scar no drag away tree. Stump not yeti stump."

"What, then?" ask Claw.

"Gnaw no know," Gnaw say. "But Hackle right. Greasefang wrong."

Claw cuff Gnaw then. But not hard. No blood even. Claw stare at stump. Claw think about stump. Claw say, "Greasefang right." But Claw think about stump.

Next day, Claw walk with Greasefang. Claw talk with Greasefang. Maybe Claw show Greasefang tree and other tree. Hackle never know.

Claw and Greasefang no come back. Never come back.

Jaggal angry. Jaggal say, "Yetis kill Greasefang! Feral Scar kill Greasefang!"

Hackle say, "Yetis move east. Feral Scar move east. Feral Scar gone. Yetis gone."

Jaggal no cuff Hackle this time. Jaggal go for Hackle's throat. Jaggal is friend of Hackle not *so* long ago—but go for throat. Jaggal pulled off Hackle. Jaggal is friend of Hackle no more.

Gnaw become Woodpaw matriarch. Jawstretcher become Woodpaw brute. More trees gone. No shade. No squirrels. Game scarce. Gnolls should have known then.

Finally, ogres attack. Gordunni ogres attack Woodpaw camp. Big surprise. Gnolls not ready to fight ogres.

Wordok and Marjuk are like brutes for Gordunni. Ogres no call Wordok and Marjuk brutes, but Wordok and Marjuk are like brutes, lead attack on Woodpaw lands, on Woodpaw clan. Jawstretcher fight. Gnaw fight. Jaggal fight. Jaggal brave. Jaggal fierce. Kill ogre. Hackle fight. Hackle brave for pup. No kill ogre, though. And many gnolls die. Only three ogres die. Jaggal kill ogre. Jawstretcher kill ogre. Gnaw kill ogre. No kill Wordok, though. No kill Marjuk. Wordok and Marjuk no die. Three *other* ogres die. Gnolls no eat ogres, though. Ogre meat rancid.

Ogres chop trees. Ogres hunt game. Ogres and Wordok and Marjuk take gnolls as slaves for Gordok. Woodpaw lands are all stumps now. No trees. No squirrels. No shade. Streams dry up. No game. Gnolls hungry. Gnolls fight ogres, but gnolls hungry. Many gnolls die. Many Woodpaw die. Few ogres die. Not Wordok. Not Marjuk. Just a few.

Matriarch Gnaw say, "Time to move. Woodpaw must move east."

Jawstretcher nod.

But Jaggal no nod. "These Woodpaw lands. Woodpaw no move!"

Matriarch Gnaw cuff Jaggal. "Woodpaw move east," Gnaw say.

So Woodpaw clan leave Woodpaw lands. Move east.

Ogres still attack from west. Wordok and Marjuk still attack from west. Yetis defend from east. Feral Scar defend from east. Woodpaw trapped in middle.

Matriarch Gnaw say, "Time to move. Woodpaw must move south."

Jawstretcher nod.

Jaggal say, "Gnaw no fight. Gnaw always move. Gnaw afraid."

Gnaw cuff Jaggal. "Woodpaw move south," Gnaw say.

So Woodpaw clan move south.

In south, Woodpaw find new lands. Not *so* long ago. Good lands. Trees. Streams. Squirrels. Shade. Game. No hyenas. Hyenas follow ogres now.

Woodpaw fight yetis. Fight ogres. But not all the time now.

Many seasons pass. Hackle grow. Not pup now. Not pup. No grow as big as Jaggal. No grow as big as many gnolls. But not pup.

Jaggal grow big. Jaggal big as Jawstretcher. Jaggal almost big as Gnaw.

When Woodpaw fight, Gnaw lead clan. When Woodpaw fight, Jawstretcher lead battle. But Jaggal fight beside Jawstretcher. And Hackle fight beside Gnaw. Jaggal kill yeti. Jaggal kill ogre. Hackle no kill yeti, no kill ogre. But Hackle fight. Hackle warrior. Not pup. Hackle fight.

Big battle come. Ogres come. Wordok come. Marjuk come. Big battle. Woodpaw fight. Woodpaw fight ogres. Many gnolls die. Some ogres die, too. Not Wordok or Marjuk, but some.

Jawstretcher die then. Wordok kill Jawstretcher.

Gnaw die, too. Marjuk kill Gnaw.

Wordok take some gnolls as slaves. Marjuk take some gnolls as slaves. For Gordok. Ogres leave with slaves.

Hackle sad. Hackle warrior now, but Hackle sad.

No matriarch. Greasefang dead. Gnaw dead. No other gnoll female ready to be matriarch.

No brute. Claw dead. Jawstretcher dead. So Jaggal become brute. All gnolls agree Jaggal become brute. Hackle agree, too.

Jaggal turn on Hackle then. "Jaggal no need pup to agree," Jaggal say. "Woodpaw no need pup."

"Hackle no pup!" Hackle say. Maybe Hackle shout.

Jaggal nod. "Hackle no pup. *Hackle runt!*"

Hackle silent. Gnolls all silent.

Hackle finally say, "Hackle no runt." But he say it like whisper.

Jaggal say, "Who say Hackle no runt? Jawstretcher say Hackle no runt? Gnaw say Hackle no runt?"

"Jawstretcher dead," Hackle say. "Gnaw dead."

"Gnolls say Hackle no runt?" Jaggal ask.

Gnolls silent. Woodpaw silent. Even Hackle silent.

Jaggal say, "Runt no fight yetis. Runt no fight ogres. Runt no hunt game. But runt eat game. Runt live off Woodpaw. Runt take game from mouth of Woodpaw like hyenas. So Woodpaw no live with runt. Runt weaken Woodpaw. Runt must go."

Gnolls silent. Woodpaw silent.

Hackle say, "Hackle no runt. Hackle hunt game."

Jaggal say, "Hackle hunt squirrels. Hackle feed Hackle. Jaggal hunt boars. Jaggal feed Woodpaw. Hackle take game from mouth of Woodpaw like hyenas."

Hackle say, "Hackle no runt. Hackle fight."

Jaggal say, "Hackle no kill ogres. Hackle no kill yetis. Hackle no fight. Hackle hide behind Gnaw. Gnaw dead now. Hackle runt. Runt weaken Woodpaw. Runt must go. Or runt die."

Gnolls silent. Woodpaw silent. Even Hackle silent. Hackle shamed.

Jaggal cuff Hackle then. Hackle mouth bloody. Jaggal raise club. Jaggal say again, "Runt must go. Or runt die."

Hackle shamed. Hackle go.

Hackle stay away from Woodpaw. Hackle die if Woodpaw catch. Runt die if Woodpaw catch runt on Woodpaw lands. So Hackle die if Woodpaw catch.

But Hackle plan. Hackle prove. Hackle end shame when Hackle catch Feral Scar. Hackle think, *Hackle kill Feral Scar. Hackle prove Hackle no runt.*

Hackle search for Feral Scar. For yetis. But Hackle no find yetis. No find Feral Scar. Hackle search long.

Hackle hunt. Hunt squirrel. Eat squirrel. Hunt boar. Eat boar. Hunt deer. No eat deer. Deer too fast. Hunt bear. No eat bear. No find bear. But Hackle good hunter. Eat squirrel. Eat boar.

Hackle hunt for yetis. Hackle hunt for Feral Scar.

Hackle find Feral Scar!

Now, Hackle can kill Feral Scar and end shame. But Wordok find Hackle first. Wordok take Hackle as slave for Gordok. Hackle shamed again.

Hackle fight in arena. Fight murloc in arena. Kill murloc in arena.

Hackle fight Aram in arena. But Aram and Hackle are friends. Hackle no kill Aram. Aram no kill Hackle.

Hackle and Aram fight Old One-Eye. Aram and Old One-Eye become friends. Hackle no kill Old One-Eye. Aram no kill Old One-Eye. Old One-Eye no kill Hackle and Aram.

Then all fight ogres. Makasa fight ogres. Makasa fight Wordok. Even Murky fight Wordok. Makasa hurt Wordok. Hackle kill Wordok. Hackle kill Wordok, who killed Jawstretcher, Hackle's father. Hackle take Wordok's club.

Now Hackle here with Makasa, Murky, and Aram. Hackle back in new Woodpaw lands with Makasa, Murky, and Aram. But Hackle still runt to Woodpaw. Still shamed. Runt die if Woodpaw catch. Hackle die if Woodpaw catch. Makasa, Murky, and Aram die if Woodpaw catch.

Aram was stunned. He remembered the Hackle he had first met in the ogres' slave pit: bitter and defensive, angry and so very lonely. Aram realized now that Hackle had tried to tell him some of his story then. But there hadn't been time before the slaves had been called to the arena. Yet, in the pit and in the arena,

Aram had somehow managed to win the young gnoll over to his side. They had fought together against the wyvern One-Eye, whom Gordok had summoned to kill them both when each refused to kill the other. Then they had escaped together on One-Eye's back with Makasa, Murky, and a dying Thalyss. They were friends now. Fast friends. But amid all the dire acts and daring actions, Aram's thoughts had never returned to wonder about Hackle's story. No, it had taken Makasa's bluntness to wring it free of the gnoll.

She said, "All right, we'll swing wide to avoid the Woodpaw lands." She glanced at the flooded Thousand Needles canyon to the left. "We can't go farther east unless we plan to swim to Gadgetzan."

Murky said, "Murky flllurlog."

Makasa ignored the murloc. She said, "So we'll head west. As far as you think necessary, gnoll, before tacking back on course."

Hackle nodded, but Aram piped up, "Is that really necessary? We know how to deal with gnolls. Look how Greydon dealt with the Grimtail. Look at Hackle and me. We can do this. Reconcile Hackle with his people."

Murky said, "Mmmrrglllmmm."

Hackle shook his head.

Makasa said, "That's not a chance we need to take. We've made enough enemies. We have enough to do . . ." She ticked off the items on her fingers. "Finding food, finding crystals, avoiding Malus, getting to Gadgetzan, delivering Thalyss's Seed, bringing you home to Lakeshire. We don't need to engage an entire clan of gnolls in some pointless attempt to change their long-held customs."

"We don't need them to change their customs. We just need to prove that Hackle's not a runt."

"Runt *is* runt," said a new voice, catching them all off guard.

"Jaggal." Hackle growled low.

But it wasn't just Jaggal. Aram, Makasa, Hackle, and Murky were standing in the middle of the wide road—with no cover—completely surrounded by ten to twelve gnoll warriors.

CHAPTER SIX
NEGOTIATIONS

Makasa was kicking herself. She had needed to hear the gnoll's story, but how could she have been such a fool as to allow him to tell it on this open road? And how had she allowed herself to become so engrossed in his tale that she hadn't heard nearly a dozen gnolls getting the drop on her from every side?

Hackle had offered little description of Jaggal in his account, but Makasa quickly identified the brute. Though relatively young, he was by far the biggest gnoll she had ever seen, broad as a tree trunk and as tall as she at five foot ten despite his hunched posture. He had brown-and-gold fur, black spots, and a thick rust-colored mane that began behind his head and ran all the way down his back. He had only one piercing, a small iron bar near the top of one pointed ear. He sported a very big axe and a permanent sneer (the former, most likely taken off an ogre; the latter, more likely taken as a birthright).

Nevertheless, Makasa Flintwill was prepared to fight the gnoll and—though she desperately missed her harpoon—liked her odds in single combat against him. Unfortunately, she was painfully aware that any attack she might launch now could easily generate a massacre. Because, of course, the brute was not alone. There were nine other warriors, three male and six female, some as young as Hackle, some considerably older. There was also a small female pup, standing less than half an inch from Jaggal's left haunch. She held a smaller version of the brute's axe (more like a double-bladed hatchet) and sported a smaller version of his permanent sneer. (If Makasa were a betting woman, she'd have wagered ready silver that the pup was Jaggal's daughter.) Makasa could take the brute, but she couldn't possibly take down this many combatants fast enough, even if Hackle joined the fight—something she couldn't count on, given his current defeated posture. And, in any case, she'd be leaving Aram exposed.

So she stood in a defensive pose—one hand on her cutlass, the other ready to let loose her iron chain—prepared for whatever move the gnolls made next. What she was not prepared for was Aramar Thorne, who *launched* himself at the massive Jaggal. Makasa just barely managed to grab the flying tail of Greydon's leather coat, tied around the boy's waist, and pull Aram back. The gnoll's axe whistled through empty air, slicing down where Aramar's skull had been a second before.

Jaggal didn't seem to mind that he had missed. He laughed and said, "What dumb boy doing?"

"Boy not dumb. Boy is Aram," Hackle said. "Aram attack to prove Aram worthy to talk to gnoll."

Jaggal turned toward Hackle and growled low.

The little pup barked sharply, saying in a small but almost ridiculously confident voice, "Runt no talk to Jaggal. Runt no talk to any Woodpaw gnoll."

The brute looked down proudly and patted the pup's head. He spoke to Hackle without deigning to look at him. "Jaggal warn runt what happen if runt caught on Woodpaw lands. Runt die now. Then Jaggal eat runt. Eat runt's friends, too. Runt's friends dumb for being friends of runt. Deserve to be eaten."

Aram looked stunned. *You'd eat another gnoll?*

All the gnolls shrugged, as if not quite fathoming the purpose of the question. Even Hackle shrugged. "Meat is meat," one said, and more than a few echoed the truism.

"Listen," Aram said.

Makasa stifled a groan. *What happened to the boy who could never manage to utter a single sound during a crisis?* When had this twelve-year-old become a miniature Greydon Thorne, a semi-eloquent ambassador for his father's nuanced approach to interspecies relations? Makasa had admired her captain, but Aram didn't have Greydon's skill with a sword to back his plays. Yet her brother didn't seem to understand that fine distinction and stumbled on heedlessly.

"Hackle is not a runt," he said.

"Runt is runt," the brute said with a dismissive wave.

"No. Hackle is a brave warrior. He fought in Gordok's arena. He fought beside me against the wyvern One-Eye. He killed the ogre Wordok."

This got Jaggal's attention. His head snapped up, and he growled out, "Runt no kill Wordok."

And *that* got Hackle's attention. He raised his head and spoke with pride and not a little umbrage: "Hackle kill Wordok! Hackle kill!" But then his head sank again, and he muttered, "Makasa and Hackle kill Wordok."

Jaggal laughed once more. "See? Runt no kill Wordok. Jaggal knew runt no kill Wordok."

Makasa spoke for the first time. "Hackle killed Wordok. I am Makasa Flintwill. I hurt Wordok, yes. But I could not kill him." She chose not to mention that she couldn't kill the ogre because, at the time, Murky had been hugging her and wouldn't let go. "Hackle saved Makasa. Hackle killed Wordok. Hackle took Wordok's club."

Hackle managed to perk up. He hefted the ogre's hefty war club onto his right shoulder and tried his best to look defiant. "Hackle kill Wordok," he said, nodding curtly in confirmation.

"So you see," Aram said carefully, as if trying to be logical with a child, "Hackle is no runt. Hackle is a warrior worthy of the Woodpaw clan."

Jaggal stared at Aram. Then he stared at Hackle. Then he shot a glance at Makasa, who still had one hand on her cutlass and one on her chain's release hook. He looked at Hackle again, and his expression softened, as if he could finally remember the days when Hackle and Jaggal were friends, training together with Hackle's mother, "not *so* long ago." Then the brute looked down at his pup, who clung to his leg and looked up at him with the sneer he had briefly lost. He shook his head, almost sadly. He said, "Runt is runt. Runt come back to Woodpaw lands. Runt die."

Every gnoll took a step forward. Makasa drew her sword, prepared to take the brute down and risk the result. Even Aram drew his sword.

"Runt die," Hackle said then—but his tone was not one of defeat or resignation. No, there was a calculated edge to it now. "Or runt prove runt is Hackle by killing Feral Scar."

All the gnolls—except Jaggal and the pup—took a step back as if the mere mention of the name Feral Scar had summoned the great yeti into their presence.

Jaggal, however, was not impressed. He laughed again. "Runt no kill Feral Scar. Runt not even find Feral Scar. Feral Scar hide from Woodpaw with all his yetis. He attack hunting parties, kill gnolls, then disappear into hills."

"Hackle *already* find Feral Scar. Find Feral Scar before Wordok capture Hackle. Now, Wordok dead. Hackle kill Wordok. Now, Hackle kill Feral Scar with Wordok's club."

Jaggal stared at Hackle, then shook his head. "No," Jaggal said.

"Yes," Hackle said. "Jaggal let Hackle and friends go. Hackle and Aram and Makasa and Murky find Feral Scar again. Then Hackle kill Feral Scar with war club of Wordok. Hackle swear this on Hackle's life."

One of the older gnolls, a bronze-furred female with drooping grey eyes, said, "If runt no kill Feral Scar, then Feral Scar kill runt. Or if Hackle no *find* Feral Scar, Jaggal kill runt. Either way, runt die."

Hackle nodded. "Yes. But if Hackle find Feral Scar, if Hackle kill Feral Scar, then Jaggal let Hackle and friends pass through Woodpaw lands."

This seemed to satisfy the old female. She nodded at Jaggal.

But he shook his head again. "If runt really know where Feral Scar hides, runt tell Jaggal where Feral Scar hides. Jaggal kill Feral Scar."

The silence lasted long enough that Makasa glanced over at Hackle to warn him against giving away the one piece of information that might save all their lives. Immediately, she saw she needn't have worried. Hackle was smiling broadly. His dark-brown eye squinted with mirth. His bright-blue eye almost seemed to sparkle.

Hackle laughed at Jaggal then. "Hackle not fool. Hackle tell Jaggal nothing. Let Hackle go, and Hackle kill Feral Scar."

The old female said, "Let runt go. What do Woodpaw have to lose?"

Without warning, Jaggal swung his axe toward her, missing her snout by a hairsbreadth, which seemed to be his intention.

"Karrion not matriarch," Jaggal said after the old female had stumbled back and lowered her head. "Woodpaw have no matriarch now." He glanced down at the pup. "Woodpaw have no matriarch yet." Then he slapped the flat of his axe against his chest. "So brute rule Woodpaw. Jaggal rule Woodpaw. Karrion no tell Jaggal what to do."

Karrion's head bobbed abjectly. She said, "Jaggal is brute. Karrion not matriarch. Jaggal decide for Woodpaw."

"Jaggal decide for Woodpaw," he said. He turned back to Hackle. "If Jaggal let runt and friends go, runt and friends run. No find Feral Scar. No kill Feral Scar. Runt just run. Runts always run."

"Hackle not runt," Hackle said. "Hackle no run."

"Then runt leave friend with Jaggal. If runt run, friend die."

"No!" Aram shouted.

"Jaggal say yes!" Jaggal growled back. "Runt leave friend. And runt take Sivet to confirm runt kill Feral Scar."

"Who's Sivet?" Aram asked.

Everyone ignored him. Makasa could tell exactly who Sivet was by the imperious look on the pup's face. Makasa was mildly surprised that the brute would put his own daughter at risk like this. But then Makasa remembered her own mother taking similar chances with her four children.

"What friend runt leave?" Jaggal asked.

Murky said, "Murky mrrugl. Ukle frund Murky mrrugl."

Again, Aram protested. "Murky, no! You don't have to do this!"

Murky shrugged. "Mrgle, mrgle. Murky mrrugggl. Murky mrrugl."

Hackle said, "Hackle friend Murky stay with Woodpaw. Sivet go with Hackle, Aram, and Makasa. Sivet see Hackle kill Feral Scar. Sivet come back and tell Jaggal that Hackle not runt. Jaggal let Murky and Hackle and Hackle's friends go."

Jaggal nodded, then actually shoved Sivet toward Hackle. Hackle shoved Murky toward the brute.

Aram whispered to Makasa, "I don't like leaving Murky as a hostage to these gnolls. We just got him back from Malus."

She whispered in return, "Do you see another option I don't, brother?" If he could attempt to influence her by calling her "sister," then she might as well learn to return the favor.

Aram said nothing, but his head sank a bit, which was as good as a no.

Thus, with negotiations complete, Hackle led Sivet, Aram, and Makasa down the road, away from Jaggal, his nine warriors, and the grinning, waving murloc.

CHAPTER SEVEN
THE LITTLE MATRIARCH

As soon as they were out of sight of the Woodpaw, Hackle led the small band off the road and up into the hills, setting a stiff pace. Aram—losing a few feet of ground on the others—felt light-headed from hunger.

Sivet turned to him, and with her small voice dripping contempt, said, "Keep up, dumb boy!"

Aram caught Makasa cracking the slightest hint of a smile. He said to her, "She remind you of anyone?"

Flintwill's smile instantaneously vanished. "No. Who? What do you mean?"

"There is no one like Sivet of the Woodpaw clan," Sivet said. "Sivet will be matriarch."

Hackle nodded and said, "Sivet will be matriarch."

The pup practically spat out, "Runt no talk to Sivet. Runt no talk at all until runt kill Feral Scar. *If* runt can kill Feral Scar. *If* runt can *find* Feral Scar."

Hackle said nothing. But he had clearly recovered some of his own. He smiled, uncowed. Aram wasn't sure if Hackle was truly confident of being able to kill the yeti. But the young gnoll warrior seemed quite sure he could find the beast.

Makasa asked him, "Are you sure Jaggal won't follow?"

Sivet said, "Jaggal send Sivet. Jaggal no need to follow runt and dumb humans."

Makasa's movement was swift. In an instant, she had torn the small axe from the young gnoll's grip and wrapped a strong hand around her throat. She said, "I am Makasa Flintwill of Stranglethorn Vale. I am no runt. And you are not yet matriarch. Learn respect for your elders and betters, pup, or you will get no better and no older."

Sivet didn't struggle. She fearlessly looked Makasa in the eye and nodded once, respecting the human's speed and strength.

Makasa released the gnoll and proffered the pup's axe. Sivet took it. Makasa turned on her heel and walked on alongside Hackle. Aram, just behind Sivet, was briefly worried that the pup might choose to plant the weapon in Makasa's back, but instead Sivet sped up to flank Makasa, glancing up at her with no little admiration. Makasa looked down at the pup and nodded to her, respecting the respect she was now being shown.

Aram shook his head. He walked behind the other three, pondering what might have happened if he had responded that way to Second Mate Flintwill's angry contempt aboard *Wavestrider*, and whether he might not have gained her respect sooner.

Just at sundown, they paused at a stream. All four slaked their thirst—the humans cupping the water to their mouths with their hands, and the two gnolls getting down on all fours to lap it up with their tongues. Makasa also refilled Thalyss's canteen.

Sivet sat back on the dirt. From a small pouch on her belt, took out a strip of boar jerky and ripped off a good-size chunk with her teeth. Her companions—even Makasa—stared at the jerky as if prepared to worship at its altar.

The pup smirked. She pulled another long strip from her pouch and offered it to Makasa. She watched Makasa tear a piece off and give it to Aram. But when Makasa tore a second piece off for Hackle, she barked out, "No! Runt no get Woodpaw grub!"

Hackle hesitated. So did Makasa. She said, "Hackle takes us to the mighty Feral Scar. Hackle will kill Feral Scar for Woodpaw. So Hackle must be made strong with Woodpaw grub."

Sivet clearly didn't like this, but she respected Makasa and nodded reluctantly. Makasa held the piece of jerky out to Hackle, who took it and quickly shoved it all into his mouth in case either female changed her mind.

As Hackle led them forward again, following the stream up a rocky slope, Aram gratefully chewed on his strip of the salty and flavorful dried meat, while marveling at Makasa's ability to handle Sivet. He became more and more convinced that Makasa knew how to influence the gnoll pup, because in looking at Sivet, Makasa was basically looking in a mirror. Not that they actually were anything alike in appearance. They were different ages, different species, different physically in almost every way. But Aram felt sure that, by observing Sivet, he was getting a kind of glimpse of Makasa as a child. He imagined a thin young girl in Stranglethorn Vale, imperious and unstoppable. He'd have wagered that precious piece of jerky that her three older brothers had had no small amount of trouble keeping her in line.

Hackle led them to the northwest, down into a hollow and then up another hill. Aram was keenly aware that they were now trudging in the exact opposite direction of Gadgetzan—and, in fact, were vaguely heading back toward the ogres of Dire Maul. Still, he wanted to help Hackle and ransom Murky, so he never even considered objecting. He did worry—assuming Feral Scar was as dangerous as the Woodpaw seemed to think—whether or not Hackle would really be able to bring the creature down. But he relied on Makasa to help Hackle during the fight and set the table for their gnoll friend to go in for the final kill.

Final kill? That phrase gave Aram pause. Should killing really be the goal?

Aram thought of the wyvern One-Eye, whom he and Hackle had regarded as merely a monster that needed killing so they might survive—before, in fact, discovering she was the *mother* of a litter of cubs captured by the ogres to force her to serve Gordok's whims. In the end, Aram had found a way to save those cubs and ally with One-Eye against their common enemies.

It was one of Greydon Thorne's favorite lessons, expressed over and over in a hundred different ways, but mostly boiling down to this: "There is always something worthwhile— something to treasure—in every species."

And as further evidence, wasn't that also true of the gnolls themselves? The first time Aram had seen a gnoll clan, he had definitely regarded them as nothing more than monsters. Now, he counted a gnoll among his best friends.

So if his father's wisdom applied to gnolls and wyverns, might it not also apply to yetis?

Cautiously, he asked, "Are we sure the yetis are our enemy?"

Sivet rolled her eyes. In fact, she rolled her entire head and yipped out, "Of course, yetis are enemy! Yetis kill gnolls, dumb boy!" She glanced anxiously at Makasa—her new hero—to confirm that the woman approved of her name-calling.

Makasa was grimacing. Aram guessed she was probably torn. More than likely she had no problem with him being called "dumb boy," especially as his question would strike her as absurd, since she regarded nearly everyone—no matter the species (humans not excepted)—as a potential enemy. (Makasa

Flintwill was, in her own way, as egalitarian about potential enemies as Greydon Thorne was about potential friends.) But she also hated eye-rolling on principle, and Aram knew from personal experience it particularly grated on her.

So while she scowlingly searched for her response, he forged on: "Yes, yetis killed gnolls. But didn't gnolls kill yetis as well? If all the killing stopped on both sides, couldn't—"

"Killing no stop," Hackle said, absently scratching behind his ear with his free paw. "Killing never stop." The young gnoll sounded neither sad nor gleeful. He was simply stating a fact, as he saw it.

But Aram saw things differently. Or he was coming to, anyway. He talked of his father's lessons. He brought up One-Eye. He described his father's encounter with the matriarch of the Grimtail gnolls.

Hackle grunted some begrudging acknowledgment. But Sivet gawked at him incredulously.

Aram reached back to remove his sketchbook from his pocket to show the gnoll pup the good magic therein. When presented with the commonalities between species, most everyone saw things in a new perspective. *(In any case, it had always worked before!)* But Makasa stayed his hand.

She said, "And what did you find to 'treasure' in the Gordunni?"

This instantly stumped him. He racked his brain but could summon up nothing worthwhile in the bloodthirsty behavior of even one of the ogres.

He gaped up helplessly at his sister and was surprised to find her looking down on him kindly. She said, "You can't save everyone, Aram. And not everyone *deserves* saving, either."

He found himself nodding in agreement—then grew angry with himself for acquiescing. Yet he couldn't summon up the evidence to defend his position from her argument—and that grieved him.

Sivet chose that particular moment to snicker at his fallen expression and his fallen ideals, which in turn caused him to briefly question whether this particular arrogant pup deserved saving.

But that question would get answered soon enough.

Soon enough, Hackle was leading them along the knife-edge of a ridge that had been blocked from view by a ring of tall pines. The ridge curved around a hidden canyon, small but deep, rocky but accented with green. Some millennia ago, a mighty river must have carved a gulch out of this granite terrain. The gulch became a ravine; the ravine, a canyon. Now all that remained of the river was a small nameless stream far below them on the canyon floor. It was further proof to a morose Aram that nothing in this world stayed the same—not even things as seemingly constant as stone or mighty rivers . . . not even his own constancy in the lessons of his father.

The sun had set. The White Lady had not yet risen, but the Blue Child—or seven-eighths of it, anyway—crested the treeline. Though Aram was only halfway through his current sulk, the artist in him saw the little stream glittering blue in the moonlight and couldn't resist whispering, "Beautiful . . ."

Hackle and Sivet both looked over their shoulders at Aram. Like the stream, the gnolls' eyes eerily reflected back the Child's azure light. Sivet stared at the human boy for a bit, then barked out her small, contempt-filled, yipping laugh.

Hackle hushed her, whispering, "Shhh. We right above yeti caves, above Feral Scar cave."

As they had already trudged over halfway round the canyon, Sivet glared at Hackle and growled, "Runt lead Sivet in circles. Runt lie about Feral Scar. Runt no know where Feral Scar is."

The "runt" was afforded no time—or need—to respond. Because at just that moment, a huge hairy hand smashed up out of the chalky ground, grabbed ahold of Sivet's legs, and yanked her down and out of sight—seemingly into the bowels of Azeroth—all before she even had time to scream.

CHAPTER EIGHT
FERAL SCAR

Raising his club over his head, Hackle yelled, "Hackle follow Sivet! Cave entrance below! Go!" Then he brought the war club down, smashing and expanding the hole in the ground until it was as wide as his shoulders. Instantaneously, he dropped through it and out of sight.

Aram stood there stunned. He stared down into the hole but could see only darkness. He turned to exchange a glance with Makasa—but she was gone.

Where?

Below!

Belatedly, he scrambled toward the edge of the ridge and looked over. Below, Makasa seemed to be vanishing into the side of the mountain.

Aram couldn't see the entrance to the cave from above, but having finally gotten his head around what had happened, he knew the cave must exist. The ledge before its entrance was about ten feet beneath him. He hadn't seen how Makasa had gotten down. He imagined now that she had jumped. He tried to steel himself to do the same but couldn't quite work up the nerve. So he grabbed the stone at the edge of the ridge and swung himself over. Fully extending his arms, he hung down, then dropped the last five feet or so to land in a crouch before the yawning entrance of the dark cave.

He stood, drew his cutlass, bit his bottom lip, and raced inside.

The cave was rank with the smell of musk. Blue moonlight shone down through the hole in the ceiling, eerily illuminating the scene before him. An immense creature of fur and muscle—presumably the yeti Feral Scar—had Sivet in the grip of his impossibly enormous right fist. She was conscious but straining, her arms pinned to her sides. Aram spotted her small hatchet-size axe on the cave floor.

Hackle was hanging by one paw from the rightmost of the two long horns that emerged horizontally from the beast's great head. The young gnoll warrior used his free hand to swing Wordok's club at the yeti. It thudded against the monster's right shoulder with little observable effect. Certainly, it wasn't making him drop Sivet.

Makasa was before the beast, her sword in one hand, her chain in the other. The latter hung limply at her side. She didn't—couldn't—swing the iron chain, because Feral Scar held Sivet out in front of him. It flashed through Aram's mind to wonder:

Is this supposedly dumb animal blessed with dumb luck? Is the beast simply holding Sivet away from Hackle and only inadvertently thwarting Makasa's most devastating attack? Or does the yeti know what he's doing?

Aram could almost hear Makasa wishing she still had her harpoon. And at first—aside from the regular muffled thumping of Hackle's club on Feral Scar's thick, fur-covered hide—there was little else *to* hear. None of the combatants made a sound. Feral Scar swung his head back and forth, trying to shake Hackle off his horn, but Hackle held on. The yeti reached his free left hand across his body to grab the gnoll, but Hackle swung his legs out of range. And all this was done as a kind of pantomime. Sivet didn't scream. Hackle and Makasa let loose no war cries. Aram hardly breathed.

And the yeti didn't roar.

This surprised Aram. He had imagined a beast that size would roar loudly enough to shatter the stone walls of the cave. But the creature made no sound. Hackle was hanging from one of the yeti's horns (which one would think was quite uncomfortable for the yeti), yet the creature made no sound. And what was that expression on the beast's face? *Determination?*

Sivet emitted a strangled, barely audible cry. Aram realized her tiny body was being crushed in the monster's grip. It looked a bit like her head might pop off any second.

Aram came up even with Makasa. He wanted to help but

70

wasn't sure how and didn't want to get in his sister's way. They exchanged a glance. He could see Makasa had no clear idea of what to do, either.

But Hackle did. He growled out, "Go low, Makasa."

Aram didn't understand, but Makasa Flintwill did. She stepped back to swing her chain in tight circles. Now, Aram definitely saw the yeti move the hand holding Sivet in Makasa's direction. Feral Scar was using the tiny gnoll as a shield to protect his head. But Makasa wasn't swinging for the beast's head. Without warning, she crouched down and let the chain swing toward the monster's legs. It wrapped around a tree-trunk-thick ankle. The chain went taut, and Makasa pulled, trying to yank the beast off his very big foot. But the creature didn't budge. She gestured with her head, and Aram, suddenly understanding, joined her to help pull on the chain. Straining loudly, their efforts breaking the silence, both pulled with all their might.

Still, Feral Scar could not be moved. His glowing yellow eyes squinted a bit into an expression resembling contempt. It was the only reaction they got. The yeti raised Sivet up toward his huge toothy maw. If her head hadn't yet popped off, he looked ready to bite it off—or perhaps simply to swallow her whole.

Amid the renewed silence, there finally came a sound. Not from within the cave but from without. It was the kind of roar one might expect to hear from a bear being attacked by hounds:

angry, plaintive, deadly, frustrated. Aram thought he could hear all those sounds in this bellow.

Feral Scar heard something more. Suddenly, he was no longer content to calmly vie with Makasa's chain or Hackle's club. Roaring now himself—though more in response to the call from outside than toward his current combatants—he charged forward, forcing Makasa and Aram to dive to either side. With a tilt of his head, the yeti slammed Hackle hard against the wall of the cave, finally dislodging the gnoll from off his horn.

Makasa tried to trip the beast with her chain, but a massive foot stomped down upon it near the handle, tearing it from her grip. The beast was about to exit the cave—with the chain still trailing from one ankle and Sivet still being crushed in one fist—when Hackle pushed off a wall and leapt across, bringing his war club down on the monster's wrist. Feral Scar didn't scream in pain—in fact, he made no noise at all. But he dropped Sivet, who fell to the cave floor, inhaled, winced, and then snatched up her small axe and found her footing—faster than Aram had found his—ready to do battle with the creature.

But by then Feral Scar was gone.

The four of them exchanged a series of glances, and then Makasa and Hackle led the way out of the cave, followed quickly by Sivet and Aram.

"Are you all right?" Aram asked the pup as they ran.

She muttered something—and just muttering seemed to make

her wince in pain again. But she kept running. Aram hadn't been able to make out what she said, but *dumb boy* was high on his list of probables.

They emerged from the cave. Above them, the White Lady now appeared below the Blue Child. Her bright light illuminated Feral Scar's progress—indicated predominantly by the smashing of trees that had blocked his path—down the canyon.

Breathing hard, Sivet said, "Hackle must kill Feral Scar."

Hackle said, "Hackle know." If the young gnoll warrior took any notice that Sivet had called him by name, he gave no indication.

Aram looked at Makasa. She was seething. "The beast has my chain," she said. She had lost her harpoon. She was not going to lose her blasted chain, too. She leapt off the ridge and skidded downhill. Hackle followed. Then Sivet. Then Aram.

The beast. Was Feral Scar just a beast? Aram's instinct to find another way besides killing—suppressed by Makasa's discussion of the ogres—was reasserting itself. Feral Scar was no mindless beast. He had used strategy. He had expressed determination and contempt, even patience. And killing them had clearly not been his priority. He hadn't fled. He wasn't running *away*. He was running *toward* . . . something. He had been summoned, likely by another yeti. As the quartet of humans and gnolls scrambled and tumbled down the steep grade, Aram became more convinced than ever that their small hunting party was on the wrong path . . .

Feral Scar's path was easy enough to follow. They had lost sight of the yeti, but not his swath of destruction. He had taken a direct route down the canyon, letting nothing stand in his way: not the four of them, not massive trees, not the nameless stream. Even boulders had been pushed aside as he had begun heading uphill on the far slope of the deep ravine. The foursome followed, quickly as they could, not even pausing when Makasa found her chain, discarded beside a fallen oak, torn up by its roots for the crime of being in Feral Scar's way.

With a grim smile, she scooped up the chain and continued forward, saying, "He's in a hurry."

Four minutes later, Makasa, Hackle, Sivet, and Aram stopped before the entrance of another cave. Feral Scar's footprints led the way in.

"Could be many yetis inside," Hackle said.

"Could be," Sivet said. "But Feral Scar inside for sure."

Hackle nodded and advanced. Sivet followed. Then Makasa. And again, Aram took up the rear.

There was dim light at the end of the tunnel: a cool bluish-silver glow. But it took them some time to cross through the mountain. Every twenty feet or so, the tunnel forked, and they had to stop—at least briefly. But it was easy enough to follow Feral Scar's large, fresh footprints in the dirt.

Makasa said, "He could be leading us into a trap."

Aram said, "I doubt he's giving us a second thought. That's not what's drawing him on."

She glared at him, clearly ready to demand how he could be so sure what the great beast was thinking. But even in the dim light, one look at his face told her just how sure he was, and she said nothing. There were certain things she had an instinct for, and certain things *he* had an instinct for, and both had learned to respect the other's intuition. Up to a point, anyway.

Finally, the tunnel opened up onto a shallow valley on the other side of the ridge. This, Aram knew instantly, was the yetis' retreat, their haven. That knowledge, however, required no instinct or intuition, because a hundred yards below them, a raiding party of Gordunni ogres stood amid a killing ground littered with ogre and yeti corpses. The ogres' commander, easily as broad of back and shoulder as Wordok, had placed the surviving yetis in chains. Two dozen or so of Feral Scar's kin, males and females, old and young—a couple even smaller than Aram himself—were set to become slaves for the late Gordok's gladiatorial arena.

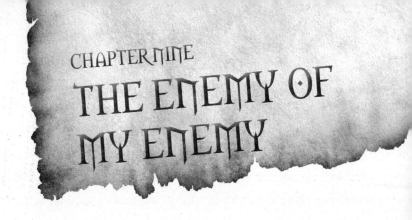

CHAPTER NINE
THE ENEMY OF MY ENEMY

Gordok send Wordok west to find slaves. Send Marjuk east. Gordok say to Marjuk, "No come back without new slaves."

Slaves are stupid, Marjuk think. Do nothing. Fight in arena, sure. But slave fights dull. Marjuk think Gordok use slave fights to keep dumb ogres happy. Dumb, happy ogres no challenge Gordok. Marjuk think Marjuk challenge Gordok. Marjuk become new Gordok. Soon. But not yet. Gordok still too strong.

So Marjuk go east. Marjuk look for new slaves. Look for gnolls. Look for yetis. Find gnolls before. Find yetis before. Find tauren, even.

This time Marjuk no find gnolls. No find yetis. No find tauren. Marjuk no find murlocs, even. But Marjuk no go home to Dire Maul without new slaves. So Marjuk keep looking.

Finally, Marjuk spot yeti. One yeti. Small yeti. Marjuk could take small yeti. But Marjuk no take yeti. Marjuk follow yeti. Find many yetis. Marjuk have about twenty ogres in Marjuk's command. Marjuk order attack.

Yetis no want to be new slaves for Gordok. Yetis fight. Ogres fight. Marjuk fight. Marjuk kill two yetis. Marjuk not happy. Dead yetis no fight in arena. Also, some ogres die. Not too many. Some. That okay. Marjuk must come back with new slaves. Marjuk no need to come back with all his ogres. Plenty ogres in Dire Maul.

Too many yetis die. But Marjuk chain some yetis. Yetis make good slaves for arena. Fights not so dull. Gordok be happy. So Marjuk happy.

Then come Feral Scar. Then come human boy. Then come gnoll. Then come human woman. Gnoll pup, even . . .

Feral Scar kept to himself. He loved his tribe. But the valley of the haven was small. And Feral Scar was big. He needed space to range his body. He needed space of his own to range his mind. To consider what to do.

He had his own cave outside the haven. Close, though. Close enough to hear the call of his tribe. But far enough away to consider what to do.

He missed the yeti lands. Not the lands they had left. Those had become dead lands. He missed those lands from *before* the ogres cut down all the trees, chased off all the game, killed yetis or took them away.

Those lands-of-before were rich and wide. Those were lands on which a yeti could range. On which Feral Scar could range. There were gnolls nearby, but there was space enough for gnoll and yeti. And if a gnoll got too close, gnolls were easy enough to kill.

But that was before.

Once the ogres destroyed the lands, destroyed the trees, destroyed the game, Feral Scar knew the yetis had to move. They moved through gnoll lands and had to kill some gnolls. They kept moving. They found the haven.

The haven was too small for his tribe, he thought. It was safe, hidden from ogres and gnolls. But the yetis needed to range. They did not—could not—stay in the haven all the time. The yetis ranged. But when they ranged, Feral Scar knew they might be followed back. This was a problem. This was the problem that Feral Scar considered from his own cave.

And while he considered, Feral Scar listened for the call of his tribe.

Instead, he heard footsteps above his cave. He heard voices. He heard speech. He heard gnolls. He heard them right above his head. Feral Scar thought, *These gnolls have not found the haven. But they are too close. These gnolls must die.*

He smashed his hand through the ceiling of his cave and grabbed the closest, loudest gnoll. He pulled her down. She was just a pup. Barely worth eating. Barely worth killing. Then another gnoll dropped down through the hole that Feral Scar had made in the ceiling. This gnoll was little more than a pup, too. He hung from Feral Scar's horn but barely weighed enough to be annoying. Then two more gnolls ran into the cave. These were strange-looking gnolls. Skinny gnolls. No fur. A female and a male pup. The female had an iron chain. She began to swing it toward Feral Scar's head. But Feral Scar held the smallest gnoll pup out, and the bigger, strange-looking gnoll stopped swinging. She let the chain fall. She didn't know what to do. Feral Scar thought she must not be very bright. Maybe these two weren't gnolls at all. Maybe they were tiny ogres. Very tiny ogres who thought they could use the chain to pull Feral Scar off his feet.

But, no, these were not ogres. Ogres and gnolls would not fight together. Maybe they were ugly elves. He stared at them with contempt. Ugly elves, and not too bright.

Then he heard the call of his tribe. The haven was under attack. Ogres—real ogres—were attacking the yetis. Feral Scar had been playing with the gnolls and ugly elves. But there was no time to play now. He knocked the one gnoll off his horn and left. He almost forgot he was carrying the pup. The male gnoll hit Feral Scar's wrist with his club. It stung a little. Feral Scar dropped the pup. He didn't have to, but he didn't want to be burdened with her. Not when he was in such a hurry to return to the haven and his tribe.

He wasted no time. A straight line down the canyon, a straight line up. If anything was in his way—trees, rocks, anything—he moved them. Feral Scar was big. Moving trees was simple. He had forgotten about the chain wrapped around his ankle until it fell off. He didn't even look back.

He came to the long cave. He didn't stop. He knew the way. He crossed through the mountain and came out the other side. Only then did Feral Scar pause.

It was worse than he thought. Worse than he had hoped. The ogres had discovered the haven. Many yetis were already dead. Sister Heart was dead. Brother Sinew was dead. Strong warriors and wise elders were dead. Cubs dead.

Many ogres dead, too, but not enough. The ogres had put what remained of his tribe in chains.

Feral Scar *ROARED* as he raced down the slope! He pulled the head off the closest ogre without slowing or stopping. He gored two more with his horns. He waded into the rest. He tore off limbs. He bit and thrashed. But some of these ogres were big, nearly as big as Feral Scar. They had weapons. Hammers. Spears. They hammered at him. They stabbed at him from a distance. He knew he would not be taken. But he thought that now he would die. He would fight until he died. And then he could range far in the afterlands of the yetis. He was ready for the afterlands . . .

Then came the ugly elf boy. Then the male gnoll. Then the ugly elf female with the chain. Even the little gnoll pup . . .

*   *   *

"Hackle's work done for Hackle," Sivet had said.

Hackle had nodded, frowning. He said despairingly, "Hackle be runt forever."

The little matriarch seemed slightly flummoxed by this revelation. Her regard for him had clearly undergone a drastic change.

Feral Scar had waded into the ogres and had already done much damage. But there were just too many. It was clear to Makasa that the beast would not surrender, that he was fighting to the death against too many enemies led by too fearsome a commander. And it was equally clear that—although he might take half the ogres with him—the great yeti was indeed going to die. This would have been fine with Makasa, except he wouldn't die at Hackle's hand, which would complicate retrieving the murloc.

Suddenly, Aramar Thorne was running downhill. Makasa had tried to grab him, but he was just out of reach. He was *not* out of reach of the length of her chain, but stopping him with *that* would have somewhat defeated the purpose. (Which didn't mean she didn't briefly consider the option.) Within seconds, she and Hackle had joined the fray. Even Sivet . . .

Dumb boy dumb, Sivet thought.

Hackle brave, but Hackle follow dumb boy, so Hackle dumb.

Makasa Flintwill brave, but Makasa Flintwill fight beside dumb boy and Hackle. So maybe Makasa Flintwill dumb.

So Sivet fight.
Sivet probably dumb now, too.

Aram had taken off practically before the impulse had crystalized in his mind. An ogre with a spear was aiming for Feral Scar's back. Aram ran up and slashed at the ogre's arm.

Aram's attack didn't cut deep, but it did cause the ogre—a big tawny-skinned creature with large tusks that seemed to stretch his mouth wide—to turn toward the source of the annoyance. His eyes widened in surprise at the sight of the small boy. Then the resigned ogre all but shrugged his shoulders before raising his spear again, this time to skewer Aram.

Aram glimpsed something flying over his head. It was Hackle, who had leapt from above him on the incline. With the gnoll's entire body weight behind it, the swing of Wordok's club crushed the skull of the tawny ogre. Aram cringed involuntarily. He took a step back and watched for a good two seconds as the gnoll balanced on the dead ogre's shoulders—before leaping off with a loud keening cackle and wading into battle against the other Gordunni.

The tawny ogre came crashing to the ground, and Aram—belatedly realizing that he was just standing there like an idiot—was nearly skewered by the monster's spear for a second time. Makasa barely managed to yank the boy out of the way.

"Stay on the perimeter!" she yelled. Though, of course, it wasn't advice she intended to follow herself. Her cutlass was out.

Her chain was swinging in its wide arc. And despite the danger, Aram felt certain the tide would turn.

Makasa was furious with Aram. But that reckoning would have to wait. She made quick calculations. Judging by the quantity of ogres already lying deceased on the valley floor, she didn't think the Gordunni were holding any warriors in reserve. A party of about twenty, she thought. And between the initial battle and Feral Scar, about a dozen ogres were already dead. Hackle had just killed another. That left . . . five, six, seven. The seven biggest—including their *especially big* commander—but still only seven. (Seven, of course, being quite preferable to twenty.)

She swung her chain. It wrapped around the massive biceps of the closest ogre. She pulled and—unlike pulling Feral Scar—when she pulled, the ogre stumbled off his feet and onto the point of her blade. That left six.

She crossed swords with another. Or rather, she crossed her sword with the ogre's axe. He was large and strong but slow. She carved him up. Five.

Their entry into the battle now commanded the ogres' attentions. A couple turned from Feral Scar. A clear error. They should have finished the beast off while they had the chance. The yeti's claws ripped out the spine of the first ogre to turn his back on him. Four.

Out of the corner of her eye, she saw that crazy gnoll Hackle single out the largest ogre of all, the commander, nearly as big as the ogre king Gordok. This ogre regarded the smallish gnoll with the huge club in stunned amusement. Then he actually laughed out loud when Sivet ran up to join Hackle, brandishing her tiny double-bladed axe. The ogre commander had his own considerably larger double-bladed axe, which he swung with enough force to slice off both gnolls' heads at once. But he clearly wasn't accustomed to fighting opponents quite so *short*. Hackle easily ducked beneath the swing, and Sivet didn't even have to bother. Moving under the ogre's extended arm, Hackle slammed the club down on the commander's foot. The ogre howled, glaring at Hackle and the war club. He shouted, "That Wordok's club! Where little gnoll get Wordok's club?!"

Hackle barked out, "Hackle take club off Wordok's corpse! When Hackle done with Marjuk, Hackle take Marjuk's axe, too!"

The commander, Marjuk, roared, swung his axe up over his head, and brought it down hard and fast. Hackle and Sivet leapt to either side.

Makasa knew they'd need her help. But she was busy with two ogres of her own—an eight-footer and a ten-footer—and she was trying to keep an eye on the hopeless Aram as well.

The boy had, in fact, moved to the perimeter upon her command, but he hadn't stayed there. He had again rushed forward to help Feral Scar, *again* slashing at an ogre about to strike at the yeti from behind. *Again*, the blow had done only superficial damage

84

to his opponent, who instantly turned and slapped Aram's cutlass out of his hand. But *again*, Aram's actions had distracted the ogre long enough for the yeti to turn and snap the ogre's neck. Three.

She thought she saw the boy and the yeti exchange a glance. *Did the beast just nod a thank-you to Aram? No! That's insane!* At least losing his sword had forced Aram to run back to the perimeter to retrieve it.

She briefly lost track of the others, however, as the two ogres she kept at bay with her chain attempted to flank her. She executed an old but consistently reliable trick. Turning her back on the ten-foot female, Makasa tilted the rotation of her chain toward the eight-foot male in front of her. The ten-footer moved in low to club Makasa under the chain. Makasa instantly corrected her swing, and the chain connected with the rearward ogre's jaw, stunning her and sending her reeling. The forward ogre rushed Makasa—but was tackled by Feral Scar, who brought him to the ground and went to work with his claws. Two.

This freed Makasa to turn back toward the ten-foot female. While this ogre was still shaking off the blow to her jaw, Makasa stabbed her through the heart. One.

That "one" was Marjuk, the ogre commander. He had found no success trying to kill the two young gnolls, but they had found none, either. The difference, of course, was that Feral Scar and Makasa were both now free to come to the gnolls' aid. Marjuk was surrounded on three sides. His earlier mirth had melted away. He swung his axe in long sweeping arcs, not to kill but to stall for time while his ogre brain struggled to come up with a plan. Feral Scar wasn't inclined to give him that time. When next the axe swung past the yeti, he moved in.

But Hackle yelled, "No! Feral Scar no kill Marjuk! Marjuk kill Gnaw! Kill Hackle's mother! Hackle kill Marjuk!"

The yeti actually stepped back. Makasa might have wondered then how much the beast understood, but at that moment, she was too busy mourning once again the loss of her harpoon. Her preference would have been to ignore Hackle's demand and kill Marjuk from a safe distance before things got out of hand.

Still, she was semi-prepared for this. She had planned to help Hackle kill the yeti. The same plan would work even better on the ogre commander. The next time the ogre swung his axe, Makasa swung her chain. The iron links cracked against Marjuk's elbow and wrapped around his arm. She pulled the bellowing ogre off balance, and Hackle slammed his club against Marjuk's knee. The knee buckled. Marjuk dropped onto it. Hackle swung the club upward; it cracked against the ogre's jaw. Feral Scar's claws slashed at Marjuk's back. The ogre roared again—this time in pain. Sivet raced in, swinging her little hatchety-axe. Marjuk brought his free hand up to protect his face and lost a couple of thick fingers.

* * *

Aram had been forced to scramble a dozen yards to recover his sword. An ogre had easily—too easily (and not for the first time)—knocked the blade from his hand. It was embarrassing, and Aram preferred to blame the cutlass itself. *It's not really mine*, he told himself. It had belonged to Old Cobb, the sailor who had betrayed Aram's father to Malus. During the battle for Greydon Thorne's ship, Cobb had cornered Aram and was about to run the boy through—when instead, *Wavestrider*'s mast had come crashing through Cobb. As Aram had already lost two cutlasses in the battle, he had been forced to pry the one he now carried from Cobb's dead hand. Yet a somewhat superstitious Aram didn't quite trust the blade. Deep down, he thought it still loyal to Cobb, that maybe it *liked* slipping from his hand and still longed to fulfill Cobb's last desire: to see Aramar Thorne dead.

Nevertheless, it was the only sword he had, so he ran to recover it. By the time he turned, the others were already engaged in fighting the ogre commander. From his vantage behind and to the left of Makasa, Aram grimaced. He had little sympathy for any ogre—particularly one who had killed Hackle's mother—but in his heart, he knew this was hardly a fair fight. Four against one was bad enough, but when one of those four was the yeti of all yetis and another was Makasa Flintwill and a third was a vengeful Hackle, he couldn't help feeling a little bad for this Marjuk. But only a little. Barely a little. Still, he was about to intervene, to say . . . something. But as he struggled to find the words, the means to reconcile everyone, Marjuk turned his head to the left and to the right, taking a last look at the odd collection of species bent on taking his life. Then he turned toward Hackle and spat out, "Gnaw easy kill."

Hackle brought down Wordok's club as hard as he could, and it was over. Commander Marjuk was over. And Aram never did find the words.

There was a pause. Then Makasa moved in to release her chain from around the dead ogre's arm.

Feral Scar moved toward his fellow yetis to free them from *their* chains.

But Hackle called out, "Feral Scar!"

Everyone turned. Hackle had Marjuk's axe now. He faced Feral Scar, who—grumbling irritably—raised himself to his full height to face the gnoll.

Sivet watched eagerly, ready to see if Hackle could regain his name once and for all. With nearly the same fervor with which she had quite recently held the "runt" in contempt, she now seemed to be silently rooting for him.

Makasa stepped back to allow this last conflict to run its course.

But Aramar Thorne had other ideas, and this time he was ready with the words . . .

"**S**ugl."

"Jaggal."

"Sugl."

"No. JAG-gal"

"SUG-gul. Suggul."

Jaggal growl out, "Close enough." But not close enough. Only been one day and one night, but Jaggal starting to hate little murloc hostage. All day and all night, jabbering murloc follow Jaggal, scampering behind Jaggal all over Woodpaw village. Come morning, when Jaggal bring wood to woodpile, find murloc sitting on woodpile, jabbering. Jaggal burn wood in hearthfire; murloc jabbering at hearthfire. Jaggal fetch water from river; murloc sleeping beneath river. (*Murloc not even swim away! At least murloc no jabber while asleep.*) Jaggal go to nap in hut; see murloc dancing and jabbering on *roof of hut!*

Jaggal yell up at murloc. Murloc come down. Jaggal grab

murloc to tie murloc up. Murloc see rope. Dumb murloc happy. Murloc say, "Murky flllurllog mgrrrrl!" Dumb murloc dance around some more. Take rope from Jaggal. Murloc start tying rope in knots. Dumb murloc making mess of rope.

Karrion say, "Murloc want nets. Make nets. Fishing nets important to murlocs."

Murloc say, "Mrgle, mrgle. Murky flllurllog mgrrrrl! Mmmurlok flllur mgrrrrl!"

Jaggal throw up arms, say, "Give murloc rope. Let murloc make nets. But keep murloc away from Jaggal!"

Jaggal go in hut. Jaggal lie down for nap. Jaggal no nap. Jaggal no sleep. Jaggal hear murloc jabbering with Karrion outside hut.

"Kurun."

"Karrion."

"Kuron."

"No. KAIR-ee-on."

"Kur-EEE-un. Kureeun."

"Close enough."

Inside hut, Jaggal growl.

Murloc is hostage. Jaggal know Jaggal need to trade hostage for Sivet. But murloc is dumb hostage. Jaggal think maybe Jaggal let murloc hostage go free. Or maybe Jaggal kill murloc hostage. Killing murloc hostage risk Sivet. But murloc no make only nets. Murloc make Jaggal crazy, too.

Jaggal no nap. Jaggal go outside, to kill murloc hostage, probably.

"Suggul!" murloc call when murloc see Jaggal. Dumb murloc happy to see Jaggal.

Jaggal pick up axe and stalk toward murloc . . . just as Sivet emerge from forest . . .

If I can pull this off, Aram thought, *it'll be my best magic yet!*

He had told Sivet to go first. And she practically skipped into the lead. She wasn't simply compliant; she was *enthusiastic*. It hadn't taken much to convince her, either. When Aram had started to explain—as best as he understood—why Feral Scar had attacked her, why the yeti had felt the need to protect his people from hers, Sivet had quickly grown impatient, had interrupted him, had said, "Sivet know this, dumb boy." *She's a convert*, he thought. *A convert to the teachings of Captain Greydon Thorne.*

Entering the gnoll village, she called out to Jaggal and ran to him, rubbing her furry head against his furry side.

Aram and Hackle followed in time to see Jaggal's expression change—or rather melt—from aggravation to pleasure. Jaggal did shoot one last evil glance Murky's way, but Murky was already loping past the brute and his daughter to embrace his friends.

"Urum! Ukle! Frunds! Nrk mlggrm Mrksa?!"

"Shhh," Aram said, patting the murloc on the head as he watched Jaggal saunter over with Sivet wedged under one arm.

Jaggal smirked down at Hackle, who carried something in a large burlap sack. "Runt carry head of Feral Scar?" he asked, voice dripping with what passed for gnoll sarcasm.

Hackle shook his head slowly.

"Ha! Jaggal knew! Runt not even find Feral Scar!"

"Hackle find Feral Scar," Hackle said, his voice quiet, calm, and even.

Jaggal snorted again, and looked down at little Sivet, expecting her to deny it.

But she said, "Hackle find Feral Scar."

This clearly caught Jaggal off guard. He stared at her, and she nodded. Slowly, he turned back toward Hackle. Once again, he said, "Hackle carry head of Feral Scar?" But this time the question was sincere, and—whether he noticed it or not—he had followed Sivet's lead and called Hackle by name.

Hackle shook his head again.

A disgusted Jaggal waved him off. "Then runt still runt," he said.

So far it was going exactly as Aram had planned.

Hackle said, "Hackle no kill Feral Scar . . ." He opened the burlap sack and dumped the head of Marjuk onto the ground at the brute's feet. "But Hackle kill Marjuk."

Jaggal stared down at Marjuk's head. So did Aram at first. But he quickly turned away. The sight of the thing, with its semi-crushed skull and mayflies buzzing around it, was, frankly, nauseating.

Slowly, the brute shook his head. "No. Runt no kill Marjuk. Human woman kill Marjuk. Where is woman?"

But Hackle said, "Hackle kill Marjuk."

And again, Sivet confirmed Hackle's truth: "Marjuk kill Gnaw. Gnaw Hackle's mother. So Hackle kill Marjuk with club of Wordok."

Hackle reached into the sack again and pulled out Marjuk's massive double-bladed axe. Dropping the sack, the young gnoll knelt before Jaggal and lowered his head submissively; he offered the weapon up to the brute. "Hackle take Marjuk's axe. Hackle no keep axe, though. Hackle give axe to Woodpaw brute. Hackle give Marjuk's axe to Hackle's old friend Jaggal."

Putting down his own axe, Jaggal took a halting step forward and slowly reached for the weapon. He wrapped his paws around it, clearly liking the feel of the thing. He lifted it over his head and laughed.

But when he looked at Hackle again, his smile faded—not into anger or contempt, but into regret and sadness. He lowered the axe and shook his head. "Runt do good, killing Marjuk. But that not deal. Runt promise Feral Scar to regain name, to save friends. Runt no deliver Feral Scar. Runt and friends must die."

Hackle shrugged and said, "Hackle bring Feral Scar."

As every revelation left Jaggal more and more amazed, he looked around and howled out, "Where? Where body of Feral Scar?!"

On cue, Makasa emerged from the trees, leading the body— the very large and very alive body—of Feral Scar. Karrion and the other gnolls backed away from the huge yeti.

But Hackle, Sivet, and Jaggal did not. The latter stared at the beast, then gazed down at Hackle with a look of pure, almost beatific, gratitude. He swallowed and spoke the following words of love: "Hackle give Jaggal axe of Marjuk so Jaggal can kill Feral Scar. Hackle true friend."

It was finally Aram's turn. He said, "Jaggal cannot kill Feral Scar. Or yetis will kill gnolls."

Feral Scar let out a low growl, and on every side of the village, yetis emerged from the forest, leaving Jaggal and his gnolls completely surrounded.

Jaggal, angrier now than he had been happy moments before, roared out, "Traitor!" He raised the axe to strike at Hackle. "Jaggal kill traitor runt. Jaggal kill humans. Jaggal kill murloc! Jaggal kill Feral Scar! Jaggal die! All gnolls die! But traitors and humans and yetis die, too!"

"No," Aram said. "No one dies. The yetis aren't here to kill you. They're not here to kill a single gnoll. Yetis are *not* the gnolls' enemies. *Ogres* are the gnolls' enemies. Ogres are the yetis' enemies. So gnolls and yetis should be friends. Allies. They should fight together against the Gordunni ogres. They should share lands without killing."

"No!" Jaggal snarled.

A small but confident voice said, "Aram right, Jaggal."

"What?!" The brute turned and raised his paw to cuff his daughter.

Sivet didn't flinch. She said, "Sivet saw. Sivet saw gnolls, humans, yetis fight together against Marjuk and Gordunni ogres. Twenty ogres. Gnolls would die fighting twenty ogres. Humans would die fighting twenty ogres. Yetis *did* die fighting twenty ogres. But together, humans, gnolls and yetis kill twenty ogres. Gnolls and yetis and humans are stronger together. Aram right, Jaggal."

Hackle nodded. "Aram right, Jaggal."

Murky said, "Urum mmmml," which nearly set Jaggal off again. But he swallowed his annoyance and looked around the village, unsure.

Sivet slipped out of his reach and strode over to Feral Scar. She took his huge paw and pulled the beast toward her father. Feral Scar followed mildly, stopping when she stopped.

Here was the moment of truth. Feral Scar and the Woodpaw brute, Jaggal, face-to-face. One holding his newly gifted battle-axe. The other with practically every natural weapon one could conceive. Everyone seemed to be holding his or her breath . . .

Then Jaggal nodded.

And Feral Scar grunted.

And just like that, an alliance was sealed.

The gnolls all cheered. The yetis roared to the heavens. Aram breathed a heavy sigh of relief. It was *good magic*, indeed. But he hadn't accomplished the trick alone. He put an arm around Hackle's shoulder, and they exchanged grins.

Sivet approached, also grinning. Aram said, "Sivet, you'll make a great matriarch someday."

Hackle said, "Yes."

Even Makasa, shaking her head in sheer disbelief at what had been accomplished, said, "A great matriarch."

Sivet beamed.

And finally, there came the feast.

The yetis had brought gifts: bear meat and venison. For a second, Aram felt a slight qualm. Thalyss the druid had taken the shape of a bear and a stag while in Aram's company. But that second passed quickly. *It can't be a night elf,* he told himself. As the gnolls said, *meat is meat,* and Aram had never in his life been quite this starved.

There were many mouths to feed this night, so the bear meat was cut into thick steaks for the yetis and Jaggal. For the rest, the venison was transformed into a huge iron stockpot of Karrion's Dragonbreath Chili. Aram watched longingly, greedily, as

Karrion poured oil into the stockpot and added peppers and onions. For five *lonnnnng* minutes, she cooked the vegetables until they were brown and soft. Then she added the meat—the venison chopped fine, square chunks of bear meat, and sliced pork sausages from the gnolls' own stores—stirring it all until brown (another torturous five minutes).

Spices next: cumin and chili pepper and a pinch of something Aram couldn't identify. Then a paste made from tomatoes, some kind of gnoll ale, and a broth that had been simmering in a separate kettle. Next, beans and more tomatoes.

And then the interminable waiting. Waiting those last two hours for the chili to simmer—with the luscious smell of it emanating from the stockpot on the hearthfire—provided greater torment than being in the ogres' slave pit. And it was all made worse by the sounds of Feral Scar and Jaggal tearing into their (respectively) raw and rare steaks. Aram was so tempted to sneak one off the platter, Makasa actually had to stay his hand, saying, "Aramar Thorne, do you really want to wreck the impossible alliance you yourself have forged this day, simply for the sake of eating some few minutes sooner?"

"*Yes!*"

She glared at him.

"Yes," he insisted, but with less volume and enthusiasm.

She glared some more.

"Maybe . . ."

97

Her glare did not abate.

"No."

So they waited. And waited. And waited some more. After a quarter of an hour of waiting, he said, "This is longer than a 'few minutes.'"

He knew she could have said, *"Brat, I'm hungry, too."* Instead, she said, "Take out your sketchbook."

The sketchbook! Of course! That'll get me through this!

And it did. Beginning with Feral Scar, he noticed details about the yeti that he hadn't been able to focus on during the earlier conflicts, when all he could take in were the creature's immense size, immense horns, and immense claws. Now, he noticed that Feral Scar had thick brown fur with a slight red tinge covering his entire body, except for a snow-white belly and a snow-white beard. His face was otherwise hairless, and he had a long, eponymous scar that ran in a jagged diagonal from above his right eye to the left-hand corner of his mouth. He had crooked teeth and pointed ears, and his horns possessed subtle rings that reminded Aram of the rings on a tree.

Aram had many other fascinating subjects besides Feral Scar, including Sivet and Jaggal together, and Karrion stirring chili. He filled pages with yetis and gnolls, and while he drew, his desperate hunger and need faded—as Makasa had known they would.

Thus, before he knew it, Karrion was scooping the chili into a bowl, sprinkling cheese (made from the milk of some unknown mammal) atop it, and holding the bowl out to Aram.

He was so hungry, he nearly dropped his sketchbook into the fire. But he forced himself to carefully wrap the precious book and return it to his pocket before wolfing down his first bowl— without truly tasting a mouthful—and asking for another.

Karrion ignored him until everyone else had been served. But she served him seconds before she served herself firsts. She said, "Pace yourself, boy. This *Dragonbreath* Chili."

Aram tried to slow down. He took a bite and savored the meaty concoction. *Oh, this is heaven!* he thought. It definitely had a little kick. But both his father and his stepfather enjoyed spicy foods, and he was accustomed to the heat. (Or so he believed.) Meanwhile, he was still too hungry to truly take his time. He shoveled spoonful after spoonful into his mouth—without noticing the cumulative effect of Karrion's secret ingredient.

No, he didn't notice it at all—*until he did!* And then suddenly his mouth was aflame! He grabbed Thalyss's canteen and downed gulp after gulp of water, but somehow that only made it worse.

Karrion and Sivet and Hackle and Jaggal all laughed their hyena laughs at him. Finally, Hackle offered him a cornmeal biscuit, saying, "Water just swirl Dragonbreath around Aram's mouth. Aram chew biscuit. Biscuit absorb Dragonbreath. Then Aram swallow Dragonbreath. Make Aram strong."

CHAPTER TEN

Aram chewed gratefully, and as predicted, the burning sensation subsided.

"Furlskr," Murky was saying.

"Feral Scar," said Sivet.

"Furlskr . . ."

"No FAIR-al SCAR," she corrected.

"FUR-ul SKUR. Furul Skur."

"Close enough."

Jaggal growled low.

Seeing a potential problem, Hackle quickly asked Aram to show Jaggal and Sivet his magic book. The boy sat among the three gnolls and revealed the wizardry of his sketchbook's pages. The brute and the little matriarch were soon marveling at Aram's portrait of the two of them.

Hackle whispered something in Aram's ear, and Aram flipped back to his illustration of Cackle, matriarch of the Grimtail gnolls.

Hackle said, "This Cackle."

Sivet stabbed a finger at the sketch. "Cackle?"

"Yes!" Hackle said gleefully.

"Hackle is Hackle!" Jaggal said.

"Hackle know!"

Together, the three of them repeated, "Cackle, Hackle! Cackle, Hackle! Cackle, Hackle!" over and over, until their words dissolved into a mutual fit of hysterical laughter.

Aram never quite understood why gnolls found such a simple rhyme so uproariously funny. But he noticed that no one was calling Hackle a runt anymore. (And not because *runt* didn't rhyme with *Cackle*.)

Once Jaggal had caught his breath, he looked down upon Hackle with affection, caused, probably, by some combination of the laughter they had just shared, a full belly, the new yeti alliance, and nostalgia for their childhood friendship. But whatever the cause, the brute was ready to make amends. He said, "Hackle is no runt. Hackle is Hackle. Hackle rejoin Woodpaw."

Sivet, who was looking at Hackle the way Aram used to look at Duan Phen, grabbed up Hackle's paw. "Yes," she said, "Hackle rejoin Woodpaw."

Aram didn't even have time to think, *I'm gonna miss that gnoll*, before Hackle shook his head.

"Hackle glad to be Woodpaw. Hackle always be Woodpaw. But Hackle's place is with Aram now." He removed his paw from Sivet's.

Aram said, "You can stay here—with your people—if you want, Hackle. You will be sorely missed. But any debt you think you owe me is paid in full, my frund."

"Hackle know Hackle's place with Aram."

Jaggal nodded. Sivet sighed—then nodded as well.

Hackle repeated, "Hackle's place with Aram."

YETI AND
WOODPAW FEAST

R. Thorne

CHAPTER ELEVEN
BLOODY GOOD CHEER

Come dawn, dey could all see da wyvern One-Eye circlin' high overhead. Circlin' and dancin' tru da air in da morning sunlight wid her tree wyvern cubs. And unless da Hidden were *wantin'* ta fight dem wyverns, dis was a place where dey don' dare linger.

Zathra hissed a warning ta da ogres. "Try ta stay outta sight." Den she glanced back over her shoulder and realized how ridiculous dat request was. Slepgar—all twelve feet a him—yawned mightily before lookin' round lazily for a tree big enough ta hide his oversize self. Da rest a dem ogres—Throgg, Karrga, Ro'kull, Ro'jak, Guz'luk, and da two-headed Long-Beard and Short-Beard—were nearly as easy ta see. Certainly, from above.

Karrga leaned over ta whisper what already was obvious: "Hiding no work. Best if ogres no stay long." Karrga had led dem here, ta da foot a Skypeak, havin' guessed correctly dat da wyvern would be returnin' ta her nest wid her cubs. "Marjuk and

Wordok and Arkus climb Skypeak, take cubs from nest. Put in dome of thorns. Gordok—*old* Gordok—use cubs to force Ol' One-Eye to do what old Gordok want. But One-Eye's cubs free now. One-Eye free now. One-Eye probably kill any ogre One-Eye see. Maybe kill troll, too."

Valdread chuckled and whispered, "Well, thank the gods *I'm* safe."

All but *smellin'* da Forsaken's smug grin floatin' in from unda his hood, mingled alongside da scent a jasmine, Zathra ignored him and muttered a trio a quick, silent prayers ta her loa—Eraka no Kimbul, Lord a Beasts, and Ueetay no Mueh'zala, God a Death, and even Elortha no Shadra, Mother a Venom (who likely was keepin' da wyvern's stinger rich in poison)—askin' dat da wyvern's attentions stay focused up high. She drew out a crossbow bolt and pricked her finger, lettin' tree drops a her own blood fall ta da ground. Dey vanished instantly inta da sand, so she knew her prayers been heard.

Skitter smelled da blood and woke from her nap, clicking her thirst.

"Hush, sista," Zathra said, strokin' da scorpid dat armored her chest. "Dat blood not for you. Dat blood for da loa, for Eraka, for Ueetay, for Elortha."

Skitter clicked again but settled.

Now, Zathra scanned about, lookin' for signs, lookin' ta find exactly where da beast had left da Thorne boy and his friends.

"If dey not be up in her nest, den dey be leavin' for Gadgetzan from somewhere round here."

Quickly and easily, she found plenty a evidence a da fugitives. Near da waterfall was a fresh grave. From da length a da disturbed earth, she knew it ta be da grave a da night elf. "Been tinkin' I killed dat druid," she murmured, sportin' a serious grin. Two bolts ta da kaldorei's back from her crossbows had put him in da ground.

Leadin' away from da grave, she found tracks: da boy, da woman, da murloc, and da gnoll. Clear as day ta someone who knew how ta look.

"Dis way," she whispered, and led dem forward.

Karrga, Throgg, Valdread, and da rest a Gordok's Elite followed.

Zathra glanced up one last time. Da four wyverns continued deir dance round Skypeak, none a dem even bodderin' ta look down. "Tank you, my loa," the troll whispered. "Next chance I get, I be feedin' you more dan just a few drops. Maybe I be feedin' you da Thorne boy and all his friends . . ."

The Thorne boy and all his friends breakfasted on fresh sliced palm-apple. It was sweet and juicy, light and refreshing.

By this time, Jaggal was a changed gnoll. All notion of Hackle not deserving Woodpaw grub had vanished. Now, the brute was practically *forcing* supplies on his old friend. He gave Hackle a leather pack with two whole palm-apples already inside, not to mention two good-size packets of Aram's favorite boar jerky and a thick slab of bear steak, roasted the night before and wrapped in a giant gunnera leaf, for that night's supper.

Everyone seemed to be in a very good mood. The yetis had left during the night, but the gnolls scampered about the village as if a pall had been lifted, which, in fact, it had. Now the yetis were the gnolls' friends and, better still, their allies against the ogres. (Plus, the worst ogre slavers—Wordok and Marjuk—were no longer a threat.) The adult members of the clan went about the business of the morning with a significant spring in their collective steps. Pups smaller than Sivet raced about, some with diminutive weapons, pretending to be grown warriors, while others brandished their little claws, pretending to be their new yeti friends. (Honestly, few sights are quite as adorable as a tiny gnoll pup imagining himself as Feral Scar while fighting off invisible ogres.) Cries of "ROAR! ROAR!" and peals of cackling laughter crackled throughout the camp.

Aram was fairly proud of himself for having negotiated the peace between gnoll and yeti. Makasa was clearly proud of him, too, though she was semi-desperate not to show it, lest it go to his head—and semi-desperate to get on with their journey, lest Malus catch up with them. Jaggal and Hackle were laughing together and cuffing each other (with relative gentleness). Sivet took turns showering admiring looks upon Makasa and Hackle and her father. And though she didn't throw the same looks toward Aram, she had stopped regarding him with contempt, which was something, anyway.

Murky was off to the side, slurping up the occasional slice of palm-apple, but mostly concentrating on weaving new nets for himself.

Karrion studied his work and nodded approvingly.

Aram smiled, quite self-satisfied.

Within the hour, they were off, once again following the compass southeast toward Gadgetzan. They had walked a good mile before Aram noticed that Murky didn't have his nets. Instead, he was carrying an extremely short spear. The kind the gnoll pups had been play-acting with.

"Murky, your nets? Where are your nets? Did you forget them?"

"Nk, nk. Murky fllmm Kureeun mgrrrrl fr mmmm mrrugl mrrruggl."

Makasa grumbled, "What did he say?"

"I'm not sure," Aram said. "But . . . Murky, did you trade your nets to Karrion . . . for that spear?"

The murloc said, "Mrgle, mrgle," and began pantomiming his own battle against invisible ogres. "RRRgrrrs nk mlgggrrrr Urum mmgr Murky lggrm!" He poked at the air with his new spear.

"Those were good nets," Makasa said with bewilderment. "He traded them for a toy?"

Aram considered this for a moment, then said, "Makasa, those nets were very important to him. But he traded them so he'd have a *weapon* to help us fight."

Hackle nodded. "Spear look like toy to Makasa, but spear a real spear. *Small* but real."

Makasa's expression changed then. She nodded to the murloc, who grinned broadly at the tiniest hint of approval from her. But there was something else in her expression . . .

Aram guessed, "You're thinking you should have traded for a long spear."

She almost shrugged. But then she shook her head. "No, I'll wait until I can find a real harpoon to trade for. Assuming I have anything to trade."

They walked on.

Baron Reigol Valdread slid his hood back off his head and looked up at the display before them. As always, his thin, pale skin was stretched taut over his skull into a skeletal grin, which matched his mood. He was, in a word, *delighted* by what he saw, which made for a nice change—given how dull he found most sights generally. A headless ogre was hanging from a tree, a thick rope looped under his armpits and wrapped around the trunk.

The others in his party were not half so pleased by the sight.

Except, perhaps, Karrga, who whispered in Throgg's ear, "That Marjuk."

Throgg's face darkened with confusion. He said, "Karrga know Marjuk even though Marjuk no have head?"

"That Marjuk," she repeated with certainty.

Throgg nodded and said, "Huh. Throgg no kill Marjuk then." He sounded disappointed that he couldn't do Karrga this favor.

"It be a warning ta da Gordunni," Zathra said. She was studying the body. "Hmm. Head cut off with axe. One swing. After death."

"And before death?" Valdread asked in his cheerful whisper.

"Before death . . . claw marks . . . from a yeti."

"Interesting," the baron murmured slyly. "I've never known a yeti to use an axe before."

"No, mon. Yetis not be usin' no axes. But a yeti not be killin' dis ogre by his lonesome. Here, on da arm, dere be bruises from da human woman's iron chain."

"Ah. Our Miss Flintwill does always seem to be in the thick of things, doesn't she?"

Zathra nodded, frowning. "Ogre also hit wid war club . . ."

Karrga interposed, "Like club gnoll take from Wordok."

". . . and fingers cut off by a smaller blade. Maybe da boy's cutlass. Maybe."

Valdread whispered, "So a real *team* effort, then." The undead swordsman sounded absolutely tickled—mostly because he was.

"And young Squire Thorne and his friends now number a *yeti* in their company?" He was trying very hard not to laugh—since a good laugh tended to dislocate his jaw.

"Don' know, mon. Dis not be da battle site. No human tracks round here. No murloc tracks, eider. Only gnoll and yeti."

Guz'luk said, "Gnolls and yetis working together? Gordok no like that." The old ogre thought about this for a moment before adding, "'Cept Gordok dead now."

"I hardly think the *new* Gordok will much care for the news. Please say I can be the one to tell him? Oh, and I simply *must* be the one to tell Ssarbik just as soon as we rendezvous. I'm sure the arakkoa's reaction will be absolutely apoplectic. And absolutely priceless."

"Put your hood up and stop your grinnin', Valdread," a chagrined Zathra barked. "I lost deir trail. And dis corpse been hangin' here for at least two days." The baron watched her waken the scorpid and send the creature off to search for signs of their prey. This afforded some mild amusement as each of the ogres, save Throgg, shrunk from the skittering Skitter and seemed to be attempting to *simultaneously* pick both feet up off the ground to avoid her.

Valdread looked up at Marjuk one last time. "Do we cut the poor fellow down?"

Slepgar yawned and said, "Why? Valdread hungry?"

The Forsaken laughed so hard he did indeed dislocate his jaw.

CHAPTER TWELVE
BEST-LAUGHED PLANS

For once, they had an actual plan. Their map of Kalimdor had shown a night elf outpost, New Thalanaar, right along their route, on the coast of the flooded Thousand Needles canyon. They'd stop there for the night, inform the night elves of Thalyss Greyoak's passing, resupply again, and maybe hire a boat to take them across the water to Gadgetzan. Even Makasa thought it a good plan, nodding with satisfaction as Aram folded the map.

But as *Wavestrider*'s first mate, the odd and cheerful dwarf Durgan One-God, used to say, *"We plan. The Life-Binder laughs."*

Now, two days later under a midmorning sun, our quartet stood on a hill overlooking New Thalanaar, having found the outpost under siege. Three contingents of warriors surrounded New Thalanaar on three sides—that is, every side but the side facing the waters of Thousand Needles. Elf sentries and archers manned New Thalanaar's makeshift battlements, but no arrows were being loosed, at least not currently.

Hackle pointed at the raiders and said, "Grimtotem tribe. Tauren."

Aram found this nearly incomprehensible. He thought of his friends, the night elf Thalyss Greyoak and the tauren Wuul Breezerider, and saw no reason why night elves and tauren shouldn't get along famously. He said, "I know the kaldorei are Alliance, and the tauren are Horde, but—"

"Most tauren are Horde, yes," Hackle said, "but Grimtotem hate Horde."

"So the Grimtotem joined the Alliance?" Aram asked, more confused than ever.

"No," Hackle said, sounding bored. Then he knelt down so he could scratch the back of his neck with his hind foot. Eventually, he stopped and added, "Grimtotem hate Alliance. *And* Grimtotem hate Horde. Grimtotem hate everyone. Grimtotem even hate tauren."

"Well, that makes it all as clear as mud," Aram said, frowning. But the frown faded quickly. The wheels were already turning. Without being conscious of it, he took a half step forward.

Makasa grabbed him by the collar, growling out, "Oh, no you don't!"

"What?" Aram asked, only somewhat disingenuously.

"I can read your mind, brother. See it on your face. You're thinking you united the gnolls and the yetis. Now, flush with that success, you think you can march down there and broker a peace between night elves and tauren."

"Is that *so* impossible?"

"We'll never know. Because I'm not letting you anywhere near either side, even if I have to hog-tie you to stop you."

"But—"

"No."

"You don't even have any rope," Aram said mopily.

"I'll wrap my chain around your neck and drag you away behind me."

Aram looked at both Murky and Hackle for support, only to find both nodding absently, as if Makasa's proposal made indisputable sense.

"You will not risk your life and ours on a fool's errand," she continued evenly. "You cannot bring peace and palm-apples to all of Azeroth simply because you think that's the way it ought to be."

"You wouldn't say that to our father."

"Captain Thorne was an idealist. But he was never naïve. Not *that* naïve, anyway."

"Makasa—"

"You forget. Malus is likely still after us, and we've already lost enough time. There are limits, Aramar, to what even a Thorne can accomplish."

*　*　*

Aram was trying hard *not* to sulk as they walked west, some distance out of their way, in order to skirt the raid. They crested a hill and looked down on a very wide stream (or a very thin river) that they could see ran south around New Thalanaar before turning east to feed Thousand Needles just below the outpost. If they remained in the trees on the far side of the stream, they could avoid all the tauren and continue on to Gadgetzan.

But here, that meant fording the rushing water to get to the western side. Aram's reluctance was palpable—and not caused by any lingering desire to bring peace and palm-apples to elves and tauren. Rather, the water itself made him nervous. In the last month, he had nearly drowned twice. Once, while attempting to swim ashore from the *Wavestrider*'s dinghy, and once when trying to rescue Murky from a stream (or river) much like this one. Aram felt he didn't have good luck with water, but he said nothing. He figured he was being, well, silly.

Murky enthusiastically swam across on his back, holding his little spear out of the water, above the flow. Makasa, the tallest of them, followed, carrying the majority of their supplies, including Hackle's war club, which he had reluctantly relinquished to her. The water was up past her knees, but she was always surefooted. Hackle nodded to Aram, who nodded back, smiling uncomfortably, and waded in. After three steps, the water was practically up to Aram's waist, but he kept walking forward. The riverbed stones felt slippery under his boots, and once he nearly lost his footing before recovering. He swallowed hard and looked up. His eyes met Makasa's, and he thought he could see her dawning realization that he was afraid.

She called out, "Take it slow, one step after another!"

He nodded to her and took it slow, one step after another. He glanced back over his shoulder. Hackle had followed Murky's lead and was swimming—dog-paddling—across. He paused, treading water, waiting for Aram, who was now about halfway to the other side.

Suddenly, Aram thought of the sketchbook in the back pocket of his breeches, which was currently right at the waterline. It was wrapped in oilskin, which had always preserved it before, even when diving off the dinghy or rescuing Murky had completely submerged him. So he continued forward, feeling confident it would survive this, too.

But what of the acorn?!

The Seed of Thalyss was in a leather pouch tied to his belt. It, too, was wrapped in oilskin. But how well wrapped? Thalyss had used his dying breath to warn Aram not to let the fist-size magic acorn get wet. Now, Aram was dragging it through the water. He stopped and reached for the pouch. Then he stopped himself from doing that, too. The pouch was already damp. Either the oilskin was doing its job—or it was already too late. Checking on it now would only risk soaking a seed that was potentially still dry.

Makasa called out again, "One step at a time, Aram!"

He started forward with a new determination to get to the other side and onto dry land—where he could safely check the acorn—as soon as possible. And pretty much instantly, he slipped.

His right foot found no traction and was swept up by the current, the toe of his boot almost clearing the water. He fell backward. Hackle was right there and tried to grab Aram, but buoyed up by his clothes and with no purchase at all on the riverbed, Aram was quickly washed downstream out of Hackle's reach.

The water was cold, but he'd been in colder. The stream was flowing fast, but he'd fought stronger currents. His head disappeared beneath the waterline a couple of times, but never for very long, and he was always able to surface quickly and grab a breath.

He'd been so afraid of this exact thing that when it wasn't quite as bad as he'd imagined, he actually gained confidence. The river (or stream) was deeper here: he could no longer touch the bottom with his feet. But he felt certain he'd eventually be able to make it ashore without drowning, so he tried to swim.

He looked back and saw Hackle swimming after him, only ten yards or so behind. He looked toward shore and could see Makasa running alongside, ready to dive in. He couldn't see Murky at all, and then suddenly, Murky emerged from beneath him. The murloc wrapped one thin but surprisingly strong arm around Aram's chest and kicked with both webbed feet to propel them toward Makasa.

Within seconds they were stumbling up onto the sand. Hackle followed. Aram coughed a couple of times but mostly just felt embarrassed. "Sorry, sorry," he said. Then he thanked Murky and apologized again to all three of his companions.

Murky seemed truly glad to have helped Aram and thanked him—"Mmrgl, mmrgl!"—for providing the opportunity to be of use. Makasa actually patted the little murloc on his head: *high praise indeed!* She didn't even wipe his slime off her hand until after his attention had shifted back to Aram.

Hackle shook himself from head to haunch, spraying water everywhere, including all over his three compatriots. It reminded Aram of his dog, Soot, after a swim in the Lakeshire quarry, and brought a smile to his face.

"You're sure you're all right?" Makasa asked.

"I'm fine, I swear," he said, while confirming that the compass was still around his neck. Then his thoughts returned to the Seed. He moved farther from the stream (or river) and reached for the soaking-wet pouch, still firmly tied to his belt. "I just want to make sure the acorn didn't get wet."

"Stop," she said. "Your *hands* are wet."

He tried to dry them on his breeches, but, of course, they were soaked through.

She grumbled something unintelligible and then turned around and removed the shield from her back. "Use the back of my tunic," she said with enough distaste for him to notice.

He rubbed his palms and fingers on the dry material, then carefully, cautiously, untied the leather pouch. The crystal shard was there. And the oilskin-wrapped acorn. The oilskin seemed to have done its job. Water beaded on it and slid off as he lifted it up. Carefully, cautiously, he unwrapped the acorn. It was dry. He breathed a heavy sigh of relief. All four of them exchanged a smile. *Everything's fine*, Aram thought. *I didn't drown. The acorn didn't get wet. This is just a minor inconvenience. That's all.*

He began to rewrap the Seed in its oilskin. Then somehow—*somehow*—it started to slip. He bobbled it, trying to hold on. Makasa, Hackle, and Murky all gasped. All four lunged to grab it, but all four missed. And the acorn fell . . . right toward a large puddle forming at the feet of the dripping-wet Aramar Thorne.

It landed in the shallow water with a visible and audible *SPLASH!*

PART TWO:

NAVIGATING THOUSAND NEEDLES

CHAPTER THIRTEEN
BLOSSOMLING

Aram stood there, frozen, staring down at the acorn in the puddle. They all did. Then, a good three seconds later, they all simultaneously bent to pick it up, knocking their heads together like players in a traveling comedy.

Thus, a chorus of "ows" was the first sound to greet the hatchling of the Seed of Thalyss. (Or perhaps the correct term might be "blossomling.") In any case, the acorn cracked and then practically turned itself inside out, like a kernel of corn dropped in a firepit. A flower of lavender and cyan emerged from the inverted shell and rapidly grew on a stem of royal purple.

But the stem began to take on form and substance. It widened and lengthened, grew hair and skin to form over bone and muscle. Soon, two big green eyes were staring into Aramar Thorne's brown eyes. In fact, their eyes locked in on each other with such intensity that by the time this new entity blinked (allowing Aram to finally shake off the contact), he had missed much of the process of her growing.

Now, however, he could take her all in—take her in, in all her splendor. She smelled simultaneously of his mother's flower bed in spring and fresh-cut grass. But what truly struck him first were the colors, all the fine shades she brought forth, like an entire hothouse of orchids displayed together in a single petite form. (For she was, in fact, an inch or so shorter than he.) She had purple-rose skin and burgundy hair, which faded to mauve, then to violet, indigo, and light blue, the farther it grew from her scalp. She had pointed elf ears the color of a ripe peach, turning to cherry-blossom pink at the tips. She had those big green eyes, but her features were otherwise subtle, and the overall effect of her face was quite pretty.

The original flower—which by this time had a blood-red (or perhaps magenta) center, surrounded by white petals tinged with pale yellow and pink—now appeared to decorate her long locks, though in point of fact, it was a part of her. There were more flowers, too: baby-yellow blooms and light-pink posies around her neck, and cherry blossoms with yellow centers discreetly covering her small chest. Mauve leaves, which covered her midriff, flared out into a leafy belt of deep ocean blue around her waist, dividing her upper body from her lower half.

As if that delineation were necessary—as if the split between her top and bottom halves might go unnoticed otherwise—since from the waist down, she was something akin to a four-legged centaur. And yet she was *nothing at all* like the centaur Aram had seen in Flayers' Point. Those beast-men and beast-women were huge, massive and misshapen. *She* was small, delicate, and elegant, and her lower body had less in common with a horse's bulk than with the lithe shape of a fawn, painted with short, dark-purple fur hinting at rusts and more burgundies. She had tiny black hooves shaded with more dark purple, and a tail that matched her hair color with curly tendrils of teal at the back. Despite these unusual qualities, this . . . *girl* (for in appearance, she seemed to be about twelve years old, that is to say, roughly the same age as Aram himself) fascinated our young hero, which in part explains why he stood there, staring into her eyes once again, with his mouth hanging open.

To be fair, he wasn't the only one staring rather foolishly at the newcomer. Makasa Flintwill, her mouth also hanging open, stood behind this strange child of nature. Hackle and Murky stood to either side. Their mouths hung open, too.

The newly blossomed youngling opened her mouth to speak in a voice that was almost musical in its tone, timbre, and clarity. (Aram would later decide she sounded much like the wind chimes Robb Glade made to sell at market on slow days at the forge.) She said, "Spring has come!"

Aram managed to squeak out three words: "You can talk!"

"Yes," she said, "and so can you!" She sounded quite impressed with them both.

He nodded stupidly, as if he were also impressed with his own (currently meager) ability to form words. Actually, he was struggling to remember exactly what she had said. Failing, he rather cleverly asked, "I'm sorry, what did you say?"

"I said you can talk, too."

"No, before that."

She thought about this for a moment. "Hmmm. Oh yes! I said, 'Spring has come!'"

"Actually, it's summer. Late summer, even."

She shook her head as if he were being quite silly. "Summer is coming."

It didn't seem to be a point worth arguing. Instead, he asked, "Sorry. Um. What are you?"

She said, "I am a dryad."

And still Aram nodded stupidly. He'd never heard the word before but guessed that was her species.

Perhaps sensing his ignorance, she added, "A daughter of Cenarius."

Again, he nodded. He vaguely recalled Thalyss mentioning something called the Cenarion Circle and assumed it had something to do with this dryad's father, but that was all he could glean.

Drella

She smiled again, as if she were taking benign pity upon him, and said, "My name is Taryndrella. But for beings such as your-selves, perhaps that is too long for regular usage. So, you may call me Drella."

"Durula," Murky said.

"Drella," she corrected.

"Durula," he attempted again.

"No, DREL-la."

"DRH-la. Drhla."

"Close enough," she said cheerfully. She looked about at her new companions, even turning around on four delicate hooves to take in Makasa.

"You are all so beautiful," the dryad said. "And all so different."

"Uh . . . thank you," Makasa muttered.

"Which of you is Thalyss Greyoak?"

Four sets of eyes fell under her inquiring gaze. Then three of those sets turned toward Aram. So she turned as well.

His mouth was dry. He swallowed and said, "We're sorry. But Thalyss . . . died."

"Oh," she said.

"It'll be all right." He thought of reaching out a hand to com-fort her but wasn't sure if that was, well, *allowed*.

She shrugged. "All things die."

He bristled a bit at her coldness. And yet, there was nothing particularly cold in her demeanor. Quite the opposite.

She said, "Still, I will miss our little talks."

Makasa said, "You talked to Thalyss? When?"

"Well, I suppose *I* did not talk. Not in a way you four would understand. But at night—every night—he would whisper to me. To my acorn, that is. And in many different tongues. That is how I know how to speak to all of you." She turned to Murky and asked, "Drhla mrrrgl mmmm nurglsh? Mmmurlok mrrrgle?"

"Mrgle, mrgle," Murky said, nodding happily. "Murky, Murky," he continued, pointing at himself. Then, in turn, he pointed out, "Urum, Mrksa n Ukle."

Aram quickly reintroduced himself and the others as "Aram, Makasa, and Hackle."

"It is lovely to meet each and every one of you. Thalyss mentioned you, Aram. And you, Makasa. And Murky. He was quite fond of you three." She turned her smile on Hackle and said, "You never came up."

Hackle looked a bit dejected, but Aram spoke up, reminding him—while informing her—that "Thalyss died shortly after meeting Hackle. He probably didn't have the opportunity to mention him. But I promise you, he liked Hackle a lot."

Hackle seemed pleased by this, and Drella seemed satisfied, or at least unperturbed.

Aram was still having trouble swallowing. He croaked out, "Thalyss asked us to bring you to Gadgetzan, to a druid tender there named Faeyrine Springsong."

She nodded. "Thalyss mentioned her, too. Considerably more often than he mentioned *any* of you. He was *very* fond of Faeyrine. It was almost embarrassing."

"Uh huh. Yeah. I got that sense. A little. Maybe."

They were all silent for a while.

Eventually, Aram said, "So, um, we'll bring you to see Faeyrine, okay?"

"If you like," the dryad replied.

They all stood there for a while.

Finally, Drella said, "Do we go now?"

"Yes!" Makasa said, eager to be moving on. "This way!" She led them into the trees beyond the stream (or river), remembering her desire to keep them out of sight of the Grimtotem.

Drella's eyes scanned everything with intense curiosity. "I just love these trees! And that bush! And those wildflowers!" She scampered from one wonder to the next with Aram chasing after her.

When the party stopped briefly to consult Aram's map, the original foursome looked up to find their new fifth gone. Makasa ordered, "Find her!" simultaneously to Aram calling out, "We have to find her!"

They split up, heading in four different directions. Aram

found her within a few minutes, conversing pleasantly with a hive of bees. Keeping his distance, Aram said, "There you are."

She maintained focus on the bees but answered, "I am always where I am."

"Uh, right, but . . . you shouldn't wander off like that."

"Why?" she asked, coming to him and away from the bees (to his immeasurable relief).

"Well, there might be tauren patrols in the area, and—"

"Oh, I have never seen a tauren. Let us go find one!"

"No, see, they're not friendly."

"Why? Thalyss said very nice things about tauren."

"Actually, all the tauren I've met have been pretty nice."

"Well, then?"

Aram was flummoxed. How had he come to be arguing against his own earlier arguments? There was still a part of him that very much wanted to walk up to the Grimtotem and convince them that all this fighting and sieging were completely unnecessary. But the greater part of him now felt he couldn't risk Taryndrella. *I have to protect her!* So, instead of answering, he called out (rather desperately) to Makasa—all while Drella smiled at him charmingly, and he nevertheless wished he could stuff her back in that acorn until they reached Gadgetzan.

Makasa, Hackle, and Murky soon rejoined them, and their hike continued.

As the dryad turned her attention to rubbing the various black spots amid Hackle's yellow fur—causing him to shake his left leg vigorously with every other step—Aram caught up to Makasa and whispered anxiously, *"She thinks she knows everything but really knows nothing!"* This was hitting him hard, creating a burden considerably more stifling, more onerous, more intimidating than safeguarding compasses, crystal shards, and fist-size acorns.

Makasa looked down on him and snorted out a short chuckle.

He whispered, "We need to get to Gadgetzan and the tender fast!"

"Oh, I agree."

"I mean this was why Thalyss was so insistent. He wasn't giving us an acorn. He was giving us a person!"

"Yes, I'm aware of what we both witnessed."

"Then why are you smiling?!"

"You found a baby," she said. "Now you have to bring baby to momma. That's a lot to take on."

"Exactly!"

"And she's worthy of protection, but at the same time, you hate that you are responsible for this child."

"Yes!"

"Welcome to my world."

CHAPTER FOURTEEN
WAKE-UP GROWL

$\mathcal{S}$teering clear of New Thalanaar, their *troop*—for so Makasa had begun to perceive it (much to her endless chagrin)—had stopped for the night at the edge of the forest, with the waters of Thousand Needles shimmering under Azeroth's moons just beyond the trees. All but Taryndrella consumed the last of the bear steak they had rationed. She asked each in turn for seeds. None of them had seeds. She found a small, stunted berry bush and held her hands over it. The bush slowly began to grow before their eyes, and a few berries blossomed. But the effort seemed to exhaust her. She said, "This was much easier when I was an acorn."

"Maybe because Thalyss was helping?" Aram offered.

She shrugged.

He had his sketchbook out and had just finished adding the dryad to it. He regretted more than ever that all he had was a charcoal pencil and that he couldn't capture all of her brilliant colors on the page. But as Robb used to say, "It is what it is." Aram turned the leaves back until he found his portrait of Thalyss—in both the shapeshifter's kaldorei and stag forms. He showed the sketch to Drella.

She asked, "Who is this?"

"It's Thalyss," he said, a little confused, as he had clearly written Thalyss's name on the page. "They're both Thalyss."

"Oh, so *that* is what Thalyss looked like. He was so beautiful, was he not? I especially like him as a beast."

"You can't read, can you?"

"I never had eyes before," she said cheerfully. "Would you teach me to read? I like learning new things."

He nodded, though he wasn't exactly sure how to go about it.

"Hackle no read," Hackle said. "Aram teach Hackle, too, and Hackle learn."

"Nk Murky fllm," said the murloc. "Murky mrgggll."

Makasa said, "You'll be opening a schoolhouse next."

"Do *you* want to teach them?" Aram asked, knowing the answer full well.

"No."

Aram looked at the other three and said, "Let me think about *how* to teach you for a bit, and then we'll start."

They all seemed satisfied. Drella ate her few berries.

Makasa, as usual, took the first watch.

Aram fell asleep easily, dreaming, as he often did these days, of the Light.

The Voice of the Light called to him, "Aram, Aram, you must not let the traitor stop you. You must find your way around him, through him . . ."

"Traitor?" Aram asked. "Who's a traitor?"

"I am no traitor," declaimed Malus, who now stood, silhouetted, between Aram and the bright, bright Light. "Only death lives in that Light."

"But to be a traitor . . ." Aram mused quietly, before raising his voice with an epiphany, ". . . Malus must have once been on your side."

"Yes," the Light said.

Malus growled, "It's easy to be a fool when you're young, boy."

"Boy, wake up." Aram jolted awake and then froze. There was a knife at his throat. "Slowly, boy," growled a voice behind him.

Aram sat up slowly, looking around. It was still dark, but the White Lady's light illuminated enough of his surroundings for him to see that their makeshift camp was now in the possession of a half dozen night elves. He glanced back over his shoulder. A male kaldorei was kneeling behind him, holding a long curved blade to his throat. Two more had Hackle and Murky in similar predicaments. Makasa stood free of such things, with her cutlass held out in front of her, aimed at a female night elf with short blue-green hair, extremely long pointed ears, and a wavy scimitar, likewise pointed at Flintwill.

Aram glanced around for Drella. The elf behind him growled, "Hold still, boy," and held the blade tighter against his throat.

"Don't hurt him," Makasa said darkly, the implied threat explicit in her tone.

The female kaldorei said, "Drop your weapon, and we will consider it."

"No," said Makasa Flintwill.

The female kaldorei actually sighed then. She asked, "Why would two humans be traveling with a gnoll and a murloc?"

She didn't mention a dryad, and again Aram wondered where Taryndrella was. Part of him was glad she wasn't there, wasn't captured with them, but the other part worried what that might mean.

Makasa said, "What does a night elf care with whom we travel? What business is it of yours?"

Aram said, "You're from New Thalanaar?"

No one answered.

He went on. "Well, you can see we're not Grimtotem, can't you? We're not your enemies."

Still, no response.

"We had a good friend who was one of your people. Thalyss Greyoak."

No one spoke, but the night elves clearly reacted to Thalyss's name, exchanging glances.

Finally, the female said, "Had?"

"He was killed. By a troll's crossbow." Aram decided to take a chance: "He died saving my life."

The elf behind him growled again. "And what made *you* worth the life of the Greyoak?"

Aram thought about this for a few seconds and said, "Friendship."

Nothing changed visibly, but Aram could tell that the kaldorei were more hesitant, unsure.

Then, out of nowhere, a musical voice said, "You are all so beautiful!" Aram's heart sunk. But as all the night elves turned to face Drella—who had emerged from deeper in the forest with her arms full of roots, vegetables, mushrooms, and fruit—each and every one of the kaldorei gasped audibly. Three or four lowered their heads worshipfully.

Recognizing—if not quite comprehending—an opportunity, Aram spoke quickly. "This is Taryndrella, daughter of Cenarius. She makes up one of our party."

The female elf bowed her head slightly and addressed the dryad. "Daughter of Cenarius, I am Rendow of New Thalanaar."

"Hello, Rendow of New Thalanaar," Drella said with her usual cheerfulness. If the dryad noticed the night elves' weapons and the precarious state of her companions, she gave no indication. "I think you are just lovely."

Makasa scowled but spoke with a tightly controlled voice. "This dryad was the Seed of Thalyss. He trusted her to us upon his death. It is a trust we hold sacred."

Rendow turned back to face Makasa. "And yet you let her wander alone in this wood?"

"No, I let her escape when I perceived we were at risk from you."

Rendow stiffened. Then almost absently, she nodded. She looked around the camp at her fellows, then in one swift motion, sheathed her scimitar. A second later the other night elves had put their weapons away, too.

Makasa, however, did not. Still aiming her cutlass at Rendow, she said, "I am Makasa Flintwill. We take Taryndrella, daughter of Cenarius, to Gadgetzan to fulfill our vow to Thalyss Greyoak. Will you allow us to go on our way?"

Rendow didn't exactly answer the question. Instead, she said, "Thalyss was a friend. A dear friend to all of us. I am sorry to hear of his passing. To be honest, it is almost incomprehensible." There was still a hint of suspicion in her voice.

Makasa said, "Aram, show her the book."

Aram reached into his pocket.

Once again, the night elf behind him growled out, "Slowly, boy."

He pulled out the sketchbook and turned to Thalyss's picture. He showed it to the growling kaldorei, who growled again—but nodded.

So Aram took a few steps forward and handed the book to Rendow.

She gazed at the page for a long time. But as always, there was a kind of magic to Aram's art. Or an art to his magic, perhaps. The picture of the kaldorei hardly proved anything. And yet there was an honesty to the drawing, and the expression on Thalyss Greyoak's face clearly spoke to the plain fact that his likeness had been taken whilst among friends. Rendow seemed to relax considerably.

She said, "Gadgetzan?"

"Yes," Aram said. "There is a druid tender there."

"Springsong," Rendow replied with a nod.

"Yes. Thalyss asked us to take Drella—Taryndrella—to her." Aram heard himself speaking a half-truth and coughed to cover, but Rendow was too lost in thought to notice.

Drella said, "Thalyss spoke of Faeyrine often. He never mentioned anyone named Rendow."

Aram shot the dryad a look, but she simply smiled at him.

Finally, Rendow spoke. "My apologies, daughter of Cenarius. My apologies, Flintwill. My apologies to you all. New Thalanaar has been under siege for so long, it has placed our very thoughts under siege as well. As I said, I am Rendow. A simple merchant. I trade in leather armor. Or I did."

"You are behind enemy lines," Makasa said.

"Indeed. We are bringing supplies to New Thalanaar."

"I have supplies," Drella said helpfully, holding out the produce in her arms. "All *they* had was meat." She scrunched up her face at Aram, the way Aram's little sister, Selya, did when asked to eat liver. It was, in a word, adorable.

"Keep them, Taryndrella," Rendow said. "You are generous, but we have enough."

Just then, another night elf emerged from the forest. He stopped short, bewildered by what he was seeing. He was younger. Or seemed younger anyway. To Aram, he looked to be about fifteen. But for all Aram knew, that could mean he was only fifteen hundred years old, instead of fifteen thousand.

"Speak, Garenth," growled the growly kaldorei, who still stood behind Aram.

"I . . . um . . ." He shook off his confusion, stepped up to Rendow, and spoke with some urgency. "A Grimtotem patrol approaches. Too many to fight."

"How far away?" Suddenly, Rendow was all business again. She reminded Aram to no small degree of Makasa.

"Four minutes. Five if we are lucky."

"I don't want to count on luck," Makasa said, and Rendow nodded to her in agreement.

Rendow said, "We need to avoid that patrol and get our supplies to the outpost, and we cannot risk being slowed by you.

And you need to get the dryad to safety, which means getting her as far away from here as possible—as fast as possible."

"You have a suggestion?"

"I do." Rendow pointed toward the water. "My boat is right over there, hidden in the rushes. Though it is small, it is yet big enough to hold all of you. Take it."

"Really?" Aram asked.

"The patrol might find it anyway and scuttle it. Sail it down the canyon. All the way to Fizzle and Pozzik's Speedbarge."

"To what?"

"Do not worry; you cannot miss it," Rendow said.

"We'll find it," Makasa said.

"It sounds lovely," Drella said.

"It is not," Rendow said. "But it will serve. When you arrive, you can leave the boat for me with a human woman named Daisy, who works at the inn there. She can also arrange for you to purchase further transport to Gadgetzan."

"This is very generous," Aram said. "Thank you."

"It is the least we can do for friends of Thalyss Greyoak, let alone a daughter of Cenarius." She handed Aram's sketchbook back to him. "Now, go. We cannot stay to cover your backs. So be quick."

Aram stooped to pick up his father's leather coat, which he had been using for a pillow. By the time he stood, the kaldorei had vanished.

Makasa whispered, "Come."

Hackle and Murky followed her, but Drella hesitated. Looking pouty, she said to Aram, "I still do not understand why I cannot stay to see a tauren."

"Maybe we'll see one from the boat."

And they did.

Reaching the water, Makasa had some difficulty locating the vessel. But Murky found it right away. It was, as Rendow had promised, a small wooden boat, yet big enough for the five of them. It had oars and a pole. They all clambered aboard, though Drella was unsure on her four hooved feet and required some assistance. She dropped all her vegetables onto the floor of the boat and knelt beside them.

Hackle and Aram pushed off. Makasa used the pole to guide them quietly away from the shore. Hackle moved to take up the oars, but Makasa shook her head. "Not yet," she whispered. "Too much noise."

Hackle nodded.

Then Drella shouted excitedly, "I think I see the tauren!"

And hearing her, the tauren turned to see the boatload of them as well. And since a few of the Grimtotem had spears, *seeing* wasn't their only option.

Makasa yelled, "ROW!"

Hackle rowed, putting his powerful shoulders to the task.

Angry tauren shouted and threw their spears, but in an instant

Makasa was at the rear of the boat, using her shield to deflect any spear that came too close. Aram had never seen tauren look so menacing. Not in Flayers' Point, not even when Breezerider had threatened to *split Aram's skull for him* in the ogres' pit.

Drella said, "They are all so beautiful!"

Aram stared at her and said, "They're trying to kill us!"

"And what if they do?" the dryad said with a laugh. "All things die."

Aram shook his head incredulously; Makasa's caution was making more and more sense.

Fortunately, the tauren soon ran out of spears. Or perhaps the boat was out of range. Either way, Hackle kept rowing furiously as the boat and their party floated down the flooded Thousand Needles canyon.

They (that is, all of them but Drella) took turns rowing throughout the night, Makasa being unwilling to put ashore until she was certain they'd put enough distance between themselves and the Grimtotem. Having made that pronouncement, she was silent, but often, Aram thought, she seemed on the verge of speaking.

Still, Aram, who was by then taking his own turn at the oars, would never in a million years have predicted what came out of her mouth once she did speak: an apology.

"I'm sorry," she said. The words seemed to twist in her throat. Aram realized he had never once in seven months heard her apologize—for anything. (Of course, he also couldn't quite pinpoint an occasion when she owed anyone an apology, either.) She went on with the same difficulty. "It was *my* watch. I'm not sure how it happened. Drella slipped away without my notice. And those night elves were upon us before I heard or saw a thing."

"I was hungry," Drella said. "But I could not eat your meat."

"You can't just disappear, Drella," Aram said. "You need to tell us when you're going. You need to let one of us come with you."

"I do not see why."

The other four exchanged flummoxed looks.

Finally, Hackle said, "Hackle vow to Thalyss to protect Seed. Protect Drella."

Murky's head bobbed in agreement. "Mrgle, mrgle. Murky mrrugggl Drhla, mmmmrgl."

"Do you see now?" Aram asked. "We promised Thalyss. You are new to this world. There are things you don't understand."

She frowned. It occurred to Aram that he had never seen her frown before. She said, "I am new to this form. I am not new to this world. I am *of* this world. And there are many things you do not understand, either." She all but said, *So there!*

But Aram thought she had given him an opening. "Yes," he agreed. "There are *so* many things I don't understand. Which is why we *all* must stick together."

She considered this and then nodded decisively. "Yes. That makes some sense."

The other four breathed a collective sigh of relief.

Then she added, "After all, I must not leave you four alone to fend for yourselves. You may require *my* protection."

Aram started to respond but changed his mind. *Whatever works*, he thought.

Makasa returned to her original point as if it were a burr in her boot. "I do not believe I fell asleep. But I failed you all."

"None of us are perfect," Aram said.

She waved him off dismissively.

Murky said, "Kuldurrree flllurlog mmgr mrrrggk."

Drella translated. "He said that kaldorei move with magic. He meant that you could not have heard them unless they wished to be heard."

"Mrgle, mrgle," Murky confirmed.

Makasa said nothing, but even in the moonlight, Aram could see that her self-doubt seemed assuaged by this—at least a little.

Murky took over the rowing.

Aram said, "Jerky, anyone?"

Come daybreak, they found themselves among the great soaring "needles" of Thousand Needles, tall pinnacles of stone that emerged from the flow to rise into the sky. Aram tried to look down into the deep water, wondering just how far below the surface the canyon floor was, wondering just how tall the needles, in fact, were.

Some could hardly be called needles at all. They were mesas, some wide enough to have an entire village settled atop them. Aram's father, Greydon, had told him of this place. How tauren and centaur and quilboar and many other species had lived both on the canyon floor and atop the needles. Before the Cataclysm. Before the dragon had risen, and the world shook. Before the wall that separated the canyon from the Great Sea shattered, flooding the canyon from one end to the other, drowning villages—and many, many poor souls—indiscriminately.

But life finds its way, one supposes. The mesas survived. The way of the desert became the way of the water.

Aram took out his sketchbook and worked up a landscape of this place with so little surviving land.

As one day passed and then another, they rowed between mesas connected by rope bridges, with tiny docks carved at the water-line into the sides of the needles, and rope ladders and blocks and tackles providing access to the villages at their peaks. Scattered boats crossed back and forth from one needle to the next or trawled the water with nets. Seeing this, a mournful Murky stared down at his spear, clearly wondering if he had made a good trade. Makasa had a different response. Avoiding trouble, she kept any other conveyance at a distance.

They had plenty of jerky, but the dryad wouldn't touch it. And she actually had quite an appetite. Her roots and vegetables were soon gone, and, upon a boat in the middle of the water, she had no way to grow anything more.

By this time, they were deep in the center of the canyon, far from either shore.

Drella said, "I am hungry, Aram."

Aram turned to Makasa. Both knew they had to stop somewhere.

They passed a large mesa—the largest yet. Aram took out his map and thought it was probably Darkcloud Pinnacle. But just in case that name wasn't forbidding enough, Hackle spotted banners of the Grimtotem flying above it.

They rowed on.

Murky stared into the water. He looked up at Drella and bubbled out something like a sigh. Suddenly, he stood up and threw his spear down into the water. Aram thought it was an act of anger or frustration, but seconds later the little murloc dove into the water himself, stunning his companions. A few more seconds passed as they tried to decide what to do, and Murky emerged holding the weapon, with a fairly large fish speared on the tip. He called out, "Uuaaa!" and swam effortlessly back to Rendow's boat. Aram and Hackle pulled him aboard. Murky instantly knelt before Drella and, "Drhla mlgggrrr. Murky flllurlok fr Drhla."

She smiled at him but shook her head. "I cannot consume beasts of the land or of the water, Murky." After a moment, she added (as if to stave off some future fruitless attempt), "Or of the sky."

Murky looked stricken. He offered the fish to Aram, who said, "Thanks, Murky, but I can't eat fish raw. And we can't build a fire on the boat."

Hackle wasn't nearly so picky. And even Makasa had a little. The gnoll and the murloc split the rest, enjoying it thoroughly, bones, guts, head, fins, tail, scales, and all.

None of that, however, solved their vegetable dilemma or helped their hungry dryad.

That night, while Murky and Hackle slept soundly (and Makasa napped lightly), Aram held the watch. The boat was drifting down the canyon. The White Lady was but a sliver in the sky, but the Blue Child was at three-quarters and provided enough light to shimmer across the surface of the water.

Drella touched Aram's chest. "What is that?" she asked. "It calls to me."

Aram looked down. For the first time in days, he pulled his father's compass out from under his shirt. The crystal needle still pointed southeast . . . *and it glowed!* With excitement, he nudged the others awake and showed them.

"We're close to another shard," he said.

"A shard of what?" Drella inquired.

Aram tried to explain about the crystals and the compass, but Drella asked question after question, most of which the boy could not answer. The interrogation left her unsatisfied and him somewhat demoralized. There was still so much he didn't know.

Morning of the next day, they approached another large mesa. Again, Aram took out his map. "I think this one might be Freewind Post," he said, liking the sound of the name. They saw no banners—Grimtotem or otherwise—so Makasa swallowed her natural reluctance to trust anyone and rowed them toward it.

CHAPTER SIXTEEN
UNEXPECTED GUESTS

They were welcomed at Freewind Post with *so much* warmth that both Makasa and Aramar were suspicious of it.

Rendow's boat was tied to a small makeshift dock by a rather matronly female tauren with short horns, a short muzzle, and light-brown fur. She introduced herself as Thalia Amberhide. As his father had taught him, Aram greeted the tauren in the custom of her people by gesturing first to his heart and then to his head. Pleasantly surprised, she returned the greeting and instantly took it upon herself to act as their guide. A sturdy rope ladder was offered to Aram and his friends, but such a means obviously didn't suit Drella. Aram said as much, but Amberhide seemed distracted. She was studying the sky. When he spoke her name to get her attention, she practically fell over herself to make other arrangements. Soon, Thalia, Makasa, Murky, and Hackle were climbing the ladder—while Aram stood with Drella upon a shaky supply platform that was raised to the top of the mesa by strong tauren muscles tugging ropes through pulleys. It occasionally bounced against the needle's stony side. Aram felt completely off balance, and Drella put a hand on his shoulder to steady herself—or perhaps to steady him.

Once topside, Amberhide led them first to a small market, where Aram—*before Makasa could stop him*—pulled out a gold coin and tried to use it to pay for Drella's vegetables. But the grimacing quilboar peddler couldn't come close to making that much change. He seemed impatient—not to make a sale but to end the transaction, one way or another. Thalia generously used a single copper to purchase more than Drella needed.

Drella was very pleased. Pleased to have something she could eat and pleased to finally see a tauren—any tauren—up close. The dryad thought Thalia particularly beautiful. Then again, the dryad also thought the grimacing and impatient quilboar beautiful, so as usual, her standards of beauty didn't seem particularly exacting.

The quilboar, all bristles and snout, kept glancing toward the descending sun and pawing the ground with his right hoof. As soon as they moved from his stall, he began packing it up for the day.

Thalia invited the five of them to her home for supper. She claimed to be eager for news of the world beyond Freewind Post and thought she'd also invite some friends who would be just as interested. She pointed out her canvas hut and told them to meet her there at sundown. She took off at a fast jog—then looked back and noticed her new acquaintances watching. She slowed to an amble, as if in no particular hurry to extend her other invitations.

Before Makasa could reprimand him, Aram said, "I shouldn't have shown that gold coin. I'm sorry."

"It's done," she said. "But it means we have to stay alert. Amberhide saw you had gold. So did the quilboar and another tauren, the female lingering by the fish stall."

"They might not be thieves."

"They might not. But they might mention your gold to one who is. Plus . . ."

Hackle finished her thought. "Amberhide too nice."

Drella said, "I did not know one could be 'too nice.' Thalyss never mentioned such a thing."

Murky nodded. "Mrgle, mrgle." He was agreeing with someone, but it wasn't too clear with whom.

Aram was silent. He looked at Drella. Like her, he wanted to believe Thalia Amberhide was exactly who she appeared to be. But his responsibility to the dryad had made taking anyone at face value difficult. He turned to Makasa. "We have the vegetables. Should we skip supper and go?"

Now, Makasa was silent for a time. When she did speak, she chose her words carefully: "There are questions I want to ask. Or at the least, *answers* I want to get. Something in this place is not right. I can feel it. Taste it."

"What does 'not right' taste like, Makasa?" Drella sounded slightly cross.

Makasa ignored her but continued. "I want to know *what's* not right. Want to be sure that whatever it is won't follow us if we leave."

"*When* we leave," Aram said.

"Yes. I'm going to look around. Ask around. But I want you four to stick together. Do you understand that, Drella? Stay with Aram, Murky, and Hackle."

Drella said, "Yes, you want me to protect them."

"If necessary. Please."

"I can do that, Makasa."

"Thank you, Drella. I'll meet you all back here before sundown."

Makasa moved off, but not before shooting a look at Hackle, who nodded back to her, clearly taking responsibility for protecting the others.

Aram's cheeks burned. *After all this time, his sister* still *didn't trust him. Not really. She was still his babysitter, the way he was now Drella's. This hurt. He knew he wasn't the greatest fighter in the world, but hadn't he proven himself in one dangerous situation after another?* "C'mon," he said, revealing more anger than he cared to. "We're looking around, too."

*　　*　　*

The four of them came to a rope bridge that connected the Freewind mesa to another across the water. And—visible on this clear day—to another mesa and another beyond, reaching perhaps all the way back to Darkcloud Pinnacle, held by the Grimtotem. *Was that what was wrong with the place? Was the bannerless Freewind some kind of bait, luring in unsuspecting travelers? And if it was, if Thalia was secretly Grimtotem, and her dinner party the spring of the mousetrap, what would the Grimtotem want with the likes of them? Their gold? Their freedom? Their lives?* The questions multiplied and threatened to drive him mad. He *hated* thinking this way. He knew that Greydon had always taught him to see the best in everyone. But Aram also knew Makasa was right. He too could taste something in the air. *What was it? Fear? Yes, fear.* Everyone—from the kind and obliging Thalia to the gruff and grimacing quilboar merchant—was afraid of something.

Meeting up with Makasa a good twenty feet from Amberhide's hut and a good twenty minutes before sunset, they compared notes. Most of Freewind Post's inhabitants were either tauren or quilboar, two races that couldn't well stand each other—and it showed. And yet, there was no open fighting. Makasa had seen a large male of each species nearly come to blows, before begrudgingly refraining at the last second.

"Is that not good?" Drella asked irritably. It wasn't

Freewind putting her in a bad mood; it was her companions' responses to it.

"It would be," Makasa answered, "if we knew *why* they were suddenly behaving so well."

"Fear," Aram said.

"Fear, yes," Hackle said. "Hackle smell fear everywhere."

Murky shook his head violently. "Murky nk mrrrgle. Flggr flll-lur mmml?"

Drella answered him, "Mrgle, mrgle. Fear does have a smell. But I smell nothing, and I have a very sensitive nose." She crinkled and twitched it, as if to prove her point. It was, once again, adorable—but not particularly convincing.

Aram put a hand on her shoulder and spoke as reasonably as he could manage. "Is it possible you haven't been around enough fear to recognize the scent . . . *yet*? I mean, *you've* never been afraid."

She considered this. "That is true." She straightened her back. "Nothing scares me, Aramar Thorne."

"Everyone just stay ready," Makasa said. She led them into the hut.

Thalia was there, wearing a new dress of brown and red and blue, setting the table with the help of an ageless, tall, and graceful female high elf, a quel'dorei, whose presence took Aram's breath away. Before he could speak, she said, "I have seen you before, boy."

Aram nodded and pulled out his sketchbook. "In Flayers' Point." He was soon searching its pages for a particular sketch.

"Yes," the elf said, her light-grey eyes widening with some surprise. "You have a good memory for a human. You could not have laid eyes on me for more than a few seconds."

"You make an impression, Lady . . ."

"Elmarine. *Magistrix* Elmarine."

He found the page he was looking for and showed it to her, saying, "It doesn't do you justice, I'm afraid."

Drella said, "You do not smell afraid."

"It is a good beginning," Elmarine said, smiling down at Aram's unfinished sketch of herself.

"I drew what's there from memory, but I always do better when my subject's in front of me. Perhaps, Magistrix, you would allow me to finish it now?"

He glanced at Makasa, expecting some disapproval, but she nodded. She knew the power of Aram and his book. Together, they might just loosen some tongues.

Thalia said, "I can finish setting the table. Sit, Elmarine. Pose for the boy."

Just then a young and burly quilboar female entered in a bit of a rush. She had rust-colored bristles, bulging muscles, and mismatched tusks. Her right tusk pointed up, but her left angled outward dramatically.

Thalia said, "Ah. Shagtusk. I'm glad you were able to come."

Makasa said, "Is everything all right?"

Shagtusk stared at Makasa without speaking.

Thalia stepped between them. "Shagtusk, this is my new friend, Makasa Flintwill. You know Magistrix Elmarine. And this is Hackle, Murky, Taryndrella, and Aramar Thorne."

Shagtusk still said nothing. She stared at Thalia's other guests, studying each in turn.

Once again, Aram made use of his father's lessons, and when Shagtusk's eyes fell on him, he snorted loudly, the traditional quilboar greeting.

Almost automatically, she snorted back. Then she scowled—more at herself than at him—and took a seat at the rear of the hut, facing the doorway. It was the seat Makasa would have chosen, which was somewhat telling.

Makasa sat beside the quilboar and said, "Aram, after you're done drawing the magistrix, you might want sketches of Thalia Amberhide and Shagtusk, too."

"I would like that, if both are agreeable."

"Certainly," Thalia said with a slight declination of her head.

Shagtusk looked confused, but she nodded.

Aram turned to the high elf. "Magistrix?"

"If you wish. Should I sit or stand?"

"Stand, if you don't mind."

"I do not."

Aram sat and immediately got to work.

Drella, Hackle, and Murky helped Thalia finish laying the table. It was a generous supper: firefin snapper on a bed of spinach leaves, mashed yams with melted butter, and fresh-baked bread. Aram ate while sketching Elmarine first, and then Shagtusk and Thalia together. It seemed odd to see a quilboar and a tauren breaking bread side by side. Thalia appeared quite comfortable, however. And Shagtusk appeared equally *uncomfortable*.

Makasa leaned past Shagtusk to question their hostess under the guise of giving her the desired *news of the world beyond Freewind Post*, saying, "The Grimtotem lay siege to New Thalanaar."

"Yes," said Thalia Amberhide, "Thalanaar has been besieged for months."

"We also saw Grimtotem banners flying over Darkcloud Pinnacle. At least, we thought it was Darkcloud."

"I'm sure it was," Thalia confirmed.

"Any problems with them here?"

"Who?" Thalia said, darkening.

"The Grimtotem."

Aram leaned forward to see if Thalia showed any indication that she was hiding something. Or to see if she'd exchange conspiratorial glances with either Shagtusk or Elmarine.

But she didn't hesitate or consult the others in any way, speaking as if it was all old news and not particularly interesting news at that. "Oh, we've had our problems with the Grimtotem. Without a doubt. They laid siege to Freewind, as well. But the Grimtotem are so universally . . ." Here, she did pause.

Shagtusk spoke for the first time all evening: "Despised."

"I was going to say 'feared,'" Thalia corrected. "The Grimtotem are dangerous enough that all of Thousand Needles is wary of them. The other shu'halo and the local quilboar banded together to expel them from Freewind."

Makasa said, "Quilboar and tauren working together. And now living together. How . . . rare."

"Yes," said Elmarine. "As you can imagine, it is an extremely uneasy détente. A delicate and fragile détente. In part, that is why I am here. To help keep the peace."

Aram looked up from his sketchbook to study the tauren and quilboar. "I suppose it helps to have a common enemy. But if gnolls and yetis can live side by side . . ."

Elmarine scoffed, "Gnolls and yetis? Impossible."

Hackle said, "Not impossible. True. Aram make peace."

The magistrix turned from Hackle to study the boy again. She said, "Have you drawn a self-portrait, Master Thorne?"

Aram frowned but nodded, saying, "It's a poor likeness."

"Might I see it?"

He nodded again, but instead showed her the finished portrait of herself. He thought it had turned out nicely and wanted to make a better impression first.

"Very good," she said. "Perhaps slightly exaggerated. But I will not complain about that, since it works in my favor."

Aram felt stricken. "Exaggerated—"

"And the self-portrait?"

Sulking a bit, he flipped the leaves back to himself.

"It is a fine likeness," she said. "Very telling." She held her hand, palm down, an inch or so over the page as if trying to glean something of its essence. "Yes, very telling, indeed. But I should not be surprised. Two humans traveling with a gnoll and a murloc is hardly commonplace."

"Hardly," Makasa said.

"But for the four of you to be in company with a dryad . . . well, it is nothing short of astounding."

"Is it astounding?" Drella asked. "Why?"

"You are a daughter of Cenarius, Taryndrella."

"Yes, I know."

"It makes you sacred to the druids, and it is odd enough to find you out of their company, and out of their protection."

"I do not require protection."

"Is it spring or summer, Taryndrella?"

"Spring!" Drella answered, grinning.

"I thought as much."

Aram started to ask about this, but a look from Makasa stopped him. She subtly tugged down on her ear. *Listen first*, she was saying. So Aram listened.

"When summer comes, Taryndrella, your powers will begin to mature. You will be largely immune to magicks. You will be able to abolish harmful sorcery and mystic affronts to nature. Formal training from a druid tender will help with that, as well."

"And in spring?" Drella asked. When the magistrix hesitated, Drella implored her to go on: "Please. I am very curious. Very curious about all things, really. But I am *especially* curious about myself. I find myself quite fascinating. In fact, I believe I am the most fascinating individual on Azeroth."

Elmarine smiled. "You may be at that, child."

"Then please tell me about spring."

"In spring, Taryndrella, you are immature and untrained. You are unsure of your abilities."

"I am not."

"That is untrue, little dryad. You have great potential, certainly. But like any babe in the woods, you are not yet who you will be."

"I am not yet who I will be," Taryndrella repeated, not unpleased with the pronouncement.

Aram said, "We're taking her to a druid tender in Gadgetzan."

"Springsong?" the magistrix asked. And when Aram nodded, she said, "It is well."

Drella giggled at this, which seemed odd to Aram—but before he could even form a question, his thoughts were interrupted by a prodigious *screeching*!

Magistrix Elmarine

A. Thorne

Amberhide slammed her fists down. "No, no, no, no, no, no, no!"

She pushed away from the table, reached behind her cookstove, pulled out about a dozen long spears bound together by a wide leather strap, and stampeded outside. Aram and Makasa exchanged glances and followed. They all followed.

Aram emerged into the night, unsure what to look for. Then another screech from above snapped his eyes upward. Four female creatures—with light-green skin, winglike arms, taloned feet and hands, and rows of dark-green feathers running down their scalps, backs, arms, and legs—circled above Freewind as if riding upon the moonlight. Suddenly, one swooped down behind a hut and swooped back up holding a young male tauren in the talons of her feet.

"Corewind! That harpy's got Corewind!" Thalia growled. She snapped off the leather strap and dumped the spears on the ground—all but one, which she threw with all her might (and a deep, angry grunt) at the kidnapper.

The spear pierced the harpy's left wing, and she dropped the tauren. He landed with a soft thud on the thatched roof of another hut. A second later, the roof collapsed under him, and he vanished from sight. But assuming he didn't break his neck falling that last distance, Corewind had to be better off out of the harpy's grasp.

But their little dinner party wasn't better off. All four harpies turned their attention toward Amberhide and her spears. They swooped down in a tight aerial phalanx. Murky ducked. Hackle swung his club but missed. Staring upward at the terror-birds, Aram was reaching blindly for his cutlass, then glanced down briefly to find its handle. He heard Makasa call out, *"ARAM!"* and looked up in time to see her using her shield to block a harpy's talons from snatching him away. He drew his sword as Makasa grabbed up one of Thalia's spears and threw it with all her might (but no grunt).

The spear pierced the back of the offending harpy who had tried to grab Aram. The harpy seemed to hang in the air for a good three seconds before crashing to the ground dead, ten feet in front of them.

The magistrix stepped forward, chanting something brief in Thalassian. Suddenly, a second harpy burst into flame. She flew off, screeching and burning, diving down below Aram's line of sight—presumably into the canyon waters to douse herself.

By that time, Thalia, Makasa, and Hackle were all throwing spears into the sky. (Thalia threw two at a time!) None of them found their targets, but the barrage was enough to chase the two remaining harpies into the night.

Aram breathed a sigh of relief. He exchanged grateful smiles with Makasa and Hackle. He looked over at Murky, who held his short spear at the ready. Then he turned to check on Drella.

But the young dryad was nowhere in sight.

CHAPTER SEVENTEEN
THE LONG MARCH

Gordok's Elite stood over the bodies of the Grimtotem they had just killed. Five dead tauren and barely a scratch on even one ogre. Baron Reigol Valdread had lost an arm, but he was already reattaching it. That was one of his special skills. Most of the undead Forsaken could survive losing a limb, but Valdread knew of very few capable of reattaching theirs, of making the skin turn briefly liquid, of making muscle knit and bones click back together. Most Forsaken were, quite frankly, a mess. Valdread held no illusions about how pleasing he was to the eye: he knew he was a walking, waking nightmare. But he was a *functioning* walking, waking nightmare. And he had, for the most part, maintained his sense of humor about the whole thing.

If not always his attention span. He was, he had to admit, easily bored. He had to practically force himself to focus on what Zathra was saying . . .

"Dey boarded a boat here. All four a dem, da woman, da boy, da gnoll, and da murloc."

"And the yeti?" Valdread asked hopefully.

"No, mon. But it lookin' like dey be herdin' a live deer or fawn wid dem. Ta eat later, I suppose."

"Could be night elf," said Long-Beard. "Night elf shift to stag and go on boat."

"Yes," Valdread whispered, using dead lungs to force air up through his windpipe. "The night elf that we found buried back near Skypeak dug his way out of his grave, raced us here to meet his friends, and then decided *boat travel* is made more convenient when voyaging in the form of a stag."

"Oh," Long-Beard said, "Long-Beard forget night elf dead." Short-Beard whapped his other head on the nose. "Ow."

Slepgar yawned and said, "Maybe dead elf leave grave to walk."

Guz'luk nodded and pointed at the baron. "Yeah. Like you."

Zathra cut off the discussion impatiently. "Dese tracks not be stag tracks, bruddas. Dis not elf."

Slepgar and Guz'luk both said, "Oh."

Karrga, who had something of a pleasing knack for cutting to the chase, said, "What now?"

Zathra hesitated. Valdread, bored again, decided to speed things along. "With access to a boat, there are three routes to Gadgetzan from here. They can hug this shore and make their way via Tanaris. They can sail right up the center of the canyon. Or they can cross to the opposite shore."

"Ya, mon," Zathra said, having made her decision. "We be needin' ta split up. I gonna stick ta dis side. Throgg, you take da dead tauren's boat dere and da central route. But first you sail across and drop off Valdread. He gonna take da far way."

Throgg asked, "Who take ogres?" Then, blushing, he quickly added, "Throgg take Karrga."

Zathra said, "I be takin' Ro'kull and Ro'jak wid me and Skitter. You and Valdread divide up da rest."

Valdread scowled. The last thing he wanted was to be burdened with numbskull ogres. He whispered, "You can keep them all, friend Throgg. I don't require companionship—or a transport ship, for that matter." And to prove his point, he strode right into the water, leaving the rest of the Hidden behind . . .

Marching across the submerged floor of the flooded canyon was slow going. But the baron appreciated the silence and solitude after months of associating with ogres, trolls, arakkoa, and monomaniacal humans. Being dead was terminally boring, but being around the living grew tiresome, too. In fact, everything grew tiresome eventually.

He passed a village and the skeletons of drowned centaur picked clean by the marine life.

Life. There was that word again.

He missed life. Or living, anyway. Not this travesty of existence he whispered his way through now. His voice was a whisper. His movement was a whisper. His effect on those around him—even as a stone-cold killer—was hardly more than a whisper. He wasn't a man any longer, but some kind of Whisper-Man.

It hadn't always been that way. Once, long ago, he had led a life of boldness. He was SI:7. Stormwind Intelligence. One of the elite. (Back when the word *elite* meant something and wasn't given out to every group of ogres serving at the whim of some minor, even temporary, despot.) No, Reigol Valdread had reported directly to and served directly under King Varian Wrynn of the nation of Stormwind. Served so well, in fact, that His Majesty had made Valdread a baron of the realm.

The baron had been a rogue, certainly. But a patriotic rogue. Based in Stormwind, assigned to Lordaeron, he gathered intelligence that benefited the kingdom of his birth at great risk to life and limb (back when his limbs weren't reattachable). He was a dangerous man, and he took many lives, but he had principles then and killed only those that threatened king and country.

And the women . . .

He had been roguish in that pursuit, as well. Ghoulish as he was now, Reigol had been considered quite handsome in his day. But he was not unkind. Perhaps there were one or two former companions who had wished him dead when their time together had ended (though he doubted even *they* would have hated him enough to wish him *un*dead). But he thought most would look back on their time together warmly. Even after becoming Forsaken, he had run into a pirate he had once loved after his fashion. And she had bravely brushed a kiss upon his cold, thin, stretched, pale lips for old time's sake. It was the only touch of affection he'd been shown since dying. And though he had barely felt the contact, he thought back on it fondly. Almost as fondly as their original encounters nearly twenty years ago.

But, oh, those years, those intervening years . . .

Some eight or nine years ago, he had been at Stormwind Keep, relating intelligence of Lordaeron to the king.

Grateful as always, Varian had wondered with a smile if Valdread was ready to retire. After all, the baron was pushing forty, which made him nigh on ancient, *relative to most of his SI:7 peers. "I gave you a title, my friend," His Highness had said. "But you've taken no time to enjoy it. Should you wish it now, I would reward you handsomely for prior service and ask no more of you."*

And Valdread had considered it . . . for about sixteen seconds, at most. No, he enjoyed the work too much—and he enjoyed the pleasures and other perquisites that accompanied it.

So when word came of a plague in the north, Baron Reigol Valdread volunteered to investigate. He found a mystic disease that brought both death and undeath. And then came the Scourge, the Lich King's undead army, murdering everything in its path. And once dead, its victims rose again to join *that army.*

Valdread never severed so many heads in his life. But it mattered little. The plague weakened him, and even before he had succumbed to it, the tide of the Scourge washed over him, and four Scourge swords pierced him from every side. He breathed his last and fell.

And then rose.

Reigol Valdread had always been strong in body and mind. Strong enough in the latter to know he no longer controlled his own actions. He was a walking puppet of flesh and bone, prey to the puppet master Lich King's every whim. He killed people he had once loved and barely had enough self-possession to notice, let alone stop himself.

This was the darkest time. A small piece of him still had wished for a true death. But that piece was buried deep and had no force behind it. He shambled on and on and on . . .

Thank the gods for the Banshee Queen!

In life, Sylvanas Windrunner had been a high elf and the ranger-general of Silvermoon, capital of the kingdom of Quel'Thalas in northern Lordaeron. Defeated by the Lich King's champion, she had been raised into undeath. But somehow, she found a way to break the Lich King's hold on her mind and will. Tearing herself away from the Scourge, she sought out others among them whose souls were merely buried—not obliterated.

She found Reigol Valdread. Her power freed his mind, his will, his soul, but could not restore his body or his life. He became Forsaken, swearing fealty to the Banshee Queen. He fought at

Windrunner's side against the Scourge and those who did or would control them. He marched against them throughout the north.

But at some point, it became clear that the march would never end.

He grew bored with killing the dead. He knelt before Sylvanas and asked her to release him from his vow. She was—begrudgingly— willing. Though she demanded loyalty, she would not hold her agents in thrall. She understood the call of freedom better than most. But she warned him that few in Azeroth would accept him as the Forsaken had. Even the most open-minded, who understood that his was not a condition he had chosen for himself, would ne'er be able to stay in the same room beside him for long due to the stench of death he carried with him everywhere he went.

Nevertheless, Baron Valdread took his leave of the Banshee Queen and the Plaguelands.

He doused himself—practically bathed himself—in jasmine water and traveled across Azeroth, looking for something, anything, that could hold his interest for a time. He became a mercenary and paid assassin (though he had little need of money), because the jobs acted as little puzzles to occupy his mind.

Eventually, he encountered Malus, who offered a decent purse and tasks of superior complexity as a member of the Hidden. It was spy-work and death-work, the closest he had come to his days as a living man in SI:7. His new companions—Zathra, Skitter, Throgg, Ssarbik, Ssavra, and Malus himself—provided drama and amusement. And the individuals they were hunting, Captain Thorne and his son and the talented Makasa Flintwill—now, of whom did she remind him?—*provided serious challenges to success.*

It was not life. But it was a living.

For the length of two days—or so he estimated without confidence, *since what meaning could time have to such a one in such a place?*—he marched on through the cold, watery grave of a great many poor, drowned souls . . . and felt a kind of numbness not brought on by the frigid temperature.

He finally emerged on the far shore of Thousand Needles. He stripped to dry his clothes, trying hard not to look down at the withered, white, and ravaged mockery of the man he once was. He opened a brand-new sealed bottle of jasmine water and sprinkled it liberally over himself.

Then he dressed and moved on, marching onward swiftly—*for the dead don't tire, do they?*—in search of Aramar Thorne, Makasa Flintwill, their gnoll, their murloc, and the compass.

For what better occupation could a thing such as himself be expected to find?

CHAPTER EIGHTEEN
THORNE AMONG THORNS

Thorns. The entire shoreline was composed of a grand barricade of colossal thornbushes that curved up and over into a massive dome of razor-sharp thorns, admitting no entry to the quilboar lands of the aptly named Razorfen Downs. Aram was instantly reminded of the ogre king's unnatural dome of thorns—much smaller by comparison—that held prisoner the cubs of the wyvern One-Eye in Dire Maul, where Thalyss had been mortally wounded. He said a silent prayer that their sojourn into Razorfen would not be as costly.

The White Lady was taking her monthly rest, and the Blue Child was playing peekaboo amid dark clouds, allowing the two boats (and their grateful passengers) to approach under cover of darkness. Amberhide, or rather her silhouette, signaled from her boat, indicating the only place of entry, an arched gap in the dome, nearly invisible to any who didn't know where to look.

It was guarded by two quilboar sentries. But the magistrix, or rather *her* silhouette, removed a hand from the pocket of her robe. She held her palm out flat, and Aram saw her lean in and heard her blow upon it. A kind of dust or powder floated into the air, sparkling in the minimal light and wafting toward the sentries. One coughed. The other sneezed. And in Rendow's boat, Aram, Makasa, Hackle, and Murky waited . . .

When the harpies had fled and Drella was found to be missing, her sworn protectors had all raced back into Thalia Amberhide's hut, hoping against hope that the dryad was safe inside. But instead of Taryndrella, they found a large hole torn right through the hut's canvas rear wall. Thalia and Elmarine seemed briefly convinced that a harpy had ripped her way inside and taken Drella. But Makasa wasn't buying it. For starters, the wall was damaged from the inside out. Also, harpies were sky raiders and would never risk being confined indoors.

Finally, Drella was not the only one missing. Shagtusk was also nowhere to be found.

Makasa had become violent then, slamming the substantial Amberhide down into a wooden chair with enough force to buckle the thing, leaving the tauren on the floor among shattered fragments of wood—with Makasa's cutlass at her throat.

Makasa wanted answers and wanted them now.

Thalia cooperated, answering every question without hesitation. Elmarine helped to fill in the blanks. The rest came down to logic.

The travelers had not been wrong. Everyone on Freewind Post was afraid. But not, as was now plain, of the Grimtotem—but of the harpies, who attacked irregularly, but easily once every three or four nights. This had little to do with Drella, except that the bird-women had provided the perfect distraction for her true kidnapper.

It was Shagtusk who had most likely taken Drella, and Elmarine thought she knew why. There were rumors of unnatural magicks being practiced in the quilboar lands on the far shore of the canyon. Because of the dome of thorns there, the rumors were hard to confirm. Elmarine had sought to learn more by questioning Shagtusk on several occasions. The young quilboar scout was, well, reticent, to say the least. But her silence spoke volumes to Elmarine of Shagtusk's grave concern over the activities of her fellow quilboar in Razorfen.

And here, Elmarine accepted the blame for what happened to Drella. In relating Drella's abilities at dinner that night, Elmarine had presented Shagtusk with a possible solution to the problems in Razorfen. The magistrix now believed that Shagtusk had abducted Drella in the hope that she could fix things there. That was the good news. Shagtusk needed Drella and would not harm the dryad.

And the bad news?

Drella was young, immature, and inexperienced. Her ability to cleanse Razorfen of all unnatural magic, particularly when there must be one or more quilboar magi intentionally practicing that magic, was going to be limited at best. And when Shagtusk discovered that this particular daughter of Cenarius was not as useful as had been suggested, would she still keep Taryndrella alive?

They had to act fast.

Within minutes, Aram, Makasa, Hackle, and Murky were in Rendow's boat, following the tauren and the quel'dorei in Amberhide's boat. Thalia had explained that neither she nor Elmarine could enter Razorfen with Aram and the others. If a magistrix from Freewind or any of the post's tauren were caught—dead or alive—in Razorfen, then the Freewind Post détente would collapse. Makasa thought this a convenient excuse for them not to trouble themselves with solving a problem they had largely created, so they offered to do what they could: they'd guide the travelers to the gap in the barricade, deal with the sentries, and secure Rendow's boat so that Drella's rescuers would have a quick means of escape—assuming they could find their way to Drella, rescue her, and then find their way back out again.

Makasa was still far from impressed with this offer, but Aramar had pointed out that it was better than nothing. So the two boats headed off together.

*　　*　　*

The two quilboar sentries were snoring. One had plopped down onto his rear and, still holding his battleaxe, had *slowwwwwly* tilted back until prone. The other was asleep standing up, leaning on his long lance, as his axe clattered to the ground. But before Makasa had disembarked, the lance snapped under the quilboar's substantial weight, and the creature fell forward, bloodying his snout against the stone floor of the entry—all without waking.

Carefully and quietly, Makasa led Aram, Murky, and Hackle to shore. Hackle threw the boat's rope to Elmarine, and Amberhide rowed softly away, towing Rendow's vessel behind her own, to wait in the shadows for the rescue party to return.

Aram knew Makasa didn't like trusting them even that much. *But*—again—*what choice did they have?* They tiptoed past the snoring sentries and entered a virtual *labyrinth* of thorns.

Within minutes, Hackle—like Soot on the trail of a rabbit—had Drella's scent. With Aram holding his heavy club, the gnoll skimmed the ground on all fours, sniffing his way through the twisting thorn passages with a certainty that amazed and impressed his companions.

Some of these alleys were quite narrow, and more than once Aram caught a sleeve or some skin on the sharp thorns to either side of him. But he stifled any cries of frustration or pain. The last thing they needed was to attract attention.

Fortunately, at this late hour, the dome seemed nearly deserted. One large quilboar male, stumbling around drunk, forced them to duck down a side passage. He passed, belching and farting loudly, without any sign he was aware of their presence. Minutes later, a large quilboar female, also drunk, completely blocked their path as she stood there, swaying back and forth to the rhythm of some unheard music. Makasa borrowed Hackle's club from Aram and clocked the quilboar on the back of the head. She'd wake up tomorrow morning with an even bigger hangover than she deserved.

They saw no one else . . . until Hackle led them straight to Shagtusk, who sat on the ground—holding her knees to her chest—in a cramped cell of dense razor-sharp thorns. The thorns surrounded her on all sides within an inch of her fur and with barely enough room for her to raise her head and stare up miserably at Drella's four friends.

"Where is she?" Makasa hissed dangerously. "Where's the dryad?"

Shagtusk shook her head and moaned out, "Gone."

CHAPTER NINETEEN
SPURS OF THE MOMENT

It had been a wild impulse. Nothing more.

At supper, Shagtusk had listened to the magistrix talk about the powers of the dryad and how those powers were stronger now while it was summer. The quilboar didn't understand why this Drella would be less powerful come spring, but spring was months away, so that didn't seem important.

What seemed important was what the dryad could do. Destroy unnatural magic. That was what her tribe needed. Chugara was out of control, and Blackthorn . . . Blackthorn was just insane.

Then the harpies came. It was part of the détente with the blasted tauren that a quilboar scout be posted at Freewind every night to help fight the blasted harpies. But Shagtusk was sick of fighting the bird-women. So when Amberhide rushed out with her bundle of spears, Shagtusk took her time just to rise from the table.

When she did rise, she looked up to find everybody else was already outside. The tauren, the elf, the humans, the gnoll, and the murloc. The dryad stood in the doorway, watching the harpies' attack and Amberhide's counterattack.

And that was when the impulse hit. This wild idea. There was no plan. Almost no thought. Before Shagtusk knew what she was doing, she had wrapped her big mitt over the dryad's mouth and lifted the little creature bodily off the floor.

It occurred to her now that Drella hadn't struggled at all. No muffled screams. And the look in her eyes had been pretty much only a look of . . . *curiosity?*

Anyway, Shagtusk had lowered her head and stampeded toward the hut's back wall. It was only canvas. She tore right through it without stopping.

Still carrying the dryad, Shagtusk passed between two tauren totem poles and crossed the rope bridge to the next mesa. There were no sentries on either side. They had probably left their posts to ward off harpies. She found a short length of rope and tied it around Drella's waist, warning the little thing not to shout.

The dryad tilted her head and asked, "About what?"

Shagtusk ignored the question, wondering briefly whether the creature was simple. Then the quilboar led the dryad down a dirt ramp that circled the mesa, crossed another bridge to the next mesa, went down another ramp, across another bridge, and down the final ramp, where she had left her boat on a sliver of shore.

Shagtusk put Drella in the craft, pushed it off the sand, climbed in herself, and quietly rowed away.

Two hours later, they docked and came ashore at the entrance to the thorny dome. Whistler and Bristlemaw were on sentry duty but knew Shagtusk and let her pass. They might have raised a couple of eyebrows over Drella, but aside from a belch or two from Bristlemaw, they said nothing.

Tugging on the rope, Shagtusk led the dryad into the maze of thorns—turning left, then right, right again, then left—until they were no longer within earshot of the sentries.

Shagtusk stopped, looking around and listening for the sound of approaching quilboar.

Drella said, "Should I have stayed with Aram? I believe Makasa wanted me to protect him."

Shagtusk said, "You're needed here, dryad."

"Am I?"

Shagtusk nodded. "You see these thorns? Thorns are sacred to the quilboar."

"Why?"

"They just are."

Drella nodded sagely. "Many things just are. It is not unusual for things just to be."

"These thorns were shaped by quilboar thornweavers. Most of this dome was shaped by Charlga Razorflank."

"She must have thought thorns were *very* sacred." Drella looked around. "There are many, many thorns here."

"Now *Chugara* Razorflank weaves the thorns. Charlga trained

Chugara to maintain the dome, but Chugara has surrendered Razorfen to the Death's—"

Drella cut her off with an annoyed wave of her hand. "You have taught me the meaning of boredom, Shagtusk. I do not understand what this has to do with *me*."

Shagtusk's bristles rose with annoyance. She said, "The magistrix said you can undo unnatural magic."

Drella perked up. "Yes!"

"I need . . . The *quilboar* need you to undo that here. Return Razorfen to its natural state."

Drella looked around. She said, "I do not see any unnatural magic here in your dome. I do not sense any. The thorns here are extreme but have long been part of these lands. They have as much right to exist as anything in nature."

"Not *here* here," Shagtusk gruffly pleaded. "In the Spiral of Thorns. In the Caller's Chamber. In the Bone Pile."

Drella considered this. "All right," she said. "Show me these places. They sound curious, and I like curious things."

"And you'll help?"

"*If* you are right, I will help. But after that I really should get back to protecting Aram. Also, he promised to teach me to read."

Shagtusk nodded. She still held the rope tied around Drella's waist. Drella didn't seem to object to it. So Shagtusk led Drella by this cord and by the dryad's own curiosity.

They barely made it ten paces.

As they approached a T in the maze, Shagtusk knew to turn left, but there was no leftward opening—just another wall of thorns. She stood there, staring. She was raised in these thorny corridors, knew them like the tip of her snout. *Turn left at the T.* Yet there was no left. This was no T, but an upside-down L. *She must have made a wrong turn in her haste to put some distance between herself and the sentries. But where, exactly?*

Well, there was no choice in the matter now. She'd make a right turn instead, positive that soon enough, she'd recognize the pattern. She turned and started forward, but the thorns grew up right in front of her, creating another wall before her eyes.

Shagtusk turned around fast. Drella was staring at the new thorn-wall, too, looking a bit queasy. She said, "Oh, that does feel unnatural. The thornbushes were screaming over being grown so fast and so large. They do not like it."

But Shagtusk wasn't listening—because standing behind the dryad were five quilboar. And not just any quilboar, but Thornweaver Chugara, Death Speaker Blackthorn, and three of his Death's Head minions in their black leather uniforms. One of these relieved Shagtusk of her battleaxe.

Blackthorn spoke, his voice a low rumble. "You bring this creature into our sacred space?"

Shagtusk said nothing.

Blackthorn said, "Then you must have brought her as a gift to *me*."

Shagtusk said nothing.

Blackthorn turned to Drella and said, "You my prize?"

"No," Drella said. "I am no quilboar prize. I am the dryad Taryndrella. I have been brought here to undo your deviant work. I was unsure such twisted magicks truly existed. But you reek of the unnatural. And you reek of death. Or something worse than death."

Blackthorn chuckled then and said, "I am Death Speaker Blackthorn, and you have value to me here. Thank the traitor for bringing such value, Thornweaver."

Chugara chanted, and the thorns grew up and around Shagtusk, arching over her head to enmesh themselves with more thorns growing from behind. The spurs slashed at her hide, tore at her ears. The thorns grew downward, forcing her down onto her backside, forcing her to draw her knees up tight to her chest, forcing her to hold them there, and forcing her to lower her head. They weren't as dense as a wall; Shagtusk could see out. But they admitted no possibility of escape.

Blackthorn watched Chugara at work, smiling his death's-head grin. He thanked the thornweaver and turned back to Drella, who looked ill and on the verge of tears.

Shagtusk watched him gesture his arcane gestures and chant his arcane chants at the dryad.

Perspiration was forming on Drella's forehead, but she attempted to laugh it all off bravely. "You seek to enslave me with your spells, but I am immune to your unnatural powers, Death *Reeker* Blackthorn."

He bristled—literally—and growled out, "But you're not immune to Death's Head steel."

The first minion brandished Shagtusk's axe.

Blackthorn snatched up the rope still tied to Drella's waist and handed it to the minion. "Take her to the Bone Pile. But don't kill her. She is not for you. She is for the Coldbringer."

The minion nodded obediently and—flanked by his two fellows—led Drella away. As usual, Drella didn't struggle. She simply followed where she was led.

Farting loudly, Blackthorn turned to face Shagtusk and Chugara. He smiled unpleasantly. He said, "We leave you here to think on your betrayal, Shagtusk."

Chugara said, "We leave you here to starve."

Then they turned and walked away.

The story related, a deal was proposed: if the four travelers released Shagtusk, she would lead them to Drella and fight beside them to free her.

As usual, Makasa didn't care for the idea of partnering with anyone, let alone Drella's abductor. Makasa was initially more inclined to trust Hackle's nose and leave Shagtusk to rot.

But Hackle shook his head. "Hackle only smell death now."

"Then follow the smell of death."

"Death smell everywhere. All directions."

Shagtusk said, "That is Blackthorn. He belches death. He farts death. Death for everyone. In all directions."

Aram spoke the obvious, needful truth: "Makasa, look what they did to her. I don't like trusting her, either, I promise. But we need her, and it's clear she's no friend to Drella's kidnappers."

"*She's Drella's kidnapper!*" Makasa whispered (in order to keep herself from yelling).

"Drella's *new* kidnappers, then."

So Hackle slipped back to the dome's entrance and liberated two battleaxes from the sleeping sentries. Then he and Makasa went to work, freeing Shagtusk. Bits of thorn went flying, sticking the quilboar over and over. Makasa not only didn't care, but she smiled, grimly pleased.

Aramar said, "We have seen thorns like this before. In Dire Maul."

Shagtusk was keeping her head down but answered, "Yes. The ogre king Gordok paid Chugara to build his dome of thorns around the wyvern cubs. I was there, a scout in her honor guard."

"What did Gordok pay her with?" Aram asked, wondering if it might be a crystal. He pulled out his father's compass and cupped his hand over it to hide its glow. The needle still pointed southeast toward the next crystal shard (and toward Gadgetzan), but the glow had faded some. There were no crystals here.

Shagtusk responded, "Slaves for the Murder Pens. For the Caller's Chamber. In the end, for the Bone Pile."

By this time, Makasa and Hackle had hacked through the thorny cell. The hole wasn't quite big enough for Shagtusk, and Aram thought Makasa probably knew that. But he said nothing, merely wondering why he could not bring himself to temper Makasa's ire. He realized belatedly he was angrier with Shagtusk than he had known.

Seeing that her egress wasn't likely to get any wider, Shagtusk crawled out of her tiny prison. Thorns and spurs tore at her sides, but within a minute she was free and standing. She held out her hand for one of the axes.

Makasa shook her head. She said, "When we have a common enemy, you will have a weapon. Until then, you will have none."

Shagtusk scowled but nodded. Then she strode forward. Makasa kept one of the axes. Hackle hefted his new battleaxe over one shoulder and hefted his war club over the other. They followed close behind the quilboar. Aram, his cutlass drawn, and Murky, brandishing his tiny spear, followed close behind.

CHAPTER TWENTY
CONVERGENCE PILE

Shagtusk indeed knew the passages in the dome like the tip of her snout. Aram was positive he'd have been hopelessly lost within seconds, and a glance up at Makasa's face suggested it wouldn't have been much different for her. In fact, the *real* difference between their expressions was that his revealed his begrudging gratitude for Shagtusk's presence, whereas his sister's revealed her resentment that the quilboar was necessary to their success at all.

Ten minutes later, the five of them stood before a fork in the maze, where Shagtusk turned leftward but hesitated. "This is the fastest way to the Bone Pile," she said.

Makasa glared at her. "But?"

"Takes us through the Caller's Chamber."

"And . . . ?"

"And Arachnomancers are there. Maybe Aarux."

"Who's Aarux?" Aram asked, while wondering whether or not he should know what an *Arachnomancer* was.

"Giant spider," Shagtusk answered. "Arachnomancers grow them like thornweavers grow thorns. Aarux is the biggest spider of them all."

Aram swallowed hard. He had *never* liked spiders. Willy and Stitch, his best friends in Lakeshire, both collected dead spiders—mostly, Aram suspected, because they knew spiders made him jump. And those were just dead spiders. Little spiders. Little dead spiders. So the giant living variety had even *less* appeal.

Makasa jerked her head to the right, asking, "And this way?"

"Takes longer. But no spiders."

"How *much* longer?"

"Another hour."

Aram said, "It could take us at least that long if we have to fight our way past this Aarux."

Makasa nodded, and Shagtusk led them to the right. They walked on carefully and quietly, the five of them—plus Aram's sense of guilt. *Had he nudged Makasa onto the rightward path because he* believed *in the practicality of what he'd said to her . . . or because he was too afraid of spiders to go to the left? And what if that added hour cost Drella her . . .* He couldn't bring himself to finish the thought.

They walked along a long, wide, arcing passage with walls of thorns to either side. Every hundred feet or so, a low-burning torch lit the way. But the curve of the corridor meant that very little light reached them for long stretches at a time. Though he knew they had avoided the path of the spiders, the *idea* of the arachnids was now firmly lodged in Aram's head. He felt— or thought he felt—cobwebs brush across his face. He felt—or thought he felt—tiny spiders drop down into his hair and scamper down his neck beneath his shirt. He was itchy all over. Twitchy all over, too. It was going to be a *long* hour.

As soon as Death *Reeker* Blackthorn entered the chamber known as the Bone Pile, he took Drella's rope from his minion and tied it to an iron post upon which hung the skeleton of a kaldorei. Suddenly, Drella did not like the rope. Though it had seemed of no consequence moments before, it now felt constricting, like the air in this section of the dome, like the iron and sulfur taste of the dark and twisted magicks that suffused the space. Taryndrella knew the word *nauseated* from Thalyss Greyoak and now understood what it meant. She untied her end of the rope from around her waist and let it fall.

Blackthorn and Thornweaver Chugara stared at the rope, still tied at the other end to Blackthorn's post, as if they could not quite fathom how she had escaped it. Then they stared at her as if she had performed some sort of miraculous sorcery by untying it. She wanted to laugh at them, but bile rose in her throat. She choked it back and swallowed. Acid burned her esophagus. She wished she were with Aram and the others. Perhaps she should not have left them alone.

They found more rope and restrained her hands, tying her securely to the post of iron. For a second, it almost felt as if the rope were afire, searing her skin, burning her leaves, scorching her fur. She nearly screamed, but when she looked down, she saw no flames, felt no actual heat.

She began to admit to herself that she was scared.

She looked around. The space was cavernous, but there was not much to see. The thorny dome arched over the dirt floor. The iron post stood beside something she believed might be an altar. And, of course, there was the immense pile of bones that filled more than half of the chamber and gave the place its name. She peered at it with curiosity. (She took refuge in her curiosity, for it seemed to tamp down her fear.) Most of the bones were quilboar. But there were human bones and tauren bones, centaur bones and animal bones (mostly boar, hyena, and bear). She thought maybe she saw the bones of a harpy. Maybe the bones of a wyvern. Maybe yeti bones and gnoll bones. *And was that the skull of a dragon?* She had never seen a dragon, so she could not be sure. But she decided that if she *did* ever see a dragon and then got to see the dragon's skull, it would look much like that.

She asked, "Are there any dryad bones in your Bone Pile?"

Blackthorn laughed ominously.

Drella continued, "Because if there are, I would very much like to see them."

Blackthorn stopped laughing abruptly. Once again, he looked stunned.

Drella frowned at him. She wondered if he was of low intelligence. He seemed so easily shocked. She said, "Do you not understand? I am very curious to see what my bones look like."

Chugara grumbled darkly, "That can be arranged."

"Good," Drella said.

Huffing angrily, the thornweaver advanced on the dryad. But Blackthorn held up a hand to stop Chugara. "No! She is for the Coldbringer."

"I am hardly ready for winter yet. It is still spring."

One of the minions scrunched up his snout and said, "It's summer."

"Silence!" Blackthorn bellowed. He turned to Drella. "No one speaks of seasons. You and your power are to be sacrificed to Amnennar the Coldbringer, a lich of the undead Scourge!"

"Ah," Drella said, considering this. The truth was she did not truly understand Blackthorn's words. "Amnennar" and "Coldbringer" and "lich" and "undead" and "Scourge" all meant very little to her. Thalyss had never used such words when whispering to her, at least not in any context that made much sense now. She thought she could decipher "Coldbringer" and "undead." (The perverted magical energy of this place was cold and unnatural, like a withered plant *forced* back into the green.) She decided Amnennar must be this Coldbringer's name. She wondered if "lich" might be short for "lichen." She *liked* lichens. If this Amnennar was a lichen, perhaps he would not be so terrible. And Scourge? Was Blackthorn talking about some kind of blight? It was all very confusing. She shook her head and flatly stated, "No, thank you."

Chugara said, "You sure Chugara can't kill her now?"

"Yes, I'm sure," Blackthorn said, though he seemed to regret the fact. "The ceremony doesn't take long to prepare. Less than an hour. Watch her."

He turned his back on them to face the altar and began to chant in a baritone whisper. He raised a mask painted to look like a bleached white quilboar skull and donned it over his own quilboar head.

Drella's throat had gone dry, but she squeaked out, "Makasa will not be happy that I am not protecting Aram."

Makasa was not happy.

She didn't like following Shagtusk, didn't like trusting her not to lead them into a trap. *Yes, we found the quilboar imprisoned in a cage of thorns, but what if that was merely a show for our benefit? What if that was done specifically to engender our trust? Shagtusk must have known we'd be coming after Drella, so putting herself in that position was a sure way to ensnare us.*

This is Aram's fault, she thought. *He insisted we trust Drella's abductor—as he insisted on trusting blasted near everyone!* Makasa glared at Aram. He caught the look and absorbed it with a little shrug. He was used to such looks from her. *It's too commonplace, that's the problem. I need to be stingier with my disapproval so he'll feel it on occasion . . . that is, when it counts. But it's hard to be stingy when he earns my scorn so often. I know deep down that my brother is a good kid. Even a bit of a miracle-worker, if truth be told. But being a miracle-worker and a* fool *isn't mutually exclusive!*

But it was hard to maintain her anger at the boy. *It isn't his job to keep us safe. That's my responsibility. Captain Thorne had commanded that of me. It was the man's final order, and he had gone so far as to call upon the life debt I owed him for saving my own life years earlier.*

And why are we both in danger now? Because I have not been equal to the task of protecting Aram. We needed Thalyss to keep Aram safe. But Thalyss's help had come at the cost of taking on the burden of Taryndrella, who has only managed to put us at further risk.

She glanced over at Hackle. He nodded to her. She nodded back. She had come to rely on the gnoll as her good right arm. *But that's infuriating, too! The price of Hackle's arm has been risking life and limb against more gnolls and yetis!*

And then there's Murky, who was captured by Malus! It never ends! Every additional companion on our journey—EVERY ONE—has added complications and dangers that could not possibly be anticipated.

She thought, *I need to be more self-sufficient. That's the answer. No more dependence on others. From now on these burdens will be mine and mine alone. Period. Blast, I miss my harpoon!*

Aram thought it was getting colder with each passing step along the curved path. His sweater and coat were still tied around his waist. He longed to stop and put them on, but he imagined that might be a difficult task to accomplish while holding a cutlass—assuming anyone would even be *willing* to stop. Frankly, *he* wasn't willing to stop. He had no idea what they'd find at the other end of this corridor. But he knew they didn't dare waste any more time. Not while Drella was still at risk.

Hackle like having club and axe to grip. Hackle wonder if Hackle strong enough to wield club and axe at once. Hackle think wielding club and axe together would be good. Hackle practice wielding club and axe together after Hackle help save Drella.

Murky worried about Drhla, but Murky was brave and determined. And Murky had a spear now. Murky would spear Drhla's enemies like flllurlok!

What is that feeling, that dread, which draws me on?
He reached the entrance to the dome and found its two quilboar guards snoring before it.

Well, that must portend something . . .

Of course, he had no idea if this path would lead to what he sought, what he had been commanded to seek.

But it blasted well leads somewhere, doesn't it? There's a flavor here I cannot identify but somehow recognize. The taste of something I don't much care for, and a screaming in my head, warning me to turn away. Yet, at the same time, a summons, calling me forward.

Ironically, it was the *summons* that nearly made him skirt the area. But in the end, he followed its call into Razorfen, because *knowing* would—at the very least—present opportunities for a little diversion.

And so they all converged upon the Bone Pile.

CHAPTER TWENTY-ONE
·SORTED·

Shagtusk signaled for them to stop and pointed toward an archway. From beyond it, Aram heard some kind of noise, like rain on the roof of his family's cottage in Lakeshire—but it stopped and started, regular and rhythmic. Shagtusk mouthed the words *the Bone Pile.*

The other four nodded.

Shagtusk held out her bristly hand for an axe.

Makasa smiled a grim smile and mouthed, *Not yet.*

Shagtusk glared at Makasa, then turned and barreled her way through the arch.

Caught briefly off guard, Makasa raced in after, with Hackle at her heels. Aram and Murky reacted a tad slower, but soon they were inside, too.

Four smoldering torches dimly illuminated a cavernous chamber with a ceiling of thorns. There was, of course, an immense pile of bones in the center. Aram didn't need the nose of a gnoll to know the place smelled like death.

"Aram!" Drella called.

He turned to see the dryad tied to an iron post beside an altar of fire-scarred black wood. She was between two quilboar, one male—presumably Death Speaker Blackthorn—and one female—presumably Thornweaver Chugara Razorflank. Blackthorn was wearing some kind of quilboar mask and holding the biggest rattle Aram had ever seen. Aram shouted back to Drella, "Are you all right?!"

"Of course," she said, sounding suddenly pouty and almost disappointed in the question. "I am always right!"

"No, *all* right—"

Blackthorn shouted, "I need more time! Kill them!"

Two other quilboar in matching tunics of grey and black exchanged glances and advanced. But, frankly, the odds didn't look good for them. Shagtusk, snorting and blowing, was already standing over a third uniformed quilboar, pummeling him into unconsciousness. She straightened up, and Makasa tossed her the axe while unhooking and unleashing her iron chain, which she immediately began spinning in tight circles. Hackle, meanwhile, dropped the axe he'd been carrying into the dirt and raced forward, bearing his club with both hands.

Within seconds, both uniformed quilboar were dead, lying

beside their unconscious fellow. That just left Blackthorn and Chugara between Drella and her rescuers. The thornweaver confirmed her identity by chanting and drawing down huge branches of thorns from the walls of the dome, which expanded to halt—if not trap or kill—the rescuers.

But Drella, pulling one small hand free of her bonds, reached toward Chugara and cried, "Stop that. Can you not hear those thornbushes screaming? Listen!" The dryad put one hand on the thornweaver's back, and in an instant, it was Chugara who was screaming. She dropped to her knees, breathing hard and . . . *sobbing?* The branches of thorns ceased their advance.

Blackthorn roared something in unintelligible frustration. Then he squealed like a pig and shouted, "The Coldbringer comes to taste of his sacrifice! His power fills me!" He shook his rattle at the pile of bones. "They must not steal the Coldbringer's sacrifice! Kill them for the Coldbringer!"

In response to the Death Speaker's rattling, the Bone Pile itself began to rattle and shake, and the pile's bones began to rapidly assemble—*klik, klik, klik, klik, klik*—sorting themselves into skeletal warriors that advanced—unburdened by trifles like muscle, organs, sinew, and skin—toward Shagtusk, Makasa, and Hackle.

Makasa actually took a step back. But her hesitation lasted only a moment, and her standard determination *klik'd* in. She swung her iron chain in swift, broad circles. It smashed through the bones of undead quilboar, tauren, humans, and centaur. She swung the chain high, and it knocked off quite a few skulls. Unfortunately, the skeletons didn't seem to require heads for their current calling, and continued their advance.

Hackle, who was considerably shorter than Makasa, focused his war club more on thighbones and pelvises, and met with more long-term success.

Shagtusk, in her typical fashion, just barreled through the crowd, using her bulk to bash skeletons back into their component bones and swinging her axe to split what remained.

Aram and Murky hung back. There wasn't much Aram could do with his cutlass, and less Murky could accomplish with his little spear. At first, that hardly seemed to matter. Makasa, Shagtusk, and Hackle were routing the enemy.

But it soon became clear victory wouldn't be quite that easy. To begin with, more and more skeletons were forming from the Bone Pile, hyenas and gnolls, a bear, a wolf, and boars of all sizes. Harpy bones formed into two skeletons that took to the air, swiping their talons from above at Makasa and Shagtusk. What's more, the skeletons already dealt with refused to stay down. *Klik, klik, klik,* they formed new combinations. A centaur with the upper torso of a tauren. A human with the head of a quilboar. And more. Even the skeletons with shattered legs wouldn't rest, using bony fingers to drag themselves forward toward Blackthorn's chosen prey.

Shagtusk, who had waded in farther than even the length of Makasa's chain, soon found herself overrun. The skeletons climbed over her, pulled at her, tried to drag her to the ground. They had no real strength, and she was practically all muscle, but they had the numbers—and soon she was barely holding her own.

Hackle wasn't faring much better. The skeletons were unarmed, but many still had teeth and a few had claws. Hackle growled loudly as hyena jaws bit down on one leg. He shattered the creature's skull, but more creatures were coming.

Makasa's chain kept all larger opponents at bay, and by tilting it upward briefly, she even clipped the wings of one of the skeletal harpies. It crashed to the ground, shattering into miscellaneous bones. But many of those bones were soon *klik, klik, kliking* back together, and the result began crawling toward her, beneath the arc of her iron swings. This and others would be upon her soon.

And some of the skeletons circled wide—or sorted themselves back together beyond their first line of opponents—to attack Murky and Aram. A skeletal boar rushed at the murloc, its long, sharp tusks prepared to skewer Aram's friend like a fish on a spit. Murky pointed his spear at the thing but realized it would do him little good. He squealed out, *"Flllur mgrrrrl! Flllur mgrrrrl!"*

and ran in a serpentine pattern that seemed to confuse his pursuer. It tried to cut left to follow him, and one of its legs snapped. It continued to drag itself after Murky on its three "good" legs, but Murky saw an opportunity. He ran around behind the beast and jumped, landing on his butt upon the creature's back, causing its bones to shatter and scatter beneath him. When Murky stood up, he was holding the boar's spine and swinging it like a club.

This inspired Aram. A gnoll skeleton had rushed at him, and he had barely managed to parry its swipes with his cutlass. Now, sheathing his sword, he launched his entire body at the creature, knocking it backward onto the ground. As with Murky's boar, the bones scattered apart beneath him. Aram picked up a good, thick thighbone and swung it at the next skeleton—a legless human—that crawled toward him.

But the numbers still favored the bone warriors.

As Aram whacked at skeletons, he called out to Drella, who remained tied to the post between the low-chanting Death Speaker and the kneeling, sobbing thornweaver. "Drella! Can you stop this?!"

"Yes!" she called back as she struggled to free herself. It was said with enough unthinking confidence to cause Blackthorn to look her way (and even make his *mask* appear concerned). But then she paused, looked confused, and shouted, "How?!"

Blackthorn actually snorted out a laugh, and Aram groaned.

At which point, a new arrival made things look even worse. Aram smelled him before he saw him. *Is that jasmine? Jasmine in this desolate spot?* It could only mean one thing. One person . . .

Baron Reigol Valdread, the Whisper-Man, entered through the archway. Short of Malus himself, the Forsaken was the worst possible person at the worst possible time.

He spotted Aram first, swinging a thighbone at skeletons. "Well, well, young squire, what have you gotten yourself into now? Throw me the compass, Aramar Thorne, and I might just . . ." He trailed off and slowly pulled down his hood to reveal the pale stretched skin that covered his skull-shaped head, which seemed to mark him as a comrade to Blackthorn's skeletal army. And as if further proof of his compatibility were necessary, the second harpy skeleton swooped toward him—only to veer away shy of attacking. Aram glanced back at the Whisper-Man as he studied the chamber, bugged-out eyes scanning from bone warrior to bone warrior, taking in Murky and Hackle and Shagtusk, pausing briefly on Makasa, before passing over Chugara and Taryndrella, and finally landing on the Death Speaker.

"You!" the baron called, pushing his voice to the limit of its volume. "What is your game?!"

Blackthorn's mask revealed little, but it seemed he was only now noticing the newcomer. "What are you?!" he shouted back.

"I am Baron Reigol Valdread, and I am—"

"FORSAKEN!" roared the Death Speaker. *"ABOMINATION!"* (The two words were clearly synonymous to Blackthorn.)

"Whom do you raise, lunatic?" Valdread hissed, while the skeleton of a huge bear lumbered toward him, only to veer away at the last moment as the harpy had.

"I raise Amnennar the Coldbringer! And when he comes, you will once again find yourself under the yoke of the Scourge!"

"Over my undead body."

"So be it!" Blackthorn yelled, before chanting something low, which caused the bear-skeleton to pivot back toward Valdread.

The Whisper-Man's black sword was out, slashing through bear bones and making very short work of them, actually.

But he had become Blackthorn's new priority, and Blackthorn had become his. Every skeleton in the place broke away from Drella's rescuers to converge on the baron, whose black sword sliced through bones like butter as he fought his way toward the Death Speaker with murderous intent.

Even during the battle, the irony wasn't lost on Aram. One of his greatest enemies was aiding their cause because the evil of the Scourge inspired more hatred in the Whisper-Man than any fifty casks of jasmine water could drown.

Free of her skeletal opponents, Shagtusk reached Drella first, yanking the rope that bound her free of the post and scooping her up as if she weighed less than a feather.

Makasa was right behind her, her cutlass out and poking into the quilboar scout's ribs. "Lead us out," Makasa growled, "and don't try anything funny."

Shagtusk grunted and led the way, skirting wide round the battle of bones. Neither the Whisper-Man nor the Death Speaker nor the still sobbing thornweaver seemed to notice that the Coldbringer's sacrifice was being carried off. The bones were once again piling up beneath Reigol Valdread as—compass forgotten—he sought to keep the Scourge from gaining another foothold on Azeroth.

Only as the group reached the archway did Blackthorn realize what he was about to lose. "No! The sacrifice!"

"If a sacrifice is required," Valdread whispered, "then let it be you."

It was the last Aram heard of either of them, as he followed Shagtusk, Drella, Makasa, and Murky out of the chamber. He looked back once to confirm that Hackle was behind him (which he was) and that none of the skeletons were following (which they weren't). Then he glanced down at the thighbone he still held in his hand. A tiny spider scurried along its length.

Aram screamed and chucked the bone away.

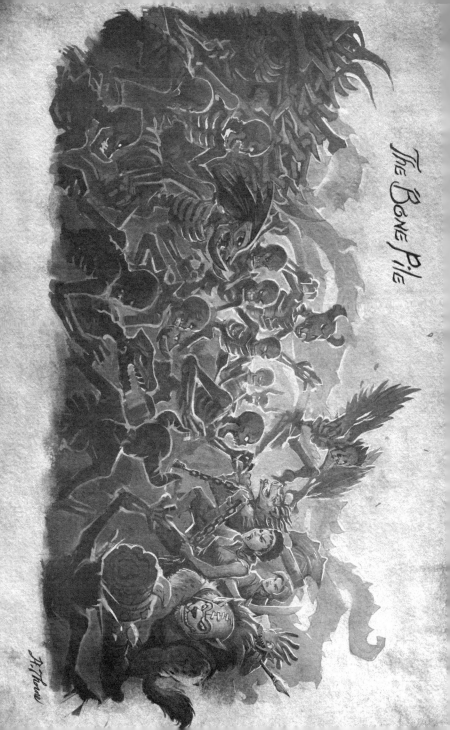

The Bone Pile

CHAPTER TWENTY-TWO
BACK ON TRACK

They didn't stop running until they were back at the entrance to Razorfen. The two sentries, Whistler and Bristlemaw, were *still* snoring contentedly right where they'd been left. Makasa whistled for Amberhide and Elmarine. Shagtusk put Drella down.

"Thank you, Shagtusk," the dryad said. "That was a new and interesting experience. For the most part."

Shagtusk stared at her. The others stared at her as well.

Drella started to look uncomfortable. She said, "I am sorry. Is it possible I have disappointed you? I could not bring all the unnatural magicks to an end."

Shagtusk grunted and said, "If you taught Chugara something, you've done more than anyone else has managed."

Makasa cleared her throat.

Shagtusk added, "And I'm sorry I got all of you into this mess."

Aram said, "You made up for it. Or did your best to, anyway."

The tauren and the high elf rowed up, towing Rendow's boat. Both stared up at Shagtusk angrily, causing Aram to repeat, "She made up for it."

Thalia Amberhide nodded but seemed less than convinced. Elmarine kept her own counsel.

Makasa growled, "Let's get out of here. Now." She climbed down into Rendow's boat.

Shagtusk picked Drella up again and lowered her into Makasa's arms. Aram, Hackle, and Murky followed.

Drella stretched and yawned demurely. "Excuse me," she said. "I am a little tired." She curled up in the center of the boat and was asleep before they'd said their good-byes and pushed away from shore to continue their journey toward the Speedbarge and, ultimately, toward Gadgetzan.

Maluss and Ssarbik, meanwhile, were taking their own route to Gadgetzzan.

Ssside by ssside, they walked down the ssstepss leading away from the war room of the Masster of the Hidden, after ssspending nearly a week in the highlord'zz gloriouss pressencce.

Maluss pauzzed at the bottom, painfully pulling an iron gauntlet over hizz left hand, while ssstaring acrosss the dessolation of rock, debris, and flame that encompasssed Outland. In the disstancce, the campss and campfirezz—or more accurately, bonfirezz—of the Burning Legion were jusst barely vizzible through the sssmoke and hazze.

Ssarbik was almosst giddy with pleassure over the reprimand Captain Maluss had recceived from the dreadlord of the Legion for not having already achieved the compasss. The arakkoa glee-fully exxpresssed hizz hope that Maluss had learned the error of hizz wayzz—and wazz, at lasst, properly motivated to complete the tassk at hand.

But truthfully, Malus required no reprimand or punishment to achieve the compass. He felt no need to justify his actions. Not to himself. Not to the Hidden's Master. And certainly not to Ssarbik. *This is about completing what I started*, he repeated to himself over and over. *Else, why did I do what I did at all?* He glared down at the giggling bird-man and shut him up with a slap from his new gauntlet. The arakkoa squealed out in pain, and Malus's own hand stung from the effort—though he would not even allow himself a grimace, let alone a grunt.

The captain did take some pleasure in knowing he remained in command of the Hidden on Azeroth. Not because it would have changed anything for him. He would do what he must no matter what His Highlordship decided or declared. But Malus knew Ssarbik coveted his command, and thwarting the bird-man brought a begrudging smile to the big man's face.

He said, "Time to get to it. Open a portal," while he thought,

After all, what's my alternative? Admit I committed a terrible—
He wouldn't allow himself to complete the reflection.

Ssarbik, now considerably less giddy, began his chant . . .

The portal opened on the deck of Malus's ship, the *Inevitable*—
an elven destroyer, tar-black in color. Malus and Ssarbik emerged
to face the latter's sister, Ssavra.

"Greetings, Captain," said the bird-woman, her voice crisp
and precise like that of most arakkoa—nothing like the hissing speech of Ssarbik. "What says our dreadlord of the
demonic Burning Legion? What says the Harbinger of the Dark
Storm?"

"He says little," answered Malus before Ssarbik could respond.
"He wants the compass. Nothing else required saying."

Ssavra nodded. But in the next instant, her imperious indigo
eyes cast a questioning glance down her long curved beak at her
brother. She was a few inches taller than Ssarbik but held herself
straighter, so appeared taller still.

The hunched Ssarbik anxiously snuck a peek at the iron
gauntlet on Malus's left hand, then decided it was worth the risk,
saying, "Our captain wazz casstigated for hizz failurezz." He
flinched involuntarily, but Malus moved not.

"For my tardiness," Malus corrected with equanimity. He
strode across the deck, leaving the two arakkoa to catch up. "So
you'll understand my sense of urgency. Heading?"

This last word was spoken to his helmsman, Sensiago Kryl, a human with ebony skin, one good eye, and a burn scar that covered the entire right side of his head. "Gadgetzan, Captain," Kryl said. "Two days out."

"Good. I want to beat the Greydon-spawn to the city."

"Then why wait?" the helmsman whispered. "Have the bird-beaks portal you there. Blast, Captain! Together maybe they can open a portal big enough for the whole blasted ship to sail through."

Malus smiled a strained smile. He said, "Doesn't work that way. From Azeroth, they can only portal to Outland."

"We can brave that foul place!"

"You don't want any part of Outland, believe me, Kryl. Besides, from Outland, each arakkoa needs the other to act as an anchor here. So even ignoring the detour, they can only portal back and forth between each other."

"That what they tell you?"

"Yes. And that's what I believe."

"If you say so, Captain. I just don't trust them bird-beaks. They be lookin' to stab you in the back, you ask me."

"He didn't," interjected Ssavra, who had slid up behind them. "But I'm sure he appreciates the warning, helmsman Kryl."

Sensiago shuddered and said, "Yes, ma'am."

Malus turned toward her. Her feathered head, black with a deep-purple sheen, tilted slightly to regard her captain with some amusement. He glanced over her shoulder. Her brother stood a safe distance away, his sneering head bobbing in expectation of a confrontation. "You had something to say?" Malus asked Ssavra casually.

"Only this," she hissed. "I am not my brother. I will not be growled or slapped into submission. Complete your assigned task, or I will kill you and complete it for you."

"Your Master might not approve."

"I would risk the highlord's wrath in order to fulfill his wishes," she said with a surprisingly pleasant grin.

"These threats are unnecessary, Lady Ssavra. I have no intention of failing."

"As long as we understand each other."

"We do."

"Oh, and one more thing . . ."

"Yes?"

"I am no lady."

Malus laughed and turned back to Sensiago Kryl. "To Gadgetzan, helmsman."

"Aye, aye, Captain!"

CHAPTER TWENTY-THREE
A GLOW AMID THE SHIMMERING

Aram, Makasa, Murky, Hackle, and Drella spent the next day aboard Rendow's boat. They passed between high canyon walls and tall, rocky plateaus. Enthralled, Aram spent much of his time sketching, inspired to attempt something he had never tried before: to sketch from a point of view other than his own. He sketched those canyon walls and a couple of the spires, then placed the *entire* boat upon the water (not just what he could see of the vessel from where he sat upon it). Then he sketched in his four companions. Finally, he added himself. This last part was the most difficult for Aramar. He had no looking glass with which to study his own face. He'd look down at his clothes—and their ragged condition—and occasionally he'd try to catch a glimpse of his reflection in the water. But the boat's own movement disturbed or distorted any view of himself. So, resignedly, he did the best he could. He tightened up the pencils last and, in the end, was fairly satisfied with the result. He did wish he could do better justice to the scene by using color, that is, by painting what he beheld in all its subtle shades. And he still felt his attempt at Aramar Thorne was feeble, but it didn't seem right not to include himself on the voyage. He showed the sketch to the others. Murky, Drella, and Hackle were all very impressed.

Makasa scowled and said, "It's good."

Aram scowled and asked, "Then why are you scowling?"

She lowered her head to whisper in his ear, "Because there are too blasted many of us on this blasted boat."

Aram whispered back, "Haven't they all proven themselves useful now and again?"

"And all proven themselves trouble now and again, too."

Aram was certain that Makasa didn't dislike any of their companions, at least not anymore. It was just that she hated relying on them. And the more of them there were, the more complications tended to arise, and the more she then *needed* the others to help solve them. For the Mighty Flintwill, it was a vicious circle.

She sighed quietly, nostalgic for the days when she only had herself and Aram to worry about. *Perhaps*, he thought (without really believing it), *nostalgic for the days when she only had Makasa Flintwill to worry about.*

Thus Aram passed his time, while Makasa passed *hers*—small surprise—on the alert for trouble. Hackle, taking his cues from her as usual, was likewise watchful as he rowed them down the

Sailing through Thousand Needles

A. Thorne

canyon. Drella conversed with Murky in his native tongue. Makasa frowned over what she perceived as their babbling, but it made Aram smile. It reminded him of the exchanges Murky used to have with Drella's former keeper, Thalyss Greyoak, who had somehow managed to teach the murloc language to the dryad's acorn simply by periodically whispering to her in that tongue. When Drella talked to Murky, Aram felt to some small degree that Thalyss was still with them. That he was alive in Taryndrella, that some of her quirks were Thalyss's quirks.

"What's he saying?" Aram asked the dryad.

"He talks about many things. Well, no, actually. He talks about two things. He talks about his friendship with the four of us. And he talks about his nets. Mostly, he talks about his nets. He is in some mourning for his nets."

"Yes," Aram said. He patted Murky on the murloc's oily head, then wiped his hand on his breeches. "He has twice made a great sacrifice in giving up his nets to help our band."

Murky nodded. "Mrgle, mrgle."

Come late afternoon, with the sun still fairly high, Aram had put away his sketchbook and was splashing cool water onto his face. He leaned back in the boat to let the warm summer breeze dry his skin. He shut his eyes. He felt a tug on the front of his tunic as Hackle called out, "There! Look!"

They all turned. The canyons had opened up into the Shimmering Deep, revealing before them what could only be the Speedbarge—Fizzle and Pozzik's Speedbarge—which came into view a mile farther down the canyon. Rendow had said they wouldn't be able to miss it, and it seemed she hadn't been joking. The Speedbarge looked like a cross between a city-size ship and an artificial island, with its own set of docks on either side and a warren of buildings—or perhaps machines—built atop it.

"That must be it," Makasa said.

"Mrgle, mrgle!" Murky said.

Aram thought the Speedbarge was surrounded by more boats than he'd ever seen in any one place—including Stormwind Harbor. Someone was still tugging on his shirt, as if trying to get him to look at what he was already observing. He glanced down to see who was doing the tugging. But it wasn't a hand tugging from without. It was the compass pushing from within!

The compass! He hadn't checked it in . . . how long? It seemed like days, though really it had been less than twenty-four hours. Nevertheless, he hadn't thought about it since before they'd recovered Drella, and now that they were traveling by boat rather than on foot, they were advancing at a greatly accelerated rate. He pulled it out. Even with the sun shining down on its face, he could tell that the needle was glowing brightly. He leaned forward over the water, and the enchanted device yanked hard downward with enough force to all but pull him off the boat.

The needle was spinning wildly, and Aram knew exactly what that meant. "Stop," he called out. "Stop the boat."

Hackle pulled the oars out of the water. All eyes turned toward Aram.

"There's a crystal shard here," Aram said in a tense whisper (as if Malus might have spies listening from beneath the surface).

"Where?" Makasa asked.

"Right here. The compass says—I mean, it's telling me there's a shard right beneath us now," With a tight grip on the compass, he leaned over the side again to look down. The others all did the same. Unsurprisingly, nobody saw anything but shimmering water. *Deep* shimmering water. (Hence, the name of the place.)

Aram started to take off his boots, burying his fear of drowning beneath the responsibility he felt toward his father's quest. "I guess I'll have to dive in."

Murky said, "Nk, nk."

Makasa said, "He's right, Aram. It's too deep."

Murky then began speaking very fast. Too fast for Aram to follow a word he was saying. So Aram looked to Drella for help. She met his gaze, smiled back at him—but said nothing.

Aram said, "What's Murky saying, Drella?"

"Oh. He does have a new topic of conversation, which is of some note in and of itself. He speaks of your compass and its crystals. Things I still am not sure I understand. Can you tell me anything more about this compass? Can you tell me anything more about these crystals? I do not believe you have been entirely clear on the subject."

Murky started up again.

Drella stiffened. "Now he says that you can tell me more later. He seems very impatient with me, actually. I do not believe Murky has ever been impatient with me before. I do not believe that I like it."

Murky said, "Drhla!" and Aram said, "Drella!" at virtually the same moment.

"Now you are both impatient," she pouted. "Fine. Murky says he can take the compass and dive down and recover the crystal."

"That actually makes some sense," Makasa said.

Aram nodded slowly but found himself reluctant to comply. He didn't like turning the compass over—to anyone. Maybe because Malus and his minions were constantly trying to take it from him, or maybe because his father's last act was to trust the device to Aram's care alone. Whatever the reason, he had to force himself to see the logic in what Murky was offering. Slowly, he removed the compass chain from around his neck. Murky held out his hand. But Aram still hesitated.

Finally, he handed the compass to the murloc and closed Murky's oily fingers around it. "Hold it tight," Aram said.

Murky grinned, stood, and dove down into the Shimmering Deep . . .

*   *   *

Murky positively loved to be of actual use to his frunds. He knew he wasn't much of a fighter. Not like Mrksa or Ukle. And he knew from his uncle Murrgly that he wasn't even particularly clever, like Urum or Drhla. But he was loyal. That much he could be for them all. So this opportunity to help, truly help, kept a grin on his face the whole way down to the bottom of the Deep.

The Shimmering Deep was dark and, well, murky. But the little murloc had excellent underwater vision and could see in near pitch blackness. Even so, he wouldn't have needed such a gift to see the compass, which he checked every few seconds. Its crystal needle glowed brightly—the more brightly the deeper he swam. If it spun in a circle, he knew he was right on top of the crystal. If the needle stopped spinning, it would point him back in the right direction. So he made swift progress, taking barely a moment to appreciate how nice it was to be swimming freely, without his nets wrapped tightly around his torso. (He felt a bit guilty about this, however. He knew—again from his uncle— that a murloc without nets was not a true murloc at all.)

He also resisted any temptation to eat. There were many tasty delicacies swimming within view—almost within reach. But he was helping Urum find his crystal. He would not let a simple thing like his gnawing, unending hunger divert him from his course. (All right, fine. There was that one *tiny* perch that he grabbed and stuffed in his mouth. But that wasn't his fault; it had practically swum right up to him.)

A whale shark—gargantuan and potentially quite dangerous—swam lazily past, sluggish from the summer sun heating the water. She ignored Murky, so Murky ignored her.

Finally, he reached the bottom. What had once—before the Cataclysm's flood—been called the Shimmering Flats lay open and revealed to the murloc. There were stone houses scattered about, and over a hundred . . . well, Murky wasn't sure what they were. Some kind of metal tubes. They had padded seats inside them for sitting, one seat each, occasionally two. Each had an odd wheel inside that faced the seat and had nowhere to roll. But there were wheels on the outside of the tubes, as well, like the wheels of a mule cart, only smaller and more compact. Murky, ever curious, sat down in one of the tubes and grabbed the interior wheel with one two-fingered hand. He couldn't budge it. And he couldn't use both hands because of the compass he held in the other.

The compass! Murky cursed himself aloud as a selfish fool (and the bitter words sounded crisper underwater, as that was where his language was meant to be spoken). He swam out of the tube and immediately checked the compass. It pointed just toward his right, toward a pile of stones that had once been some kind of structure—but that likely collapsed when the floodwater of the Cataclysm came rushing in.

The little murloc swam among the stones until the swiftly rotating crystal needle glowed brightly enough to fill the gloom below. Murky placed his free hand over the face of the compass to block its light, allowing him to see a matching glow emerging from beneath the wreckage. *The crystal!*

He put the compass chain around his neck, or at least he tried to. But his head was too big, so he wore the thing like a head-band, with the compass sitting like a third eye in his forehead, its glow lighting the work he set himself to. He moved a small stone here, and a small stone there. He tried to move a bigger slab but couldn't lift it. He tried to push it sideways across another slab that lay underneath it. It wouldn't budge. He put his back to it, digging his webbed feet into the silty bottom, but even working every single muscle in his little body, he couldn't shift it an inch.

So he swam down beneath the lowest slab and tried to dig it out. But that was no good, either. He could dig his way beneath the slabs, but the crystal wasn't there. It was between the two heaviest slabs, and Murky just wasn't strong enough to move them.

He was going to need some help . . .

CHAPTER TWENTY-FOUR
BARGING IN

The five of them, *all* grimly brooding over what to do about the sunken crystal shard, silently docked Rendow's boat at the floating artificial island that Rendow had called a "Speedbarge" (whatever that meant). Though the sun was setting, the place was still awash with activity. Gnomes and goblins and a handful of humans were buzzing about like bees after a rock had been thrown at their hive. Moving from one of the floating outer docks across a gangway of wooden planks to the barge itself, they looked around for the inn. Every inn or tavern Aram had ever seen, right down to the Tanner's Bed in Flayers' Point (which was nothing more than a wooden lean-to with walls of canvas), had a sign outside the door to bring in customers. But they saw nothing that resembled a sign anywhere.

Makasa separately asked two gnomes and a goblin to point them toward the inn, but each raced past her without acknowledging her question, let alone stopping to answer it. Finally,

Makasa drew her sword and planted herself in the path of a small gnome male with big ears and a big red nose. Makasa demanded directions, and with her cutlass out, the gnome pointed the way. The five travelers moved off; the gnome with the big red nose raced on.

This was the biggest port Aram had visited in months. (Captain Thorne favored more obscure landings for *Wavestrider.*) And more than that, this was the oddest, *strangest* port Aram had ever laid eyes upon. The structures were incredibly bizarre, with thick tubes running everywhere, tubes that pulsed and stretched—almost breathed—like giant lungs. Boats came in; boats went out. And some of these boats were like no boat any of them had ever seen before. They had strange, insect-like carapaces, roared like lions, and skimmed across the water as fast as any fish could swim. Normally, Aram would have been fascinated with every sight, every sound. He'd be reaching for his sketchbook to draw every gnome and goblin within view. And every one of those odd boats, too.

But not now.

Now, Aram was focused on the crystal shard and the seeming impossibility of recovering it.

Aram had waited impatiently for Murky to surface. He'd stared down into the water, as if looking away for even an instant might put the murloc's return at risk. Over and over, he'd absently reached for the compass that was no longer around his neck, and each time he had to check a moment of panic and remind himself why the device wasn't there. Nervously, he wondered aloud, "He's been down there a long time, don't you think?"

"You asked that before. Four times *before*," Drella said. "Is your memory experiencing difficulties?"

He had once again explained to her what little he knew about the compass, its crystal needle, and the crystal shards they seemed designed to seek out. It wasn't clear whether or not she grasped their importance, since—to be fair—Aram wasn't exactly *sure* why they were important, either. But the dryad did seem to grasp that Aram and the others regarded the crystals as important, so she became as silent as the rest, awaiting Murky's return.

Of course, when Murky did return, he didn't bring the shard— or any good news. He did bring back the compass and chain, which was somewhat comically wrapped around the top of his head, and which Aram snatched back to put around his neck before Murky could get a word out. When Murky did speak—with Drella translating—he apologized for failing them for a good five minutes before they managed to force out of him an actual explanation of their new dilemma. Aram, Makasa, Hackle, and even Drella were all more than willing to jump into the water to help the murloc push the slab aside and retrieve the shard. But Murky explained

223

that the bottom was just too deep. None of them could possibly make it all the way down to the crystal before needing to come back up for air. Instead, Murky suggested they get a very, very long rope. He could then tie one end to the slab and the other end to the boat, and maybe if Makasa and Hackle rowed very, very hard, they could pull the slab aside. Makasa and Hackle both frowned and shook their heads, but neither could offer up a better solution.

Ultimately, Makasa made the command decision to head for the Speedbarge. Aram protested, but Makasa pointed out that they weren't going far and that maybe a solution would come to them.

But as yet, none had. Aram found himself scanning his surroundings for very, *very* large coils of rope.

In the meantime, they headed down into the bowels of the Speedbarge, where they found the inn's saloon, mostly by following the noise made by its boisterous crowd. They were looking for "Daisy," Rendow's contact aboard the Speedbarge. All they knew about her was that she was human and worked there.

Upon crossing the threshold, Makasa had to instantly yank Aram out of the way of a flung pewter tankard, thrown by a tallish (four-and-a-half-foot) goblin at a shortish (two-and-a-half-foot) gnome. The tankard was—inevitably—aimed too high for the little gnome and thus came darn close to clocking Aram on the forehead. But beyond that, the throw also seemed to be the first volley in a full-scale brawl between goblins (and a couple tauren) espousing the strength of the Horde, and gnomes (and a few humans) equally promoting the power of the Alliance.

Or at least it would have become a brawl. But just then, music began to play. Attention turned immediately toward a young yellowish-green goblin, sadly and sweetly playing a fiddle. Beside the goblin, an attractive pair of bare legs swung back and forth. All eyes followed those legs upward to find them attached to a very comely human woman with long strawberry-blonde hair, who was sitting atop the bar as if waiting for something.

She didn't have long to wait. The brawl—or its beginnings— ended abruptly. The gnomes, goblins, tauren, and humans quickly found seats.

Makasa, Aram, Hackle, and Murky took four chairs at a table near the back of the tavern (while Drella curled up at Aram's feet). Makasa tried to ask a female gnome with big ears and a big and veiny blue nose whether the woman seated on the bar was Daisy. The gnome ignored Makasa's question (and existence) as the woman on the bar began to sing. In fact, the entire clientele of the place had gone pin-drop silent as the melancholy fiddle and the woman's sweet voice told of love and loss during the Cataclysm. Makasa was on the verge of drawing her sword on the blue-nosed gnome to get the information she required, but Aram put his hand on Makasa's arm and whispered, "Better to wait until the song ends. We'll likely have more luck then."

Makasa nodded begrudgingly, and they all sat back to listen . . .

The flood . . . chang'd ev'rything I knew.
We sank below the deluge,
And our great love was through.

The flood . . . has wash'd away my past.
A cataclysm so huge
That I am sinking fast.

I held on tight as waters rose high,
So high I thought 'twould never end.
I fought for breath as our love did die,
And felt my spirit break and bend.

The truth . . . is water's thick as blood,
When there's no port, no refuge
To save us from the flood.

The yellowish goblin boy played on. The room and its occupants were otherwise silent, save for the scattered sounds of sniffling. Aram looked around and saw that the simple song had greatly affected the tavern's patrons. The blue-nosed gnome wiped away a tear, and she wasn't the only one so afflicted.

The singer began again . . .

> *I held on tight as waters rose high,*
> *So high I thought 'twould never end.*
> *I fought for breath as our love did die,*
> *And felt my spirit break and bend.*

> *The truth . . . is water's thick as blood,*
> *When there's no port, no refuge*
> *To save us from . . . the flood.*

The singing ended. The fiddle played on for a few more measures; then it, too, stopped. There was silence in the barroom. Aram admired the song and the singer but didn't immediately understand the effect both were having on the crowd. He looked around . . . at the backs of heads lowered in sorrow, at the profiles of tough humans, tougher goblins, gnomes, and those two tauren, all with tears streaming down their faces, and he realized that these were all survivors of the Cataclysm, that each and every one of them had lost someone when the seawall fell and the Great Sea poured into the Thousand Needles valley, washing away the Shimmering Flats and replacing it with the Shimmering Deep.

Suddenly, the loss of a shard of crystal seemed of little significance in the grand scheme of things. There were much greater losses in the depths of the Deep.

The little goblin boy was moving through the crowd slowly, with his fiddle case open. The tavern's clientele dropped coins into the case with universal generosity. Eventually, the goblin found his way to the five travelers. Makasa held up a gold coin—so that no one but Aram and the goblin could see it. The latter's eyes went very wide. Makasa said, "I expect some change."

He nodded and held up the fiddle case, whispering, "Take it all."

"Not here," she said. "Your mistress. The singer. Is her name Daisy?"

"It is for a coin of gold."

She scowled, and he backed up a step. Aram knew that scowl and its power, and had to cover his mouth with a hand to hide his smile.

The goblin said, "Yeah, yeah. She's Daisy."

"Arrange a meeting for us. Somewhere private."

"You bet."

"No. I don't bet. I don't gamble. I expect guarantees . . . What's your name?"

"Me?" He asked the question as if no one in the entire history of Azeroth had ever been interested in his name before. "I'm Hotfix."

"Well, Hotfix, can you guarantee this private meeting?"

"Uh huh." He stood there, his green eyes still staring at the gold piece, until Makasa slipped it back in her pocket. Then he stared at her.

"Tell Daisy that Rendow sent us."

"Uh huh."

"Now."

"Right, right." And he was gone.

They watched him rush behind the bar, where he was too short to be visible. The singer, Daisy, was now acting as a smiling barkeep, serving grog to her increasingly rowdy clientele. The catharsis of her song had loosened their spirits and their purses, and they were exchanging coin for liquor at an astounding rate, one with which she seemed to effortlessly keep pace. For a few seconds, she leaned down and to one side, and Aram could picture little Hotfix whispering up to her. She straightened, and without ever losing her smile or ceasing to distribute ale, she scanned the bar until she spotted Makasa. Still smiling, she nodded.

Makasa nodded back.

It took a good half hour for the rush on the bar to slow, at which point Daisy made her way around the wooden counter with a bar rag, Hotfix trailing her with a tray. She'd wipe down tables and place empty glasses, mugs, goblets, and tankards on the tray until it was a miracle the little goblin could stand beneath the mountain of pewter and glassware he was carrying. But he staggered along in her wake, until she slowly made her way back to where Makasa, Aram, and the others were seated. Without stopping, Daisy signaled with her eyes toward a door in a dark corner. "I'll join you in three minutes," she whispered, and moved on.

Makasa leaned toward Hackle. "Stay with the others. Watch the door," she said. "If anyone other than the woman enters, be there with your club."

Hackle nodded, proud to be her second.

Makasa nodded to Aram, and they both stood. Drella stood, too. Makasa said, "Drella, stay here with Hackle and Murky."

Drella said, "I would prefer not to."

Makasa didn't quite know how to respond to that.

Aram said, "Drella . . ."

The dryad said, "I believe your conversation with this Daisy will be much more interesting than anything I might see here. In addition, I think it wise that you take me with you for your protection. The last time I let you out of my sight, events became very complicated. Or have you already forgotten what happened in the Bone Pile?"

The not uncommon occurrence of Drella's companions staring at her, flabbergasted, was once again put on display for all to see.

Makasa gave up. "Fine," she said. "But listen. Do not speak."

Drella waved off the advice. "That would be ridiculous. I am a very good speaker. I have a beautiful voice and a large vocabulary, especially when you take into consideration that it is springtime."

"It's summer," Makasa murmured under her breath. Still, she made no other objection and led Aram and Drella into the back room.

Makasa quickly took the measure of the small, bare space. There were no other doors or windows and nowhere for anyone who might covet her gold to hide. Just the one door, which Hackle was watching from the main room, a long table, and six chairs. Makasa and Aram took two of the chairs facing the door, and Drella stood beside them.

Precisely three minutes after Daisy had given her instruction, she entered with Hotfix. Hackle was right on their heels, club at the ready, asking Makasa, "Goblin all right?"

Makasa said, "Send your boy away."

Daisy said, "Send yours away, and I might consider it."

Aram, feeling a little insulted, straightened to his full height. He noticed Hotfix doing the same.

Makasa said, "This is my brother, Aramar Thorne. I am Makasa Flintwill."

Drella, not appreciating being left out, said, "I am Taryndrella, daughter of Cenarius."

Hackle shrugged and said, "Hackle is Hackle."

From somewhere behind him, Murky's voice chimed in, too: "Murky lggrm."

Daisy smiled and said, "My name is Daisy. This is my very good friend Hotfix. I keep him close. I'm sure you understand."

Makasa grumbled, "Fine," and nodded to Hackle, who departed with Murky, closing the door behind them.

Daisy took a seat opposite Makasa. (Hotfix climbed into a chair beside his mistress.) The two women stared each other down. Daisy with a smile. Makasa with a scowl. Daisy seemed to smile as easily as Makasa scowled. But there was a similar strength behind each woman's expression. Aram thought that maybe Makasa had finally met her match. (Not on the field of battle, perhaps, but at this negotiating table—if that was what it was lining up to be.)

Both women waited. Eventually, Daisy's smiling eyes glanced in the direction of Makasa's pocket. Makasa took out the gold piece and put it on the table.

Hotfix whispered, "She expects change."

Daisy put a gentle hand on his head and said, "Well, let's see what she needs, and then decide how much change she deserves." She turned to Makasa and asked, "So. You know Rendow?"

"Yes," Aram said, feeling the need to prove himself to be more than just *Makasa's boy*. "She lent us her boat and asked us to turn it over to you when we got here."

"How do I know you didn't *steal* it from Rendow?"

"If we stole it," Makasa said, "why would we give it to you?"

Drella said, "Rendow offered us the boat because kaldorei always seek to be of use to a daughter of Cenarius."

"That is true," Daisy said. "And other than taking charge of my friend's boat, how might this humble flower be of use to Cenarius's daughter and her friends?"

Makasa said, "Rendow said you could arrange transport for us to Gadgetzan."

"That's easy enough. A ship leaves every day for Gadgetzan."

"There's one other thing," Aram said, tentatively. "We lost something in the water. It fell to the bottom. We need to find a way to get it."

"Didn't I see a murloc among your companions? Can't he swim down and get it?"

"He tried. But something heavy is on top of it. He couldn't budge it by himself."

Daisy's amused smile became somehow more pointed as she said, "You dropped something in the water, and *then* something heavy fell on top of it?"

Aram didn't respond right away. Finally, he said, "My father—" He looked at Makasa and corrected himself. "*Our* father once told me that salvage operations take place in the Deep all the time. People looking for things lost in the Cataclysm. Is that also something easy enough to arrange?"

"I can make introductions."

"Thank you. The sooner the better."

"It can happen tonight. I know just the goblin. Is that all, then? The boat, Gadgetzan, and your little salvage mission?"

"We'll need two rooms," Makasa said. "And five hot meals."

"Easier still."

"No meat, please," Drella said.

"No meat for her," Makasa said. "But—"

"But the rest of you are carnivores of the first order. I understand." Daisy slid the gold coin back to Makasa. "I'll set up a tab. For a friend of Rendow, I trust we can settle up before you leave for Gadgetzan."

"Of course," Makasa said as she again pocketed the coin.

Hotfix showed them upstairs to adjoining rooms: one for Makasa and Drella, the other for Aram, Hackle, and Murky. Each room had two small beds and two pallets of straw on the floor. A few minutes later, the little goblin returned with his mistress, carrying five trays of food and drink between them.

Aram had his sketchbook out, finishing up the view of the Speedbarge from his window, which didn't seem to do it—in all its bizarre magnificence—justice. He longed to be once again upon the back of the wyvern One-Eye, soaring above the floating island so he could sketch it from there. But he did his best to capture the living, breathing lungs of the place, its hustle and bustle, its cornucopia of races, and the many, many boats that surrounded it. When Daisy placed his tray down, her eyes lingered upon the sketch.

She said, "That's quite good, um . . . I'm sorry, I've forgotten your—"

"Aramar," he volunteered loudly, and then blushing and quieter: "Or, um, Aram's fine."

"Well, Aram, you have ability."

He flipped back to the sketch of Elmarine to show Daisy a sample of his portraiture skills and said, "I'd love to sketch you, if you have time." Then, glancing over at Hotfix, who was placing a tray of raw fish before Murky, Aram added quickly, "Both of you."

She said, "It's not the first time someone's offered to draw my likeness. But it might be the first time I've felt instantly comfortable saying yes. The time suits me now, if you don't mind sketching and eating."

"I don't mind."

Daisy sat down on the other bed and beckoned Hotfix to climb up next to her. Aram sketched them in between spoonfuls of hot stew, strips of bread, and sips of hot spiced apple cider.

And in between the sketching and the eating, Aram exercised his boundless curiosity to find out more about the Speedbarge. Daisy told him that the reason the floating island was currently a jam-packed blur of activity was because Fizzle and Pozzik's Speedbarge was hosting the Annual Fizzle and Pozzik's Speedbarge Boat Race, and everyone was rushing around like crazy in order to be ready for it in five days' time. (The strange boats Aram had seen earlier were called "speedboats," which, it turned out, were boats with mechanical engines, designed to move very fast across the surface of the water. Aram hadn't known such things existed.) The competition had brought literally hundreds of gamblers, racers, and members of MEGA to the barge.

"What's mega?" Aram asked.

"M. E. G. A. MEGA. The Mechanical Engineers' Guild of Azeroth."

"Oh," Aram said, nodding. And then: "Um, what are mechanical engineers?"

"They build things like, well, like speedboats. Fizzle and Pozzik are both members, and MEGA sponsors this race and races like it all across Azeroth. Gives their engineers a chance to show what they can do."

"You mean to show off," Makasa said from the doorway to the adjacent room.

Daisy smiled. "Is there a difference?"

"What a waste of time," Makasa grumbled.

"Don't let him hear you say that."

"Who? Him?" Makasa pointed at Hotfix.

"No. The goblin who's going to help you salvage your lost treasure. He's sponsoring a boat in the race. And, trust me, he doesn't think he's wasting his time."

"What's his name?"

"Gazlowe."

CHAPTER TWENTY-FIVE
GAZLOWE'S CONCERN

Night had fallen, but all across the Speedbarge, torches—housed inside what looked like giant, mirrored half clamshells—shone with an intensity that nearly approximated daylight. Aram thought them brilliant, both literally and figuratively. The clamshells could be turned to aim the focused mirrored light wherever the shell-turner chose.

Daisy and Hotfix led Makasa, Aram, Drella, Murky, and Hackle across a gangway to one of the outer docks. A lone goblin male stood between two clamshells that aimed their reflected illumination out onto the shimmering water. He was staring down at an odd-looking pocket watch in his hand—in much the same way Greydon Thorne used to stare down at his enchanted compass, which is to say with a vague look of disappointment.

Daisy smiled and said, "Gazlowe, there are some people I'd like you to meet."

The goblin Gazlowe was about forty years of age. He was a muscular four feet tall, with bright-green skin, bloodshot yellow eyes, a prominent chin, an impressive nose, long pointed ears, steel-toed boots, and fingerless gloves. He didn't look up from his watch but said, "Not a good time, Daisy. Come back in nine minutes."

Daisy said, "It seems to me you have nothing to do for at least eight of those minutes except listen to what they have to say. Especially since they'd like to pay you for your services."

He chuckled. "Ain't that the truth?" He looked up at Daisy's new acquaintances and said, "You got seven minutes and thirty seconds."

Daisy quickly made introductions.

Gazlowe said, "Ugh. Too many names. I'll never remember 'em all. Just state your business."

Makasa nodded to Aram, who—acutely aware of the time pressure—took a deep breath and tried to speak clearly and to the purpose: "We've lost something in the Shimmering Deep about a mile up the lake. It's trapped under a slab of stone that's too heavy for our murloc friend to budge. Daisy tells us you've performed salvage operations here before. This one should be fairly straightforward, I'd think."

"Sounds like it," Gazlowe said. "So here's the deal. I take a thirty percent cut of whatever we find. Plus a ten percent equipment fee and a ten percent finder's fee. Deal?"

Aram shot Makasa a panicked look and said, "It's . . . it's not something we can split. It's one thing. And it's little. Honest."

Gazlowe studied the boy, perhaps trying to divine whether that one word, *honest*, was, well . . . honest. "Let's say I believe you," he said. "What makes you think that in this great expanse of water, we could find your little thing in less than a thousand years?"

"We know exactly where it is. Murky, here"—Aram turned to indicate the murloc—"can guide us right to it."

"Mrgle, mrgle."

"We just need a way to move the stone."

"This must be a pretty valuable little thing."

"It is to me. It's part of a gift my father gave me before he died."

Gazlowe chuckled again. "Your father gave you a gift, then died; then the gift wound up at the bottom of this flooded canyon; then a slab of stone landed atop it? That's *awwwwwwfully* complicated, kid, and not a little bit unlikely."

"But it is the truth," Drella said. "You can trust Aram. He would not lie."

Gazlowe looked extremely unconvinced, so Aram raced to say, "I might lie. But I'm not lying now."

Drella looked appalled. "Well, *I* do not lie. Ever."

"Of course you don't, Drella," Aram said while maintaining eye contact with the goblin.

"All right," Gazlowe said. "But if I can't get my cut, how would this work? I don't work for free, boy."

"We can pay you."

"How much?"

"A gold piece."

"You mean twenty."

"We don't have twenty."

"How much *do* you have? And keep in mind, we're talkin' 'bout a very valuable gift from your father. So don't hold out on ol' Gazlowe."

Aram looked to Makasa, who was scowling but said curtly, "We can pay you three gold coins. We have a fourth, but we need some portion of that to pay Daisy for services and accommodations, some of it for passage from here to Gadgetzan, and some for passage from Gadgetzan to Stormwind Harbor."

The goblin exhaled. "Five of you traveling from Gadgetzan to Stormwind for less than one gold coin? Where you plannin' to bunk, with the bilge rats?"

"If necessary," Aram said.

"Murky mrrrgle rrrdhs mmm," Murky said, licking his lips.

They all ignored him, but Gazlowe said, "It don't matter. Or put another way, that part ain't my business. Here's the part that is: I mount salvage missions for entire pirate ships, where my take is somewhere in the neighborhood of a thousand gold coins and at least as many silver."

Aram pleaded: "But our mission would be much easier, don't you think?"

"That's why I was willin' to do it for twenty gold pieces. Anything less just ain't worth my time."

"But—"

"Look, kid, I can see you're sincere, and I'm even sympathetic. But three gold pieces wouldn't cover my expenses for this sorta thing. The answer's no."

"But—"

"And your seven and a half minutes are up." Gazlowe turned back toward the water, checked his pocket watch, and growled, "Long past up, blast it all!"

Aram turned to Daisy. "Isn't there anyone else we can talk to?"

Daisy smiled sadly. "There is. But none who'd offer to do it for less. Or if one did offer, it would only be to stab you in the back and take your prize."

Gazlowe chuckled and said, "Ain't that the truth?"

Aram slumped down onto a mooring post and looked up at Makasa. "What do we do?"

"We'll come up with something," she answered with a determination that offered no concrete solutions.

And just as she said that, Aram had an idea. He stood again and pulled his sketchbook from his back pocket, hoping it could work its magic one more time. But before he could show it to Gazlowe, one of the speedboats, fantailing water in its wake, pulled to a stop right in front of the goblin, dousing him, Murky, Hotfix, and Hackle. Aram was partially drenched, too, and just barely managed to save his sketchbook by whipping it behind his back.

With a hiss of steam, the speedboat's carapace flipped upward, revealing the pilot: *a head inside a large glass jar!* The head looked vaguely gnomish, but the skin was a brighter green than any goblin skin Aram had ever seen. It almost seemed to glow. The eyes, however, *definitely* glowed, green and luminous in the night. The head had short dark-green hair and looked . . . young.

Drella backed away, moaning, "No, no, no, no, no, no, no . . ."

The head frowned at her and spoke crossly, its voice echoing slightly within the glass jar: "I'm coming out." Aram could hear something pumping within the jar and the harsh, in-and-out echo of the head's steady breathing.

"No!" Drella practically screamed.

"Of the boat. I'm coming out of the boat," said the head.

Aram, who had seen the undead Whisper-Man and scores of animated skeletons, still couldn't quite fathom a severed head— jar or no jar—scowling and speaking aloud. But then the head-in-a-jar began to rise, and Aram realized that it wasn't *only* a head. The jar was attached to a metal body that unfolded long, steam-driven metal arms and legs. Whatever it was climbed out of the speedboat and onto the dock. Straightening to its full height, the head's eyes were now an inch or two above Aramar Thorne's.

Aram looked around at his companions. Murky was hissing. Hackle growled low. Makasa was silent and stoic, of course, but she had one hand on her sword and the other on the latch to her chain. Daisy smiled benevolently. Hotfix looked bored. Gazlowe looked just as cross as the metal man's head.

Drella was covering her face, still moaning softly. Then she looked up at the head and took a couple tentative steps forward, murmuring, "I should . . . I think I should . . ." But she seemed to lose her courage and turned away. Aram thought he heard her crying.

He was about to say that he didn't understand, didn't understand what this creature was, didn't understand why it upset Drella so. (Drella, who was so curious and naïvely imperturbable about nearly everyone and everything she encountered.) He didn't understand any of it—and then, suddenly, he did!

"It's a suit! A suit of metal and steam and glass!" Excited by his epiphany, he turned to Makasa, almost beaming. "And there's a little gnome inside the suit's, uh . . . chest!"

The gnome growled, "I'm not little!"

Makasa said, "Leper gnome."

Horrified by those words, Aram quickly turned to look at the gnome again. His father had told him of leper gnomes: irradiated and driven insane, they were locked away or banished. *And they were potentially contagious!* Aram saw a small blister on the gnome's face burst, and he took a few steps back himself.

Gazlowe held up his hands in a calming motion. "It's fine. It's fine. The suit contains the bad stuff. The suit protects him, us, and the world." Then he turned to the gnome and barked, "What it don't do is let you pilot that boat at anythin' like a winnin' speed!"

"Gazlowe, listen . . . ," the gnome began, but the goblin wasn't in the mood.

"No, Sprocket. You said one more chance, and I gave it to you. C'mon, now. Be realistic. You built us a terrific little filly here, but the jockey's too blasted heavy. We both know you need to run this course in less than twelve minutes to win. The boat can do it. But not with *you* in it. That was your best time just now. You wanna know what it was?"

"Fifteen minutes and fifty-two seconds," said the gnome mournfully.

"Fifteen minutes and fifty-two seconds," said the goblin angrily, and he pounded a fist against the gnome's metal chest.

Daisy stepped between them. She said, "Where are my manners? Gimble Sprysprocket, I'd like you to meet my new friends, Aramar Thorne, Makasa Flintwill, Hackle of the Woodpaw clan, Murky, and Taryndrella, daughter of Cenarius. Ladies and gentlemen, this is Gimble Sprysprocket."

"Just call me Sprocket," Sprysprocket said with a dismissive wave of his large metal hand. "My full name takes too long to say." Then to the goblin: "Gazlowe, I'll cut the weight. I'll streamline my containment suit."

"You did that already."

"I'll do it again."

"How? By takin' out some of them gears and motors that let you move? You do that, how you gonna steer?"

"The breathing apparatus—"

"What, you gonna hold your breath for fifteen minutes and fifty-two seconds?"

"Then I'll increase the engine's output."

"If you could do that, you'd've done it by now." Gazlowe shook his head. "Kid, I'm sorry."

"Fine," Sprocket said, looking away. "Razzle's still on his way."

"Nah, kid. I ain't buyin' that line no more. You lied to me."

"No, I—"

"Stop. I get it. You built her; you wanted to pilot her. So you tell me you got your cousin Razzle lined up for the gig. And I fall for it. That's on me. Shoulda hired my own guy. Didn't."

"Razzle *will* be here. Tomorrow or the next day."

"Yeah. For a record-holdin' pilot, somehow Razzle's always runnin' late. And while we wait, you'll just put our baby through her paces. Maybe convince me you're just the gnome for the job. But Razzle ain't comin'. Was never comin'. And you ain't gonna convince no one. Meanwhile, I got *three hundred* gold coins invested in this boat and *two thousand* wagered on this race. And now I only got *five days* to find a new pilot."

"I'll do it," Aram said.

All eyes turned to stare at him. He had almost surprised himself with the offer. He swallowed hard and tried to speak the goblin's "language," saying, "You got a lotta coin riding on this, right? If I pilot your boat, it's gotta be worth the twenty gold pieces you were gonna charge us to salvage my father's gift."

Gazlowe chuckled. "Ain't that the truth?"

Belatedly, a stunned Sprocket and an even more stunned Makasa shouted, "NO!"—practically in unison.

Ignoring the gnome, Aram turned to his sister. "Why not?"

"It's too dangerous."

"It's a boat race. Compared to everything else we've faced over the last few weeks, it'll be the safest thing I've done." Given his recent experiences in water, he sounded considerably more confident than he felt, but he said, "This gets us the . . . thing. And it won't cost us a copper. Then in five days we can be back on our way to Gadgetzan."

"And if the Whisper-Man or one of the others gets here in *less* than five days?"

"That's always a risk. But . . ." He didn't feel the need to add, *what choice do we have?*

To her frustration, Makasa couldn't find fault with his argument.

But Gimble Sprysprocket could. "What do you know about being a pilot?"

"I've raced boats before."

"Where?!"

"Lake Everstill."

"What kind of boats?"

"All kinds."

"All kinds of rowboats, I'm guessing."

"And rafts."

Sprocket turned his metal body back to Gazlowe, who was thoughtfully sizing Aram up. "You can't be considering this."

"Can't I? The boy's gutsy. Knows what he wants and knows how to get it. I like his style." Gazlowe stepped forward and wrapped his arms around a surprised Aram, who at first thought the goblin was giving him a hug. Instead, Gazlowe *lifted* Aram off his feet and held him in the air for a good five seconds before putting him down. "But mostly, I like that he weighs almost nothin'!"

"No!" Sprocket shouted, his voice echoing inside his jar. "He *knows* nothing! Nothing about piloting a speedboat—let alone the fastest speedboat ever engineered!"

"Aw, c'mon, Sprock," Gazlowe said with a mocking tone. "You sayin' a genius like you can't figger out a way to train him with five whole days left before the race?"

"I didn't say that."

"But that's it, ain't it? You're not up to it. Okay, I'll find someone—"

"I didn't say I couldn't train him. I could train *the murloc* if I wanted to."

Murky nodded. "Mrgle, mrgle."

Gazlowe rolled his eyes and muttered a sarcastic, "Sure you can."

"Of course I can!"

"Please. I'll bet you fifty in silver you can't make a winnin' pilot outta the boy."

"You're on!"

Gazlowe turned to Aram, waggled his brow ridges, and whispered, "Too easy." Then louder: "Kid, you got yourself a deal!"

They shook on it, and Gazlowe said, "What's your name again?"

CHAPTER TWENTY-SIX
·DRRRUGG ɅɅ
RRRGRRRS

Leper or no leper, Gimble Sprysprocket was one clever gnome. And not just clever. He was brilliant. Too smart to be fooled—or to fool himself—for very long. Half a second *before* his boss had said, "Too easy," Sprocket realized he had been shamelessly manipulated into training this human boy. It was a sad little bit of self-knowledge, but Sprocket knew he was practically incapable of passing up on a dare. Now, he had silver riding on it. Silver he didn't have—and wouldn't have—unless his boat, his invention, the *Steamwhistle*, won the race and he received his ten percent cut of Gazlowe's prize. That meant Sprocket had to either (1) turn this boy into a winning pilot or (2) convince Gazlowe the boy was a disaster so that Sprocket could pilot instead. (Gazlowe had been right about Cousin Razzle, whom Sprocket had never contacted at all.) Sprocket's clear preference was (2). But in another morsel of unhappy self-knowledge, the gnome had to admit that his mechanized suit was indeed too heavy to score a winning time.

He was proud of the suit. Most leper gnomes were slobbering wretches, unable to interact with society, unable to accomplish anything at all. But Sprocket had engineered and constructed a thing of genius—*if he did think so himself*. Actually, he had engineered and constructed an entire series of brilliant devices that together made up the complex containment suit that allowed him to safely walk among his fellows and continue to prove his extraordinary talents. He could do almost anything with it. He could do almost anything *in* it. (Except, of course, cure his cursed and shameful condition.)

But even his amazing suit had its drawbacks. It was too heavy. And five days' time wasn't going to be long enough to fix *that* problem. So (1) it was. But that didn't mean he was going to make it easy on this Thorne.

They began bright and early the next morning. Thorne seemed eager to hop into the *Steamwhistle* and test her out. But Sprocket wanted to make sure the kid was sufficiently impressed with—or intimidated by—the magnitude of what he was undertaking. So he pulled out the boat's blueprints and insisted on going through every intricate detail of his invention. To Sprocket's surprise, Thorne *was* impressed, studying the blueprints with extreme focus, praising their draftsmanship, and asking numerous pertinent questions. Instead of being pleased, Sprocket felt strangely disappointed, even mildly annoyed. And he became more annoyed when Gazlowe made an appearance, forcing the gnome to allow the boy to finally step into the boat. Instantly, Sprocket could see that the *Steamwhistle* was sitting considerably higher in the water than it had for himself, meaning Thorne weighed considerably less than Sprocket in his containment suit, meaning Thorne might theoretically be able to race considerably faster than Sprocket.

This just might work. Which was somewhat annoying as well.

Makasa watched Aram work with the leper gnome. She didn't like seeing her brother so close to the contagious creature, suit or no suit. Drella's clear . . . *distaste* for the gnome didn't help. The young dryad couldn't seem to stand being anywhere near Sprysprocket, so Makasa asked Hackle and Murky to take Drella for a walk around the Speedbarge.

Minutes later, Murky and Drella were back. Murky was dripping wet and frantic, and Hackle was nowhere to be seen.

"What happened?" Makasa demanded.

Murky said, "RRRgrrrs! DRRRugg n RRRgrrrs!" And Makasa knew exactly what he meant.

Throgg, Karrga, Guz'luk, Slepgar, Short-Beard, and Long-Beard spend three days aboard Grimtotem boat. Boat cramped, not comfortable. Slepgar too big. Slepgar too sleepy. Throgg spend much time with Slepgar's big feet in Throgg's face. Only good bit is boat so crowded, Karrga forced close to Throgg. Throgg like when Karrga close.

Boring on boat, too. Give Throgg time. Time for Throgg to think. Throgg no like thinking. When Throgg think, Throgg remember. Throgg no like remembering.

Throgg young. Throgg strong. Throgg fight for Horde with Throgg's clan. With Mahrook ogre clan. Mahrook warriors kill many Alliance soldiers. But Mahrook warriors fooled. Mahrook warriors cornered in box canyon by Alliance. By many humans and dwarves. Too many. Mahrook warriors kill many Alliance soldiers. But more Alliance soldiers come. Too many. Mahrook warriors slaughtered by Alliance. Only Throgg left. Only Throgg alive to fight. Throgg keep fighting. Arrows in Throgg. Many arrows. But Throgg have two hands then. Pull arrows out and stab humans with arrows. Smash dwarves with mace. But too many Alliance soldiers. Throgg know Throgg will die. Die with rest of Mahrook warriors. Throgg think this death good death.

Then orcs come. Orcs enter canyon behind Alliance. Orcs fight Alliance soldiers from behind. Orcs kill humans, kill dwarves. Alliance soldiers turn from Throgg to fight orcs. Now Throgg kill Alliance soldiers from behind. Finally, Alliance soldiers all dead like Mahrook warriors. Orcs and Throgg meet in middle. Meet over bodies of Alliance and Mahrook. Throgg see orcs. Throgg see orcs only have one hand.

These orcs Shattered Hand. Not many Shattered Hand left in Azeroth. Not many Shattered Hand orcs left. No Mahrook ogres left. Throgg see Shattered Hand orcs are great warriors. Shattered Hand orcs see Throgg is great warrior.

Shattered Hand orc Teremok look around at dead. Shattered Hand orc Teremok nod head at Throgg. Teremok say, "This ogre's a fighter. Strongest of his clan."

Mahrook warrior Throgg nod at Teremok and say, "Throgg strongest of all."

Teremok say, "The Shattered Hand could use an ogre like you, Throgg. Join us. Join us few. We band of brothers. Become Shattered Hand, and you become our brother."

Throgg look down at Thrull. Thrull was Throgg's brother. But humans kill Thrull. Thrull dead now. All Mahrook dead now. Throgg no got brothers left. Throgg say, "Throgg need brothers. Throgg join Shattered Hand."

Teremok nod. Teremok cut off Throgg's hand with axe. Good hand. But gone now. Throgg only got one hand now. Throgg is Shattered Hand now.

Shattered Hand blacksmith Ulmok put metal stump on Throgg where no hand is now. Give Throgg quiver with many weapons. Show Throgg how to screw weapons onto metal stump. Now Throgg have one hand and one weapon all the time. Different weapons, too. If Throgg bored with mace, Throgg screw on pike. If Throgg bored with pike, Throgg screw on axe. Throgg no miss old hand too much. Not too much.

Throgg fight Alliance with Shattered Hand orcs. Throgg kill many Alliance soldiers with Shattered Hand. Then Ulmok killed by Alliance elf. Ulmok was Throgg's friend in Shattered Hand. Ulmok was Throgg's brother. Throgg kill elf. Throgg miss Ulmok.

But Throgg still fight with Shattered Hand orcs. Throgg kill many Alliance soldiers with Shattered Hand. Then Teremok killed by humans. Take five humans to kill Teremok. Teremok was Throgg's friend in Shattered Hand. Teremok was Throgg's brother. Throgg kill five humans. Throgg miss Teremok.

Now Throgg look around Shattered Hand. All orcs and Throgg. Teremok dead. Ulmok dead. Throgg have no friends in Shattered Hand. Orcs no like Throgg. Throgg too strong. Throgg too good a warrior. Orcs treat Throgg bad. But Throgg swear oath to Teremok and Shattered Hand. Throgg think Throgg Shattered Hand for life. But Shattered Hand not Throgg's brothers anymore.

Shattered Hand work with Hidden to find stupid compass. Work with Hidden to find Greydon Thorne. Throgg meet Malus. Throgg watch Malus. Throgg see Malus is strong. Throgg see Malus is great warrior for Hidden. Malus watch Throgg. Malus see Throgg strong. Malus see Throgg is great warrior for Shattered Hand. Malus see Shattered Hand orcs no treat Throgg like brother. Malus say, "Throgg, I'm leaving tomorrow. You should come with me."

Throgg say, "Throgg swear oath to Shattered Hand. Throgg no leave."

Malus say, "Nothing would make you forswear your oath?"

Throgg say, "Nothing."

Malus say, "Nothing, ever?"

Throgg say, "Nothing. Never."

Malus nod at Throgg. Malus no say anything else to Throgg.

But Malus talk to Garamok. Garamok not strong as Throgg. Garamok not brother to Throgg. Malus ask, "Does Garamok want an ogre among the Shattered Hand orcs?"

Garamok say, "No. No ogre can ever be true Shattered Hand."

Throgg burn inside when Throgg hear what Garamok say.

Malus say, "Release Throgg from his oath. I'll take him with me."

Garamok shrug. Garamok say, "No, human. Throgg's good for carrying supplies on his back."

Malus say, "I'll pay you twenty silver pieces if you release him."

Garamok shrug. Garamok say, "No, human."

Malus say, "Thirty."

Garamok shrug. Garamok say, "Yeah. Good."

Garamok release Throgg from Throgg's oath for thirty pieces of silver.

Malus say, "Throgg, now will you join me? Will you join the Hidden?"

Throgg say nothing.

Malus say, "Will you swear an oath to the Hidden? Will you make all the Hidden your brothers and sisters?"

Throgg say nothing. Throgg think and remember. Thrull dead. Teremok dead. Ulmok dead. Throgg no have brothers. No ogre

brothers. No orc brothers. Throgg say, "Throgg swear oath to
Hidden. Throgg be Malus's brother."

Malus still Throgg's brother. But Throgg no like what Malus do
to Gordunni ogres. Throgg know Karrga no like, either. Karrga
no like that Malus force all ogres from home in Dire Maul.
Karrga no like that human is new Gordok.

Throgg think Karrga like Throgg. Throgg want to make
Karrga happy. Throgg want to fight by Karrga's side. Throgg
want to fight *for* Karrga. Throgg like Karrga but no want to be
Karrga's brother. Throgg want . . . *more.*

But Malus still Throgg's brother. And Throgg swore oath to
Malus and Hidden. So Throgg follow Malus's orders.

Makasa glanced at Aram, who was sealed beneath the carapace of
the speedboat, safely out of sight as he took his first spin around
the Speedbarge with Gazlowe and Sprysprocket watching.

So Makasa turned back to the matter at hand. With Drella's
help, getting details from Murky wasn't difficult. Murky, Hackle,
and Drella had been taking their stroll when Hackle had spotted
ogres docking a Grimtotem boat.

Drella had said, "I do not believe I have ever seen an ogre in
person. Let us go say hello."

Instead, Hackle had grabbed Murky and dove into the lake so
that neither of them would be spotted.

The ogres—five of them, including Throgg (or as Murky called him, DRRRugg)—had walked right past Drella. She had even introduced herself. She said they stared at her pleasantly but said nothing and walked on.

Hackle and Murky had resurfaced. Hackle told Drella and Murky to return to Makasa. Then the gnoll had followed the ogres, keeping his distance, keeping out of sight.

With a wave from the leper gnome, Aram went around again. Before he could go around a third time, Hackle returned with Daisy and Hotfix.

Now, the ogres were in the tavern, searching for Aram and his friends, questioning everyone—at the point of a sword. So far, no one had spilled. Gnomes and humans weren't likely to cooperate with ogres, and goblins preferred payoffs to threats.

"But I'm afraid it's only a matter of time," Daisy said with a resigned smile.

Just then, Aram passed again in the boat. Gazlowe hooted loudly and held up his pocket watch, shouting, "That's eight laps in fourteen minutes! And the boy barely knows what he's doin'!"

Makasa and Daisy conferred with the goblin. Daisy finished with, "We'll have to find them new accommodations."

"We have to get off this barge," Makasa insisted.

Gazlowe eyed Makasa. "Why are ogres huntin' you?"

"Does it matter? They're ogres. If they catch us, they'll kill us."

"Ain't that the truth? All right, fine. But you don't gotta go far. We'll put you up on my yacht. And we'll keep alla you under wraps."

"Wait," Makasa said incredulously. "Do you think we're staying?"

"You gotta stay. The kid and I have a deal."

"His name is Aramar, and the deal's off."

"Is it, now?"

"Yes."

"I don't think so, girl. Leave before the race and you can forget salvagin' your father's whatever-it-is. Don't know if *you're* okay with that, but I doubt the boy will be."

Makasa glowered but said nothing.

Gazlowe put a hand on her shoulder. "Don't worry. I like the kid. We'll be careful. I promise."

He sounded sincere, but Makasa knew his sincerity had its limits. Gazlowe might legitimately like Aram—but not enough to value her brother's life over his racing profits. And as far as she could tell, the goblin *still* couldn't remember Aramar's name.

After eight more laps, Thorne was coming around again. Gazlowe was still talking to Daisy and the tall woman, so Sprocket was timing the run. Thirteen minutes and thirty-four seconds.

This just might work.

CHAPTER TWENTY-SEVEN
ALL VERY ROUTINE

So began their new routine.

They never went back to the tavern or the inn, which turned out to have been a wise choice. Daisy and Hotfix rowed out in Rendow's boat to let them know that the ogres had found a drunken goblin who didn't mind telling them that two humans, a gnoll, and a murloc matching their descriptions had been at the tavern the night before. The sloshed goblin also told the ogres that the four fugitives had a dryad with them, meaning Drella wasn't safe on the Speedbarge, either. The ogres came to the inn and demanded to be taken to Aram's room. Daisy complied—there was no reason not to—and then tried to convince them that Aram and his friends had only stayed one night and had then taken a boat to New Thalanaar the next morning. She thought that might get the ogres to leave the barge while sending them off in the wrong direction. But she feared now she had overplayed her hand, because the ogres had not left, had clearly not believed her.

"If I had told them Gadgetzan, they might have been convinced. They seem to know you're headed that way."

The five travelers took up residence on Gazlowe's yacht, which he kept anchored a few hundred feet from the Speedbarge. They shared a single large cabin and largely kept off the deck so that they couldn't be spotted from the barge. This made all of them—but especially Makasa—fairly stir-crazy, but there was no remedy for it.

Sprocket was also on the yacht, and every morning, just before dawn, he would put Aram in the *Steamwhistle* and watch through a telescopic attachment on his containment suit as the boy raced the course. Over and over and over.

Inside the speedboat, Aram would lower himself into the seat, which was halfway below the waterline. The seat had a double-belt that he fastened crisscross over his chest. It reminded him of how Makasa wore her chain, and it made him feel a little like a warrior. As did the helmet Sprocket had given him to wear. "Why do I need this?" Aram had asked.

"In case you crash," Sprocket answered.

"I'm on the water. If I crash, I get wet. I suppose I might drown, but how does a helmet help with that?"

Sprocket stared at him and said, "You're a simpleton, Thorne. Put on the helmet."

"You know, it's all right to call me Aram."

"That's two syllables. Thorne is only one. It's more efficient."

"So Aramar is out, then?"

Sprocket ignored him.

Having settled in, Aram would pump a lever until the engine caught and turned over. When it had worked up a head of steam, he'd pull another lever, and the carapace would lower down over his head. When it was nearly shut, he'd pull down hard on a handle until the carapace click-locked into place, sealing him in.

There was a long, slim slot in the carapace that allowed him to see out but wasn't wide enough for anyone to see him inside the boat from even the smallest distance. So Aram could safely run the course within a few yards of the Speedbarge without any risk of being spotted by Throgg and his very large friends.

Next, Aram would push up on another handle, which Sprocket called a throttle. True to its name, the *Steamwhistle* would whistle steam as the boat began to accelerate. There was a wheel for steering, smaller than but not unlike the wheel of the *Wavestrider*, which helmsman Thom Frakes had taught him to use. But because *Steamwhistle* was smaller and sleeker, it was much more sensitive to the wheel's spin. One of the first things Aram had to learn was not to oversteer.

Then came the course, which circled Fizzle and Pozzik's Speedbarge: there were two straightaways to the north and south, and two slaloms between pylons on the eastern and western sides. Aram began to understand why Sprocket had wanted the pilot job so badly. *This is so much fun!*

The boat flew across the water like a skipping stone. The speed was intoxicating. The fact that Aram controlled the craft's slightest movement was intoxicating. Swishing back and forth between the pylons was intoxicating. He absolutely, positively *loved* this.

Every night, they all ate together: Aramar, Makasa, Hackle, Murky, Drella, Gazlowe, and Sprocket. (Daisy and Hotfix stayed away, because the ogres—suspicious of her lie—had begun to follow her. Fortunately, the creatures were too big to make a subtle job of it, so they were an easy tail to spot.)

Gazlowe liked to eat well, so his guests ate well, too. Meals on the yacht were something akin to a feast. There was roast turkey and roast pork. There was raw fish for Murky, and plenty of fruits and vegetables for Drella. Once served, the dryad would pick up her plate and move as far from the leper gnome as she could. Yet throughout the meal, she would periodically start to inch *toward* Sprocket—then seem to lose her nerve and move away again.

Gazlowe also had a sweet tooth; thus, there was always a whole selection of individual pastries, pies, and cakes for dessert.

On the third night, Gazlowe finished his Dalaran brownie and asked Aram how it was going.

Aram, who had just stuffed an entire bloodberry turnover into his mouth, swallowed and answered, "Great! I think I've really got the feel of the *Steamwhistle* now."

Gazlowe shot a glance at Sprocket, who somewhat begrudgingly nodded confirmation before using a mechanical arm to open a panel in his suit's metal chest. He inserted a plum cake and closed the panel. Then through the suit's glass helmet, Aram could see Sprocket's actual gnomish hands feeding his face.

Gazlowe turned back to Aram and said, "And you're learnin' the course?"

"Better each time." By the end of the first day, Aram had reduced his time to thirteen minutes and three seconds. By the end of the second day, after nearly one hundred trips around the raceway, he'd gotten it down to twelve minutes even. By the end of the third, eleven minutes thirty-two. A potentially winning time. "I think by race day, I can get under eleven."

"That's fantastic," Gazlowe said. "Now, tomorrow . . . I want you to slow down."

"What?"

"There are a lotta folks watchin' you practice."

"I know. But the ogres can't see me inside the boat."

"I'm not worryin' 'bout ogres."

Makasa shot him an angry look.

Gazlowe said, "I mean, I'm not *talkin'* 'bout ogres. I'm talkin' 'bout my competitors and fellow gamblers. Keep gettin' the feel of the boat and the course, but let's not give away just how good you think you can be. Hold back now, just a bit. We want to surprise 'em all when it counts."

Aram nodded, though he was somewhat unsure he'd be able to exercise that much discipline. He *liked* pushing his time.

Aram took his sketchbook out to continue work on a memory sketch of the goblin and the leper gnome arguing over who would pilot the *Steamwhistle*, which was visible in the background. Aram had chosen to depict the moment when Daisy intervened between sponsor and engineer, because, well . . . because he just liked drawing Daisy. And he had stuck little Hotfix in there, too, off to the side. For no good reason, he had drawn Hotfix playing his fiddle, even though the little yellowish-green goblin hadn't even had his fiddle with him at the time. But Aram liked that he was feeling freer and more imaginative with his sketches. Drawing from memory had become easier, too. Yes, he'd glance up at Sprocket and Gazlowe now and again, and he also referred to the sketch of Daisy and Hotfix he'd already completed. (It was definitely helpful having the reference and two of the subjects currently before him.) For the most part, however, he just drew what he remembered and what he was feeling.

"One more thing," Gazlowe said. "Tomorrow night . . ." He hesitated and snuck a glance at Makasa.

"What?" she said darkly.

"Tomorrow night, our pilot needs to board the Speedbarge to officially register for the event."

"You do it," Makasa said. "He's not going anywhere near that barge. And, yes, I *am* worrying about the ogres."

Gazlowe, Sprocket, Daisy, and Hotfix

R. Thorne

"Sprocket and I are goin', but the boy has to come, too, or we're disqualified. But it's routine, and I got just the thing. A hooded cloak I, uh, *liberated* from an actual member of SI:7. So it's a real spy cloak. Perfect for the job." And before Makasa could object again, he added, "We'll be in and out."

"Then I'm going with," she said.

"I don't got two cloaks," he said. "And trust me, girl, *you* do not walk about unnoticed. In fact, you cut quite the figure wherever you go. So you stay behind, or you put the boy at greater risk."

"His. Name. Is. Aramar."

"Right, right. I know that."

"Say it."

"What? Why?"

"So I know you know he's a real person. So I know you care enough about him to at least learn his blasted name."

Gazlowe straightened and stood. He then leaned over the table to look Makasa straight in the eye. He said, "My pilot is Aramar Thorne. And the truth is, I'm kinda fond of the ki—of Aram. I won't let nothin' happen to him on the barge. You got my word."

Makasa considered for a moment what the word of a goblin was truly worth. Then she nodded, satisfied. Satisfied that Gazlowe would make blasted sure nothing happened to Aram . . . at least, not *before* the race was run.

Gazlowe and Sprocket, towing the *Steamwhistle* behind them, took Aram over to the Speedbarge in a rowboat.

Having docked, Aram tried to stand but stepped on the hooded cloak he was wearing and nearly knocked his brains out against a mooring post. The cloak was made for someone a good foot taller than Aram, and, worse, it reminded him of the Whisper-Man's cloak. He kept imagining he could smell Valdread's jasmine water saturating the fabric.

Walking between Gazlowe and Sprocket, Aram tried not to trip as the three of them joined the line waiting to register with the gnome Fizzle Brassbolts and the goblin Pozzik. The cofounders of the Speedbarge sat behind a long wooden table and entered names in a large tome.

"Boat?" Fizzle asked.

"The *Guzzler*," said a goblin.

"Sponsor?" Pozzik queried.

"Razzeric," said the goblin, now sounding slightly annoyed.

"Engineer?" Fizzle inquired.

"Razzeric," the same goblin said again, with frustration.

"Pilot?" Pozzik demanded.

"Razzeric!" the goblin roared. "You know blasted well who I am, the both of you!"

"Move along," Fizzle said, with a dismissive wave.

Aram watched a grumbling Razzeric move to stand in front of his green-and-red speedboat. Another goblin—older but quite distinguished, even handsome—took up position in front of Razzeric *and began sketching him and his boat!* This goblin artist worked quickly. It didn't seem as if he was trying to finish the sketch; rather, he was just putting enough lines—enough information—on the page so he could finish it later.

"Boat?" Fizzle asked.

"The *Annihilator*," said another goblin, this one with a nose ring.

"Sponsor?" Pozzik queried.

"Griznak," said the nose-ringed goblin.

"Engineer?" Fizzle inquired.

"Mazzer Stripscrew," said a gnome.

"Pilot?" Pozzik demanded.

"Rizzle Brassbolts," said another gnome, one who looked an awful lot like . . .

"Move along," said Fizzle Brassbolts, with a dismissive wave.

Griznak, Stripscrew, and Rizzle then went to stand in front of their yellow-and-black speedboat. And once again, the distinguished goblin moved in to sketch the trio. And once again, Aram marveled at the goblin artist's speed and efficiency.

"Boat?" Fizzle asked.

"*Freebooters' Fire*," said a male troll, wearing a black bicorne hat with a white skull-and-crossbones painted on it.

"Sponsor?" Pozzik queried.

"Admiral Tony Two-Tusk," said the troll pirate.

"Engineer?" Fizzle inquired.

"Jinky Twizzlefixxit," said a petite female gnome.

"Pilot?" Pozzik demanded.

"Rugfizzle," said a well-dressed goblin with a topknot.

"Move along," said Fizzle.

This was the oddest racing team yet. (Almost as odd as *Steamwhistle*'s.) The troll, gnome, and goblin moved in front of their black-and-white speedboat (which also bore the skull-and-crossbones), and again the handsome older goblin went to work on their picture. Aram looked forward to meeting and talking with another artist. His own sketchbook was burning a hole in his pocket, and on the one hand, he was dying to show it to the distinguished goblin. But on the other hand, he was a little bit afraid to show it, too. *What if it's not any good?*

Gazlowe interrupted the boy's growing crisis of confidence by nudging Aram forward.

"Boat?" Fizzle asked.

"The *Steamwhistle*," Gazlowe and Sprocket said in competitive unison. They glared at each other briefly.

"Sponsor?" Pozzik queried.

"Gazlowe," said Gazlowe.

"Engineer?" Fizzle inquired.

"Gimble Sprysprocket," said Sprocket.

"Pilot?" Pozzik demanded.

"Wait," Fizzle said, looking up from the tome to glare at the leper gnome. "You need to be a member in good standing of MEGA to register as an engineer in this race."

"I *am* a member in good standing of MEGA," Sprocket growled.

"Maybe you were once," Fizzle growled back. "But I don't know no leper gnomes that can keep their heads together long enough to—"

Before he could finish the sentence, one of Sprocket's mechanical arms slapped a card down on the wooden table. Fizzle picked it up and studied it. He eyed Sprocket again. "All up to date," Fizzle acknowledged, and held the card out for the mechanical arm to snatch it back. Fizzle wrote *Gimble Sprysprocket* down in the tome.

"Pilot?" Pozzik demanded again.

"Aramar Thorne," whispered Aram.

"What? Speak up, boy."

"Aramar Thorne," Aram said in a fuller voice.

"Move along," said Fizzle Brassbolts, with a dismissive wave.

And move along he did. But not over to the distinguished artist. Suddenly, Murky was standing before him, shouting, "Urum! RRRgrrrs! *Flllurlog!*" A stunned Aram turned and locked eyes with a potbellied ogre he recognized from the arena in Dire Maul. The rotund ogre lifted a ram's horn to his lips, distended his cheeks to an impossible degree, and blew. Seemingly from every side, more ogres rushed toward Aram, Murky, Sprocket, and Gazlowe. So the little murloc did the only thing he could do: he grabbed Aram and pulled him over the side.

Aram hit the water, struggling to swim in the long, hooded cloak. He managed to take a deep breath—just before Murky yanked him down below the surface, *deep* below the surface. Murky pulled Gazlowe's prized spy cloak off his friend and then swam with him underwater toward the yacht—*and under it!*

Aram was pretty desperate for air when Murky finally guided him back toward the surface. Light-headed, Aram cleared the waterline, gasping for breath. *Why am I always on the verge of drowning?!* They had swum to the far side of the yacht and could no longer be seen from the Speedbarge.

Murky said, "Urum mmmm?"

"I'm good," Aram said, breathing hard. "Thank you . . . my frund."

Murky smiled.

*　　*　　*

"You gave me your word you'd keep him safe!" Makasa's voice was low, barely above a whisper, which—if you knew her—was measurably scarier than when she yelled.

Gazlowe didn't know her that well but got the message anyway and backed up a step, saying, "I promised nothin' would happen to him. And nothin' did."

"Nothing?" Her outrage was palpable.

Still not trusting the goblin completely, Makasa had ordered Murky to swim over to the Speedbarge during registration, with instructions to remain in the water, watching for signs of trouble or ogres.

If she hadn't . . .

"Okay," Gazlowe was saying. "So the kid got a little wet. Big deal. *I'm* the one who lost my spy cloak."

Makasa actually started to draw her sword then, but Aram put his hand on hers and stopped her. He turned to Gazlowe and said, "Make it up to us."

The goblin cocked his head, intrigued. "I'm not adverse. Whatcha got in mind?"

"Salvage. Tonight."

"That wasn't the deal, kid."

"His name is Aram," Makasa growled.

"Fine. That wasn't the deal, *Aram*. I help you salvage your father's whatchamacallit *after* the race."

"You have my word I'll still pilot the *Steamwhistle*. I want to. But with those ogres lurking, we're not going to be able to stick around after the race is over. We need to get the crystal tonight."

"Crystal?"

"Never mind," Aram said, kicking himself over the slip. "Are you still not adverse?"

Gazlowe smiled.

Throgg not happy. Throgg say, "Boy gone. Compass gone."

Karrga say, "Boy not gone. Boy in race. Boy race in blue boat-thing. Blue boat-thing with red stripe. Throgg still get boy when boy come to race."

Throgg smile.

Murky was back in the water—this time with Aram's compass—leading the unanchored yacht back to where the crystal shard was trapped. When he signaled they had arrived, Gazlowe broke out two diving suits for Makasa and Aram. They looked a bit like Sprocket's containment suit, but even larger and bulkier, despite having no mechanical appendages. Aram and his sister exchanged nearly identical glances of discomfort.

Gazlowe said, "It's perfectly safe." Makasa frowned, distrusting the goblin more or less on principle now. But she and Aram allowed Gazlowe and two members of his goblin crew to fit them out.

It took time. Aram and Makasa would not be seated (like Sprocket) inside the suits' chest units. There were arm sleeves and gauntlets. Leg sleeves and boots. Chest plates and helmets with a single caged glass panel in front. And all of it required careful fitting to make sure the seals were watertight. Partway through the process, Sprocket joined them. He had made some adjustments to his own containment suit in preparation for the dive.

The last step was attaching long tubes—air hoses—to each of the three divers. The hoses were fastened to a steam pump aboard the yacht, which would pump fresh air to the trio after they hit the water.

Once sealed in, Aram felt like he could barely move. The five clunky steps to the portside rail nearly did him in right there. The suit was so heavy, and movement in it was so awkward, he didn't see how he'd be able to accomplish anything down there. He said as much, but his voice was so muffled behind the glass plate of his helmet that no one could clearly understand what he was saying. Communication was largely limited to flashing a thumbs-up or a thumbs-down.

Looking over the side, Aram saw Murky directly below him. He looked up again to see Gazlowe waving the murloc out of the way. He had to turn his head and shoulders to look to the other side and see Hackle and Drella watching. The dryad was staring at Sprocket with her usual discomfort. The gnoll was shaking his head. Although Aram heard no distinct sounds beyond his own breathing, he imagined he could hear Hackle growling low.

Sprocket went first, demonstrating what he had already told them: that the best way into the water was to face away from it and gently fall backward. He vanished beneath the surface. Makasa immediately followed.

Despite all the piloting Aram had done over the last few days, he still maintained a morbid fear of drowning—but he swallowed hard and leaned back. The weight of the suit tipped him all the way over instantly—and he was in the water. He felt a moment of panic! But he recovered quickly. In fact, the buoyancy of the water seemed to help. Basic movement was no longer such a struggle. He looked over and saw Makasa and Sprocket. Due to the weight of their suits, all three were sinking rapidly. Murky swam around them in fast circles as they descended, with the compass chain wrapped around the top of his head, and the compass itself once again glowing like a third eye on his brow. Sprocket, who had never seen the compass before, stared from inside his suit and reached out a mechanical arm to touch it. Murky slapped the metal hand away with his webbed foot.

Aram's level of anxiety was high. It didn't seem like he was in mortal danger—not as when ogres or skeletons were trying to bash his brains in. On the other hand, everything—the suit, the water—seemed to be crushing in on him, and he could *feel* his heart racing in his chest. But slowly, as he descended, he listened to the regular *inhale* and *exhale* of the air pump, and it calmed him considerably.

In no time at all, they were at the bottom. Murky led the other three over to the pile of stone slabs and pointed out the one they needed to move: it was immense. On land, it would have taken a team of horses to drag it even a foot. But underwater, the four of them just might have a chance.

They set to work. They couldn't lift it but found that by rocking the slab back and forth, they could slowly inch it off the other slab beneath. Aram was nervous that the crystal might get smashed into dust between the two slabs, but the glow from the slab-covered shard continued steadily.

Murky helped Urum, Mrksa, and the strange, sickly gnome-in-a-box to rock the stone back and forth, but he couldn't help thinking he had forgotten something. Just then a small perch swam past, and Murky remembered . . . with the summer sun warming the water, she had been sluggish and lazy and had let him swim by. But now it was night. The water was cool. It was feeding time.

Something grabbed Aram from behind. Grabbed him and shook him violently. Aram had no peripheral vision inside the suit and no idea what was attacking. He struggled to free himself, but he was being shaken so hard, his head was banged around inside his helmet, leaving him stunned. His diving suit's metal reinforcements seemed to be protecting him somewhat, but water was seeping inside the suit from multiple punctures. He caught glimpses of Makasa, Sprocket, and Murky coming to his aid, but he quickly lost sight of all three. Someone screamed and kept screaming. *Who was screaming? And how was he able to hear it?* Suddenly, he realized *he* was the one screaming . . .

Makasa had never seen anything like it. After a moment of stunned horror (and half again as much time to mourn her missing harpoon), she sprang into action, pushing off with her feet and swimming over to free Aram. But Murky intercepted her. Grabbed her hand and pulled her above Aram and the mouth of the creature. He let go of her and slammed both his fists down on the beast's long, flat, squared snout. Makasa got the message and did the same. It didn't seem to have much effect. Then the leper gnome joined them and began slamming his metal mechanical fists down on the creature's snout over and over. Murky and Makasa redoubled their efforts.

Just as he stopped screaming, it was over; Aram was released from the grip of whatever had held him.

He turned in the water and saw what "whatever" was: the biggest fish he'd ever seen in his life, grey and immense, with a mouthful of long knives for teeth. He could hear Greydon's voice in his head, telling him it was a *whale shark*, and he felt like telling his father to *shut up, shut up, shut up! That thing nearly ate me!* The creature was so big, he couldn't take it all in from any one angle . . .

*   *   *

Snack have hard shell. Hard to crack. Bit down, but snack have no taste. No blood. Murloc attack with other snacks. Murloc hit snout. Pain. Snacks hit snout hard, over and over. More pain. Not like this kind of snack. And not that hungry, anyway.

The whale shark turned and swam away into the dark water. With a new urgency, Aram swam back over to the stone slab. He wanted to get the crystal shard fast and get back aboard Gazlowe's yacht faster. Makasa swam to him and held on to his helmet so she could look through her glass and into his, into her brother's eyes. He could feel water slowly seeping into his diving suit, but she seemed unaware of this, so he nodded and gave her a thumbs-up. She looked understandably dubious. But he pointed to the slab, and she and Sprocket and Murky got back into position.

Together, they rocked it back and forth some more. And then Murky vanished from view, popping back up a second later *with the glowing crystal between his claws!*

By the time they surfaced, Makasa could see that Aram's face-plate was a third full of water. It had risen over his mouth, and her brother was struggling to keep his nose from submerging as well. When Gazlowe's crew—straining due to the added weight of the water-filled suit—finally managed to pull the boy out of the lake and dump him roughly onto the deck, everyone could

see half the Shimmering Deep leaking out of multiple puncture holes in Aram's suit.

Gazlowe said, "What happened to my diving suit?! That thing costs, y'know?!"

Makasa was seriously ready to kill the goblin—even as Aram's diving suit drained and his risk of drowning ebbed—but was hampered by her own diving suit. In the time it took for her and Aram to get out of their suits, Makasa had managed to bury her more murderous impulses toward Gazlowe. But everything about the entire day had added to her frustrations. She hadn't been with Aram on the Speedbarge when the ogres attacked. She hadn't known how to save him from the whale shark when it attacked—especially without her harpoon at hand. In both scenarios, she had been completely dependent on Murky. *Murky, of all creatures!!* Sucking on her lower lip, then biting it between her white teeth, she was more determined than ever to regain control over their journey. Only she could truly keep Aramar Thorne safe. She would not, could not continue to depend on others. Period.

Alone in their cabin, the five travelers gathered by candlelight. Gazlowe had sent cookies and milk in a minor attempt to smooth things over. (Belatedly, he had realized that "the kid" had nearly died, *again*, while doing something the goblin had promised was "perfectly safe.") He wanted to keep his pilot happy, and his pilot's sister nonviolent. A midnight snack was the best idea he could come up with.

Aram sat on the floor with the new crystal shard, comparing it to the shard gathered from below Skypeak. The new shard was bigger, almost as long as the boy's pinky finger. Both shards glowed, as did the crystal needle on the compass, which was back around Aram's neck and pulling toward the other two pieces of crystal.

"Stop it," Aram said (having been through this before), and the compass obeyed. Its needle continued to glow and point toward the other shards, but it ceased pulling and yanking on him.

Drella was excited. "It does what you tell it to do!"

"Mostly," Aram said. He was studying the two shards, turning them over and over in either hand.

Drella said, "If all things did what *I* told them to do, I am quite sure the world would be a better place."

Hackle said, "What Drella tell things?"

"Hmmm," she murmured, clearly not having thought that far ahead.

Suddenly, something clicked for Aram. He turned the larger shard over, turned the smaller shard around, and placed them next to each other. They fit together perfectly, their glow increasing in intensity, shining brightly, until . . .

*　　*　　*

Light. All was Light. The Voice of the Light said, "Do you see, Aram? Do you see?"

"All I see is Light," he responded.

"See what brings the Light," said the Voice. "See what makes the Light."

"See your death," said the silhouette of Malus, backlit by something other than the bright white Light. Backlit by red and orange flames.

The Voice said, "Fear him not. You are on your way. Two have become one. Soon Seven will become One."

Malus growled, "One, at least, will never be part of Seven again."

But the Voice of the Light only repeated, "Seven will become One."

Makasa was holding Aram up. "Another vision?" she asked.

"Yeah," he said breathlessly. He held the shards in one hand. Only they weren't *shards* (plural) anymore.

"Learn anything?"

"Yeah." Where the two shards had fit together, there was no longer any sign they had ever been apart; not even a seam was visible. The two were now one (and no longer glowing). Aram said, "I'm constructing something. Or . . . *re*constructing something." He looked up at her. "There are five more pieces. Five more shards."

"Check the compass," she said.

He did. The needle, which had also stopped glowing, was now pointing south. Not southeast anymore. Just south, directly south. He showed her. He showed them all. Then he took out his map of Kalimdor. Gadgetzan was directly south of the Speedbarge. "It still wants us in Gadgetzan," he said.

"Then we leave tomorrow," she said.

"*After* the race." He wanted to be certain she knew he planned to honor that commitment.

"If the ogres have their way, there won't *be* any 'after' to the race."

"Then we'll come up with a plan to make sure there is."

CHAPTER THIRTY

EIGHT LAPS

Eight laps around the Speedbarge. That was all Aram had to do. He had his helmet on already, hoping against hope it would obscure his face and identity, hoping against hope that no ogre would spot or recognize him. But even at his most optimistic, he didn't think that likely.

And he was right.

All eighteen speedboats were lined up for the race. All eighteen pilots had to cross a small gangway to board them. Makasa had asked if Aram could start the race in the boat with the carapace down so that he was never in clear view. But Gazlowe had explained that the gamblers liked to see the pilots walk to their machines, that many a last-minute wager was based on a pilot's swagger.

Aram had said, "I have to swagger?"

Gazlowe had said, "No, boy. Let 'em all think you don't stand a chance. I'll pick up a little extra action that way. So I *want* you to act afraid."

Now, Aram was thinking, *It's no act.*

He crossed the gangway behind a goblin named Juliette, pilot of the purple-and-green *Queen Mae*, and ahead of Razzeric, pilot of the green-and-red *Guzzler*. He found himself strangely unstartled by the sound of the ogres' horn, and surprisingly prepared for the pounding of their fast-approaching footsteps.

He looked up slowly. There was Throgg, at the head of a party of four or five more ogres, loping across the deck of the Speedbarge toward the gangway where Aram stood with the other seventeen pilots.

Fortunately, Gazlowe's preparations, for once, worked like a charm. *Steamwhistle*'s sponsor had persuaded Fizzle and Pozzik that the small troop of ogres prowling about the Speedbarge was intent on disrupting the race. Since that was patently unacceptable, precautions were taken.

Before the ogres could reach the gangway, their path was blocked by Fizzle and Pozzik's Brute Squad, ten enormous purple-skinned hobgoblins, known around the Speedbarge as mooks. Gazlowe had said, "They're dumber than an ogre with a hangover, but they'll do the trick."

The Brute Squad had been given one order: *don't let the ogres anywhere near the pilots.* And the mooks, each armed with a massive warhammer, seemed to have just enough brainpower to follow that order. Maybe.

Aram bit his bottom lip and held his breath . . .

*   *   *

Gazlowe watched the lead ogre pull up short, shoutin' at the mooks to get "out of Throgg's way!" He had a warhammer of his own, screwed onto his right wrist.

The mooks said nothin'. For the first time, Gazlowe noticed that the mooks' two front teeth curled over their lower lips, even when their mouths were closed. Made 'em look like chipmunks. Giant mutated chipmunks. All they were missin' were bushy tails.

Throgg said, "Hobgoblins move, or hobgoblins die."

Behind the ogres, Gazlowe shouted, "They're attackin' the pilots!"

Raphael, a gnome Gazlowe had slipped a couple coppers to, shouted, "The ogres are trying to stop the race!"

That was all it took. The crowd began to turn ugly. Too many people on the Speedbarge had too many coins wagered on the race to risk ogre interference. And many of the biggest spenders had their own bodyguards, as well. This wasn't just a crowd of curious spectators. There were paid mercenaries aboard: worgen and trolls and everything else. Two-Tusk had half his blasted pirate crew on-site.

Pozzik approached Throgg and said, "No one goes near the pilots before the race."

Throgg said, "Throgg not no one. Throgg Throgg."

Pozzik said, "Look around you, Throgg. You think you can take down my mooks, and maybe you can. But can you take down everyone on this barge? Cuz you take one more step, and we'll have a riot on our hands."

Throgg looked ready to risk a riot. But the lone female ogre leaned in and said, "Goblin say ogres no go near pilots before race. What about after?"

Pozzik shrugged. "Who cares about after?"

Gazlowe groaned audibly.

The female ogre whispered somethin' in Throgg's ear. He shook his head violently. She whispered somethin' again. His shoulders sank. He scratched his forehead horn with the edge of his hammer. She whispered somethin' more. He smiled and nodded. The ogres moved off. Throgg was unscrewin' his hammer from his wrist.

So far, so good. Gazlowe turned to watch the start of the race . . .

Breathing hard, Thorne joined Sprocket, who helped him descend and buckle into the *Steamwhistle.* The gnome was about to shut the carapace when Thorne said, "Aren't you going to wish me luck?"

Sprocket stared at the human and said, "You don't need luck. You have my boat." Thinking, *Simpleton!*—but not saying it, since at three whole syllables it would have taken too long—he closed the carapace on the boy.

* * *

Aram guided the boat up to the starting line on the north side of the Speedbarge, between the *Queen Mae* and the *Guzzler*. Daisy, looking lovely from her elevated perch atop a small raised barge, was standing in front of the largest speaking trumpet Aram had ever seen and holding a flag in one hand. With a flourish, she raised the flag high . . . and with another flourish brought it down!

The race was on!

Lap One.

From experience, Aram knew that *Steamwhistle*'s strength was not a fast start. Gunning the engine didn't help. He'd build toward her top speed and keep building.

He took the first quarter turn in the middle of the pack, glad he hadn't begun even farther toward the rear. The four slalom pylons on the eastern side of the Speedbarge were wide apart, and he took them easy, hugged them close, and made up some distance on the leaders, leaving one or two boats in his wake.

Then came the south-side straightaway, which really allowed him to pour it on. He was the stone skipping over Lake Everstill, in the moment, above the fray. (There were no thoughts of ogres or compasses now.) Aramar Thorne was free.

By the time he swerved around the Speedbarge to its western side and began maneuvering through its eight tight slalom pylons, he could see only three or four speedboats ahead of him.

And as the *Steamwhistle* curved back round to the straight-away on the northern side, he sped past the black-and-white *Freebooters' Fire*. *Steamwhistle* came even with Daisy's barge. Aram couldn't make out the barkeep's words over the roar of engines and water, but he spotted her up there, talking through the speaking trumpet . . .

Lap Two.

"Guzzler *is in the lead, followed by* Lightning Fish, Queen Mae, Steamwhistle, *and* Freebooters' Fire.

"*They're taking the first turn and—goodness!* Freebooters' Fire *is living up to its name! It's literally on fire! Burst into flames! It's slowing down, being passed by* Annihilator *and* Swordfish! *They're all holding position through the first slalom and into the second turn.*

"Queen Mae *is challenging* Lightning Fish *on the far straight-away. They're neck and neck for second place behind Razzeric's* Guzzler *into the third turn.*

"Mae *seems to have the advantage on the tight slaloms; yes, she's slipped past* Lightning Fish *for second place, into the fourth turn.*

"*Now, here on the northern straightaway, we have* Guzzler, Queen Mae, Lightning Fish, Steamwhistle, Swordfish, *and* Annihilator, *with* Corkscrew *coming up fast to join the front-runners!*"

* * *

Lap Three.

Gazlowe liked what he saw. Okay, sure, he'd like it better if the kid was in the top three and guaranteed to finish in the money, but fourth wasn't bad with three-quarters of the race still left to run. Plus, he liked that the admiral's boat was already dead in the water, that *Stormwind's Pride* had nothing to be proud of, and that *Kessel's Run* was runnin' dead last and bein' lapped by the frontrunners.

He liked how the kid took the turns, tight and sweet. Liked how his machine was handlin' the slaloms on the east and west sides.

And he liked how it was makin' small gains on the three tubs in the lead durin' *every* straightaway . . .

Lap Four.

"Steamwhistle *is making a move, trying to get out of fourth and right into second by passing* Mae *and* Lightning Fish. *But the other two have* Steamwhistle *boxed out, while* Guzzler *increases her lead on the northern straightaway.*

"At *the turn, it's* Guzzler *in first,* Mae *and* Fish *neck and neck in second again, and* Steamwhistle *still in fourth, putting some distance between those top four and the rest of the pack. In fifth place,* Corkscrew *leads a clump of machines that include* Swordfish, Annihilator, *and* Raptor's Revenge *in sixth, seventh, and eighth.*

"The frontrunners have taken the second turn, lapping five or six also-rans on the southern straightaway.

"Coming out of the third turn, it looks like Raptor's Revenge *is trying to cut off* Annihilator *into the slalom, and—OHHHHH!!!* Raptor's Revenge *has annihilated the* Annihilator, *which has crashed into the first western pylon.* Revenge *is spinning out to avoid the wreckage. Trying to recover . . . It's back in the race! Oh, but it's been passed by both* Pollywog *and* Death-Machine!

"At the halfway point now, it's still Guzzler *in first,* Queen Mae *in second,* Lightning Fish *in third, and* Steamwhistle *in fourth!"*

Lap Five.

Sprocket didn't like what he saw. This was why *he* should have been the pilot. Thorne was too inexperienced. He'd allowed himself to be boxed out of the lead by *Mae* and *Fish*.

The leper gnome watched the boats take the first turn and lost sight of his *Steamwhistle* as it entered the eastern slalom still in fourth. He waited now, struggling to follow Daisy's voice through the speaking trumpet. But between the distortion of the trumpet and that of his own containment suit, he couldn't clearly make out what she was saying, so he turned to the west so he could see the frontrunners as soon as they emerged from the far side of the Speedbarge into view.

Turning, he saw the ogres milling about the dock that would soon act as the winner's circle, where the trophy and the prize money would be handed out. That lead ogre was screwing a pike appliance onto his stump. Sprocket's mouth twitched. He briefly acknowledged to himself that they were there to grab up—and probably kill—Thorne. Well, if the boy didn't take the lead, Sprocket might just kill Thorne himself.

The first boat came into view. *It was blue!* Thorne had done it! No, wait, that wasn't a red stripe. It was gold. *Stormwind's Pride?!* How did *Pride* take the lead? No, no. There was the green *Guzzler* lapping *Pride*. That made more sense. Razzeric's machine was always going to be the one to beat. The one for *Steamwhistle* to beat. If she wasn't *still* stuck behind *Mae* and *Fish*!

Lap Six.

"*Guzzler is out front and increasing her lead.* Queen Mae *and* Lightning Fish *are still vying for second and boxing out* Steamwhistle. *But if one of those second-placers doesn't make a move soon, they're basically giving the race to* Guzzler.

"*At the turn, it looks like* Mae *may have heard me . . . She's making her move on the inside, speeding ahead of* Lightning Fish *for the second time, and—oh, that was the break* Steamwhistle *needed! She's slipped past* Lightning Fish *into third place! She's taking the eastern slalom very tight and is right on* Mae's *tail at the turn!*

"Steamwhistle *has pulled up even with* Queen Mae *on the straightaway, but* Guzzler *is already making the third turn.*

Lightning Fish *is in fourth.* Pollywog *is now in fifth.* Corkscrew *in sixth, with* Raptor's Revenge, Swordfish, *and* Death-Machine *in seventh, eighth, and ninth. That's half the field. The rest of the boats either are no longer running or have been lapped at least once by the frontrunners.*

"*We're on the tight western slalom now, and . . .* Steamwhistle *is running it tighter than* Queen Mae. Steamwhistle*'s pulled into second! But* Guzzler *has a pretty impressive lead at this point.*

"*At the end of lap six, the race's three-quarter mark, it's* Guzzler *in first by four entire lengths,* Steamwhistle *in second, just ahead of* Queen Mae. *Followed by* Pollywog, Lightning Fish, *and* Corkscrew *in fourth, fifth, and sixth.*"

Lap Seven.

Aram's heartbeat was now in perfect synch with the steam pump. He no longer felt like he was piloting the *Steamwhistle*— he felt like he *was* the *Steamwhistle*! He could see the green boat, *Guzzler*, up ahead. Too far up ahead. He opened up the throttle and thought he gained a little before the turn.

Now came the first slalom. He took it so tight and fast, he could literally *hear* the pylons buzz past like hornets.

The southern straightaway. He and she—Aram and *Steamwhistle*—were giving it all they had, and it was paying off. Now, he was *positive* they'd gained on the green. It was looming larger, closer, bellowing dark clouds behind it.

By the end of the second slalom, they were practically riding up the *Guzzler's* stern. That was good—but not good enough.

They took the northern straightaway, drafting in the green boat's slipstream. But drafting wasn't passing. Jumping the lead boat's wake, they still couldn't get around her. *Guzzler* was bigger, had more muscle. Aram knew they'd only get one shot at this . . .

Lap Eight.

"As we go into the final lap, it's Guzzler *in first with* Steamwhistle *right behind in second.* Queen Mae *is three lengths behind them both in third.* Corkscrew *is . . . three more lengths behind* Mae *in fourth, with* Pollywog *and* Lightning Fish *in fifth and sixth. The rest are either out or too far behind to seriously vie for even third prize. They're taking the turn . . .*

*"*Guzzler *has the power, but* Steamwhistle *seems to have the greater maneuverability, using the slaloms to catch up and keep close.* Guzzler *seems to be taking a conservative tack here, using her bulk to keep* Steamwhistle *from passing. That worked for* Mae *and* Lightning Fish*, until they gave the sleek little boat an opening. Will history repeat . . . ? Well, not so far; they've taken the second turn with no change to the standings . . .*

"And the southern straightaway tells the same story. Steamwhistle *cannot get around* Guzzler*. Third turn now . . .*

"Heading into the final slalom of the day, and . . . oh, that doesn't

look good! Big mistake there. Steamwhistle *has gone very wide on the first pylon. Don't see how she can cut in time to make the second—and OHHH, she did it, pulling just inside of* Guzzler. *My friends, that was no mistake of* Steamwhistle's; *that was* strategy! *They are coming out of the slalom with* Steamwhistle *no longer trapped behind* Guzzler *as they head into the final turn and race for the flag . . .*

"Steamwhistle *has cut inside on the turn and has pulled up even! They are neck and neck, heading for the finish line! It's* Guzzler *and* Steamwhistle! *It's* Guzzler *and* Steamwhistle! *It's* Guzzler *and* Steamwhistle! *IT'S* STEAMWHISTLE!!! *THE WINNER IS* STEAMWHISTLE!!!"

Lap Nine.

"Steamwhistle *is taking a well-earned victory lap around the Speedbarge. Yes,* Steamwhistle *has won the Annual Fizzle and Pozzik's Speedbarge Boat Race!* Guzzler *takes second place;* Queen Mae, *third.*

"All three winners are taking a leisurely wind-down spin around the Speedbarge. Let's see. In third place, the Queen Mae *was sponsored by Dracos, engineered by Hildy Bufferpolish, and piloted by the Speedbarge's own Juliette. They'll each take home a nice little purse today.*

"Now, Guzzler *was sponsored, engineered,* and *piloted by Razzeric. You know, folks, even taking second, he may just take*

home more gold than anyone, since he won't have to share! No? Ha-ha! I can hear you from here, Gazlowe!

"*That's right.* Steamwhistle*'s sponsor, Gazlowe, is telling me I'm not taking the wagering into account. True. True. Where was I? Oh, yes.* Steamwhistle *was engineered by Gimble Sprysprocket, known as Sprocket to his friends. And her pilot is the amazing Aramar Thorne.*

"*And here comes Aramar and the* Steamwhistle *now . . .*"

The *Steamwhistle* cut its engines and glided up to the winner's circle. Almost before it had come to a stop, Throgg and Karrga were there, with Guz'luk, Slepgar, and the Beard Brothers watching their backs for hobgoblins.

Throgg's pike-hand stabbed into the carapace (and Sprocket shouted in horror, almost as if the pike had stabbed into his chest). The spiked carapace was ripped free and flung away, exposing the helmeted individual inside. With his left hand, Throgg yanked the young speedboat pilot out of the cockpit by the scruff of his neck, growling into his terrified face, "Now, Aramar Thorne belong to Throgg . . ."

PART THREE:

SURVIVING TANARIS

CHAPTER THIRTY-ONE
LAP NINE

Long-Beard lean in over shoulder of Throgg and say, "Aramar Thorne not what Long-Beard expect." Short-Beard whap his brother on nose.

Lap nine was the key. Lap nine and the amazingly brave little Hotfix.

It had all been planned in advance, of course. But no one made Hotfix volunteer. That he did on his own—even against Daisy's wishes (though she was prepared to do her part, as well).

Gazlowe cooperated, too—on the prior condition that Aram actually win the race.

So before dawn, Makasa, Drella, and Hackle hid under blankets in Rendow's boat, while Murky swam beneath the surface, slowly towing it around the Speedbarge to the southern end.

Hotfix, meanwhile, was keeping a close eye on the ogres. Days before, Gordok's Elite had failed to follow Daisy and Hotfix without being noticed, but it was quite literally child's play for Hotfix to follow them without even one of the massive creatures having a clue. Once he confirmed that they were all gathered on the northern side of the Speedbarge to keep an eye on *Steamwhistle* before the race, Hotfix raced to the southern side, where he leapt aboard Rendow's boat before it even had time to dock. It docked anyway, however, to pick up Pozzik, who had been paid a quite handsome sum by Gazlowe to come aboard.

Of course, there was always the chance that one or more of the ogres might head south during the competition, but Daisy kept an eye on them and was ready to slip a warning—the code word *gigantic*—into her duties as race caller, using the speaking trumpet to be heard over the din of the crowd and the engines. Fortunately, it never became necessary, as the ogres all stayed on the north side.

Next, Aram did his part by winning . . . and by taking that victory lap. When he pulled around to the south side of the Speedbarge and came even with Rendow's boat, he slowed down and popped the carapace open. Makasa threw him a line, and soon *Steamwhistle* and the rowboat were side by side so that Aram and Hotfix could trade places.

That was why Gazlowe had paid Pozzik to be there: to authenticate that the registered pilot of the *Steamwhistle* had, in fact, finished the race and had not exited the boat until *after* the eighth lap was complete. (Gazlowe had no problem with Aram escaping with his life—as long as it didn't disqualify Gazlowe's boat from taking home the prize money.)

The switch took a little time, but Daisy kept her banter going to distract anyone from noticing *just* how long that ninth lap was taking. Hotfix untied the rope and put on Aram's helmet, which was way too big for the little goblin's head but not quite wide enough for his long ears, which were uncomfortably pressed down against his cheeks. Still, without complaint, he closed the carapace and piloted the boat back around to the north side.

He pulled up to the dock, to the winner's circle, where Throgg rather kindly "helped" him out of *Steamwhistle.*

Two very separate protests were lodged.

For starters, the ogres seemed rather unhappy that the pilot was a goblin and not Aramar Thorne. Throgg clumsily tore off Hotfix's tunic looking for the compass, as if the goblin boy and the human boy might have traded more than places. Finding no compass, there was a moment when it seemed likely the ogre might squish little Hotfix like a grape. But the goblin bit Throgg unexpectedly. Throgg dropped Hotfix, who fell into the water and vanished below it. At this point, Throgg and his companions grew quite angry and started smashing things and hitting mooks. The mooks hit back, until both sides were bruised, bloody, and breathing hard—and actually a bit happier for having had the opportunity to blow off a little steam.

Meanwhile, Razzeric led a long line of pilots and sponsors to protest the results of the race with Fizzle, claiming that *Steamwhistle* should be disqualified for switching pilots. But Pozzik soon arrived, having been dropped back off at the southern dock, to confirm the switch hadn't happened until after the race was over.

Gazlowe looked quite proud of himself.

Now, the pilot's share was a fraction of what Sprocket made as engineer (an amount increased by fifty pieces of silver, since the leper gnome had won his bet with Gazlowe). And Sprocket's share was a fraction of what Gazlowe himself made as the *Steamwhistle*'s sponsor, which in turn was a fraction of what the goblin made betting on his team. Nevertheless, Gazlowe dutifully collected Aram's little share of the prize. From that amount, the goblin then subtracted the fee he paid Pozzik, the full replacement value of Rendow's boat, the money Makasa owed to Daisy, and the price of repairing *Steamwhistle*'s carapace (not to mention—because he *didn't* mention it—the cost of fixing the punctured diving suit Aram had worn the night before). Yet, even after extracting those expenses, Gazlowe still had nine gold coins, fifty silver, and twelve copper, which he was keeping in trust for the boy—with the promise that he would sail his yacht to Gadgetzan the day after the race and meet the travelers there . . .

As for Aramar Thorne, Makasa Flintwill, Hackle, Murky, and Taryndrella, they were all back on Rendow's boat, following the compass south toward Gadgetzan . . .

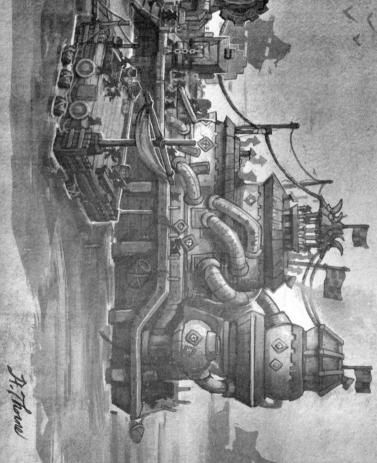

Fizzle and Pozzik's Speedbarge

*　　*　　*

It had been a warm day on the water. Aram had again spent most of it sketching. He had begun by drawing the receding Speedbarge horizontally across the page. When he finished, he tried to draw the Brute Squad from memory, but as he outlined the silhouette of the first hobgoblin, another impulse pushed his coal pencil another way. Before he even really knew what he was drawing, he had finished. It was an image from his dream, his nightmare: the silhouette of Malus blocking Aram's path to the Light. He looked at it, shuddered, and put his sketchbook away.

Now, Aram yawned, stretched, and took out his map of Kalimdor. He stared at it. Squinched his eyes shut and stared some more. He felt like an idiot. He swallowed hard, cleared his throat, and said, "We need to turn to the east."

"What? Why?" Makasa said. "You said Gadgetzan's directly south."

"It is. But it's not on the coast."

"It is. It's a port city."

"It's on the coast of the sea. Not on the coast of this lake. We need to sail east to get through the break in the seawall. Then we head south and southwest along the outer coastline to Gadgetzan. Otherwise, we'd have to cover the last leg across a mountain pass . . ."

Makasa's eyes burned through him. "And risk leaving a trail for the ogres to follow. Show me."

He had to climb over Murky, Drella, and the rowing Hackle to get to her. He showed her the map.

"We've already overshot the seawall gap. You could have mentioned this before," she said bitterly.

"I—I should have noticed it before," he said, embarrassed.

"Ships to east," Hackle said, "heading this way." He pointed.

They looked up. There were three ships on parallel courses, heading more or less in their direction. In the fading sun, the ships' sails looked red as blood.

"Bloodsails," Makasa growled.

Aram looked again. It wasn't a trick of the light. The three ships' sails *were* red as blood.

"We can't go east," she said. "In fact, your mistake may have saved us."

"But—"

"Those are Bloodsail Buccaneer ships," she said. "Pirates."

Aram had heard of the Bloodsail Buccaneers. His father had called them the most notorious, bloodthirsty pirates on the seas.

Makasa turned the rudder until the boat was heading west. She glanced down at the map, still open on Aram's lap. She said, "The Bloodsails appear to be headed southwesterly, probably looking to land here, at the mountain pass that leads straight to Gadgetzan. So we'll make landfall in Tanaris, here." She pointed to a spot on the map—on the western coast of the Shimmering

Deep. "As far away from those ships as we can get. We'll cross to Gadgetzan over land."

Aram studied the map and said, "That'll add days to the journey . . ."

"There's no remedy," she said sharply. "Row, Hackle."

Hackle was already rowing, but he redoubled his efforts obediently.

Drella said, "You really seem to dislike these Bloodsail people."

"They're not people," Makasa whispered. "They're murderers."

Something about the way she said "murderers" caught Aram's attention. He looked up at her, looked into her eyes, and somehow, *somehow*, he knew. "Your brothers," he said.

She nodded.

"Can you tell me?"

She was silent for a time. Then she nodded again . . .

CHAPTER THIRTY-TWO
BABY GIRL PIRATE

Makasa Flintwill was the fourth child of Marjani Flintwill, captain of the pirate ship *Makemba*. Captain Flintwill was tough and independent and not a little bit deadly, whether armed with cutlass, harpoon, iron chain, or her bare hands. Her four children—Adashe, Akashinga, Amahle, and Makasa—had four different fathers . . . or more accurately had no fathers whatsoever. Marjani was mother *and* father to them all.

The *Makemba* operated out of Booty Bay as part of the Blackwater Raiders' fleet, and Makasa grew up to know that port like the back of her hand. However, Makasa and her three older brothers were raised not onshore but aboard ship, to the life of a pirate. Their mother was not a woman to knit sweaters or bake pies. She was tougher on her spawn than a hundred Greydon Thornes. The four children rose at dawn, worked their ship, and learned to fight, almost before they could walk or talk. Marjani was capable of tenderness. But only at the end of a good day and only if her children pleased her well.

Adashe was the oldest. He was handsome and smart, and he was being groomed to become a Blackwater captain in his own right. Makasa admired him, but he was so far above her star that she rarely spent time with him.

Akashinga was Makasa's favorite. Though second-born, he was the tallest of the three brothers. When Makasa was little, she'd beg to ride upon his shoulders. She would pretend he was the mast and his shoulders were the crow's nest, and she'd call out, "Land ho!" or "A ship to plunder!" until her mother yelled at her to hold her tongue.

Amahle was only two years older than Makasa, and they fought like Alliance and Horde. Strong as an ox, he'd hold her down and tickle her until finally she willed herself not to be ticklish anymore. This came as a great shock to all three brothers. Makasa believed that Adashe and Akashinga never forgave Amahle for eliminating that particular form of torture through overuse.

And Makasa was the baby. The baby and the only girl. Marjani Flintwill was particularly tough on her daughter, but every member of *Makemba*'s crew knew this was only because the captain saw herself in her youngest. And not simply because Makasa looked like a miniature version of her mother. No, there was a steel to the child that matched Marjani's. If anything, little

Makasa was even tougher and less forgiving than Captain Flintwill. Marjani thought that someday Makasa might rule the Blackwater Raiders and, with them, every sea and port in Azeroth.

The Blackwater Raiders were pirates, thieves, and warriors. But they were *not* murderers. If a ship surrendered, they'd raid its stores—taking absolutely anything of value—but they'd leave its crew and passengers unharmed and their vessel as undamaged as possible. Some called this a matter of honor. Marjani Flintwill believed it a matter of practicality: "If you burn a ship and kill its crew, that's one less ship and one less crew to steal from the next time. Besides, a crew tends not to surrender if it knows the only reward for such cowardice is death."

The Bloodsail Buccaneers took the opposite approach. No one survived a Bloodsail attack. So they were without a doubt more feared, but they were also without a doubt less wealthy. This engendered some frustration and envy toward the Blackwater on the part of the Bloodsails. Thus, there was no love lost between Buccaneers and Raiders.

By the time Makasa turned fifteen, she was already five foot nine. She had been taught to fight by her mother and brothers and the rest of *Makemba*'s crew. She could and did hold her own on raids of many a merchant vessel. She had taken lives—but only when necessary (by the lights of the Blackwater code). She took no joy in killing. But she wasn't shy about it, either. It was said, "She doesn't have Adashe's smarts or Akashinga's size or Amahle's strength. But she's swifter and thus deadlier than all three of them put together."

Adashe Flintwill had finally earned his captaincy. Blackwater Fleet Master Seahorn himself presented Adashe with the *Sea King*. Many volunteered to join his crew. And the tauren Seahorn assigned the new Captain Flintwill his first mate: a worgen from Gilneas—a former Brashtide pirate—known as Silent Joe Barker. Adashe accepted Barker, of course, but his priority was to choose three he knew would be both competent and unquestioningly loyal: Akashinga as second mate, Amahle as third mate, and Makasa Flintwill as ship's lookout. If it bothered Marjani to lose all four of her children from her own crew, she gave no indication. In fact, she simply shrugged and said, "I can always make more."

Still, upon their departure, she kissed each on the forehead, wishing them "calm seas and rich pickings." It was the last time she'd see any of them again.

Only a few weeks into its first voyage, the *Sea King* had just completed the successful plunder of the merchant ship *Winter's Knot*—with no casualties on either side—and once the *Knot* had been sent on its way, the crew of the *King* was partaking of the three barrels of Lordaeron wine they'd taken aboard. Makasa Flintwill knew she should be back in the crow's nest, but Second

Mate Akashinga Flintwill urged her to enjoy herself. She looked to her captain, who winked at her, and even Third Mate Amahle Flintwill said, "Stay." (First Mate Silent Joe said nothing.) So Makasa lingered . . . *fatally*.

Two Bloodsail ships, the *Orca* and the *Killmonger*, were upon them with little warning. They boarded from both sides, and within minutes had the semi-drunken crew of the *Sea King* dead or in chains. The captain, his three mates, and his lookout were among the latter group.

By this time, the *Orca* had sailed off with its share, and Captain Flintwill was on his knees before *Killmonger*'s Captain Ironpatch. The huge orc had a long, scraggly black beard, pointed ears, long lower tusks, and, of course, an iron eyepatch over his right eye. He also carried the biggest sword Makasa had ever seen. He held the tip of his blade beneath Adashe's chin, used it to lift that chin up. Adashe matched his glare but spoke no words of defiance. There wasn't time. Ironpatch had Adashe Flintwill's head off before Makasa's eldest brother could speak.

Makasa bit her lip until it bled, but Akashinga and Amahle—despite their chains—rose up and rushed the orc. It so caught *Killmonger*'s captain by surprise, they were able to knock him to the deck. Akashinga's size and Amahle's strength were something to behold. They had their chains pressed to his neck and were choking the life out of him. But he was hardly the only Buccaneer aboard. Within seconds, they had been pulled off by half *Killmonger*'s crew (and it took half its crew to manage it). Within minutes, Captain Ironpatch was back on his feet and plunging his giant sword through both brothers' chests.

The surviving crew of the *Sea King* shook their heads at the waste of effort—if not the waste of life. But it hadn't been a waste. The altercation had created its own distractions . . .

Ironpatch scanned the chained saltbeards before him, and his single eye alighted on Makasa. Perhaps he saw the dangerous hatred in *her* two eyes and decided he couldn't risk leaving her alive for one more second. Perhaps he simply noticed the family resemblance between her and the three men he had already dispatched. Or perhaps it was merely a whim, her turn to die. In any case, he next raised his sword high, as if he would split her right down the middle. But he never got the chance.

Greydon Thorne parried aside that killing blow with nothing but his cutlass.

The crew of the *Wavestrider* had snuck aboard in silence. When asked later why he had intervened in a conflict between pirate and pirate, Captain Thorne would shrug and say, "I'd witnessed the attack through my periscope. It had been two ships against one. Didn't seem quite fair, so I decided to even the odds." His crew had boarded and secured the *Killmonger* first, where only a skeleton crew remained. But now, on the deck of the *Sea King*, they had a real fight on their hands.

The first order of business was to get some help, which meant freeing *Sea King*'s chained crew. This was done by the dwarf Durgan One-God and the human Mary Brown. As soon as his heavy chains were shed, Silent Joe likewise shed his human form. Within seconds, he had transformed into the wolflike worgen beast and was slashing his way through the Bloodsail crew like sheep brought to slaughter.

But he was nothing compared to Makasa. Unchained but weaponless, she snapped the neck of a Buccaneer, took his axe, and went to work. And bloody work it was. Her goal was the orc captain, who was busy going toe to toe with Greydon Thorne, a clear master of the cutlass. She couldn't get to them through the mass of combatants, but she did manage to get her hands on her eldest brother's iron harpoon. She took aim and threw . . .

The harpoon pierced Ironpatch in the chest. The orc fell backward over the rail and plunged into the sea, never to surface again.

With their captain gone, *Killmonger*'s crew was soon finished.

The spoils of both boats now belonged to *Wavestrider*'s captain. But Greydon Thorne would have none of it. "I'm no pirate," he said.

"Then take me," Makasa Flintwill replied. "You saved my life. I offer it to you now as a life debt."

"And the offer is appreciated. But I require no life debt from you, girl."

Silent Joe, in human form again, cleared his throat and growled, "It is the custom of her people. You cannot refuse."

Thorne had looked around then. He had lost his second and third mates in the battle. And he had seen how the worgen and the teenage girl had fought. He conferred briefly with One-God, then said to Joe, "I will take her on as ship's third mate, if you will join my crew as second."

Joe scowled, mostly because he knew he was going to have to speak yet again. He said, "I was first mate aboard this ship and failed my captain. I do not deserve to be second mate aboard yours. But she is Makasa Flintwill, daughter of Captain Marjani Flintwill, sister of Captain Adashe Flintwill. She will be your second mate. And if you take her as such, I will be your third."

It was agreed.

Sea King's quartermaster, O'Ryen Jones, took command of the *Killmonger*. Boatswain Enric Torque took command of the *King*. With skeleton crews aboard each, they'd limp back to Booty Bay and get word to Seahorn and Captain Marjani Flintwill—*after* Adashe, Akashinga, Amahle, and the rest were buried at sea.

From the deck of *Wavestrider*, Makasa stood between Joe and One-God, watching her life as a pirate sail away, as minutes earlier she had watched her family sink into the deep. She was too hard, too flinty, to cry. But when Captain Thorne had come up behind her and put a hand on her shoulder, she came very, very close.

He said, "Come to my cabin, Second Mate, and tell me of your life."

And she had. And he listened. And he offered her words of comfort. And for the first time—and from that point on—Makasa Flintwill knew the love of a father. That is, until Malus and *his* crew had taken Greydon Thorne from both his children.

Now, she ran from the Bloodsails, as fast as Hackle could row. A part of her would have loved nothing more than to turn Rendow's boat around and row *toward* the pirates, sneak aboard each and every ship and take vengeance on their crews for the deaths of her brothers—no matter the consequences to her own life and limb. But her care for her *new* brother instructed her to take a different course. So she kept her eyes facing west. They'd sneak away and land ashore. It would be a longer trek to Gadgetzan, but a safer one.

Aram was quiet. Hackle was quiet. Even Murky and Drella were quiet.

Makasa had held Aram's eyes throughout her tale. Now she looked away. But careful to block the others' view with his body, Aramar Thorne took his sister's hand and gave it a little squeeze. She squeezed his back, offered him up a sad smile . . . and exhaled, as if for the first time in years.

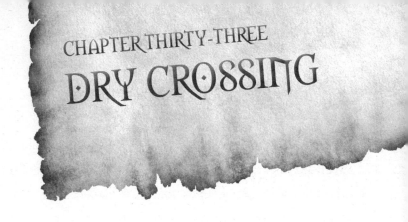

CHAPTER THIRTY-THREE
DRY CROSSING

They came ashore on the far western edge of the Shimmering Deep. Rendow's boat had served them well, and Aram walked away from it with some regret. Rendow herself would get a *new* boat from Daisy, paid for by Gazlowe out of Aram's share of the Boat Race purse. But Aram had a certain sentimental attachment to things and worried the kaldorei would not be happy that she wasn't getting her own boat back.

There was no remedy for it, however, and they left the sturdy craft behind to walk up into the mountains bordering the desert of Tanaris. It took the rest of the day to reach the summit.

They made camp and even risked a cooking fire. They had plenty of food stores (and other supplies provided—at a cost—by Gazlowe) in Hackle's leather pack, but water was becoming a problem. They had left the Speedbarge with two full canteens, and Drella had somewhat miraculously homed in on a tiny spring at the foot of the mountains, where they refilled them.

But since beginning their climb, they'd found nothing but dry streambeds. Even the dryad sensed naught. They rationed what they had.

Sitting round the fire, Aram was thirsty but knew better than to complain. Makasa and Hackle said nothing, of course. Even Murky held his tongue, though Aram guessed that their amphibious companion was probably suffering more than any of them.

Drella said, "I am very thirsty, Aram. Thirsty down to my roots. May I please have another sip of water?"

Aram handed her a canteen. Makasa warned the dryad not to drink too much, while—to Aram's mild surprise—handing the other canteen to the parched murloc.

Murky shook his head. "Nk mllgggrrrr," he said, which Drella translated as, "Not thirsty."

Makasa scowled and said, "It won't do any of us any good if you collapse on us, murloc. Take a drink."

He nodded and breathed out a single, "Mmrgl."

He took a swig, and she urgently barked, *"Not too much!"*

Aram smiled and pulled out his sketchbook. He attempted to draw Rendow from memory. It came out all right.

Before dawn the next morning, hoping to beat the heat, they broke camp and continued their trek across the mountains. They did not beat the heat by much. In fact, the heat soon caught up and overcame them mightily.

Still no water.

The path beneath their feet was dry and cracked. Aram's throat felt likewise.

Ultimately, Makasa decided to stop. "Sleep now—or rest, at least," she said. "I'll take the first watch. When the sun goes down, we're on the move again."

Thinking he wouldn't be able to sleep, Aram sat in the minimal shade afforded by a rock and started to draw Freewind Post from memory. But the oppressive heat began to work on him. He couldn't hold the pencil straight, gave up, and turned over . . .

The Voice of the Light whispered that Aram was getting closer.

Aram whispered back that he was thirsty.

The silhouette of Malus chuckled and said quite clearly, "They'll find your parched bones in the desert."

Aram said, "Who'll find them?"

This seemed to stump Malus, and Aram laughed . . .

He woke up coughing.

Night fell. They started out again beneath the White Lady in profile. It was definitely cooler. Aram was still thirsty and imagined that Drella and Murky were thirstier still. But the crisp night air made the crossing easier. Traveling at night like this, maybe it wouldn't be so bad.

*　　*　　*

But come morning, it looked pretty bad.

When the sun rose, it shone down on a vast expanse of desert to the east. (It looked much vaster now, in any case, than it had on the map.) They'd have to cross that desert to reach Gadgetzan.

"We will definitely need more water," Makasa said.

Drella, for once, said nothing. She looked around, then closed her eyes and reached out with her dryad senses—or whatever they were—and found nothing. She shook her head.

Hackle panted, tongue hanging out of his mouth.

Murky tried to suppress a moan.

Aram said, "Let's look for some shade."

They continued on, and the path began to slope back downhill. Before they spotted any shade, they spotted structures, buildings—*a village* surrounded by sandstone walls—at the foot of the mountains, half a day's walk away.

Aram said, "The village must have a water source."

"Yes," Makasa said hesitatingly. "But whose village is it? And will they be friends or foes?" Her dark tone made it fairly clear which she thought likely.

Aram racked his brain, trying to remember whether the answer existed among the many lessons his father had tried to teach him aboard *Wavestrider.* Perhaps it was the heat, already soaring under the morning sun, but he was drawing a blank.

Drella stated the obvious. "We cannot cross this desert without water."

Makasa nodded, saying, "But we approach with caution."

They didn't wait for nightfall but continued their descent.

By late afternoon, they were at the base of the mountain. They hid behind some rocks and stared toward the village. Aram pulled out his map. He thought the village might be Zul'Farrak, though the map made Zul'Farrak look like a huge city, and this wasn't that. At least, not anymore. No inhabitants came into view, and he wondered if the place was as deserted as the rest of the landscape. Zul'Farrak, he now remembered from Greydon's lessons, was home to the Sandfury trolls. Aram recalled with clarity the Sandfury troll with the orange-gold skin who was among Malus's crew. She'd killed Thom Frakes and Thalyss Greyoak both. He whispered, "Maybe we *should* go around it."

"We're not going anywhere," Makasa whispered back, "until nightfall."

At sundown, Aram finally spotted some movement. He looked to his left . . . and saw three giant turtles—desert tortoises, most likely—crossing the sand. He watched them saunter past the village. He smiled. When he and Makasa were lost at sea aboard *Wavestrider*'s dinghy, giant sea turtles had helped guide them to shore. He thought, *They're my lucky charms!*

He said, "I think the village is deserted. We can risk checking for water."

Makasa said, "If it's deserted, it's probably because there is no water anymore."

Drella said, "There is water. I feel it."

Murky's cracked voice said, "Mrgle, mrgle," though it might have only been wishful thinking on his part.

"All right," Makasa said. "We'll check it out. Once it's dark."

It never got all that dark. The White Lady was still only at half strength. But on this cloudless night, she shone down brightly on the village sandstones. "This is as dark as it's likely to get," Makasa said. "Let's move. Carefully."

She led the way. Hackle took the rear. Everyone had his or her weapons out and at the ready, except the unarmed Drella.

It didn't matter.

They cautiously entered the walled village through its lone gate. Aram barely had time to register a cold central firepit and a few sandstone huts before a voice said, "Oh, my loa gonna be likin' dese treats, brudda."

They were completely surrounded by two dozen adult trolls, all heavily armed with short swords, long spears, or crossbows. Makasa reached for her chain, but a female troll, backed by twin ogres, aimed her own crossbow between Makasa's eyes. Aram could barely breathe. There she was. Thalyss's killer. Malus's troll. *And because of those stupid tortoises, I convinced Makasa to lead us right into the troll's hands!* Her breastplate shimmied, and Aram realized that what he had taken at first to be armor plating was actually some kind of living creature.

The troll poked the air with her crossbow and said, "I not be likely ta miss you from here, sista."

"I'm not your sister," Makasa said darkly. But she lowered her hand from the iron chain's clasp.

"No," said the troll. "You be my sacrifice ta da loa. You *all* be dat. Right, Chief?"

"Ya, Sista Zathra," said a huge male troll with dark skin and a ponytail. His face was painted white. He turned to the travelers and said, "I be Ukorz Sandscalp. *Chief* Ukorz Sandscalp. And y'be prey for Eraka no Kimbul, morsels for Elortha no Shadra, an' subjects ta Ueetay no Mueh'zala. Y'belong ta da loa now."

"Dat true," said Zathra. "But first . . ." Keeping her crossbow aimed at Makasa, she approached Aram and—without looking—reached her dry hand under his shirt, pulled out the compass, and yanked its chain from his neck.

She held it up. The White Lady's light glinted off its brass case. "It be over, brudda. Over an' done."

CHAPTER THIRTY-FOUR
WHISPERING SANDS

In a procession a torches, dey marched dem sacrifices west 'cross da sands from da old village ta da older, sacred city. Zathra thought, *Been too long since dis one seen Zul'Farrak.* Her ancestors were buried here. Grandmutha afta grandmutha afta grandmutha. An' her own mutha, too. Dat was when she left. Dat was da last time she was here. When her mutha died, Zathra had left ta make her way.

Now she returnin' in triumph. Wid dem ogre bruddas flankin' her, Zathra passed tru da first gates and unda da holy arch.

Zathra had da compass in her grip, right in her hand, wid da chain wrapped twice round her wrist. She knew she and dem ogres should be takin' da ting ta Gadgetzan and takin' it now. Malus was waitin' on it and waitin' hard. She knew dat.

But Chief Ukorz Sandscalp was doin' *his* ting tonight. Zathra done served up dese sacrifices on a platter fo' da chief. Dere gonna be gratitude fo' dat, fo' sure. Whispers 'mong da udder trolls told her as much. Hadn't been a sacrifice in four times four moons. But tonight, a few drops a blood at midnight when da White Lady was right above dem all, an' da loa, her loa, would almost certainly appear. She longed ta see 'em, too. Eraka no Kimbul, God a Tigers, Lord a Beasts, King a Cats, Prey's Doom. Elortha no Shadra, God a Spiders, Mother a Venom, Death's Love. An' most of all, Ueetay no Mueh'zala, Father a Sleep, Son a Time, Night's Friend, God a Death.

Was it hunger, too, dat kept her dere? Fine. Maybe. Da loa gonna take da sacrifices' blood fo' sure. Da blood an' some meat. But dem loa fill up easy; dem loa generous ta her people. Wid five sacrifices, dere'd be leftovas aplenty. And after da loa and Ukorz, she'd be gettin' da first share. Prime cuts, fo' sure.

So as dey walked 'em tru da second arch, an' da third, an' da fourth, she found herself runnin' her reasonin' tru her mind once again: *Where be da harm, Zathra? One more night. Ol' Malus'll never know. He be glad ta get da compass at all. Be givin' me a bonus a gold for it. One more night. Twelve more hours. Dat's all. Stay.*

So she stayed.

She left Ro'kull and Ro'jak outside da last arch. No ogres—none dat were not sacrifices, anyway—allowed at da sacred ceremony. Den dey all—trolls an' sacrifices—climbed da long sandstone stairs a da pyramid a da sacred city. Da pyramid a Zul'Farrak. When she was but a little sista, too little ta be allowed at da ceremonies, she thought da pyramid must stretch all da way ta da clouds. Even now, she could feel da strength a da Sandfury trolls dat built da ting in every step she took. It felt good walkin' up dem sandstone stairs. It been too long.

Sandscalp's retainers piled da weapons a da sacrifices togedder in front a da sacred fire: a shield, a couple swords, a club, a hatchet, da human woman's iron chain, even da murloc's tiny spear. Dey not gonna be needin' dem weapons anymore, but dey'd be buried in da sandpit wid deir skulls, outta respect for da sacrifice a da sacrifices.

Dere was a bit a shovin' ta get dem all in just da right spot. Ta line dem sacrifices up right where da Lady'd shine down on 'em clean, lightin' dem up for da loa ta find 'em. After dat, da loa not gonna be needin' no light for what followed. Now, all dat remained was da waitin'. Zathra's mouth was waterin'; she could almost taste da blood.

They waited.

Aram couldn't believe it was ending this way. Blood sacrifices to the gods of the trolls? After all they'd been through?

There were bloodstains on the stones, some dark, some faded. Scratch marks, too. Scratches of desperation, of humans and others dragged away against their will. And great claw marks in the solid stone made by whatever had done the dragging. Sand had been scattered across those stones to soak up that blood, to fill in those scratches.

Zathra, Ró'jak, and Ró'kull

Aram's mouth was dry as sand. He was afraid. When the ogres had taken him to Dire Maul, he had not been this afraid because Makasa had remained free to save him.

He kept looking over at Makasa now, and he could see her turning the problem over and over in her mind. Waiting for her moment. Waiting for her chance. But logically he knew that moment wouldn't come. That chance wouldn't appear. Her weapons were tantalizingly close. Twenty paces wasn't far when compared to the distance they had already covered. And yet those twenty paces might as well have been twenty leagues. There were probably fifty armed trolls atop that pyramid with them. And easily a hundred more on the stone steps. Probably twice that many at the pyramid's base. Zul'Farrak—for now they must certainly be in Zul'Farrak—had emptied through that final arch to witness their end.

The trolls had lined them up. Makasa was on one end. Hackle next to her. Drella in the middle. Then Murky. And Aram at the other end. He had brought them all here to their deaths. He had failed Hackle and Murky, who had followed him out of loyalty. He had failed Taryndrella and had thus failed Thalyss. He had lost the compass and failed his father, as well. And Makasa? He had urged her into the village. *Stupid turtles! Stupid Aram!* He had failed them all.

He looked at his companions. Hackle's shoulders were straight, his head lowered slightly, the gnoll ready to pounce, to attack, or maybe just ready to die with honor. Drella, no surprise, seemed more curious than frightened. Aram was unclear if either she or Murky truly understood what they now faced. Murky's big eyes glanced back and forth between Aram and Makasa, waiting for one or the other to issue a command. But no command was forthcoming.

At midnight, with the moon directly above them, the troll chief approached Makasa with a wavy ceremonial dagger. He grabbed her arm roughly, perhaps expecting resistance. But the sister of Captain Adashe Flintwill would not lower herself to a feeble show of cowardice. Sandscalp cut her—barely nicked her, really—on the palm of her left hand. She didn't even flinch. He held her hand out, palm down. A few drops of blood dripped into the scattered sand.

He moved on to Hackle and repeated the process. Hackle also didn't flinch. Aram hoped he could be as brave.

Chief Sandscalp moved on to Drella, who smiled at him. When he pricked her hand, she cried out, "Ow! I do not like that at all! This is no longer amusing." Ignoring her, the troll let the drops of her blood fall and moved on . . .

Murky hissed when cut but was otherwise as brave as Hackle and Makasa.

When it was Aram's turn, he felt the sting of the blade, but it wasn't bad. He'd pricked himself worse on his mother's sewing needle. He guessed it wasn't hard to be brave for this part. But he knew staying brave through what was to follow would be much more difficult.

Ukorz Sandscalp began chanting in the language of the trolls. Aram didn't understand, but heard the names of the trolls' loa repeated over and over: Eraka no Kimbul, Elortha no Shadra, Ueetay no Mueh'zala.

"Eraka no Kimbul, Elortha no Shadra, Ueetay no Mueh'zala. Eraka no Kimbul, Elortha no Shadra, Ueetay no Mueh'zala. Eraka no Kimbul, Elortha no Shadra, Ueetay no Mueh'zala."

Soon Malus's troll, whose name appeared to be Zathra, joined in. "Eraka no Kimbul, Elortha no Shadra, Ueetay no Mueh'zala. Eraka no Kimbul, Elortha no Shadra, Ueetay no Mueh'zala. Eraka no Kimbul, Elortha no Shadra, Ueetay no Mueh'zala."

Soon all the trolls were chanting, "Eraka no Kimbul, Elortha no Shadra, Ueetay no Mueh'zala. Eraka no Kimbul, Elortha no Shadra, Ueetay no Mueh'zala. Eraka no Kimbul, Elortha no Shadra, Ueetay no Mueh'zala."

The moonlight faded away. Aram looked up. He could no longer see the White Lady or any of the stars. Yet he saw no clouds covering her or them. There was only darkness. And the torches? They still burned, but they burned low. Shadows seemed to spread across the sand like oil, dyeing it black, and out of this black sand rose three black forms, amorphous and pulsing. The trolls fell silent and bowed before their loa.

The loa didn't speak, and yet words were somehow formed. Aram could hear them, like sand blowing across the desert of his suddenly vacant and terrified mind. The words were ancient names, *Eraka no Kimbul, Elortha no Shadra, Ueetay no Mueh'zala*, and the names contained something more: *a promise of blood and meat.*

The first loa stepped forward, and his form began to take shape. It was a jungle cat, massive and muscular, black with even blacker stripes. The whispering sand called him *Eraka no Kimbul, God of Tigers, Lord of Beasts, King of Cats, Prey's Doom.* He stalked forward on four silent paws, approaching the first two sacrifices, *Makasa Flintwill and Hackle of the Woodpaw clan.* He knew their names and whispered them, too, as if—in his hunger—they were his own loa. Then he did something rather odd for a god. He . . . bowed his head. The trolls gasped.

The whispering sand of the tiger loa said, *Kimbul bows to Makasa Flintwill, and to Hackle of the Woodpaw clan. Kimbul is Prey's Doom. But Kimbul is the Doom of no Predator. I bow to honor you as my fellows. You have nothing to fear, Makasa Flintwill, from the God of Tigers. You have nothing to fear, Hackle of the Woodpaw clan, from the Lord of Beasts. Eraka no Kimbul salutes you both . . .*

And the black tiger melted down into the black sand.

Makasa and Hackle exchanged confused glances—then nods of mutual admiration.

There were murmurs from the trolls that were quickly hushed when the second loa approached, taking the form of a huge black spider that skittered forward across the black sand, straight toward Drella. Aram wanted to step in front of the dryad and defend her. That was his job, his duty. But the spider—*oh, why did it have to be a spider?*—paralyzed him with fear. He couldn't move. Aram couldn't even turn his head. But he managed to turn his eyes within his head and catch a view of Drella in profile. She looked very pretty, very sweet, very naïve. She was smiling, clearly unaware, as usual, of the danger she faced.

The whispering sand called the loa *Elortha no Shadra, God of Spiders, Mother of Venom, Death's Love.* She skittered forward on eight black legs—then pulled up short. She reared back on six legs, and her two front legs swept the air, flailing like a child having a tantrum. The sand whispered, *No. No. You are not for Shadra. You are not for me.* The trolls gasped again.

Drella strode forward with confidence. Aram still couldn't move to stop her. She said, "I am Taryndrella, a daughter of Cenarius. I am of that which grows, an avatar of bounty. There is no venom on this world that can harm me. No spider who is not my friend. And death is as natural as life. It is spring with me, spider god, and I am *not* for you."

The loa attempted to turn toward Murky, attempted to take a different sacrifice.

Murky swallowed audibly and took a step back, but Drella took another few steps forward, saying, "He is not for you, either, Mother of Venom. You will not take him. You will not have him. Not now. Not ever. So says Cenarius's daughter." And the spider

332

loa backed away from them both, nodding her head out of genuine respect—or genuine fear. The trolls began to murmur again. Some shouted objections or expletives or both. Some of them seemed to be crying. Aram felt his muscles release and unclench. He remembered Thornweaver Chugara, sobbing amid the Bone Pile. And he thought that Taryndrella contained wonders . . .

The sand whispered over and over, *No, no, no, no, no . . .* And the black spider melted into the black.

That left only one loa to whisper his names and titles: *Ueetay no Mueh'zala, Son of Time and Father of Sleep, Night's Friend. God of Death.* His shadow grew and grew and grew, towering above them. The trolls sighed with rapture—and, perhaps, with some relief. Aram tried to see what form the shadow was taking, but the loa remained indistinct. Or rather, his form kept shifting, his shadow melting from one shape into another and another. He was a twelve-foot troll. He was a giant lizard. For a second, he was Captain Malus. Then a creature of burning black flame. Aram scrunched his eyes closed, and by the time he had reopened them, the loa—now a floating whale shark—was approaching a brave Murky, who stood his ground.

The sand whispered, *A snack. A snack. This is but a little snack. Yet Mueh'zala will feed tonight . . .*

Aram had not been able to help Drella, but he'd be blasted if he was going to let this thing eat Murky. Maybe it was the form the loa had taken. Murky had saved Aram from a whale shark's maw. It was a favor he was determined to return. With more effort than it had taken to move the slab of stone upon the crystal shard in the Shimmering Deep, Aram moved his feet, one step, two steps, three—until he stood between Death and the murloc.

Mueh'zala stopped. He shifted into a new form, a red-rimmed spectre in black, towering over all he surveyed. Aram girded himself for whatever was to come. Out of the corner of his eye, he saw Makasa, Hackle, and even Drella, ready to come to his aid. He felt Murky's hand on his shoulder, gently urging him aside. But Aram was a stone that would not budge. It might not have been bravery, he knew. It quite easily might have been nothing more than paralyzing fear that kept him rooted to the spot. Still, whatever the cause, Aramar Thorne did not stir.

Ueetay no Mueh'zala swayed back and forth hypnotically before Aram. Trolls and sacrifices held their breath. Finally, the sand whispered, *Not yet, Son of Thorne. Not yet. This is not the day. That day comes. It comes. But Mueh'zala will not engage you here or now. Our battle is yet to come, yet to come . . . But it will come, child. It will come. And if you lose that battle, Mueh'zala feasts on all of Azeroth. All of Azeroth. All of Azeroth. All of Azeroth . . .*

And Mueh'zala sank from view and was gone. Aram was so stunned, he didn't even see the final loa melt back into the sand. Or notice the torches brighten and the moon shine down. The whispered words, *It will come. It will come*, echoed in his mind.

He wasn't the only one stunned by what he'd witnessed. When Mueh'zala had stopped before Aram, the trolls hadn't even gasped. They were shocked into silence. They were rocked by these unprecedented events. Sandscalp just stood there. Zathra just stood there. They all just stood there, like statues, like trees, maybe, staring at these sacrifices-that-would-not-be-sacrificed.

Drella smiled at Aram, and he found himself smiling back. Grinning foolishly. Happy.

He walked right up to Zathra. She looked down at him in something like horror. He took the compass from her hand, unwinding the chain from around her wrist. She made no move whatsoever to stop him. No one did.

He turned to face his companions. Now, all four were smiling foolishly. Even Makasa. Makasa, Hackle, and Murky had gathered up their weapons and supplies. Murky handed Aram his cutlass. Then, in full view of all the trolls, Hackle tied a harness of rope around Drella, and he and Makasa lowered her down the back side of the pyramid. The rest of them descended after, hand over hand, down the rough stones. But given the way they felt, they might as well have floated down.

They made their way into the hills, and like the loa, vanished into the night.

CHAPTER THIRTY-FIVE
RESPITE

Ro'kull gaped. A flummoxed Ro'jak said, "Ro'jak no understand. Zathra have boy. Have compass. *How Zathra lose both?*"

Zathra herself was none too sure 'bout dat. *Da loa . . . Da boy . . . Death sayin' da battle be yet ta come . . .*

She tried ta focus an' looked up. Dem two ogres were starin' down at her, confused. An' deir confusion seemed ta snap her outta her own. She barked out, "We never found da boy. We never found da compass."

The twins both said, "Huh?"

She raised her crossbow, aimed it at one ogre, den da udder. "Listen, bruddas," she said. "You tell your new Gordok dat we had da compass and lost it, den dat mon be killin' all tree of us, see?"

Dis dey seemed ta grasp. Ro'kull nodded. Ro'jak said, "Old Gordok the same way."

"An' maybe," she offered, "if we be leavin' now, we catch up ta boy an' compass an' da rest in da desert. I be a Sandfury troll.

You be big Gordunni ogres wid long strides. We can outpace dat lot, yeah?"

Dey both said, "Yeah."

And wid Skitter fretful on her chest, dey set off after da fugitives. But over an' over in her mind, Zathra heard da sand whispering, *All of Azeroth, all of Azeroth . . .*

The Sandfury troll and the twin Gordunni ogres set out with such deliberate speed that a night later they *passed* the five travelers without ever laying eyes upon them. Zathra, master tracker though she was, was so distracted (if not distraught) by what she had witnessed in Zul'Farrak, she never noticed clear signs indicating her quarry had taken a slight detour to the south.

There had been fresh water in Zul'Farrak. A stone fountain built over a deep spring. Makasa and Aram had filled their canteens and even found a jug, which they filled and stole away in recompense for the blood they'd lost atop the pyramid.

They set out across the desert, trudging all through the night. They rested all the next day and began walking again at sundown.

On this second night, with water running low again, Drella sensed fresh water to the south. It would lengthen their journey, but with little choice, they bent their path as she suggested.

Frankly, it could hardly have turned out better.

Before dawn, they had reached the eastern tower of Sandsorrow Watch, a poor structure of wood and canvas, which as it turns out was pretty much the only safe haven in Tanaris west of Gadgetzan. Here, they met the tower's master, a tall, muscular high elf with a jagged scar across his face. He was nothing short of flabbergasted to see two humans, a murloc, and a gnoll traveling across the desert with a daughter of Cenarius, and he quickly offered them shelter from the sweltering heat. The quel'dorei said his name was Trenton Lighthammer and that he was a blacksmith of the Mithril Order. Aram didn't know anything about any order, but he had apprenticed with his smith of a stepfather, so he and the elf spoke the same language of the forge. They hit it off immediately.

Sandsorrow Watch had fresh water and stores of food, carted in by the high elf and his trio of goblin friends. The travelers quenched their thirst and sated their hunger. Then, in the relative safety of Lighthammer's tent, they slept the entire day away.

On the travelers' next night at Sandsorrow, Lighthammer and Thorne sequestered themselves in the forge. Murky, Hackle, and Drella wondered why, but Makasa waved off their questions. "We all know the boy misses Lakeshire. If this makes him feel closer to home, there's no harm."

No. No harm indeed. Aramar emerged the next morning with a newly forged iron harpoon for his sister. Upon seeing it, her eyes went very wide. He put it in her hands. The balance was perfect, and so were the weight and the length. The barest touch of the tip drew a drop of blood from Makasa's index finger, which made her smile broadly. It was ten times the harpoon her first one had been, and she said as much in a quiet voice of gratitude. He thought for a moment that she was actually going to cry. Well, no. No tears from Makasa Flintwill. But the look she gave him and the whispered but heartfelt, "Thank you, brother," were more than compensation enough.

She was understandably in very good spirits for the rest of their stay and rarely let that harpoon out of her grip for more than a few seconds at a time.

Almost as an afterthought, Aram pulled the compass out of his pocket and showed its gold chain to Lighthammer. The clasp was broken. Aram had managed to repair it once, below Skypeak, but when the troll had yanked it off his neck, links from the chain were lost and the clasp was completely bent out of shape. It would no longer fasten, and he could no longer wear the compass around his neck.

Trenton grimaced and said it was not worth fixing. Aram nodded sadly—but brightened considerably when the high elf opened a crate and pulled out a good stout iron chain. Aram offered the old chain as payment, but Lighthammer wouldn't hear of it. He tossed it to Makasa, who without argument stowed the valuable (if nonfunctional) gold chain in Hackle's pack. Then Lighthammer replaced it with the chain of iron, which would never be pulled off Aram's neck unbidden.

Lighthammer even added a few iron spurs to Hackle's war club and gave Drella a small pouch of apple seeds, leaving only Murky bereft of a gift. (There wasn't much call for fishing nets in the middle of the desert.) But Murky was a good sport about it all.

When not in the forge, Aram spent his time sketching. He sketched the quel'dorei at his anvil. He finished his memory sketch of Freewind Post. He sketched Murky and Hackle laughing and wrestling over a strip of tortoise jerky. He even sketched the troll Zathra and her twin ogre companions. Then Chief Sandscalp and the pyramid of Zul'Farrak.

And he sketched the loa—though it sent chills down his spine to even think of them. He shook the shivers off and finished. He studied the drawing as if studying to avoid his own death. Then he shut the book and tightly bound it in its oilskin wrapper, as if the shadows on the page might try to escape if allowed. It darkened his mood. But not for long. It would be churlish not to enjoy this literal and figurative oasis to the fullest. And Aramar Thorne was no churl.

The following night, well rested and well supplied with both food (including apples miraculously grown by Taryndrella) and water (in *five* canteens now), not to mention the other gifts provided, they reluctantly said their good-byes to Trenton Lighthammer and Sandsorrow Watch . . . to begin their final push across the desert toward Gadgetzan.

Unfortunately, the Hidden were already there.

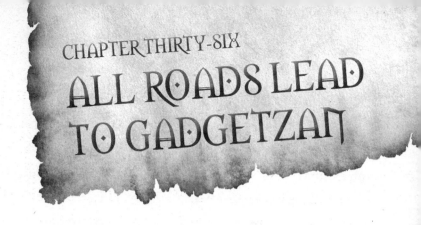

CHAPTER THIRTY-SIX
ALL ROADS LEAD TO GADGETZAN

The *Inevitable* had docked at Gadgetzan, and Malus had come ashore with Ssarbik, Ssavra, and half his crew. He scattered the Hidden across the city, placing watchers unfamiliar to Aram at every gate.

Baron Valdread arrived first. He gave an honest report of his adventure in the Bone Pile. He seemed to consider himself quite heroic for having stopped the Coldbringer from getting a foothold in Azeroth.

Of course, when Ssarbik understood that the Forsaken had been within yards of the compass and had let it go to focus on "lesss ssssignificant conccccernzz," the bird-man was apoplectic.

Reigol considered the arakkoa's reaction a bonus.

Malus considered running the baron through with his sword. But it was a tiresome exercise to kill a dead man, so his captain let it pass.

Throgg arrived next with Karrga, Guz'luk, Slepgar, and the Beard Brothers. They, too, had their near miss to relate.

Now, Malus thought he really would have to kill somebody. Set an example as a caution against future failure. But as he was about to draw his sword, Ssavra whispered in his ear, independently urging him on to just such a course. This stopped him. He could not be seen—even if it was just by the bird-woman—as subservient to another's wishes. He growled, "I don't waste manpower needlessly," and turned his back on her.

Thus, when Zathra, Skitter, and the ogre twins arrived, looking quite dejected, Malus was actually glad to hear they had never laid eyes on the boy or his companions. It kept the issue of punishment for failure at bay.

Marin Noggenfogger, baron of Gadgetzan and a leader of the Steamwheedle Cartel, was soon informed of the cascading arrival of a virtual army of humans, ogres, and more, all being led by the captain of the *Inevitable*. To say it didn't sit well with the goblin master was a bit of an understatement.

This Captain Malus was summoned to Noggenfogger's office. And this Captain Malus didn't come.

So putting in his monocle and putting on his top hat, Noggenfogger sought out Malus himself, backed by thirty hobgoblins. He found the captain at the wharf in front of his ship.

The man looked slightly familiar to the goblin, but he couldn't quite place him.

"Are you Captain Malus?"

"I am," Malus said with a touch of hesitancy.

Noggenfogger thought perhaps that Malus had recognized him, too. Marin wondered if he had met this man before—maybe long before—but under another name. Still, the baron couldn't be bothered with such trivial matters now. He was a goblin on a mission. He said, "And these ogres belong to you?"

Malus looked back over his shoulder at Throgg and the others and said, "I am their king."

"Their king?"

"Yes."

Noggenfogger had never heard of a human who was king over ogres. It sounded apocryphal, but the ogres themselves had let it pass, so the goblin did, too. He squinted his good eye at Malus and said, "I am Marin Noggenfogger, baron of Gadgetzan."

Malus's troll said, "Anudda baron? Mon, dey must be givin' dat title away."

"I certainly was given mine," whispered a hooded man who stunk of jasmine water.

Malus smiled at this exchange and smugly asked, "Can I be of some service to you, *Baron*?"

"You can be of service by causing me no trouble."

"Trouble?"

"I don't care how many men or ogres you have, Captain. I'm putting you on notice. There's to be no trouble in my city. Is that clear?"

The human did not respond. He simply stared down at Marin with the most disconcerting sneer.

"Captain—" Noggenfogger began.

"There will be no trouble, Baron," Malus stated, before turning his back on the goblin and walking up the gangway to his ship. "No trouble. No trouble, at all."

And why should there be? thought Malus. *When Arum and his friends arrive, they will be scooped up instantly. The compass will be mine. And it will be no trouble at all.*

Fortunately, Noggenfogger wasn't the only goblin on the scene. (*Blast, gaining a title had turned Marin into one pompous little baron.*) Gazlowe, who had arrived in town days before, was leanin' against a moorin' post not ten yards away. His face was shadowed by a trade ship behind him, a precaution he took in case the ogres recognized him and connected him with the kid. But the creatures never looked his way. Not even the female, who seemed brighter than the rest.

Gazlowe didn't much care for this Malus, his ogres, his troll, his arakkoa, his Forsaken, his humans, or his elven destroyer.

That is to say, they were all plenty intimidatin', and he didn't much care for what their presence boded for his young friends.

Course, if these rapscallions did get the boy, Gazlowe could always keep Aram's share of the prize money . . .

Ah, but that's chicken feed, all things considered. And the goblin liked the boy well enough to expend a little effort to see him safe. Assumin' the kid finally arrived—or in any case, arrived before Gazlowe and Sprocket had to board the *Cloudkicker* for their next MEGA competition in three days' time.

Anyway, what's the cost of expendin' a little effort to save a friend? (Especially a friend who was a damn good pilot and might win him more coin one of these days.) Gazlowe checked out every gate in the city and, by spending two coppers or less at each (money easily expensed from Aram's winnin's), quickly managed to identify Malus's hidden lookouts watching each one.

Okay, so getting the boy into the city might present a small problem. And keepin' him safe once he was here might present another. But Gazlowe didn't mind havin' a couple problems to solve. He was good at solvin' problems. Talented at it, really.

Besides, it gave him an excuse to pay a visit to *her*. To Sprinkle. To the lovely Sprinkle. To the lovely Sprinkle, one of his many former flames. To the lovely Sprinkle, one of his many former flames, who was now married. To the lovely Sprinkle

Noggenfogger, one of his many former flames, who was now married to a pompous goblin baron.

Gazlowe laughed just thinkin' 'bout it.

Malus's crewmen might have been waiting at every possible entrance to the city. But that was his mistake. Because Gazlowe's crew were waiting *outside* every entrance to the city. Far enough outside that it was child's play to spot two humans traveling with a gnoll, a murloc, and a dryad long before they were at risk. It was Sprocket himself who spied them through his telescopic lens, a good mile from Gadgetzan's western gate. He intercepted them and, per Gazlowe, warned them of the danger they faced.

If Sprocket's warning sounded almost begrudging even to his own ears, he wasn't quite sure why. All right, fine, he had wanted to pilot the *Steamwhistle*. But he could hardly argue with the end result. Or with the science that told him in clear terms that Thorne was the right choice on the basis of the weight issue alone. Or with the fact that Thorne had respected the engineering of the boat, had been a willing student and a successful pilot. Or especially with the money Sprocket had won in the endeavor.

So what was it about this Thorne that rubbed Sprocket the wrong way?

He didn't know, and it didn't matter. He left them in hiding and returned to Gazlowe.

*   *   *

On a lark, the baroness Noggenfogger decided to go on a picnic. She invited her very important husband to accompany her but was hardly surprised when he groaned that he had too much work. That was the best part of the enterprise. She could have her way, and he would feel he owed her something for it. *Hah!*

So the baroness had her servants pack up her caravan with all manner of treats. Frankly, it was enough food to feast twenty hungry goblins. Nevertheless, she left nearly every servant at home, taking only the trusted Winifred and the two most mindless hobgoblins in her husband's employ.

On a whim, she left by Gadgetzan's western gate. After about a mile, she had another whim and stopped to enjoy her picnic. *And look who was there. Why, if it wasn't her old friend—and once much more than a friend—Gazlowe. And didn't old Gazzy have some charming friends of his own with him, as well? There was his engineer, Sprocket. And a rather charming human boy named Aramar, who drew the loveliest sketch of her in his little leather book. He had a tall sister, who looked nothing like him, named Masasa or Makasa or somesuch. Then there was a gnoll and a murloc, and the loveliest springtime dryad she had ever laid eyes upon.* Her picnic was a great success.

And just to be a bit silly, she hid the humans, the gnoll, the murloc, and the dryad in the secret smuggling compartment of her caravan. (She had once had to hide a stuffed yeti in there, so she knew there was plenty of room.) They were all going to

Gadgetzan anyway, so why not have a little fun with the sentries at the gate?

So she waved good-bye to Gazlowe and Sprocket and nodded to Winifred to turn the caravan toward home.

She was the baroness Sprinkle Noggenfogger, so the sentries simply bowed their heads as the caravan passed.

There were a couple of classless humans—they appeared to be little more than brutes or pirates—who actually stuck their noses inside the caravan as if they were looking for someone or something. Of course, all they found was the baroness. She expressed a certain amount of outrage over the incident to her hobgoblins, and she thought that maybe she heard the uncouth men being soundly beaten. But really that was none of her affair.

On one final whim, she allowed Winifred to take a somewhat circuitous route home. The caravan passed through winding streets until Winifred was quite certain they had not been followed. Then it paused outside Winifred's own small two-story abode. It was here that the charming Aramar and his only slightly less charming companions chose to come out of hiding. Since they were strangers in town and needed a *safe house* to stay in, the baroness suggested that perhaps Winifred might rent them a room. Before they could answer, who should arrive on the scene but good old Gazzy himself? He offered to pay for their rooms (which was the single biggest surprise of the afternoon, until Gazzy admitted the coins he had slipped to Winifred came out of money he already owed Aramar). They waited until Winifred signaled that the coast was clear, then ran en masse inside.

Well, it was really none of the baroness's concern. She was just gratified that all her nice friends were *safe* inside the city—and that in the process, both her husband and her former beau would each owe her one. *Hah!*

Makasa eyed the goblin Winifred. Gazlowe assured Flintwill that their hostess could be trusted.

"More than I trust you?"

"Oh, yes. Considerably."

Makasa nodded.

Gazlowe said, "You'll be safe as long as you stay inside."

"There are things we need to do," Aram said hesitantly.

Gazlowe cocked his head and asked, "Like what?"

He watched Makasa and Aram exchange a quick glance before Aram said, "Um. We need to bring Drella to a druid tender named Faeyrine Springsong."

Gazlowe said, "I know Springsong a little. I can quietly bring *her* here to *you*." He got up to go. But he stopped and turned once more to reiterate, "Stay. Put."

CHAPTER THIRTY-SEVEN
SHREDS AND TATTERS

"Frrnee Srngshng."

"Faeyrine Springsong."

"Frrnee Srngshng."

"No. FaeyRINE SPRINGsong."

"FrrRHNNE SFRNGsrng."

"Close enough," said Drella.

Murky repeated, "Frrrhnne Sfringsrng, Frrrhnne Sfringsrng, Frrrhnne Sfringsrng," a few times. Then he rubbed up against Drella and cooed sadly, "Murky fflllur frund Drhla . . ."

Drella said, "He says he will miss me."

It was only then that it hit Aram. Probably only then that it hit Makasa and Hackle, too. Gazlowe was bringing the druid tender, who would take Taryndrella away from them.

Aram tried to tell himself it was a good thing. Good for Drella. Good for him. The responsibility to keep her safe had weighed heavily on him from the moment she'd blossomed.

And yet . . . And yet . . . He'd grown quite fond of her. She was naïve and self-centered, while simultaneously fearless and generous. She was charming and adorable and capable of driving him quite insane. And, yes, he would miss her terribly.

"It'll be hard," Makasa said with a wry smile. "She causes you nothing but trouble—and yet it's a trouble that's revealed something about yourself you didn't know was there. It'll be hard for you to let her go. Trust me, I know the feeling."

"You are all being quite silly," Drella said sincerely. "It will not be hard to let me go to Springsong. You will not miss me."

Murky repeated, "Murky fflllur frund Drhla." And Hackle nodded, too.

"You will not miss me," Drella insisted. "And I will not miss you."

Aram sighed. But he was distracted by a tug at his shirt. For the third or fourth time that day, he told the compass to *"settle down."* And it did . . . for now.

It had begun when they were hiding in the caravan. The compass had flat out gone crazy. Aramar Thorne was glad he wore it on Lighthammer's new iron chain, because as the caravan maneuvered through the winding streets of the city of Gadgetzan—in an attempt to lose any possible pursuers—the compass was yanking Aram left, then right, forward, then backward. It was glowing like crazy, too, and the needle was spinning like a top. Inside the secret compartment, he had told the others,

"There's another shard here in Gadgetzan, for sure. And I think it's a big one."

Now, Makasa said, "You and I should go look for the shard."

Aram looked at her with surprise. "You think it's safe enough?"

"Of course not. We'll wait for dark, but otherwise we don't have much choice. Calculated risk was your father's way. He wanted us to find those shards. So that's what we *will* do."

"What about Springsong?"

"Somehow I doubt 'old Gazzy' is in any rush to bring her. In any case, I doubt he'll bring her tonight. If he does"—she turned now to Hackle—"don't let her take Drella away until we get back. Understood?"

Hackle nodded, glad as always to be Makasa's trusted lieutenant.

A voice said, "You're not going anywhere."

They all turned to see Winifred in the doorway. She was a handsome—if somewhat stern—goblin, with pale-green skin and unusual iron-grey eyes. Like many a trusted servant, she knew how to listen at keyholes and enter a room silently. Makasa looked to be on the verge of drawing her sword—enough on the verge that Aram took the precaution of physically staying her hand. "How much did you hear?" he asked.

"Enough," she said dryly. "But you don't dare go anywhere smelling the way you do now. Even an ogre would notice *that* aroma. And you're certainly not lying down on my bedclothes filthy as you are. They'd never recover."

Murky and Hackle both sniffed themselves and shrugged.

Winifred held up a pile of white linens. "Strip off your clothes. You can put on these nightshirts while I launder everything. I have a hot bath drawn already. And there'll be four more in quick succession after the first one's done. You go first, ma'am." She held out the top nightshirt.

Now Makasa really looked ready to stab her. But she subtly gave herself a sniff and—unlike the murloc and the gnoll—clearly didn't care for the result. "I suppose I could use a good bath," she admitted begrudgingly.

Winifred rolled her eyes—nearly setting Makasa off again—and said, "Been saying that, haven't I?"

So Makasa followed their hostess out. She came back in half an hour, wearing the long white nightshirt and carrying all her weapons. Aram had never seen any one person look so uncomfortable and so relaxed at the same time. "I'm going to take a nap," she said gruffly. "Wake me at sundown." She lay down on the bed and was practically asleep before Winifred had ushered Aramar out for his turn.

By sundown, all five of them were clean and relatively cheerful. There was only one problem. Their laundered clothes, hung on a line outside in the late summer heat on the roof of Winifred's house, weren't quite dry. So all five of them sat around, waiting in five identical nightshirts. Truthfully, Makasa was the only one tall enough for the nightshirt to fit properly. (What the goblin Winifred was doing with five nightshirts better suited to worgen was anyone's guess.) Aram felt like he was wearing a ball gown. Hackle was so embarrassed, he was practically curled up in a corner, the long nightshirt tangling him up like he was wearing a cocoon.

Murky and Drella seemed delighted. Murky's nightshirt didn't fit over his head, so he had wrapped it around his torso in much the way he used to wrap his nets, which seemed to give him comfort. Drella, who generally wore no clothes except the fur, leaves, and flowers that were part of her person, was thrilled to try the nightshirt on. Hers fit over her head all right but lay bunched up on her faunlike back to no real purpose. But she liked the feel of the fabric and said as much multiple times.

Finally, Winifred came back with their clothes. Makasa and Drella left the room to change elsewhere—though, again, for the dryad, changing simply meant removing the ill-fitting nightshirt. Aram waited for Winifred to follow the other females. But she was tsk-tsking over Aram's ruined shirt. "This won't do," she said. "It's all shreds and tatters. Hmmm. Mr. Gazlowe said he has money for you in trust."

Aram chuckled. "Yes, he seems to trust himself with my winnings far more than he trusts me with them."

"Good," she said. "I'll send word. Have him purchase a new shirt. He can bring it next time he visits. Is there anything else you need?"

Aram thought about that. "Is there a boat to Lakeshire? I mean, a ship leaving for Stormwind Harbor? That's the closest port to Lakeshire."

"Never heard of Lakeshire."

"It's a small village in the Eastern Kingdoms. It's my home."

"Well, there's bound to be a boat to Stormwind. One leaves for there every week or so. You want Gazlowe to book five passages for you?"

Aram thought of Taryndrella and the coming tender and sadly corrected Winifred: "Four."

Winifred raised an eyebrow and whispered, "So you're really letting her go?"

"We made a vow," he said hoarsely. "It's what's best for her."

"If you say so," said the goblin. "All right, that's one shirt and four tickets east. Anything else?"

He looked around the room for inspiration, and his eyes alighted on his cutlass. Or rather, Old Cobb's cutlass. He picked it up and handed it to her. "A cutlass," he said. "I need a new cutlass."

She examined the one in her hand. "What's wrong with this one? It looks practically brand new."

"I don't trust it."

She didn't question that statement. In fact, it seemed to make some sense to her. Perhaps more sense to her than it even made to Aram. "All right," she said. "Mr. Gazlowe can probably get you a decent one in trade. He'll find a bargain. He'll enjoy finding a bargain, I'd guess. So that's one shirt, one cutlass, and four passages. *Anything else?*"

Aram racked his brain, and one last thought occurred. He leaned over and whispered two words in Winifred's long pointed ear. She looked at him strangely, but then nodded and left the room.

He quickly changed. His shirt really was a disaster. Washing it hadn't done the thing any favors. That is, it was cleaner than it had probably been since he left Lakeshire, but "shreds and tatters" was a generous assessment at this point. Nevertheless, he pulled his father's leather coat on over it and figured he could make do for the time being.

Under cover of darkness, Aram and Makasa ventured out with the compass to find the next shard. It was Aram's first real view of Gadgetzan, with its strange circular buildings, sand-covered sandstone streets, and perpetually scurrying populace (composed of nearly every race known to him). The latter was a boon, as no one paid much attention to the children of Greydon Thorne as they followed their odd and eccentric course. Aram kept the device in his hand and let it lead them. It glowed and tugged, and the needle would turn this way and that, as the labyrinthine streets refused to provide a direct path to their prize.

They seemed to be getting closer, however, when Makasa suddenly pulled Aram back harshly and pressed him up against a wall. They peeked out slowly and carefully. One of Throgg's ogres from the Speedbarge—the giant with the pale-red skin—was leaning against a house and yawning.

They backtracked and tried another route.

Once again, it seemed that they were getting on track when Aram—his nose practically touching the glass of the compass—pulled up short and stopped without looking, grabbing Makasa's arm.

What? she mouthed silently.

He sniffed the air, and she did likewise. An intense odor of jasmine wafted toward them on the summer breeze. Jasmine . . . and something rotten beneath it. Both of them knew what that meant: the undead Whisper-Man was near. They looked around but didn't see him. But Makasa licked her finger and gauged the bearing of the wind.

They took off in the opposite direction.

Needless to say, their lack of substantial progress was frustrating. But they kept at it.

A few twists and turns later, Aram looked up from the compass and again stopped short.

Again, Makasa mouthed the word, *What?*

But Aram wasn't looking at her and didn't notice. He was looking inside the window of a darkened shop. A bookseller's. He approached the window cautiously, as if seeing some kind of illusion that might vanish any second.

Makasa risked a whisper: "Is it in there? Is the shard in there?"

But it wasn't a shard in the window. It was a book, a large volume. *Common Birds of Azeroth*. His father had kept a copy of this wonderfully illustrated tome on a shelf in his cabin aboard *Wavestrider*. Aram leaned his head down and inhaled the leather smell of his father's coat. Between the coat and the book and the compass, he suddenly felt closer to his father than . . . well, than he had *ever* felt when the man was alive. Closer, at least, than he had since Greydon Thorne had left Lakeshire and his family on Aram's sixth birthday.

As if *Common Birds* were a book of spells that had enchanted the young Aramar, he found himself slipping the compass down beneath his disaster of a shirt, taking three steps toward the closed shop, and knocking three times on its locked door.

CHAPTER THIRTY-EIGHT
THE BOOKSELLER

"**W**hat are you doing?!" Makasa hissed.

Aram hardly knew. But he knocked again.

Through the glass window, he saw a candle floating toward the door from the back of the shop and heard a cross voice grumbling, "I'm coming, I'm coming." As the candle approached, it illuminated its bearer, a male goblin.

This cranky goblin proprietor came to the door and said, "Can't you read? We're closed. And if you can't read, why knock on the door of a bookseller?"

Aram gawked. *I know him*, he thought.

The goblin said, "I know you . . ." He unlocked and opened the door. There was a sliver of the Blue Child out, but the White Lady was almost full, and in her bright light Aram instantly recognized the distinguished goblin artist from the Speedbarge.

"You're the artist from the Speedbarge."

"And you're the winning pilot, Aramar Thorne."

"I am."

Makasa said, "Aram, we can't stay—"

But she didn't finish, because just then the goblin peered at Aram over his candle and said, "You wouldn't happen to be related to Greydon Thorne, would you?"

Makasa and Aram stared. Aram said, "I'm his son."

"Well, well," the goblin said. "The son of Greydon Thorne. Come in, come in." He opened the door wide and waved them inside. They complied, moving in ahead of the goblin, who said, "My name is Charnas."

Aram wheeled on him. "You're Charnas of Gadgetzan?!"

"For a good many years, yes," said the handsome goblin with a wry smile, all signs of his previous crankiness gone.

"You drew *Common Birds of Azeroth*?"

"I did. You sound like a fan."

"I am!"

"Your father liked that book, too." As he spoke, Charnas led them to the back of the shop and through a low door into a kind of workroom. "I remember the first time he came into my shop, he—"

"Wait! My father was here? In this shop?"

"Yes, of course. Many times. I know your father well and consider him a friend. Is he in town?"

Aram lowered his head. Charnas seemed to understand

instantly. He pointed to a couple of stools and took a seat on a chair in front of a high desk covered with half-finished sketches. Aram and Makasa sat.

Charnas said, "He's gone, isn't he?"

Aram nodded.

"That's a blasted shame. For a human, he was quite enlightened. In fact, calling Greydon Thorne enlightened is practically the definition of understatement." Charnas sighed. "He will be missed."

"He is missed," Aram said, looking at Makasa, who nodded slowly once.

Charnas nodded, too. They were all silent for a time. Then the goblin said, "He talked about you, you know." He glanced over at Makasa. "And if you're Makasa Flintwill, he talked about you, too."

"When?" Makasa said.

Charnas scratched his cheek. "Oh, now, that had to be nearly a year ago. That's the last time I saw him, I'm afraid. He talked about you then, Makasa. Aram, he'd been talking about for the last five, six years, at least. Course, I knew him long before either of you two young folk were born."

"How long have you . . . how long *did* you know him?" Aram asked.

"Ah, now, let's see. For a good twenty years. Met him the same year I opened this shop, and he was one of my first customers. Came in with his younger brother. Bought a copy of *Common Birds*. We wound up talking for hours . . ."

"Wait, wait, wait!" Aram cried. "My father has a brother?!"

Aram turned to face Makasa, but this was clearly news to her, too.

"Indeed," said Charnas. "Or at least he did. A fine, strapping young lad. Even taller than Greydon. Silverlaine Thorne, I think his name was, I remember your father was very proud of him. Said there was no better man in all of Azeroth. I only met him that one time. That first time. And he didn't stay to chat like your father did. No, Greydon and I talked on and on, all through the night. But your uncle left after fifteen minutes. To be fair, talking about birds and books isn't everyone's idea of fun. Though it is mine, I'll admit." Charnas stopped to study his new companions. Once again, the goblin seemed to intuit their thoughts. "Didn't know you had an uncle, did you?"

Aram was stunned. He had family on his mother's side—a grandmother, an aunt, a few cousins, and, of course, his half siblings. But this was the first time he'd *ever* heard of *any* family on the Thorne side, unless you counted Makasa, who cleared her throat and asked, "What did you say his name was?"

"Silverlaine. Yes, it was definitely Silverlaine. I remember now thinking, *Silver and Grey. Ha!* I even asked if they had a sister named Argent."

"Did they?!" Aram said, ready to believe almost anything could be possible now.

"No, no," the goblin said. "It was just a poor excuse for a joke, I'm afraid. But if your grandparents had had a daughter, I bet that name would have been high on their list of probables." Charnas stopped talking, no longer certain that his audience was listening.

There was another good minute of silence before the boy spoke again.

"I have an uncle . . . ," Aram whispered, his voice full of wonder. He turned to Makasa. "We have an Uncle Silverlaine."

"First I've heard of it. Is he dead?" she asked.

They both turned to look at Charnas, who shrugged helplessly. "Never heard that he was, but I must admit your father hadn't mentioned him in our more recent visits. You know there was that six- or seven-year gap in our acquaintance, when he was living in, um . . ."

"Lakeshire," Aram said.

"That's right. In the east. Anyway, I think I must have asked about Silverlaine the first time I saw Greydon after that break. I think your father said he hadn't seen him recently. But he never said he was dead."

"So he might be alive?"

"Might be. Probably is. Who knows? It's easy enough to lose track of people if the effort's not made. I remember saying *that* to

Greydon last year. Funny thing is, we weren't talking about *his* brother; we were talking about *mine*. I was saying that I hadn't laid eyes on Morbix in a decade, though once we'd been closer than two fleas on a dog's hair. Come to think of it, that got him talking about *you*, Aram. He missed you."

"He did?"

"Ah, yes. He felt bad about leaving you and your mother. 'Why'd you leave, then?' I asked. He shook off that question. 'Why don't you go back and see them?' I asked next. He said maybe he would. He said by now you'd probably be old enough to be a part of . . .'"

"A part of what?" Aram asked breathlessly, pressing a hand to his shirt and the compass beneath it.

"You know, I think I asked that, too. He had drifted off, and when I called him back, he said something like, 'A part of my life.' And I think, as far as that went, he was speaking the truth. But I got the sense he wasn't going nearly far enough. We talked a lot, but there was plenty he kept from me. We both knew that."

Makasa said, "That must have been when he made the decision. I remember the last time *Wavestrider* was in Gadgetzan. We made for the Eastern Kingdoms right after that. Trade stops along the way, but we were practically flying toward Stormwind Harbor—though I didn't realize why at the time."

Aram felt the need to pick his jaw up off the floor. He stared at Makasa. Then he turned to stare at Charnas. Finally, he said, "Thank you" to the goblin. "You sent him my way."

"Ah, now, I don't want credit for that. If your father went to see you, he went of his own volition."

Aram nodded absently. His gaze drifted over Charnas's shoulder to the sketchwork on the goblin's desk.

Charnas noticed and said, "You know, I was hired as the official illustrator for all MEGA events. But you messed me up, boy."

"Me?"

"That's right. When it came time to sketch you, some murloc pushed you into the water."

"He was saving me."

"Yeah. Them ogres were after you. That messed me up, too. Once you won, I figured I'd get the sketch in the winner's circle. But you never showed. I sketched little Hotfix instead."

Charnas turned in his chair—that is, the entire seat of the chair turned with him, though the legs of the thing never moved. As it turned, the chair jacked Charnas up a foot, putting him at a perfect level to draw at his desk. Finally, a shiny, mirrored shell cranked up out of the chair's back, focusing bright light upon his workspace. This contraption amazed Aram, but so much was amazing that night, he was hardly surprised that this distinguished old goblin had a miracle chair in his possession. If the chair had started flying, he probably would have said, "Of course." (For the record, the chair did not fly.) Charnas turned back, displaying a finished illustration of Hotfix on Gazlowe's shoulders, holding up a trophy that was nearly as big as the goblin boy himself. It was masterfully done. Precise and perfect.

Charnas said, "I don't suppose you'd sit for me now?"

Aram said, "I will if you'll sit for me."

"You draw?"

Aram was already pulling out his sketchbook and his miserable little coal pencil. The goblin frowned at the latter. "That all you got to draw with?" he asked.

Aram nodded.

Charnas leaned over and handed him three brand-new coal pencils. "Take these," he said, while he took Aram's offered sketchbook and slowly—excruciatingly slowly—flipped through its pages.

Finally, Charnas said, "Boy. You're good. Good enough that I find myself a bit jealous that you've got this skill at your tender years."

"You really think so?"

"I know so."

"You're really good, too," Aram enthused. "I mean, you're

amazing! I knew that the first time I saw *Common Birds of Azeroth* on my father's shelf."

"I'm glad he kept it. But you want to see something really amazing?" Charnas asked, nodding his head toward another door.

Aram glanced down to see if the compass was acting up, briefly wondering if Charnas had a crystal shard, if maybe his father had left a shard with the distinguished goblin for safekeeping. But the compass was calm enough for now. Next, Aram glanced at Makasa. He had thought she'd be impatient to go. Impatient like Silverlaine Thorne. But Charnas's knowledge of Greydon seemed to be keeping her engaged.

Charnas hopped off his chair with his candle, and the other two followed him through the door.

Inside the next room was some kind of machine. "It's a press," Charnas said.

"Like for pressing grapes . . . or apples?"

"It's a *printing* press. It presses something more precious than fruit, my boy. It presses ideas, words, images—all onto paper. It presses *books*." Charnas cranked a handle, and pieces of parchment whipped off the press. Charnas nodded at them, and Aram picked one up. It was a copy of the picture of Hotfix and Gazlowe. Not a second, different sketch. It was the *exact same sketch!* Aram picked up another sheet and another. They were all duplicates of the same sketch!

Charnos

"How?" he breathed.

Charnas laughed. Then he showed him how the printing press worked. Top to bottom. It was magic to Aram, but it was a magic he quickly began to understand. The plates for the artwork. The rows of type for text. The wheel of ink. The crank. By the end of the lesson, it all made sense. But that hardly made it less magical.

Aram looked through a pile of previously printed copies. There was one picture of a saltspray gull that was instantly near and dear to his heart. He told Charnas, "When we were lost at sea, I saw these gulls and knew we were close to shore from reading your book."

"You were lost at sea?!" Charnas seemed to have missed the point of Aram's story. At least, at first. But he asked the boy if he wanted to keep the copy.

Aram grinned broadly and thanked him. Then he hesitated. "Can I fold it?"

The goblin shrugged. "It's just a copy. You can light it on fire if you like. Though perhaps not until after you've left, so I don't know."

Aram folded it carefully and tucked it between two leaves of his sketchbook, saying, "I am *not* lighting it on fire. This is just the safest place for it."

Each sat for the other. While Charnas drew, he said, "I saw from your sketchbook that you've started to draw a few things from memory."

"You can tell that? I guess it's obvious. I'm not very good unless my subject's right in front of me."

"Now, hold on," Charnas said. "I never said that. In fact, I'd suggest you try it more often. It's good training, if nothing else. And a little embellishment from your imagination isn't going to hurt, either. Try it. Or rather, try it some more."

Aram smiled as he applied one of his new pencils to his book. "If you say so, I will."

When both of them were done, Charnas handed over his sketch of Aram, saying, "For me, this is just the first step. I do a bit of light sketching and finish the thing in my own time." For *light sketching*, Charnas's portrait of Aram was as precise and perfect as the rest of his work. It made Aram shy to show the goblin his own effort. But Charnas insisted and seemed quite pleased with the result. "You make me look very distinguished," he said. "To be fair, I am still the better draftsman. But to be even fairer, you've got more life to your work. It's vibrant. It puts your characters in the moment. It's partly the rough, unfinished quality, I know. But I'm telling you, boy, you have real talent. Real talent."

Aram was practically floating off his stool when Makasa said, "It'll be light soon. I'm sorry, but we need to go." .

Charnas of Gadgetzan

A. Thorne

Charnas had given Aram a copy of *Common Birds of Azeroth*, which the boy held against his chest, pressed against the compass: one treasure against another. As he and Makasa raced back to their boardinghouse in the predawn light, the latter was keeping an eye out for anyone keeping his or her eyes out for them. But Aram's mind was swirling around other concerns. He said, "I wish we had a way to contact my uncle Silverlaine. I bet he knows all about the shards. I bet he could help us."

Makasa said, "I don't bet, but I agree another Thorne would be useful."

They approached Winifred's door, and Winifred opened it before they'd even slowed down. "Come in," she said. "We have guests." Makasa reached for her sword. Winifred slapped her hand. "Good guests," she said.

She ushered them back up to their room. Gazlowe was there, and with him, a tall and beautiful night elf with silver hair, ice-blue skin, gorgeous antlers, and glowing golden eyes. She said, "Aramar Thorne, I presume." Her voice had layers. It was the only way he could describe it. It seemed to reach his ears on one level—and deeper into his soul on another.

Aram nodded breathlessly, struck by her eerie beauty and her outward resemblance to his deeply missed friend Thalyss.

"I am Faeyrine Springsong, a druid tender of the Cenarion Circle."

"Uh huh." He squeezed his eyes shut and opened them again, trying to get used to that voice and trying not to look and sound quite as stupid as he knew he currently must.

He looked around. Hackle and Murky both stared up at the kaldorei with wide eyes, big smiles, and moony expressions. Drella grinned at Aram, looking quite self-satisfied.

He swallowed hard and summoned up the wherewithal to speak. "I . . . I'm sorry if we kept you waiting. We didn't expect you so soon. But I'm glad you did wait. I wouldn't want Drella to leave without the chance to say good-bye."

Drella laughed and said, "Leave? Where would I go? And with whom? Her?" She laughed again.

Springsong smiled indulgently. "I am afraid there has been a misunderstanding. I would have been prepared to take the Seed of Thalyss Greyoak. I would have been happy to take on that burden. But I cannot take Taryndrella. It is too late."

"But . . . we got here as soon as we could."

The night elf sighed. "I am afraid I am not making myself clear. When the acorn blossomed into Taryndrella, she imprinted—*bonded*—on the first person she saw."

Drella skipped over to Aram and grabbed his arm. "That is you, silly. I told you that you would not miss me. And that I would not miss you. And so we will not miss each other. Because I cannot leave you."

Aram stared at her. "Wait, you knew this all along?"

"Of course. I know most things. I am very knowledgeable. Especially considering it is only spring."

"You keep saying that, but it's nearly autumn!" He couldn't tell if he was angry with her for keeping the secret or secretly thrilled she wasn't being taken away from him.

"She means," Faeyrine said, "that she is in the springtime of her life cycle. She is young. Very young."

"And very pretty," Drella said, turning around in a full circle for all to see and admire.

Aram started to laugh.

"This is still a serious matter," the druid said. "The daughter of Cenarius requires training with her bondmate to reach her full potential. I am not her bondmate, so I cannot train her, and you cannot train her because, well . . . frankly, you are an ignorant human boy."

Aram laughed again. "I'm sorry. I'm sorry," he said, meaning it. But he found he was a bit overwhelmed—mentally—by the quantity of surprises and revelations he had encountered over the last few hours, and the laughter seemed to vent out of him, like steam from a speedboat's pressure valve.

"*I* am sorry," she said. "I do not mean to insult you. None of this is your fault. Really, Thalyss should have warned you not to let the Seed get wet."

A sheepish Aram looked around the room. Neither Makasa nor Hackle nor Murky would meet his gaze. He said, "Uh huh. So what do we do now?"

"There is only one druid who can undo your bond with Taryndrella. Undo your bond and rebond her to him to facilitate her advancement. You must take this dryad to the druid master Thal'darah."

"Okay." Aram sighed. "Is he here in Gadgetzan?"

"No," said the night elf, hesitating.

"Dire Maul?" Aram said with another laugh. At this point, nothing would surprise him.

"Well, you are getting warmer. He is in the druid enclave in the Stonetalon Mountains."

"Which is where, exactly?"

Makasa groaned darkly. "Far away. In northwest Kalimdor."

Now, Aramar groaned.

"Specifically," Faeyrine said, "he can be found at Thal'darah Overlook."

"Well, sure. I myself am usually found at Aramar Overlook."

"This is no joke, child," said the tender.

At this point, Aram wasn't so sure. His brain was reeling.

Gazlowe piped up, "Well, it seems you gotta decision to make, boy." He fanned out four bright-green tickets. "Because, at your request, I paid good money for four passages to Stormwind Harbor aboard the *Crustacean*. Ship leaves about this time tomorrow mornin'. Now, I'm willin' to buy you a fifth passage—"

"I should hope so," Makasa said, "since it's *Aram's* money you're spending."

Gazlowe laughed. "True enough. So what's it gonna be? The Eastern Kingdoms or northwest Kalimdor?"

All eyes turned toward Aram.

"You can't take her?" he asked Springsong, half hoping the answer would be . . .

"I cannot separate her from you."

"I would not allow it," Drella said, stamping her left front hoof. "But I do not see any need to go to Thal'darah, either. I am happy to be your bondmate, Aramar Thorne."

"Yeah, me too," he replied honestly, smiling at her. "Then we could all go to Stormwind. To Lakeshire."

"Yes," said Drella. "You speak of Lakeshire often. And I would like to see it."

Faeyrine looked down . . . then slowly raised her head to meet Aram's eyes. Again, her voice spoke to his ears and deep into his soul. "She will never reach her full potential with you, Aramar

Thorne. That is not a crime. But it is . . . a sadness. A sadness she is too young to recognize now. But one that, with time, will overtake her."

Aram wondered what that meant, what Drella's full potential might be. But before he could ask, Makasa whispered, "What about the shards?"

Aram nodded. There was a shard here in Gadgetzan. Once he had collected it, the compass would tell him which direction he would need to go next. He said, "I have a day to decide, then?"

Springsong nodded. Gazlowe shrugged.

"All right," Aram said with considerably more decisiveness than he was feeling. "Makasa and I have an errand to run here in Gadgetzan. And we'll have to wait 'til after dark. So tonight, after that's done, I'll make my decision."

He glanced at Makasa. She nodded.

Drella walked right up to him and touched his cheek. "Whatever you decide, I am with you, Aram. Always."

He rested his forehead against hers. "It seems so," he said.

"And you are glad of it," she told him confidently.

He chuckled. "That seems so, as well."

Gazlowe cleared his throat. When Aram looked his way, the goblin said, "Hate to interrupt the touchin' scene, my boy, but I promised my cousin I'd meet him for a drink or twelve. And that was hours ago. So here's the other stuff you ordered." He handed

Aram a burlap sack. "I'll come back late tonight to hear your decision."

Gazlowe bowed to the druid, kissed Winifred on the cheek, and, swinging wide to avoid Makasa, was gone.

Faeyrine said, "I suppose I should leave you travelers to get some rest. Unless there is anything else I might do?"

"Is there anything else you *can* do?"

"I will contemplate that, and I, too, will return tonight."

She headed for the door. Aram looked down at the burlap sack, and it spurred a memory. He said, "Wait!"

She stopped and turned.

He said, "I think . . . I think Thalyss cared for you deeply."

"He did," she said with a slight bow of her head, though otherwise keeping her feelings to herself. "And I for him, as well." She turned to leave again.

"Wait!"

She stopped and turned again.

"There was something he said once. I mean, we saw him turn into a stag and a bear . . ."

"Yes . . ."

"But he said he could also turn into a feathered moonkin . . ."

"Of course."

"Could you show me?"

"Show you a moonkin? *Transform* into a moonkin for you? Are you serious?"

"Um. Yes."

She bristled and then stalked toward him with an air of one who had never been so insulted. "I am to do this here, as a parlor trick for your amusement?"

He swallowed hard over her displeasure but pressed on: "And for my education. And because I never had the chance to see Thalyss turn into one."

She scowled down at him. He smiled up at her hopefully—and perhaps a little longingly. And that smile melted her scowl. Soon enough she was looking on him tenderly. She said, "A feathered moonkin?"

"If it's not too much trouble."

"No," she said. "No trouble at all."

CHAPTER FORTY
END RUN

They spent the day indoors.

With dawn's light streaming in through the window, the night elf demurred, opting not to shift into a moonkin just then, but promising to do so when she returned that night to hear Aram's decision about his next destination. She departed, instructing them all to get some sleep.

Aram found he was still carrying the burlap sack. He untied the thick brown twine that held it closed and pulled out, first, his new cutlass. It looked suspiciously like the cutlass he had given up the day before, and he didn't think it unlikely that Gazlowe might have handed him Cobb's cutlass back, while charging him a fee for the "exchange." Even so, as he hefted it and sheathed it on his belt, he felt as if he had exorcised Cobb's demons by the exercise. This cutlass now belonged to him.

Next, he pulled out a new shirt. The fabric was light and sturdy and of the same off-white color that his old shirt had once been—yet considerably less shredded, considerably less tattered.

Then he looked deep into the sack and smiled. He beckoned Murky over and, with a flourish, pulled out a brand-new set of fishing nets!

Murky practically swooned! "Mgrrrrl fr Murky?!"

"Of course they're for you, my frund. Do you like them?"

Murky danced around the room, bubbling and purring with glee.

Makasa tried to grumble that now they'd be back to spending all their time untangling the murloc, but even she couldn't help smiling at Murky's rapture.

Carefully, Murky wrapped the nets round and around his waist until he was wearing them like a vest. Or almost. His thumbnail got caught in one of the loops, and soon enough—as Makasa had predicted—he was hopelessly tangled, turning in circles to get free, reminding Aram of Soot chasing his tail.

Makasa ignored the murloc and told Aram to try to get some sleep.

"After tonight? There's no way."

"You always say that. And you always fall right asleep. Try."

That was true, so he tried. For a good hour, anyway. But for once, he was right. He gave up and spent an hour turning the pages of *Common Birds*, with Drella by his side and Murky and Hackle looking over his shoulder. He remembered his promise to teach them to read and used Charnas's volume as a kind of textbook. The exquisite pictures of birds seemed to help connect the idea of, say, the image of a grackle with the sound of the word *grackle* with the letters that composed g-r-a-c-k-l-e. In any case, he was positive Drella was learning something, certain Hackle was enjoying the lesson, and satisfied Murky was happy to be among his f-r-u-n-d-s.

Afterward, inspired by Charnas's work and their earlier conversation, Aram pulled out his sketchbook and one of his new pencils—which Murky and Hackle oohed and ahhed over as if they were brand-new magic wands—and got to drawing. From recent memory, he drew Springsong looking down kindly on Drella. Then he went further back and drew their underwater salvage mission being interrupted by the attack of the whale shark. Further back still, to the Bone Pile, and the Whisper-Man fighting the skeletons while Blackthorn shook his rattle and chanted over Taryndrella. He sketched Shagtusk in her prison of thorns. He sketched Feral Scar about to swallow Sivet whole, with Hackle hanging off the yeti and Makasa at the ready with her chain. (He even put himself in that one, looking much braver and more competent with his cutlass than he had any right to look. *Well, Charnas had told him to use his imagination, so why shouldn't he imagine himself competent and brave?*) He sketched his memory of the view of Thousand Needles from Skypeak. He sketched the ogre king, Gordok, with his young female ogre servant. He sketched the entrance to Dire Maul. And then he pulled out the compass with its new iron chain and sketched that.

By this time, he truly was exhausted. He put the book away and quickly began to drift off, certain that he'd soon have another vision of the Light, another conversation with the Voice, and probably another confrontation with Malus.

But, no. Makasa roused him from a sound, restful sleep at sunset. Winifred, who had spent the day with her baroness, returned in time to serve them all a hearty meal of wild fowl (with plenty of yams and mushrooms for Drella) paid for by Gazlowe from Aram's winnings.

Then it was time to venture forth again. He put on his new shirt—Winifred insisted on disposing of the old one, saying you couldn't even make a decent set of dust rags from it—and slid his (presumably) new cutlass through his belt. With the compass in his tight fist, bucking and shifting, glowing and spinning away, he and Makasa set out to find the next crystal shard.

Far as Zathra could tell, Malus had no notion a da truth. Da twins kept deir traps shut, an' she'd managed not ta show nuttin' on her face. It hadn't hurt dat Valdread an' Throgg had both had near misses, too. She was lookin' good by comparison, just by sayin' she'd not laid eyes upon da boy.

So she was safe enough. But dat didn't put her mind at ease.

Da loa. Da loa. She'd nevah seen nuttin' like dat before. Nevah! Da human woman and da gnoll had da respect—*respect*—a Eraka no Kimbul. Da dryad had put fear—*fear*—inta Elortha no Shadra. And da boy Aramar had a reckonin'—*reckonin'*—due wid Ueetay no Mueh'zala. *What right did Zathra have ta get between such tings?*

"What we ta do, sista?" she whispered as she stroked Skitter. Da scorpid was fast asleep on her chest, but it comforted Zathra some ta talk ta her.

"What?" Guz'luk said. He was walkin' a few feet behind her. Malus still had his crew watchin' all da gates an' da docks, but he was tinkin' da boy shoulda been here by now if he'd taken a boat from da Speedbarge. (An' Zathra was tinkin' he shoulda been here by now, too, assumin' he wasn't lyin' dead in da desert.) So da Hidden an' da Elite were patrollin' da city day an' night.

"Nuttin'," Zathra said. "Keep an eye out, brudda, an' be quiet."

Da potbellied ogre grunted his acknowledgment.

Zathra thought, *Dis all be beyond poor Zathra. I be no loa. I just be a troll. Dem loa can sort dis out for deir own selves. I been paid ta do a job. So dat's what I be doin'. If da boy come in my sights again, he be one sorry human.*

And den, as if ta test her, dere he was.

Following the compass through the uncooperative twists and turns of Gadgetzan's streets, Aram and Makasa turned a corner and found themselves face-to-face with Malus's troll and Throgg's potbellied ogre. For a long moment, the four of them just stared.

Then Makasa grabbed Aram by his new shirt (tearing the collar just a bit) and pulled him back, yelling, *"Run!"*

They ran. Behind them they could hear the ogre's horn, waking half the city and probably putting all of Malus's dangerous crew on their tails. In any case, it was certain that Zathra was on their tails. Aram glanced back over his shoulder to see the troll coming round the corner, fast upon them.

Makasa had always had an excellent memory. She'd been to Gadgetzan before with *Wavestrider* and already knew the city a little. But these last two nights—in their attempt to follow the compass to the shard—had been a true education. They had slinked their way through so many byways and alleys of the place, she now knew exactly what route she wanted to take. Twists and turns, sharp lefts and hard rights. She was able to keep ahead of the enemy, despite being burdened with Aram. Without him, she'd have lost the troll by now. Or have turned and killed her. But she didn't want to take that risk with her brother beside her. She was faster than Zathra, but Aram wasn't. Fortunately, that potbellied ogre was slower still. He attempted to give chase but had fallen behind. The biggest danger from him was his horn. He'd puff his cheeks and blow at regular intervals. Malus and the others would be coming soon. She and her brother needed to get away.

Turning another corner, they were presented with an opportunity: a small two-wheeled horse cart (sans its horse). Makasa got behind it and pushed, just as the troll came around the bend. The cart slammed into Zathra. Makasa and Aram ran on.

They'd have to find the shard some other time. Right now, Makasa was just trying to get them back to Winifred's. But she needed to do it when she was sure they were no longer followed. She pulled Aram down another alley, but just before they emerged from the other end, Aram stopped short and whispered, "Look!" He held up the compass; it glowed brighter than ever and tugged hard on its chain to the right. The needle also pointed to the right, toward a refuse bin against a wall. He said, "The crystal shard's right over there somewhere!"

Makasa looked back over her shoulder. The troll and the ogre hadn't turned down the alley yet, but she knew they would any second. This was it. This was the moment of truth. She grabbed Aramar by his breeches and hefted him up and over into the refuse bin. "Stay here," she whispered. "Hide 'til they pass. Find the shard. Return to Winifred's. I'll lead them away."

"Wait, no!"

"I don't have time to argue." She shoved his head down below the level of the refuse and said, "Do what I say, brother." And off she ran.

When she got to the end of the alley and could hear the pounding of troll and ogre footsteps, she called out ahead,

"Aram, keep moving! I'm right behind you!" And she turned the corner, slowing down on purpose to confirm they weren't stopping to search the refuse bin. But seconds later, first Zathra and then the ogre emerged from the alley. Her ploy had worked. They were following her and assuming Aram was just ahead.

She knew exactly where she was going. Somewhere she could put an end to this long, long chase once and for all. Yes, she had a plan now. But in order for it to work—truly work—she actually had to give Malus's crew time to gather. So she didn't take the most direct route. Confident now—with Aram gone—in her speed advantage, she moved the race onto larger thoroughfares and streets. Soon Throgg and the blue ogre female had joined the chase. Then the Whisper-Man. She was hoping to wait for Malus himself, but she was running out of road. *It was time. Or would have to be.* She made one last turn and led them right inside the Thunderdrome.

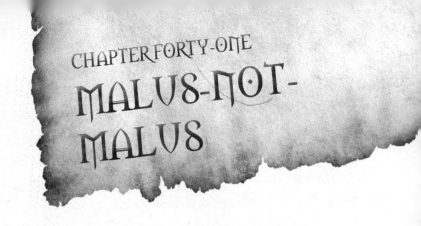

CHAPTER FORTY-ONE
MALUS-NOT-MALUS

Makasa had seen the show here once, some months before she had ever met Aramar Thorne. Her captain was off on a private errand (which she now realized was his visit with Charnas), so she had allowed Durgan One-God to drag her to the Thunderdrome. Here, Baron Noggenfogger supervised the settling of scores by combat. No fighting on the streets, unless you wanted a squad of Noggenfogger's mooks aiming hammers at your head. But fighting could and did take place in the 'drome every night. This was supposed to keep the peace in Gadgetzan, though Makasa soon suspected the true purpose was to encourage locals and visitors to bet on the outcomes and to allow the baron to take his cut of every wager.

Makasa didn't gamble, but One-God wagered a silver piece on a burly goblin, who felt her shorter but equally burly goblin neighbor had cut her wash line on purpose, dumping clean clothes in the mud. The shorter goblin eventually triumphed, and One-God lost his silver but had seemed entertained.

Yes, the Thunderdrome was a kind of gladiatorial arena, not too different in spirit from the one in Dire Maul, where Aram and Hackle had fought for the ogre king's amusement. Now, she stood in the center of the caged pitch, in the center of the 'drome, before nine rows of bleachers in the round, crowded with goblins, gnomes, humans, worgen, trolls, and a few dwarves. Another fight had just ended, with even the winner being carried out by mooks, when Makasa had entered the cage—followed quickly by her opponents. Facing Baron Noggenfogger, she stated for all to hear that "these pirates" had stolen her cheese. (It was the first lie that popped into her head.) She demanded satisfaction.

Noggenfogger leaned sideways to look beyond the tall human woman standing before him. He stared at Zathra, Valdread, Throgg, and the blue ogre. (The potbellied one was nowhere in sight, and Makasa theorized he had gone to get Malus or had finally run out of breath blowing his horn and chasing her.) Noggenfogger scratched his head and turned back to Makasa, asking, "What? All four of them? How much cheese we talking about?"

"Enough."

Standing at the edge of the ring, Noggenfogger leaned again to address the cheese-stealers. "Will you return this woman's cheese or make restitution?"

The troll and the ogres looked extremely confused. But the Whisper-Man chuckled dryly and said at the top of his rather ineffective lungs, "We will *never* return the cheese!"

"Then," Noggenfogger shouted to the cheers of the crowd, "we have a contest! Four against one! Place your bets!"

The crowd cheered, calling out wagers and odds. Makasa saw Gazlowe lean down to place a bet, handing a coin to a young gnome about the size of Hotfix. She wondered briefly whom the goblin had pegged for victory and at what odds.

In any case, Makasa *liked* her odds. Malus hadn't shown his face, but she could take out his troll and ogre, and maybe even do enough damage to the Forsaken to keep him from ever rising again. The female ogre worried her just a little. There was something in her eyes. And four opponents were, admittedly, one more than she cared to face at any one time. She thought it likely she might fall here. But at least she'd rob Malus of his top lieutenants in the process. That would be her gift to her brother, even if it was her final gift ever.

Malus liked the odds, too. He had slipped in at the back of the 'drome and scoped out the situation. He reasoned he might lose a minion or two—maybe even three. After all, he had seen the Flintwill woman fight. But in the end, his undead swordsman would bring Makasa Flintwill down. That was inevitable. Aram would be (permanently) separated from his greatest ally, and in the meantime, Malus and the two arakkoa could continue to search for Aram and the compass, which he now absolutely knew was somewhere in the city.

He slipped back outside the Thunderdrome.

Aram could barely breathe. He wasn't sure what else was in the refuse bin with him, but he was positive it must be dead, dead, dead. (Suddenly, the Whisper-Man's penchant for overusing jasmine water made a lot of sense.) Nevertheless, he waited a good five minutes before peeking out. He looked around and listened. There was no one nearby, and the sound of the ogre's horn echoed from some significant distance away. He was terribly concerned for Makasa, but he also had a terrible confidence in her abilities. He was quite aware he had held her back during the chase. Without him, she was likely to simply outrun her pursuers. The best thing he could do now was find the new shard fast and then slip back through the streets to Winifred's.

He checked the compass, which he'd been gripping tightly all this time, with the expectation that he'd find the needle spinning. It had been pointing and pulling in the direction of the refuse bin, and Aram was prepared to have to dig through it—stench or no stench—to get the crystal.

But the needle was not spinning. It glowed brightly, but it still pointed in the same direction, that is, toward the wall behind the bin. For a moment, Aram thought the crystal shard must be inside whatever building the bin abutted, and he wondered desperately how he'd manage to get inside. But when he let go of the compass to climb out of the bin, it shot straight up into the air. The heavy chain slipped right over his head, and he watched dumbly as the compass arched upward and landed with a subtle thud on the roof of the two-story building.

The shard was on the roof?

Why was that any stranger than one being in the dirt on the Feralas border or another being at the bottom of Thousand Needles' Shimmering Deep? He couldn't articulate why a Tanaris rooftop was indeed stranger, but he was quite sure it was.

Looking around again, he climbed out of the bin and stood in the alley, contemplating how to get up to the roof. He approached the wall and tried to get a grip to climb it. It wasn't exactly smooth, but there was no way to get any purchase whatsoever.

I'm so close! There must be a way to climb up!

He thought maybe there might be access to the roof from inside and turned to walk around to the front of the building to find the entrance.

There was a stairway to the second floor ten feet away. He slapped himself on the forehead and quickly ascended.

From the top of the stairs, he was able to climb up on the wooden railing. It was only slightly precarious. From there he could reach the edge of the roof and pull himself up.

He spotted the compass and the shard instantly. Only this was no tiny shard of crystal. He quickly untied Thalyss's purple leather pouch from his belt and pulled out the shard he already had: the one that combined the two shards found in dirt and water. Even merged together, they were still only as big as his little finger.

This new piece was made of the same solid crystal. But it was clearly shaped like the hilt of a sword. And a rather large sword at that. He picked up the hilt, hefted it. It had weight, substance. All that was missing was the blade. *No, that's not quite true.* There was a small pinky-size cleft in the hilt. He carefully inserted the merged crystal, and with a flash of the Light . . .

"Three have become one," said the Voice of the Light. It seemed to emerge from somewhere within him. The Voice and the Light, as well.

"Three have become one," Aram agreed. "Four left to find?"

"Seven must become One."

"So four left to find."

Laughter echoed around him. He saw he was standing in a circle of red flame, climbing higher and higher and higher. He felt strangely unafraid and wondered why. He looked down. He held the hilt of a massive crystal sword in his hand. It felt right. It felt like it belonged there in his hand.

Malus laughed again. "It always feels right. You think you're special?" By the end of the question, Malus no longer sounded like Malus. His silhouette—now burning at the edges—no longer matched Aram's memory of Malus. Malus was tall, but this silhouette was taller. Taller and slimmer. And Aram was quite sure he'd have remembered if Malus had two large horns emerging from his forehead. No, this wasn't Malus, had never been Malus. Malus was connected to this creature somehow, so Aram had conflated them. Now, he was seeing more clearly.

The Voice of the Light said, "See? You are special, Aram. Heal the Blade. Save me. Seven must become One."

"He will never heal the Blade," said the Malus-that-was-not-Malus. Wind stoked the flames, and another shadow joined the horned figure.

"You may heal the Blade. We have no objection," whispered the haunting black sands of Ueetay no Mueh'zala. "There will be a reckoning. Arm yourself however you prefer. The battle will come."

"The fire will burn," said Malus-not-Malus.

"Mueh'zala will feast."

"On all of Azeroth," they said in chorus. "On all of Azeroth."

Aram emerged from his vision with a gasp. He looked down at his hands. He held the hilt in one hand, the compass in the other, and both hands were shaking. He had to concentrate to make them stop. He looked around for the old finger-size shard, and momentarily panicked when he couldn't find it.

Then he remembered. He studied the hilt. There was no longer any cleft. The old shard (shards) had merged seamlessly. As if the cleft had never been there. As if the three pieces of crystal had never been apart. He studied the hilt some more. There was a jagged edge right near the base—all that remained . . . *of the Blade.* Four shards left to find: pieces of this sword.

He looked at the compass to see where the next one would be. The needle no longer glowed or spun. It pointed to the east, which meant it pointed toward Lakeshire. Well, that was that. He had to find the next shard. That was clearer now than ever before. *Drella had said she wanted to see Lakeshire. Guess she'll get her wish . . .*

He crossed to the edge of the roof. He looked east. Of course, he couldn't see Lakeshire or the Eastern Kingdoms from here. He could see a large dome-like structure at the far edge of Gadgetzan. And he thought he could even hear the muffled roar of a crowd cheering from inside it. For a fleeting moment, he wondered what they were cheering about, whom they might be cheering for . . .

But the moment passed. He needed to meet up with Makasa at Winifred's. He raced across the roof and, with the sword hilt stuffed into the back of his pants, lowered himself down.

Crystal Sword Hilt

A. Thorne

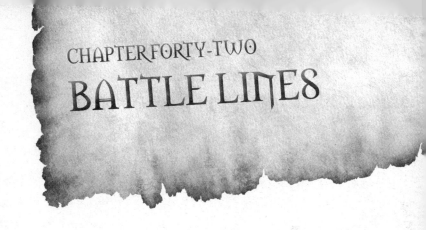

CHAPTER FORTY-TWO
BATTLE LINES

The placing of bets seemed to take some time. Gazlowe himself caused quite a delay by arguing with Baron Noggenfogger over the latter's cut of the take. For Makasa, it was just another reason to be annoyed with "old Gazzy." She was champing at the bit to get the fight started. To get it over with. She looked across the arena floor at her four opponents.

Throgg slowly screwed a mace onto his right wrist. Makasa recognized it as the weapon that had killed her crewmate Cassius Meeks aboard *Wavestrider*. Meeks was a hard worker who deserved a better end.

The female ogre drew her broadsword. Makasa thought it an odd weapon for an ogre and guessed she was a rare member of her breed to appreciate precision.

The troll, Zathra, looked nervous. After Zul'Farrak, Makasa could guess why.

Only Valdread was inscrutable, his blanched white face completely hidden under his hood.

Zathra first, Makasa thought. *Take her down with the harpoon before she finds her courage. Then dodge the swing of Throgg's mace and try the edge of my cutlass against the throat of the blue ogre. If I'm fast enough, I can get the chain unleashed and swinging before Throgg's ready for his second attempt on me. Smash his skull right then. That just leaves the Whisper-Man . . .* Somehow, Makasa knew—or thought she knew—that Baron Valdread would wait his turn patiently. He wouldn't care whether or not his companions survived, and he'd prefer to test his skills against her once they were out of the way. *The chain'll do well against him. Shatter him into pieces. Then I'll* scatter *those pieces so he can't put himself back together.* There were torches placed at intervals, all around the ring. *Set fire to each and every bit of the Forsaken.*

That was the plan. It required a lot of things to go her way, she knew. But she smiled grimly. She liked counting on her harpoon, cutlass, and chain. She liked counting on herself and no one else.

But some had other ideas.

Hackle, Murky, and Taryndrella came running into the 'drome, breathless. Out of the corner of her eye, an infuriated Makasa saw the little gnome lead Winifred and Springsong over to Gazlowe's box. They sat down beside him. Gazlowe

398

immediately sat back and told Noggenfogger that the terms of the wagering were now sufficient.

"What are you doing?" Makasa hissed as Hackle—war club at the ready—moved in beside her on her right. Murky, holding his tiny spear, took up position on her left. Drella stood between Makasa and her opponents, waving brightly. She said, "We have come to fight beside you, Makasa Flintwill. We would not have you fight our enemies alone."

"No," agreed Hackle.

"Nk," said Murky.

By this time, Noggenfogger had descended back down to the arena floor. He looked around at the newly added combatants and said, "What is this?"

With a smile playing at his voice, Valdread said, "More aggrieved individuals seeking redress. We stole a significant amount of cheese."

Zathra, Throgg, and the female ogre stared at him.

So did Murky and Hackle and Makasa.

Drella said, "I do not eat cheese."

Noggenfogger said, "Betting is closed. Four against one. Those were the terms of the wagering."

Gazlowe shouted, "So now it's four against four! I'll take the newcomers and the human woman at ten to one!"

Instantly, the entire crowd began shouting to adjust their bets.

Noggenfogger scowled, but hurried to record each new wager in order to guarantee his cut.

Makasa looked down at Hackle and said, "I do not require anyone's help."

Hackle looked up at her. "Makasa no ask for help. Makasa get help."

"Mrgle, mrgle."

"Murky agrees," Drella said. "And so do I."

Makasa exhaled—and briefly wondered just how long she'd been holding her breath. She looked at Hackle and admitted to herself that he might be useful. She didn't *need* him, but he was a tough little gnoll and not without skill. She glanced over at Zathra, who clearly didn't like facing them both together. Makasa said, "Drella, go sit with Springsong."

"No," said Drella simply. She was still standing with her back to the enemy.

"Murky," Makasa commanded, "take Drella and go sit with Gazlowe and Springsong."

"Nk," said Murky, staring daggers at the enemy while poking the empty air with his spear.

"Blast it!" she yelled. She was about ready to ignore Valdread and his lot and turn her ire against her three friends.

"Aram say we are crew. Aram's crew and Makasa's crew. Crew stand with Makasa," Hackle said calmly.

"No, I—"

"Crew is crew," Hackle said. "Makasa must learn this. Aram know this. Makasa must learn. Crew is crew. Crew stand together. Crew stand with Makasa even if Makasa no want."

Crew, she thought, calming at the word. She sucked on her lower lip, then bit it between her white teeth. The gnoll was right. Aboard *Wavestrider* or *Sea King*, she would not have hesitated to stand with her crew. She would have expected them to stand with her.

She had spent her entire odyssey with Aram resenting every addition to their crew. Resenting her need for others. *Why?* Her life had never been one lived in solitude, had never been one lived on a lifeboat. She was a creature of ships. And aboard ship, every deckhand depended on every other. *Crew.*

In a voice meant for them, but loud enough for all to hear, she said, "I am honored to stand with Hackle, Murky, and Taryndrella."

Taryndrella skipped around to stand beside Murky. "It is about time," she said.

Yes, thought Makasa, feeling as if a great weight had suddenly been lifted. *It is about time.* She smiled.

Hidden in the shadows, Malus had seen Aram's murloc and gnoll enter with the dryad that Valdread had mentioned, plus yet another night elf and a goblin. *Where does he pick up these people? He'll be traveling with a yeti next.*

Ssarbik had blustered up some more outrage over Malus's

lack of interest in the group. Malus had simply said to Ssavra, "Tell him."

The bird-woman explained to her less intelligent brother that there was no point in following Aram's allies inside. The point was that Aram wasn't with them. Meaning, *they* also were not with *him*.

"So unless he's brought that wyvern into town without anyone noticing," Malus concluded, "he's alone and friendless in this city. Now, find him."

The siblings then stood side by side—holding hands, feathered fingers intertwined—and chanted together. Malus hardly listened to the words. He felt the hairs on his arm stand at attention and watched the dark, oozing magic flow from beneath the two arakkoa's feet. It created a trail of black that burned red at the edges. It zigged and zagged along the streets, searching for what Malus and the dreadlord of the demonic Burning Legion sought.

Malus said, "Stay here. Maintain the path until it leads me to the compass, or I'll throw both your corpses at the feet of your Master."

He followed the magic, alone.

For Aram, unfamiliar with the streets of Gadgetzan, finding Winifred's house required a little luck and a lot of trial and error. But find it, eventually, he did. He entered and ran upstairs.

Makasa wasn't there. Neither was Hackle, Murky, or Drella. For some reason, he was afraid to call out for them. So he ran back downstairs but couldn't find Winifred, either. He checked the kitchen, the root cellar, the attic. He went back to his room, as if they might have magically appeared in his absence.

He had no idea what to do.

Still at a loss, he decided to go downstairs again, though whether he intended to go out looking for them or wait by the door was still an open question in his mind. But the decision was taken from his hands. Halfway down the stairs, he heard the front door open. He practically leapt the rest of the way down.

Malus stood in the doorway, looking directly at Aram with a satisfied smile. There was something at the tall man's feet, something black with red-rimmed edges. In an instant, it swept past Malus and swept over Aram . . .

Little went as Makasa had imagined.

Zathra, perhaps overcompensating for her fears, instantly fired both her crossbows at Makasa as soon as the bell was sounded. Makasa just barely managed to twist her shoulder in time for both bolts to sink into her shield as opposed to her flesh. Not stopping to reload, the troll attacked aggressively, pulling a dagger and rushing at Makasa—only to be intercepted by Hackle.

Unlike the slaves pitted against each other in the Dire Maul arena, those settling conflicts in the Thunderdrome were *not* supposed to fight to the death. But clearly, someone had neglected to inform these particular combatants.

With her unerring aim, Makasa threw her harpoon at the female ogre. But Throgg reached in and deflected it with his mace. Both ogres advanced on Makasa, but her swinging chain kept them at bay.

The only one of Makasa's predictions that seemed to be coming true was her assumption that Valdread would hang back, waiting. He did, watching Makasa and whispering, "Most impressive. You do remind me of someone. If only I could remember who . . ." But no one heard him over the roar of the suddenly bloodthirsty crowd.

On the opposite end of the arena, Taryndrella also hung back—her head tilted at an angle, one finger tapping upon her lips—as if listening, listening . . .

Zathra's nerves were still brittle. Hackle swung his large war club, driving her back. And with unloaded crossbows and a short dagger, there was little the troll could do to prevent his advance. Little except this: she clicked her tongue twice, and Skitter leapt off her chest to sting Hackle.

Out of nowhere, Murky—having dropped his little spear—*caught* the scorpid in his webbed hands. Skitter stung Murky three or four times in quick succession, as indicated by Murky's annoyed, "Ur, ur, ur!" But the scorpid's venom seemed to have no effect on the little murloc. Apparently, he was immune. Whether this was a feature common to all murlocs or something uniquely, well, Murkian, hardly mattered to Zathra, who remembered Drella's words about the murloc to the Mother of Venom. Already superstitious about Aram's little band, she began shivering involuntarily. While Murky held Skitter over his head, Hackle advanced. The troll barely managed to back away.

Valdread started laughing his dry, sandy laugh and said, "All right, all right. I suppose we should finish this." He finally drew his black sword and shale dagger.

But by this time, Makasa had seen their enemies' true weakness. They were impressive fighters as individuals, but they had no cohesion. *They* were mercenaries. Not a crew.

But Makasa had a crew. She called back over her shoulder, "Go low!" and brought the arc of her swinging chain down. Knowing exactly what she meant, Murky and Hackle—armed with a scorpid and a war club, respectively—were both short enough to safely advance directly beneath the circular spin of Makasa's chain. Not so for ogres, troll, or Forsaken.

Hackle measured the pace of the chain's rotation and swung his club upward between revolutions. It clobbered Zathra and sent her flying back.

"Murky," Makasa called, "introduce your new friend to the ogres!"

Murky raced forward and turned Skitter toward Throgg. The confused scorpid lashed out and stung the large ogre. The female ogre tried to poke at both Skitter and Murky with her broadsword, but the reach of Makasa's chain was longer than the reach of the ogre's arm and sword combined. She was forced to retreat. Throgg, reacting to the venom in his system, dropped to one knee—and was slapped across the jaw by the chain's iron links. He went down and stayed down.

This was mostly good news. Two of their opponents were laid out on the sand and sawdust. But the chain's impact with Throgg's jaw also served to disrupt its rotation, and both Valdread and the remaining ogre moved in to take advantage—with enough speed to put Makasa on the defensive, parrying the baron's sword thrusts with her cutlass, while Murky and Hackle were forced to retreat from the female ogre's now *considerable* reach.

It was at this crucial moment—with the crowd hushed and eager for a kill—that Drella could be heard saying, "Yes. Thank you. That would be lovely." She waited patiently for one second, two seconds, three. Then there was a ripple in the earth before her, and tiny sinkholes began to form. Perhaps if one held one's ear to the ground, a low rumble might have been heard. Then again, perhaps not. The dryad raised her arms, and all of a sudden, thick vines *burst* from the ground, snaring and entwining Valdread and the female ogre—and even the unconscious Zathra and Throgg. This was so shocking that Murky dropped the squirming Skitter, but before the scorpid could skitter very far, the vines had caught her up, too.

The vines snapped off Valdread's left arm and right leg, but otherwise he was held tight and immobile. They wrapped around the female ogre's arm and the entire length of her sword, preventing her from even attempting to cut herself free.

Makasa, Murky, and Hackle all turned to look at a triumphant

Drella, who said, "I am very helpful! In fact, I am impressive! I am Taryndrella the Impressive, daughter of Cenarius!"

"Indeed, you are, young one." Makasa stared at the dryad, who no longer looked quite as young as Makasa remembered. Drella seemed suddenly older, more mature. "Are you . . . taller?" Makasa asked.

"Summer has come," Drella said. "Or nearly."

Baron Noggenfogger declared them winners. Much coinage was exchanged among the spectators. (Gazlowe, as always, seemed to have done particularly well, though, of course, *no one* did quite as well as Marin Noggenfogger, who collected from winners and losers alike.) Four silver pieces were even—begrudgingly—shoved into the hands of the four victors, who snatched up their weapons and rushed out of the 'drome, not waiting for Gazlowe, Springsong, or Winifred. And certainly not waiting for their enemies to be cut down from their green bonds.

Once outside in the cool night air, Makasa stopped them. With a touch of formality, she repeated her prior sentiment: "I am honored to serve on this crew with Hackle, Murky, and Taryndrella."

"Taryndrella the Impressive!" the dryad corrected.

Makasa smiled and nodded and repeated the word, "Honored."

Sensing the importance of this moment to Makasa—and to all

of them—Hackle and Drella both said, "Honored." And Murky solemnly intoned, "Uuua."

Still smiling, Makasa said, "Come on. Aram will be wondering what happened to us."

They ran off to Winifred's . . .

None of them noticed the two entranced arakkoa, chanting quietly in the shadows before a trail of smoking red-rimmed blackness that snaked off toward Aramar Thorne . . .

Back at Winifred's, the dark magic wrapped around Aram, binding him tighter than Drella's vines. He was alone. Without Makasa. Without Thalyss or Hackle or Murky or Drella or his father or his mother or Robb. Never in his life had Aramar Thorne felt so alone—and so terrified.

A satisfied Malus advanced slowly, saying, "I gave you every opportunity, boy. You brought this on yourself. Like father, like son." Malus had killed his father. And now Malus was going to kill him.

But Greydon Thorne hadn't made it easy for Malus. He hadn't perished without a fight. The least Aram could do was try.

Aram still had one arm free. It was the wrong arm, but with some twisting of his body, he managed to draw his cutlass and point it in Malus's direction.

Malus rolled his eyes in contempt, and, oh, did Aram wish

Makasa were there to see it and respond as she was wont. Almost languidly, Malus drew his own broadsword—as if it was hardly worth the effort.

And it hardly was. The ribbons of black, burning magic were constricting around Aram and pulling tighter. It was getting hard to breathe. He tried to sever them with the cutlass, but the blade was useless against this sorcery.

Malus flicked his wrist so quickly, Aram was disarmed—his cutlass clattering against the floor—without him ever really seeing any movement of the broadsword. Malus reached his iron-sheathed left hand toward Aram's new shirt and the compass that wasn't particularly well hidden beneath it.

Desperate for air—and just plain desperate, period—Aram grabbed for the only other thing he could reach: he pulled the hilt of the crystal shard sword out from behind him and brought it into view, with some vague notion of wedging it in between the magic and his chest.

But it was Malus who briefly stopped breathing. He drew back his hand, froze, and hissed out, *"The Diamond Blade!"*

Of course, there wasn't any actual blade. Or was there? Before Aram's bulging eyes, a shining beacon emerged from the hilt, coalescing into a blade of pure, shining Light!

This shocked Malus out of his stupor. Recovering a bit, he reached for the hilt. But the Light just kept getting brighter and brighter, and eventually Malus had to use the hand he was reaching with to shield his eyes.

But Aram, trained by his dreams, did not need to look away. No matter how bright the Light became, Aram could still see. And hear. The Voice of the Light spoke inside his mind. *Once, the Light was yours to bear. Now, you cannot bear the Light.*

It took Aram a couple seconds to realize the Voice wasn't speaking to him. It was talking to Malus, who groaned miserably.

Building on Malus's misery, the Voice spoke again: *You forfeited the Diamond Blade with your betrayal. You will never possess it again.*

Malus began to growl. He struggled to raise his head, but the bright, bright Light blinded him. Moreover, it seemed to have substance that pressed down upon his head.

And yet the Light had no such effect on Aramar Thorne. He felt weightless within it. He could breathe again as the brilliance began to eat away at the dark ribbons of magic that had all but strangled him. As he had with his cutlass, Aram tried to cut his mystical bonds with this blade of Light—with much better results. The Light cut through the shadow magic like a white-hot knife through moldy black butter.

Better still, the Light continued to get brighter and brighter. Malus dropped his sword so he could use both arms to shield his vision. Again, Malus groaned deeply. And, again, the groan became a growl. The growl became a roar. And the roar became a scream of intense inner pain.

The Voice said, *Tell your Master that the Light is not yet whole. Nevertheless, it possesses more than enough power to chase away these pathetic shadows.* Within seconds, the dark ribbons were retreating as if even they were in excruciating pain.

Brighter and brighter. Brighter and brighter.

And Aram still had no need to look away . . .

By the time the Light had faded, Malus had recovered sufficiently to open his eyes, blink them furiously, and wipe the tears away. He found himself alone in the boardinghouse. There was no one there. No Aram, no Diamond Blade, no compass. Just an abandoned cutlass on the floor.

He felt exhausted, fundamentally exhausted right down to his bones. He couldn't remember ever feeling quite this tired before. He staggered forward and slumped down to rest on the stairs.

But his strength returned rapidly—and with it, his outrage. He lurched to his feet and, knowing Aram would never come back to this place, staggered out of the boardinghouse and away.

He hadn't given up. He wouldn't give up. Not now. Not ever. He had been caught off guard by how much of the Diamond Blade the boy had already recovered. *That* was why he'd faltered. But Malus would be ready next time. He would be ready. He would be ready. He flexed his left hand beneath its iron gauntlet.

The pain brought him some satisfaction. Next time, nothing would stop him. He would be ready.

Within two minutes of fleeing Winifred's, Aram ran smack into Makasa, Murky, Hackle, and Drella. He rapidly told them what had occurred and explained why they could never go back to Winifred's.

"Where to, then?" Makasa asked.

Aram thought about this. Then he pulled out the compass to see if its last reading had changed at all. It had not. Aram thought about this for half a second at most, before deciding with a firm and steady confidence exactly where they should head next . . .

Malus loomed over Marin Noggenfogger. Even backed by a score of hobgoblins, the baron found himself leaning away under the captain's threatening gaze.

And the goblin wasn't the only one feeling threatened. Ssavra had lost some of her own bravado. She still couldn't understand what had happened. She and her brother had cast their spell, and all seemed well. The shadow magic had raced forward after the compass. But some other magic must have countered it, must have plowed back along the course of their spell, tearing it asunder, until it had reached the two arakkoa and hit them like an iron hammer, knocking both unconscious.

She had awakened to Malus raging, *"What kind of spellcasters are you?! Your magicks dissolve short of their target?! Can you find the boy or can't you?!"* Dazed as she and Ssarbik were, they could not answer, which meant their answer was, effectively, no. *"Useless!"* Malus had said, before entering the Thunderdrome to find his best lieutenants—the ones who were conscious, anyway—still struggling to free themselves from the grip of dryad-generated vines. Worse, the ogre Throgg was near death from the sting of the troll's own scorpid pet.

Now, Ssavra glanced over at the swollen-jawed Throgg, pale as Valdread and unsteady on his feet. Ro'kull and Ro'jak supported him on either side to keep him upright. The Shattered Hand ogre had survived thanks to his massive bulk and to the fact that Skitter had apparently already expended much of her venom stinging Thorne's murloc (to no effect). Thus, the dose Throgg had received was relatively minimal.

Ssavra was still surprised—and not a little relieved—that Malus had not made an example of them. She assumed because he didn't want to kill *all* of his followers for their failures, he had therefore reluctantly chosen to kill none. The Hidden had been defeated at every turn that night. But one thing they now knew for certain was that Aram and his companions were hiding somewhere in the city.

So after the 'drome had emptied of spectators, her captain stood before the baron of Gadgetzan with the rest of the Hidden and the Elite arrayed about. Malus was no longer raging. He barely raised his voice above a whisper. Yet somehow that was even more terrifying. Terrifying enough that Ssavra was beginning to understand why the Master had chosen this human to lead them on Azeroth.

He said, "I want to make myself perfectly clear. I want Aramar

Thorne. He is in your city. You will find him for me. You will bring him to me."

Noggenfogger tried to rally his courage. "I am baron here. I do not take orders from you."

"I am not giving you an order. I am offering you a choice. You can bring me the boy . . ."

"Or . . . ?"

"Or I will lay siege to this city. I have those you see before you now, and they include two arakkoa with the darkest of magicks."

Ssavra thought, *Malus might not have much faith in us, but thankfully Noggenfogger doesn't know that.*

Malus continued, "I have a ship full of the most ruthless marauders in all of Azeroth. And every day, more ogres pour into Gadgetzan from Dire Maul. I am their king, and I will use them—I will use them all—to lay waste to this town."

"So not an order," the baron said. "A threat. I don't like being threatened, Captain. And Gadgetzan has fought off pirates and bandits before."

"I am neither of those minor nuisances. And I thought I was speaking to a *pragmatic* individual."

Noggenfogger chewed on this. He *was* pragmatic. In fact, he prided himself on his pragmatism. He believed this man's threats were real and significant, and he owed no allegiance to any human boy . . .

*　　*　　*

A day out of Gadgetzan, aboard the vessel of his deliverance, Aram studied his maps. He worried a little—but only a little—about whether he had made the right choice. In any case, they had escaped Malus.

The *Inevitable* was at sea, closing in on the schooner *Crustacean* bound for Stormwind Harbor. Noggenfogger had tipped off Malus that the boy and his friends had booked passage upon it. Malus had suspected a lie. But Noggenfogger was able to show him a manifest and a receipt confirming everything. Malus now suspected Noggenfogger had intentionally waited to pass the information along until *after* the schooner had set sail, thus forcing Malus to leave Gadgetzan to pursue. But the baron hadn't waited *too* long. The *Crustacean* would be overtaken in a matter of minutes. And this time, nothing would stop Malus from getting that compass and reclaiming the Diamond Blade.

It's funny where your mind goes when you have a moment to breathe, Aram thought. *I never did get to see Springsong change into a feathered moonkin. Oh well.*

He heard shouting and stood up to see what was wrong . . .

Back in Gadgetzan, Noggenfogger was still not happy about giving in to Malus's blackmail. The baroness could tell the thought disturbed her husband, and stroked his long ears to soothe him. He was indebted to her—his little Sprinkle—for these attentions, and also for being the source of their relief. Somehow she had learned about the *Crustacean* and had told her husband that the boy and his friends had booked passage upon it. He had passed this intelligence on to Malus to get that maniac to leave his town.

Sprinkle gave Marin a little kiss on his pate and told him not to fret.

After all, there was little to fret about. The pirates were gone, heading for a ship that held no one *she'd* ever met.

He said he was very grateful to her for always putting his needs first.

Hah! She smiled to herself and thought warmly of past loves.

Aram pushed open the door of the bridge to see what the shouting was about. It was Gazlowe and Sprocket, arguing at high volume over the most efficient steam quotient—*whatever that meant*—to keep their vessel moving at the optimal speed—*whatever that was.*

Aram tried not to smile as he stepped back and quietly closed the door again. He moved to the edge of the gondola and leaned out over the side, his eyes wide with the wonder of it all. The zeppelin *Cloudkicker* soared far above the shining desert sands of Tanaris, with both the sparkling waters of Thousand Needles and the deep rain forests of Feralas in clear view from this astounding height. They were heading north to Gazlowe and Sprocket's next MEGA event in some place called the Charred Vale. Aram had ridden a wyvern, but that hardly stole any thunder from what he was currently experiencing. *A ship. A ship that flew through the air! What would they think of next?*

"The view's plenty spectacular, isn't it?" said a voice behind him. "I would think it the kind of view a good artist would want to capture."

Aram turned to smile at a smiling Charnas, who was fulfilling his duties as MEGA's official artist by coming along for the ride with his cousin—*yes, his cousin*—Gazlowe.

The two artists leaned against the rail and began sketching. Aram sketched the view from *Cloudkicker* and then sketched *Cloudkicker* itself. He sketched the crystal sword hilt. And he even forced himself to sketch all his enemies together: Captain Malus; Baron Reigol Valdread, the Whisper-Man; the troll Zathra wearing her scorpid as armor; and the ogre Throgg. Not satisfied with that grouping, he sketched them all again, but this time added the bird-man; the female ogre; the ogre twins and the two-headed ogre; the potbellied ogre with the ram's horn; the towering giant who was always yawning; and towering behind them all, the shadowy horned figure with the burning edges. Putting their images to paper seemed to exorcise his fear of them. Besides, he had left them all behind in Gadgetzan, and he doubted that even Malus could find a way to follow him now.

He put his sketchbook back in his pocket and stood up straight.

Charnas said, "I've been thinking about your uncle Silverlaine. I'm fairly certain that the last time your father mentioned his brother, he said something about having left him in the north."

"Like . . . in Stonetalon?"

"He wasn't that specific. But I'm fairly certain he was referring to northern Kalimdor and not the north of the Eastern Kingdoms—nor the far north of Northrend."

"So maybe . . . maybe I might find him up this way."

"You never know."

Aramar Thorne mused on the possibilities.

Charnas interrupted the boy's musings by clearing his throat. He said, "I'm considering a new project. A new book."

"About MEGA?" Aram asked.

"Perhaps. In part. I'll cogitate on it for a good little while. Let it play round and around my brain for a bit. Then I'll let you know."

"I'd like that."

"Maybe you'd like to contribute some illustrations?"

"Are you serious? I'd *really* like that!"

"Well, we'll see."

The Hidden

Aram was practically floating—as if he could kick a few clouds himself—when he left Charnas to join his friends.

Murky, Hackle, Drella, and Makasa were all together in their cramped cabin. Makasa periodically looked out the window, shook her head, and grumbled, "Makes no sense. This thing doesn't even have wings." But when she saw Aram, she managed a smile.

Gazlowe had agreed to take the five of them north—for a minimal charge per head. Not all the way to Thal'darah Overlook. But the map Aram had studied indicated that the Overlook was little more than two days' walk from the Charred Vale. That was close enough for this crew.

Aram pulled the compass out from beneath his shirt and glanced down at it. Its needle still pointed toward Lakeshire and home. Or rather, it pointed toward the next shard, which just happened to be in that same direction.

Nevertheless, Aram had decided that helping Drella was more important than returning home right now. Even more important than his quest for the Diamond Blade. He'd return to that quest eventually. He had to. But he had no regrets—and not simply because the path he had chosen might, in fact, lead him to his father's brother, Silverlaine Thorne.

He glanced over at Drella, and thought she looked a bit older than she had when she had first blossomed. She was certainly a bit taller, her pretty, twinkling eyes now at a level with his. He looked at Hackle, who had gained so much confidence since they had first met. He looked at Makasa, no longer an island among those who cared most about her. He looked at Murky, who was currently tangled up in his nets and determined to untangle himself without any help. "There are all kinds of families," his father had once said. Aram knew this crew was one kind of family. Aram knew this crew was *his* family, as certainly as the people he still cherished back in Lakeshire were his family, too.

He thought about the path his life had taken since leaving Lakeshire all those months ago. It had hardly been straight. Often, in fact, it seemed to be spiraling out of control. Yet every step he'd taken had led inevitably toward more friends, new wonders, and a greater understanding of the world around him. And what he understood most clearly now was that it was all connected. One thing led to another. His mother had nudged him toward his father. His father had introduced him to his sister Makasa. His journey with Makasa had led them to Murky. Even their encounters with Malus had brought him in contact with Hackle and with Thalyss, who had literally placed Taryndrella's acorn in his hand. *And who knows?* Maybe Drella would lead him to Silverlaine.

Thalyss Greyoak's words resonated for Aram, now more than ever: "There is a harmony to nature, a way and a flow. Like the path of a river, like the path through the soil that a stem takes to find the sun. Do you think it is any different for beings such as we four travelers? I am not talking of guarantees. A river may be dammed. A stem may be chewed away by aphids or grasshoppers. And a traveler may be diverted in any number of ways. But the flow exists, and we are without a doubt a part of its whole."

Five travelers instead of four now, but otherwise these words seemed as true as ever—maybe truer. So first, before Aram did anything else, he knew with certainty that he must help his dryad friend become all that she was meant to be. He believed—quest or no quest, shards or no shards, Blade or no Blade—that such a path was one his father would have chosen for him. Not a straight path, certainly. Not a straight line. But a winding way and a spiral flow that would ultimately connect with all that Aram was meant to see and experience, ultimately bringing him to the desired end. Assuming there was an end—or even should be. And this rambling chain of thought gave Aramar Thorne peace.

Seeing a way clear, Aram stepped over to Murky and yanked on one end of the murloc's net with a slight spiral motion. His small green friend instantly tumbled free.

"How about another reading lesson?" he asked, to the applause of Hackle, Murky, and Drella. Makasa nodded her approval. And Aramar Thorne nodded back.

And somewhere, Aram thought, *Greydon Thorne is nodding down on me as well.*

Cloudkicker

A.Thorne

CHAPTER FORTY-FIVE
ONE LAST NOD

In Outland, the prisoner wasn't nodding, though nothing would have given him more pleasure than to nod off and dream. But this week, the dreadlord had given the order that the Burning Legion's prisoner not be allowed to sleep. Thus, every time he had begun to nod off, a blasted imp would poke him in the ribs with a red-hot brand. The prisoner thought the searing pain of the brand was less of a torture than the forced wakefulness.

But it changed nothing. By his own calculations, the prisoner had spent nearly two months chained in this deep, dank, dark dungeon. Highlord Xaraax had been trying to break his spirit all that time. In fact, Xaraax had—in one way or another—been trying to break his spirit for over twenty years.

Clearly, however, Greydon Thorne was not an easy man to break.

ACKNOWLEDGMENTS

So many people helped me complete this story. More than I could possibly list. But this, at least, is a start . . .

First and foremost, I'd like to thank Trent Kaniuga for bringing Aram's art to life in this book. Not to mention the work of Charnas, Sprocket, and others.

At Blizzard, I'd like to thank the since-departed James Waugh, who's gone on to far, far better things in a galaxy far, far away. In addition, thanks to Sean Copeland, Cate Gary, Brianne M Loftis, Justin Parker, Byron Parnell, Robert Simpson, Justin Thavirat, and Jeffrey Wong. Special props to Chelsea Monroe-Cassel for her Dragonbreath Chili recipe, which can be found in *World of Warcraft: The Official Cookbook*.

At Scholastic, my thanks go out once again to Samantha Schutz and to my new editor, Adam Staffaroni, who always has my back. Thanks also to Gayley Avery, Rick DeMonico, Lindsey Johnson, Danielle Klimashowsky, Susan Lee, Charisse Meloto, Monica Palenzuela, Maria Passalacqua, and Lizette Serrano. For producing the audiobook version of the previous novel, I'd like to thank Melissa Reilly Ellard, our wonderful narrator Ramón de Ocampo, and the folks at Deyan Audio.

the Gotham Group: Ellen Goldsmith-Vein, Julie Kane-Ritsch, Peter McHugh, Julie Nelson, Joey Villareal, Tony Gil, Heather Horn, Matt Schichtman, and Hannah Shtein.

It's also become a bit of a tradition for me to thank the folks at my day job for putting up with certain . . . distractions. And, boy, did I have a lot of day jobs this time out. At *Shimmer and Shine*, Andrew Blanchette, Farnaz Esanaashari, Dustin Ferrer, Rich Fogel, Michelle Lamoreaux, Robert Lamoreaux, Dave Palmer, and Cisco Paredes. On *Mecha-Nation*, Victor Cook, Greg Guler, Chris Hamilton, and Fred Schaefer. At *Young Justice*, Sam Aides, Brent Anthony, Jay Bastian, Christopher Berkeley, Phil Bourassa, Jonathan Callan, Mae Catt, Marlene Corpuz, Peter David, Nicole Dubuc, Joshua Hale Fialkov, Rich Fogel, Auriane Gamelin, Paul Giacoppo, Tiffany Grant, Julie Haro, Vinton Heuck, Kevin Hopps, Brian Jones, Curtis Koller, Leanne Moreau, Bobbie Page, Francisco Paredes, Tom Pugsley, Sam Register, Andrew Robinson, Jamie Thomason, Michael Vogel, Mel Zwyer, and especially my producing partner, Brandon Vietti. Thanks also to my *Rain of the Ghosts* AudioPlay producing partner, Curtis Koller.

Last but not least, I'd like to thank my entire family for their support. My in-laws, Zelda & Jordan Goodman, and Danielle & Brad Strong. My nieces and nephews, Julia, Jacob, Lilah, Casey, and Dash. My siblings, Jon & Dana Weisman, and Robyn & Gwin Spencer-Weisman. My cousin Brindell Gottlieb. My parents, Sheila & Wally Weisman. My wife, Beth, and my amazing (and very grown-up) kids, Erin and Benny. I love you all.